Not Only the Things Th̶   ̶̶̶̶̶̶̶̶

Mridula Koshy's short-story collection, *If It Is Sweet* (Tranquebar Press, 2009; Brass Monkey, 2011), won the 2009 Shakti Bhatt First Book Prize and was shortlisted for the 2009 Vodafone Crossword Book Award. Her second novel, *Bicycle Dreaming*, is forthcoming from Speaking Tiger.

Praise for the Book

'Koshy is a deft literary seamstress, intricately weaving a tapestry of voices and offering us a rich, layered glimpse into the workings of memory, community and family.' —Janice Pariat, *The Sunday Guardian*

'This novel, Mridula's first after her debut as a short story writer with *If It Is Sweet*, is light with its touch, addressing the weight of loss and the transformative role of memory…Despite its unconventional structure… the reader is pulled into the story by the sheer power and beauty of writing.' —Pooja Pillai, *People*

'Koshy's writing is dense and layered in the way of an onion: peeling involves tears and eating involves pungency, but the stinging rawness of the process is ultimately rewarding, if disquieting…The obliqueness of the many layers can be difficult to navigate, but in all its piercing poignancy the book has an edge of empathy that is perhaps the most endearing quality of Koshy's writing.' —Manasi Subramaniam, *Biblio*

'In prose that is layered and complex…the novel draws you in the way an epic does.'—Anupama Raju, *The Hindu*

'Mridula Koshy paints a complex web of memories, both real and imagined...yet the sadness of the past and the shifting sands of time don't make the world of *Not Only*...a difficult one to access. On the contrary, once you enter Annakutty's memories, it is difficult to withdraw. Instead, you sink deeper and deeper into the lives and losses that Koshy portrays so beautifully.' —Joanna Lobo, *DNA*

'*Not Only*...is a kind of literary diptych, like those artworks that consist of a pair of painted surfaces joined in the middle by a hinge, so that they face in two very slightly different directions...It is a remarkably self-assured work, and it feels slightly humbling to be in the presence of a literary talent like this.' —Anvar Alikhan, *India Today*

'[*Not Only the Things That Have Happened*] leaps nimbly between times and styles and its characters' points of view. The sheer quality of Koshy's prose is probably the best reason to read her...Such a novel could easily have fallen into the trap of being dull and worthy. That it doesn't is something of a triumph; this is a fantastic book.' —Aishwarya Subramanian, *Hindustan Times*

'The immersion in the lives of the people of this region is almost Faulknerian in its intensity, along with the milieu against which they have come of age: The influence of Catholicism, the grip of caste, trade union and Left movements and the distance between the impoverished village and the bustling city...Koshy's primary interest is in the impact of past bereavement on present-day lives and she follows her characters' befuddled journeys and their real and imagined histories with an empathetic eye.'—Sanjay Sipahimalani, *Mint Lounge*

'Motherhood looms very large – and in many forms – in the book as well. Koshy's contemplative eye takes in several maternal figures...Despite the drama, *Not Only the Things That Have Happened* is far from schmaltzy, rather feeling its way through the kinds of lack that cannot be blotted out. The novel retains Koshy's characteristically measured, poetic voice with its undertow of unease.' —Naintara Maya Oberoi, *Time Out India*

Not Only the Things That Have Happened

MRIDULA KOSHY

FOURTH ESTATE • *New Delhi*

First published in hardback in India in 2012 by Fourth Estate
An imprint of HarperCollins *Publishers*

First published in paperback in 2016

P-ISBN: 978-93-5106-998-0
E-ISBN: 978-93-5029-577-9

2 4 6 8 10 9 7 5 3 1

HarperCollins *Publishers*
A-75, Sector 57, Noida, Uttar Pradesh 201301, India
1 London Bridge Street, London, SE1 9GF, United Kingdom
Hazelton Lanes, 55 Avenue Road, Suite 2900, Toronto, Ontario M5R 3L2
and 1995 Markham Road, Scarborough, Ontario M1B 5M8, Canada
25 Ryde Road, Pymble, Sydney, NSW 2073, Australia
195 Broadway, New York, NY 10007, USA

Typeset in 12/15 Adobe Jenson Pro at
SÜRYA

Printed and bound at
Thomson Press (India) Ltd

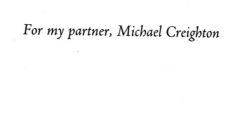

For my partner, Michael Creighton

There will be mornings like you
but with no pathways
where I'll come looking for you

—from 'Tournoiements' by Roselyne Sibille
(translated by Michael Fineberg)

PART ONE

19–20 May, 2004
Kerala, South India

*After I lost my son, I put it into my memory that he would return.
If it is real, you can remember not only the things that have
happened, but also the things that are going to happen.*

—Annakutty Verghese

1

The Sad Demise of Nina's Aunt

A fine spray of rain enters the room through its single window, bringing pinpoints of blue light into the interior dark. A bed stands low on a floor. Along one side of the bed, the spread is smooth and flat. And as flat and smooth, a woman lies stretched on the spread to a length she did not possess in life. Next to the woman, the covers crumple and raise a mountain under which Nina Scaria stirs, shifting and breaking the slope, then peeling it back.

Freed from the covers, Nina folds herself at the waist and, jack-knifed on the bed, commences a mewling and hiccupping that catches in all the sharp corners of her nearly twelve-year-old body. She wails to bring the neighbours who don't come. Her wailing is absorbed by the rain.

The rooster outside, sensitive to the least disturbance, ruffles and readies his throat, then peering about, gives up in fright. The forest beyond the coop is pressed in dark. Only the ditch where his hens scratch daily at kitchen scraps, and the red yard that slopes up from the ditch, and at the end of the yard, the outline of the larger coop that houses the two humans, show in the bits and sparkles of rain-light blowing now at this, and now at that, slant. It is not enough light by which to see the front door open, the girl shiver and cross her arms to clasp her elbows, the girl flail her arms then seat herself on the floor, far back from the door through which the rain blows.

Nina is certain morning is close at hand. The burning she tightens her legs against tells her so. She sits, willing light to outline the trees, to part the competing tides of dark that overtake one another out there where the trees should be, each tide its own texture of black. She wills light, fails herself, and hurriedly stands to yank at her underwear which is not past her thighs when she rushes to squat; the spray fans, drenching the cotton and her hands.

The Lost Boy of long ago, her Peramma had told her, could never be left alone. He would so easily get up to mischief. Once when she was preparing him for a bath, Peramma was called away. She left the little bowl of oil at his feet, and when she returned, she set to the task of rubbing him again. But now the oil was changed.

As Peramma talked, Nina entered the story, saw herself standing at the bathroom door watching the long ago boy sending his little baby jet streaming into the bowl. She saw the boy catch her eye and laugh, and she felt herself laughing with him. Midway through the oil-rub Peramma smelled the piss in the bowl. She poured the rest out and beat his little bottom.

'I never feel sorry that I beat him. Somewhere it is still serving him well.'

Peramma had smiled at the end of this telling. Other stories though have ended with the smile trembling. Nina exits Peramma's stories about her little son before Peramma can reach their end because, though divided into happy and sad, Nina knows the stories are always united by the fear that creeps into them during their telling. If Nina had let herself stay for the ending, let herself feel her Peramma's fear, she would have come to know the specific quality of that fear—the fear of ending a story in the unknown. Peramma's smile at the end of the story of her baby pissing in his bath oil pulled nearly her whole face into her mouth. Her eyes though were excluded from the smile when she said 'somewhere'. Her eyes asked, where?

Nina jerks water in swift swings from the bathroom bucket, sloshing it over her puddle, driving the puddle forward with each splash till it joins the rain-wet floor at the threshold and from there swims down two concrete steps to the yard. She can see the yard emerging in the early morning light. It is set between the fat twists of rain draining in streamers from the tin roof.

Nina turns in search of the twig broom from which Peramma used to extract a twig to keep handy at homework time. Morning enters from behind her, lit up, spelling an end to the rain, pressing itself against Nina's bent back. She swings at it with her arms and her bucket, surprising herself with the sudden knowing: mornings are not only for happiness.

Her back to the door, she sits, her height contained in the legs she pulls up to her chin. Her close cropped head is bowed, and it isn't possible to see her face, which is only as lovely as the face of any twelve-year-old child in these parts. These parts: peopled with a multitude who failed to answer her loneliness the previous night, and whose inevitable incursion she will fail to stave off. Her bent form, framed in the door, yields slow choking sounds and again she turns to swing her arms in the air behind her. Her eyes are bright with tears and she pants lightly. Through all this, her face remains smooth, an oval pearl that has not grown to accommodate overlarge teeth, a face that may be unremarkable in these parts, but would be lovely anywhere else.

2

A Late Delivery

The neighbours come. The milk, a late delivery, but still the first to arrive. Seeing her hunched in the doorway with skirt drawn over her head, Devasi knows. He trots the last few metres across the yard, picking his feet up to avoid the egg shells-onion peels-thin polythene bags flung from the door. Just shy of the girl, his feet catch on something slippery and he skates the last bit, raising a spray of muddy water. He nearly flings the metal canister on the step; landing, it rights itself, not losing one drop of its precious content. He stands over Nina wishing his wife had been the one to carry the milk here this morning. He is not a man known for his manners. When upset, he is given to a two-handed wiping at his chest, and his wife expends energy bleaching shirts that tend to carry the stains he deposits in five stripes of V.

'Your Peramma? Peramma, is it? Dead.'

He is instantly horrified; this might not be the reason the girl is crying. Nina's hands wrap themselves around him and she buries her face in the mundu wrapped around his waist. She nods her head against his belly and he pats her, his moustache working itself awkwardly as he bites at his lip.

'Girl, girl,' he comforts her.

The skirt is bunched about her waist and he attempts to smooth it down past the bareness of her buttocks. The skirt fixed, his hands attempt his chest, but Nina's head has climbed to rest there. He mutters to himself.

'We should have stayed the night.'

Just the previous evening, he and his wife had been at the house to pay a sickbed visit. The people of the area have all taken it in turn to keep Annakutty company in these last months since her illness and confinement.

'Leaving a child alone.'

He continues his muttering as if he were accusing someone other than himself. He turns twice, thinking to call out to his wife; no, better to call the priest.

'Must give the girl some food.'

He abandons thinking, and raises his voice: 'Jansy.'

He bellows, though there is little chance his voice will carry the distance. He does not think to call for those who live closer, though just moments prior to this he was delivering milk at their homes. Perhaps this is simply because, in his agitation, it is his wife who is foremost in his thoughts. Then perhaps it is also because it is only when he delivers milk at these homes that he remembers they exist. Regardless, his call carries to these homes, and eight or twelve thatched huts yield their owners and a collection of goats with bells tied to their necks. Wet to the knees of his white pants and muddy, the priest follows behind them. He is bringing the Eucharist, which he does twice a week to the homes of those who are ailing. Even now, in one of the huts, a woman lies in the dark, her breasts a raw wound of cancer, her face wreathed in forbearance.

Father Paul, recently returned from his studies in Rome, believes if priestly life is to be borne, it can only be through careful cultivation of a distaste for forbearance in women, and the skill of sipping coffee for hours on end and at no expense to his pocketbook. He hurries from the cancer-ridden woman so gifted of piety and so lacking in love. He hurries to his favourite parishioner's home from where he can hear his coffee-shop colleague, Devasi, calling for his wife. It is a home from which Father Paul has emerged in the past, an exasperated smile on his face and his burden of wafers no lighter. He hurries knowing what he will find and wanting to be done with the sudden bitterness flooding his mouth.

Devasi meets him with, 'Kunjachan, she is gone.'

'Take the girl inside.' Father Paul addresses this to one of the hut dwellers. Then turning to Devasi he replies, 'Yes, yes I know she is gone. Why else would you be shouting for your wife out here?'

He gestures to the tree limbs that lie keeled over the path he just crossed. He does not connect the destructive power of the storm with his God except in the vaguest of ways. And from this connection he draws a conclusion: 'It was Annakutty's time.'

He hurries in. His cassock, tucked into his pants to save the garment from mud, catches as he climbs the high steps, and comes loose. Those who have entered ahead of him mill about the front room. The dirt they have tracked in has adhered to the blown about-kitchen refuse, the child's paper cuttings and the scraps of fabric that had rained from Annakutty's sewing machine in the corner of the room, leaving the cement floor even dirtier than the yard. He hurries past this evidence of the poor housekeeper Annakutty was, and hurrying, he trips at the entrance to the bedroom. He sways there, caught in the eddy of a small gust, her last breath finding its way through the door he has pushed open. Briefly it is trapped in the cloth of his garments. He tugs and the cloth settles with a sigh. The story of herself she hoarded over a lifetime, the story Annakutty was gathering to herself even with her last breath, scatters to all parts. Now it will be reformed in other mouths.

All of the rest of the morning, Father Paul fusses with the cassock, trying to keep it tucked into his pants. This fussing is as much a prayer as the prayers he is already murmuring under his breath. He enters the bedroom, and in the dry manner in which he has seen his teachers in the profession conduct themselves, he bends, pretends to have creaking knees, sets aside the Eucharist, prays, and when he hears the neighbours trooping in behind him, gives over from silent prayer. Together they start into the rosary.

3

(with her last breath)

Some days if you ask him, it is idlis and nothing else will do, and other days it is anything that comes to mind. I never worry about his eating. He can eat. But today is special. A mother should make something special.

If there was just a little butter. I can get butter. But how much will it cost me; a dab of butter? It's too expensive. But idli split in half with butter and sugar is what he will want. It is what comes letting him taste these things. Who can blame him when it is I . . .

My son. My only one. Him. He. The only only only.

How is a mother to say no? To think I never knew the taste of butter till I was, how old was I when I first tasted butter? And he thinks the butter from the paper box is better than anything I make at home.

'Nina girl, how did he say it? I don't want that white colour butter, Amma. The yellow butter, Amma. I want *only* that. The way he said it. Only. The way he said that word. Only. Only. Only.'

It has to be yellow only, not white. And if I buy the butter, I will have to pay to get some jam made as well. I've heard they don't let

11

you make just a little bit of jam. It's only possible to make it in quantity. Kilos of fruit and bottles of it. Where will I get kilos of fruit? I only need a little jam for one little boy. If I could ask someone else who is getting jam made to sell me just one of their bottles. No, I can buy the butter and sprinkle what sugar there is in the house. No need to buy sugar again for a bit. Go without sugar in my coffee for the next few days. Sugar in heaps and he will never notice that I didn't buy the jam. And if I buy jam, then might as well forget sugar in my coffee for months to come. What coffee? If I buy jam, I will have to forget coffee and everything else for a long while.

It comes from giving him a sweet name. He'll want jam. My honey. My sweet. Madhu. I thought there should be a little sweet in this life. And there he was. You can think it into happening. Think what you want, and it is there in your hands. That's how it was for me with sweetness.

But the shopkeeper will ask, won't he? 'Annakutty, what's the fuss? Butter and jam is for who?' I know what they think: I shouldn't celebrate his birthday. But isn't my boy like any other child? Each birthday, new worries. If I tell him it is his birthday, naturally he will tell the other children. How much easier when he turned three and didn't even know it. He will want toffee. A bagful to treat everyone. Should I hide his birthday from him? He will want at least eight–ten toffees. There's Shekhar, Satish, Manoj and all those others. Playing with who all, that I don't even know. Boys who will tell him soon enough what he is and what his mother is, boys who will take the trouble to explain to him what the word 'bastard' means.

Oh, but he will want at least two toffees apiece. More than five he plays with, including that tall fellow. What is that one's name?

At least ten, twelve toffees are needed. It is what comes from letting him play with other children. If Manoj hadn't given out those toffees on his birthday, then my boy wouldn't even know to want toffee for his friends.

Does a big bag of toffees make one child better than another child? Does it mean he is loved more?

If I don't make him idli-butter-jam—no, it will have to be idli-butter-sugar—if I don't make anything special, then he won't know it is his birthday. Forget the appam and stew for dinner. Or don't tell him it is his birthday. Nothing special for breakfast. Otherwise the whole day he will expect more. I can make just the appam and stew at night. If I can ask for a piece of hen, it must be a leg, at the butcher's ... that way, at least the boy will eat something special for his birthday dinner. He doesn't have to know it is his birthday.

He can have appam. First with milk and sugar. Then at least one appam he must have with meat. Later I can tell him we celebrated. In a few days. Better, a few weeks. I will tell him, remember, we had stew and appam.

And no matter the cost, we will have a little bakery cake.

Almost morning. I'll go to the market as soon as he wakes up.

'Wake up. Wake up. No, no, Nina. Not you, Nina. Him. Where is he?'

A small one. With cashews. The boy likes cashews. What expensive tastes. Can he really be mine? I don't have to buy the cake with any special sugar flowers and words on top. Just melt a little sugar at home, pour it on top, won't be soft but at least I'll save that money. It is cheating the way they make a thing pretty with poisonous colours, whip some air into it, since when does air cost anything, and then charge a price for it that all the love in the world can't afford. We never had icing when I was little. Just cake at Christmas, that too given out by the priest after we forced ourselves to stay awake through three hours of that singing and listening to him mumble, and the sitting, standing, kneeling. The light blinding us. I turned my lids inside out till tears poured from my eyes. I switched from one knee to the other. If the priest saw us nodding off, then no cake after mass. A basket filled with broken pieces, and I pushed to try and be the one to get it when he reached for a big one.

Later I will say, 'Don't tell me you've forgotten our celebration. Remember we celebrated with cake in the evening, and appam at night.' Just this one more time I can fool him. Next year it won't work. But this last time.

At last he is waking. And the idlis have turned out so soft. What does it matter about butter and jam? My boy will be happy with the sugar I save from my coffee.

Son, wake up. Son. It is your birthday, son.

How it rains on your birthday. What does it mean for it to rain like this? Son, the covers are wet. The rain is coming in the window. Oh, my poor child, you will get wet.

Does she know to tiptoe in when it rains to see if you are dry? Does she know that you wet the bed if not woken on rainy nights? Will she clean you gently? Will she scold you? It's all right if she scolds you. But she must do it gently.

My dear child. My darling, why must it rain so on your birthday? How heavily it falls. No, my son, Amma is not frightened. Yes, son, I hear the trees uprooting. Listen to those explosions. But it is only coconuts falling, shaken loose by this wind.

Those stories you tell me, son, about Shekhar riding to school every morning on a horse, about his father riding up top with

Shekhar on his lap . . . Son, don't think I don't know what you are telling me. We will celebrate your birthday. I will not fool you with an idli and a sprinkling of sugar. I must run now for the butter and jam and bakery cake. If that Tamilian shopkeeper wants to know what the fuss is about, I will tell him, it is my boy's birthday. I will not hide it from the man. And he better not say two words to try and shame me. I am not ashamed of your birthday, son.

Never mind the rain, son. There will be bakery cake.

4

The Prayerful

*Eternal rest grant unto him/her (them), O Lord; and let perpetual
light shine upon him/her (them). May he/she (they) rest in peace.
Amen.*

The prayerful are crowded up against the priest, kneeling behind
him, raising their arms nearly vertically in this room which cannot
spare space for arms flung any wider. It is a rare opportunity for
the Catholics to put on a display of the true faith for the unfaithful
hut-dwellers. And they do it with little enthusiasm. The woman
laid in their midst was ecumenical in her relationships, sometimes
admired though never emulated, and those gathered sense the
hypocrisy of imposing their theology where any other might have
an equal claim.

'Hail Mary, full of Grace.

Our Lord is with thee.

Blessed art thou among women,

And blessed is the fruit of thy womb,

Jesus.'

Catholics, and those non-Catholics schooled by Catholics, reply,

'Holy Mary, Mother of God
Pray for us sinners
Now and at the hour of our death. Amen.'

Father Paul waits for the elderly, trailing their ponderous 'Amens' before beginning again, 'Hail Mary, full of Grace.' He is slower this time in an effort to slow his parishioners. He would like this rosary to possess something other than the hypnotic pendulum swing of a tide coming in to shore, receding and coming in again—something other than inevitability. The teenagers in the audience will not allow it. By the time he is at the fourth Glorious Mystery, the Hail Marys are being traded for HolyMarymotherofgods; not as the tide is, which is after all a thing of beauty, but more like soda siphoned gurgling up a straw and released back in a rush of spit and froth.

The priest is modern. He was promising once—not two years have passed since—and studied in Rome where his will to climb the ladder of success was weakened by the realization of just how many more steps lay ahead. *And why hadn't this insight been available to him in his homeland?* It was in Rome that he came to understand the magnitude of the mother church—the machinations of those wielding its power and wealth. Not, as he had expected, an algebraic expression of increase in the petty bickering and corruption of seminary life back home in Kottayam. No.

It was then it occurred to him that he should walk away. He did. And it was revealed that he could. In compensation for its earlier obtuseness, his backwaters upbringing required no higher an achievement than he return—'Rome-returned'—to the home parish and there distribute prayer cards and scapulars blessed by the Holy Father himself. Not for him the five-year side-tour of Austria, conducting mass in small university towns. In German. Not for him the year in Mexico to learn Spanish so he could be matched to the Spanish-speaking souls congregating in the United States. Not for him service to the children of the church in Tübingen and Stamford and Calgary and Perth—children God has seen fit to exempt from the call to vocation.

The call had come to Father Paul when he was fourteen and he is sure that he remembers it coming in Malayalam—not German or Spanish. He was returned to Kerala, where he was left to conduct mass in Malayalam. Kerala, where a fog rolled in to obscure his English.

In the weeks before he was Rome-returned, while the great hordes of the ambitious departed for all parts of the globe not-Kerala, Father Paul made a first and last bid for adventure. He found himself a scooter, drove the streets outside the Vatican, and drank himself silly on coffee so glorious, he felt some inkling of the spiritual. As for the women, his desire to simply be allowed to smile at them was granted many times over and with such munificence that for ever after he was ruined for anything else but smiling at women.

What remained with him on his return to Kerala was not the memory of nights in his seminary room, alone save for the fright accompanying his mulish refusal to touch the prescribed Latin text books. Instead, there was a memory of Italian streets bumping under small wheels and the sudden skittering of his scooter, the miraculous righting of itself. A woman looking up, her mouth opening, a perfect circle of dismay, then smiling as the wheels carried him from the smile. The memory of this minor accident averted is enough to send the blood tingling to his fingertips. An image of him raising the host, his back turned, in a church full of strangers, is only another version of the childhood horror of racing across the field, dribbling the ball to the accompaniment of THE WRONG WAY screams from his team-mates. So easily he might have been one thing, and here instead he is another. On his return, his mother was pleased to wear her scapular, and he was pleased to be assigned to this small village a half hour from the nearest diocesan office of any size, in Palai.

After the rosary, in an unwilled but not unanticipated move, the prayer session passes from Father Paul's hands into the hands of Deacon Thomachan. When he isn't rapping his knuckles to the tune of the day's hymn on the skulls of the altar boys at St Anthony's, Thomachan likes nothing better than to take over duties from the priests that the Palai office sends his way. Thomachan leads the flock, his sonorous voice raising prayer after prayer from the back row, each prayer detonating above the bowed heads of the sheep with a boom louder than the previous one. This is pyrotechnics that cannot be taught in any seminary.

'Oh Saint Maria Goretti, you who, strengthened by God's grace, did not hesitate even at the age of twelve to sacrifice life itself to defend your virginal purity, look graciously on the unhappy human race which has strayed far from the path of eternal salvation. Teach us all, and especially youth, with what courage and promptitude we should flee for the love of Jesus anything that could offend Him or stain our souls with sin.

'Lord, take unto you your daughter who lived a life of sin, but who in death approaches your throne on her knees, and may we one day enjoy with her and with thee the imperishable glory of Heaven. Amen.'

Now the room rushes panting through a long and blurred

parade of saints who once invoked are then supplicated to 'Pray for us'—almost peremptorily, Father Paul notes. People used to belligerence must be so even in prayer. Those kneeling, and those who forty-five minutes into it are seated on the floor with knees modestly tucked away, plead with Saint Peter, Saint Paul, Saint Andrew, Saint James, Saint John, Saint Thomas, Saint Mattias . . .

Deacon Thomachan's belly protests the delay in receiving its daily infusion of coffee. A monstrous bubble swelling and rising hard on the heels of Saint Barnabas overtakes him, so Saint Barnabas is announced to the room with a trumpeting, the gaseous reverberations of which momentarily fuddle Thomachan.

Jonikutty seizes this opportunity to unleash into the room a dazzle of saints: Saint Cupertino, Saint Ephrem, Saint Berchumans, Saint Kiklia and Saint Siprian.

The crowd likes the show. If Thomachan thinks he can outdo the priest, the crowd is happy for him to learn that this is only as expected. Shouldn't a deacon of six decades know his way around the saints? After all, the priests the Diocesan office at Palai sends their way are so uniformly young, their skulls must still bear the bruise marks of their own recent tenure as altar boys. They are, as a rule, quickly done with their tour of duty. Mostly a blur, and not easily told apart, they are known, all of them, by the affectionate and disparaging title—Kunjachan, Little Father.

And if Thomachan does his job as he should, why should he expect to be exalted for it? Is the salary he is paid to manage the affairs of the church, to sweep and mop and keep a correct count of the Eucharist ready to be blessed at mass, not enough for him, that he must also insist on competing with the various Kunjachans that come to serve them?

Jonikutty is right to put Thomachan in his place. And when Jonikutty's flow of saints threatens to turn into a deluge, they know to put Jonikutty in his place. They are unambiguously commanding when calling for Saint Corbinian to 'Pray for us!'

The command Father Paul knows is directed at him—it is time to bring this prayer session to a close. Father Paul is not sure whether to be dismayed or relieved: the belligerence of his parishioners is intended for him and not for the saints. In any case, he mumbles his way through the needful. With a collective sense of expectancy—now there will be food and coffee—the crowd looks to him to lead them out from the room.

But Father Paul kneels another moment. He feels he should address the group from outside the obscurity of prayer, and the safety of his back turned to them. So he turns, and the crowd is pleased to note the haggard face that he turns to them.

'We pray today for someone who was many things to many people. She was an elder in our community, Annamma, and an elder sister to many, Annachechi. She was young Nina's aunt, her Peramma. I knew her as my parishioner, Annakutty Verghese.'

He stops, realizing he has nothing further to offer. Then it stumbles from him, 'We pray today because the passing of our sister teaches us to remain steadfast in our faith even as we mourn.' Another moment of silence elapses, then he adds, 'I will inform Father Augustine. I will also inform Annakutty's sister in Dubai. We must wait for them, for her sister and her sister's husband. Mass and burial will not take place before tomorrow. We will keep vigil till then.'

The room rustles a vague assent.

The window lets in a breeze that finds no entry in Annakutty's nostrils. They have been sealed with twists of cotton wool. The hands that sealed her nostrils, ears and eyes, are now repositioning her head so it faces east. As if the funeral rites are already underway, those gathered pull the bed, scraping it across the floor, away from the wall it is leaned against, and an orderly shuffling processes its way around the bed. The breeze collects scents from the shuffling crowd—each particular one known so recently to the dead woman: talcum powder mealy with sweat, heavy scent of hair-oil, of rain and mud, of grease from frying caught in the folds of trailing skirts. The breeze becomes unruly, given no access to the shut door that is Annakutty's mind. Where has *she* gone? A few stray coughs are heard. A throat is cleared. Outside the house, everything speaks: crows, cows, calves, streams, stray leaves falling into yesterday's dry well. Inside, the cleared throat breaks into song.

The scented breeze—subdued in its departure from the home that was Annakutty's, the recognition that was hers, the *she* that was her—reaches the twittering sounds outside. The larger world comes to know Annakutty is no more. Led by the rooster, a moment of strict silence is observed. Then a clang, as the canister on the front steps is picked up and carried back to the kitchen from whence it came. There it yields enough milk to lighten forty cups of coffee. Word has reached Devasi's stalwart Jansy: Annakutty is no more.

Father Paul steps over tree roots ruptured from the forest floor, steps out onto the tarmac road and hitching his cassock high kicks his motorcycle from sleep. It snarls a reply. He kicks it again, mounts and speeds away.

Back in Annakutty's yard, a miserable squawking, then silence, and the rooster must call for additional mourning. How these events cascade! Now his hens are carried away to be mated with small onions, green chillies, ginger, coconut, for an evening meal to feed twice forty.

Nina will surely need till evening to stop her whimpering.

5

But Nina Refuses to Whimper

Nina wends her way through the rubber trees separating her home from the huts nearby. 'Rrroooooo'—the sound of four-year-old Kunjukuttan's game finds her. He is bound to try to force her to play. She ducks into the goat-shed and tries to feed the babies, born just the week before. But they want nothing to do with the leaves she holds out. Her own stomach growls. No one has called her to eat. She is torn between humiliation and anger at the thought that she may have to ask for food at a neighbour's.

'Not here,' she mumbles to herself, thinking of the huts and the undoubtedly poor stores of food within. But her Peramma, she knows, would not have hesitated to enter or to share a meal within.

She ducks again to hide when two children emerge dressed for school. No one can make me go to school today, she exults. She cannot help the little hop of joy. Then comes the jolt.

Oh but Perammma. She. And I forgot.

Now Nina wants to cry. Now she tells herself: but I did not cry last night. No, I did not. Not till nearly morning. No, I won't cry.

And anyway, Peramma didn't just die last night. She began dying from a year ago.

Of course, everyone is always dying from the moment they are born. It's just that from last year Peramma began to do it in a serious way. By 'serious' I mean that she lay down in bed soon after Thambi Perappan died, and what was it she said? She said she had to conserve her energy to live. That let me know she *was* dying. And from there in bed, she was sweet to me. She let me do everything in bed with her: my homework, even eating and reading. Before she started her serious dying, she would scold me if she saw me reading in bed. Before the dying, I wasn't allowed to read Harry Potter because I got scared in the second book when Mrs Norris was hung and there was blood-writing on the wall. Afterward I asked her if I couldn't read it in bed with her and then I wouldn't be afraid. She said, 'Yes.' She turned sweet, Peramma did, on the way to the end.

Thambi Perappan loved her like anything. He loved her with songs and jokes and riddles. Which made it fun to be around them. But I never thought when Thambi Perappan was alive about how Peramma must feel about him.

I have seen Perappan put oil in Peramma's hair and comb it. When he asked me to run outside and throw the hair he cleaned from the comb and balled into his hands, I always made a face of disgust, mostly just to make him laugh. But after he laughed, he would push himself up, hobble out with his cane, and through the doorway we'd see him throwing the hair high to reach the roof of the cowshed. Well, he lost his balance when he threw. If you've never known a one-legged man then you can't know that it is hard to balance and throw when you have only one leg on which to remain standing. If I felt bad and thought that I should have thrown the hair for him, I just told myself the person who really should have gone out there was Peramma.

It was a long time after he died, when she continued remaining in bed, getting out only in the evenings and that too to go sit outside in the dark without me that I understood she had loved him like he loved her.

People always said she was lucky to find him. Which I could understand because of how sweet he was. He played her head like a drum when he oiled her hair and the song he sang most often went like this:

'She shimmered her hair with musk oil
She jingled her beaded bracelets.'

He also sang a song about her being a black girl. I don't even want to think about the words in that song. He called her his black beauty. This I hated because I am black, and I don't think it's anything that needs to be noticed—whether in a good way or a bad way. He was always tugging her plait when she passed him and saying black beauty and then winking to me. This, I really hated. It was as if he thought that I would care to be called black beauty. If you want to call me a beauty, that's fine with me. But to add a word like black is no joke, in my mind. I told him this: Black Beauty is the name of a horse in a storybook. I should have known he would laugh. For a while after that, every time I was near them, he pretended to gallop using his cane and his one leg. Even Peramma laughed at me when he did this. I hated that.

I think he was trying to tell me something about how being one-legged is like being black. Or maybe it was about how being one-legged is worse than being black. If that is true, and I don't think like that of course, but if it is true in the thoughts of other people then they should have been saying *he* was lucky to get Peramma, and not that she was lucky to have found him.

Back then when Perappan and Peramma were poking so much fun at me, if I'd had a choice, I would have gone straight home, to my real home, and told my mother that I wasn't going to live at Peramma's anymore. But there was no choice since my real home's front door has a big lock on it. I had to remain.

When my mother first went to work in Dubai, it was decided I should live with Peramma. I think it was because, besides my mother, no one else in our family has a big education. All my father's relations are nice, but no one that side has an education beyond primary. Peramma went up to her matriculation, same as I will in a few years. Peramma said to forget about being an astronaut, but after my matriculation I am going to apply to ISRO, which is the Indian Space Research Organization. Peramma was surprised I knew that. Sister Bernadette says I have the most General Knowledge of anyone in my class and in my school.

Which is the brightest star next to our sun? Sirius.

Can you give another name for Sirius? Dog Star.

Which planet is the closest to Earth? Venus.

My marks in GK are very high when there are questions about space. So ISRO is easy for me.

I heard them in the kitchen. They were saying Peramma was lucky. It's the same old thing but they were saying it in an all new way. Out loud. I heard it in a new way too.

Everyone knows Peramma was waiting for the Lost Boy to come home before she died. She was even advertising in the newspapers for him to come. Nobody liked that. At Perappan's funeral the same thing was said.

'How lucky she is to have her wish not come true.'

Also they said, 'God knows not to answer all our prayers.'

People always talk about Peramma as if they are saying their prayers. The sounds come out like the sound of prayer, which is the sound of the river running. Soft and loud. Soft and loud. The loud part is the Amen. The loud part is the angry part that says: 'And to think she doesn't even know how lucky she is.'

At least I know the truth. I know the Lost Boy is on his way home. She told me last night to tell him when he gets here that she waited. She told me to say exactly the words: 'I waited.'

And I would have never known if I had not been here—here when Perappan went, and here for Peramma's passing also.

I want food. I am hungry. No one has said, Come eat, even though it is so late now and I haven't eaten since yesterday. They are saying food cannot be eaten in our house since Peramma has died. So what? I know they will do some cooking in Jansyammai's house like they did for Perappan's funeral. They can call me there. As long as they don't call me to eat, I will not ask them for food.

Kunjachan is done saying prayers and gone now to the Junction to telephone my parents in Dubai. It will take till tomorrow at least before they come in a plane. They won't bury Peramma till my mother comes, because my mother and she were sisters. Half-sisters. Tonight we will all stay awake with Peramma. I am going to sleep this afternoon so I can be awake tonight. Two nights. That will be two nights that I am awake. If no one gives me food, then I will be hungry till my mother comes. Then people will have to answer to her.

When I first came to live here I was four. I cried so hard I couldn't eat. Every time Peramma held me I stopped crying. But as soon as she stopped holding me, I started again. So she held me all day and night. How do I know about this since it happened so long ago? Peramma and Perappan always liked to talk about when I first came. To make them happy, I would ask them to tell me about it. They talked about it like it was the most important thing that ever happened to them. Which of course made me feel good. When I was little and I cried for my mother, Peramma had to put me on her lap even when she cut the vegetables, and we sat on the floor with her arms circled around me and she cut the vegetables like that. She told me to sit back and to be careful. This part I can also remember: I sat back and her body was so different from my mother's. Hers was hard and thin. My mother's was fat and good. I used to blow on my mother's stomach and make a sound like the sound of Perappan's autorickshaw horn. I never could imagine doing that to Peramma. I could tell that her stomach, with the skin so thin that it didn't fold at all, would never blow the sound of my mother's stomach.

Never once did I tell Peramma what I remembered from when I first came to live here. Never once did I tell her because I got used to her stomach and the skin of it and the colour of it, which is like my colour. It is Peramma I know. And no one talks to people that they know about knowing them, do they? We always talk about the people we don't know, who are gone, not the people who stay. It is Peramma I know, and my mother is who I remember every year when she comes home again. When I was little and my mother returned, I cried and wouldn't go to her. So Peramma must have come to know I liked being with her. But each time when my mother got ready to leave, I wanted to tie her to the iron pipe that holds up the roof of our house so she wouldn't leave. Every year I started by hating her then loving her; and now when she comes and goes, I don't cry, at least not aloud, and I don't think about tying her up. All this my mother doesn't know about me.

I know who I am; and Peramma knew me too. She must have known how even when we fought about ISRO and my wanting to become an astronaut, I always felt happiest living in this house with her. Otherwise, why would she have told me in the end that this is where I must stay even when she is gone? Here is where I am happy, and here is where Peramma's son will come for her and me. This much Peramma has promised me.

She told me a story about myself last night. She told me this story because I keep forgetting the many things that happened to me when I was little. When my first tooth started to fall out, I was five, maybe six years old. That was at least six years ago. I was so scared to pull my old tooth that my new tooth came through and stuck itself tight behind the old one. That one tooth is still a little behind all the others. Peramma told me that I used to make excuses about the old tooth still remaining there. I used to say, my eyes know it is time for my tooth to come out and my nose, it knows also; my ears know. Only my mouth doesn't know. I used to say that my ears could hear my new tooth asking for space and my eyes could go back in my head to see the tooth looking for space and my nose could smell from inside the smell of the new tooth. Only my mouth couldn't know anything because it was where everything was happening. This was the excuse I made for not wanting to pull my tooth. One day, Perappan put a string around my old tooth and stretched the string to the door and tied it to the handle there. Then, while Peramma told me to look right into her eyes, Perappan pulled the door shut and my tooth hung on the floor from the end of the string.

Peramma was busy last night telling me this story about when I was five, and I was busy remembering the story the way it really happened. I remembered, after the tooth came out, it was Peramma who scolded me for crying and Perappan who gave me sweets. And another thing I remembered was Peramma holding me so tight that I couldn't wiggle when the door was shut and the tooth was pulled. She was hard with me many times when I was little; alongside that she took care of me.

Last night, while Peramma kept breathing with her eyes shut, all I could think was I would never have remembered this story about myself if Peramma hadn't just told it. So how am I going to know about all the things that happened to me when I was little if she is not here to tell me the stories? When she was here, she would start a story and I would remember it better even than her. But without her, I don't know the start of the stories. So she is not an old tooth that I can pull out and toss on the roof and forget about. She is my Peramma who knew me.

After the story about the tooth, there was a long time for silence. I started counting, tick-tick one, tick-tick two, tick-tick three. Peramma woke up from her heavy-breathing sleep and asked me to think about my life without her. I tried to last night and I didn't feel what she was asking me to feel. And I still can't.

Before she died, my Peramma said it's important to remember not only the things that have happened. She said it is important to remember what will happen. I am worried about remembering just the things that have happened. How am I to remember what has not happened yet? She said if you remember it, it will happen. That it is a way of dreaming. If that's true then I should be able to dream about being an astronaut. But she said I can't be one because no one from Kerala has ever dreamed of anything like that. She wants me to dream about becoming a nurse. Before you know it, she said, you will grow up. As if that has anything to do with anything. I didn't want to fight with her. I just told her, I am not going to grow up.

She said, remember the Lost Boy has grown up without me for so many years.

I didn't tell her this but when she was talking about him last night, I could see everything she was seeing. Her words and my dreaming got mixed up, I saw her Lost Boy. He was grown-up and a stranger. He spoke in English even though he should have been speaking in German, which is the language of his German mother and German father. I wish he would have taken a decision like me to not grow up. Or maybe to grow up just a little so he is as old as me, but not older. Then I could teach him the games of here, and he would give me marbles from Germany.

Tonight they will be singing hymns. If Perappan were here, he might sing the Black Girl song. When he went, Peramma sang it as we sat with his body. Everyone pretended to be shocked at her. All the stuff about, 'Lay her down, she is overcome,' and all the whispers about, 'Now she will go mad,' it was all just pretend feelings. Really, everyone was happy for her making a drama. Tonight there will be a high number of pretend feelings. I don't have Peramma's courage to sing a song like Black Girl. But I have courage for other things that I will eventually do. And I was brave last night.

Yesterday after evening prayer, Peramma told everyone to leave. They did. Right then I started being brave. The room smelled like meat roasting. Her stomach was bloated and she wanted me to press on her stomach so she could pass wind. It was horrible to be near her. But I went when she called me. I stayed with her. Everyone left the house. Then she talked again. She forgot who I was. She called me by many other names. She even called me by her lost son's name. Then she called me by my name and told me to close the window before the rain got in. I was afraid of the window being open. The shutters kept banging against the wall outside. But I was also afraid to put my hand out into the dark to pull them shut.

Sometimes at night if I get cold I have the feeling of wanting to get up and pull the cover from the foot of the bed, but at the same time it is impossible to push my way out of sleep. I stay asleep and feel cold all night.

After I got out of bed to act like I was closing the window I said, 'It's closed, Peramma.'

I got right back into bed. Then I realized she was resting for a long time and I waited even after I was pretty sure she wouldn't talk again. She never came back. Then I knew for sure.

Before she died, she told me she might die soon. She told me not to be afraid. I was not afraid till it was almost morning. I did not cry till it was almost morning.

6

(with her last breath)

My stepmother cuts my hair off. She cuts it close to my head. I want to beg her, Saramma, please don't. I don't beg. And the cutting isn't enough for her. She takes a razor into her hand. It is my father's razor. I want to beg my father, Acha, please. He looks away from me. He is her husband. He is my father. The same man. He doesn't know how to be both. Saramma shaves my head.

Why do I bow my head?

She wipes the blade on the edge of the bed. I sit on the floor, hunched between her legs. My hair is spilled around me. I look up to see the legs crowding the door. They have come to stare at me. I travel up the legs to the eyes that stare at me. I stare back at them.

She thinks if she cuts my hair, my love will no longer look at me. No, that's not it. She thinks if she cuts my hair, I will feel too ugly to go to him. And yes, that he won't want me. She doesn't know. I have given myself to him. And he to me. He will take me from my father and from her, from Saramma. We will have our own home. My hair will grow.

Here is my love. Here he is. Mine. Dropping something to the ground, bending down to look at me through the thicket of legs. He looks at me in shock. He looks at me in shame. I want to look at him as if I am stone. The rain is a curtain between us. He swims in the door.

I move my tongue to tell him to go. I move my tongue to beg him to stay, but the words that come—

'Nina girl, close this window before the rain gets in.'

'Nina,' I call again. That girl doesn't know to answer when she is called. I will tell my sister. 'Tessie, take your daughter. I can no longer raise her.'

No, I will not tell Tessie. Let the girl grow as she is. Disobedience has its place.

'Nina, listen to me. You will catch a cold from this rain.'

But how is it that Saramma is here? And my father? That was so long ago when I was a girl and we lived in Cochin. Oh my father! Oh, he will hear Saramma scream. She will alert those who sleep. My father, the whole village, they will all know. Wait, that was in Cochin she shaved my head. Then we went to her village. And where am I now?

'Nina, where am I?'

Oh, but Saramma, don't. Please. You were right. He wanted nothing more to do with me. You have already punished me. No more.

And Saramma screams: 'Catch her. Where is the girl going? Jose, I told you. You didn't believe me. Now you see her. Now you see her go.'

7

Annachechi Leaves Tessiebaby
Without a Story

Tessie is at the nurse's station, hunched over the phone. Her back is to the hallway, empty of everything save the artificial yellow light that bathes it from the ceiling.

In her mind she cries, 'Chechi, Chechi, Annachechi' and the cry that never found utterance in all her past crying for her sister, 'Don't goooooooo.'

'Who are you?' she whispers into the phone. 'Why do you say such a thing?'

When he doesn't reply immediately, she shouts: 'Who are you to say such a thing?

All the while, a hand trembles, tries to loosen pins from her hair. From far away, over the phone line, comes the sound of rain in Kerala, but outside the hospital's double-paned windows, there is no weather. Only the dreary grey of tinted glass casting its pall over the endless Dubai lawn; grey blurs the outline of a Dubai cat crossing this Dubai lawn. Grey, the Dubai bird that taunts her from across a stretch of the Dubai lawn. It is not yet time for Tessie to remember that her daughter Nina has lost the aunt who raised her. All Tessie can feel is disbelief. All she can hear in her head is her long ago cry from when she first lost her elder sister—'Chechi, Chechi, Annachechi.' The only other person at the nurse's station, a Filipino nurse whom Tessie despises for the fact that she is Filipino, doesn't know that in a few seconds a phone will fly through the air, just miss hitting her and scatter the contents of the tray of suture material she is listlessly assembling.

When Tessie is a baby, she is known as Tessiebaby. It is her half-sister who names her, and it is her half-sister, not her mother, Saramma, who carries Tessiebaby on her hips everywhere. Accordingly, Tessiebaby longs for her Annachechi with the hopelessness a child usually reserves for the mother. And when Tessiebaby's mother is cruel to Annachechi, torn between the two loves of her life, Tessiebaby is lifted right out of her golden skin. She observes the world from the vantage point of someone terrified that she will be asked to choose. Tessie's eyes see as early as four or five what everyone around her has missed. She sees that Annachechi is extraordinary. Beautiful. Wrapped in black. Slipped easily into night.

Tessie is not six when Annachechi gets up one night from the bed they share to slip away in the dark as she often does, but this time there is shouting, a lamp is lit and Annachechi is dragged back inside. Tessiebaby's mother, who is her Amma but somehow not Annachechi's, pulls at Annachechi's clothes till they tear from her body. Annachechi shouts, 'Go ahead and take my clothes from me, Saramma, I will leave the house like this.' Annachechi does not return to lie next to Tessiebaby that night, or ever again.

Yes, Annachechi is that love that forever leaves, chased by the angry voice in the night: 'Catch her. Where is the girl going? Jose,

I told you. You didn't believe me. Now you see her. Now you see her go.'

After Annachechi is gone, Tessiebaby asks 'why' and 'where', and is slapped by Amma for asking.

Soon afterward, consulting her memory, Tessiebaby discovers she no longer remembers her Annachechi's face. Now she turns to the women in the village, trading information they want, particularly about her mother Saramma's life in Cochin city, in return for information that will help her remember.

'Yes, when we lived in the big city, in Cochin, Amma went far away to work and our Achan had already left us and gone, so Annachechi had to become my mother and search for a father for us. But luckily Amma and Achan both came back. Is that why Annachechi has gone?'

Tessiebaby's memory becomes layered over with the neighbours' stories. She remembers a game of ant-funeral and Annachechi crying. Annachechi's hair was beautiful then; so long, Tessiebaby could hide inside it.

She tells the neighbours, 'Yes it was when we were in Cochin that Amma shaved Annachechi's hair. No, I don't know why Amma did that. But after that, we came here to the village, and Annachechi's head grew thorns.

'Still, Annachechi was beautiful. Wasn't she? But a few nights ago, Amma tore Annachechi's clothes up and then Annachechi shouted, "Saramma, I will leave the house like this." Then she looked ugly, and Amma had to lock her in the bathroom.'

The neighbour women are interested in Tessiebaby's story, but Tessiebaby needs something back from the women if she is to share more. Tessiebaby is smart, she is.

'Wasn't Annachechi beautiful?' Tessiebaby asks one woman.

Tessiebaby tries to remember something of her sister's beauty. She tries to reason where her sister comes by her beauty. It is an important question to concern herself with. Overheard, the half-uttered exclamations—'such an ugly thing . . . how could . . . an ugly thing like her, and black, attract anyone'—provide a clue to Annachechi's vanishing. She is not, and was never, ugly; they must not be, cannot be, talking about Tessiebaby's Annachechi. Perhaps, then, her sister is still here, hiding somewhere in the village. She searches, but all that remains is a memory of feeling her sister beautiful. Her sister's face is gone, and the story she gathers from the neighbourhood as a substitute for it is not beautiful.

Annachechi's father, Jose Verghese, marries Tessiebaby's mother Saramma John, then takes her from the village to his home in the city of Cochin. At that time, Tessiebaby is far from being born. But Annakutty is there in Cochin, waiting for her father to come home with a new mother for her. Annakutty is just old enough at two to run full tilt behind mongrel dogs, which is what she is doing when Saramma first sets eyes on her stepdaughter.

Tessiebaby nods at the neighbour-woman. She has heard the story many times now but is still unable to digest the idea of a time when she was not yet born. The story is a jumble for another reason. It is impossible to picture Annachechi as a baby.

Running, the baby's feet mash soft turds that fall to the ground unhindered by the cloth that has come loose from a string tied around her waist.

Tessiebaby likes this never-before-heard detail in the story. In this version, Annachechi is not just any old baby; she is a baby with a loose nappy. 'That was Annachechi, was it?' she asks.

The story reverts to what Tessiebaby has heard before, the story Saramma has told in the village, the story of her heroic efforts on behalf of her stepdaughter: in the new mother's care, the child is finally clean. And everyone approves of the widower taking himself a new wife.

Tessiebaby is bored. She interrupts: 'But when did I get born?'

Nine years go by before the new wife bears her own child, prompting eleven-year-old Annakutty to ask, 'When did I get born?'

'Annachechi asked that same question I just asked?'

And many years in the past, Saramma answers Annakutty with what she has not asked to know—that her mother had been prone to sadness in giving birth and that this had killed her soon after Annakutty's birth. Saramma speaks with equanimity. 'Four times. That is how many times your mother miscarried before you came along.'

Tessiebaby interrupts again, 'You can't die from being sad.'

The storyteller is impatient with Tessiebaby's interruptions, and tells her so. 'Enough. I have work to return to.'

Tessiebaby is once again alone with her imperfect memory.

At fourteen Annakutty's hair falls to her knees, and when she bends to a task, she likes to let it sweep the floor. Bending over Tessiebaby's game of ants marching to ant-funeral, her hair falls around little mounds outlined in flowers and twig crosses.

'Let's pretend this is a mother whose babies have died and now she is so sad she is going to die.'

Tessiebaby watches her sister take over the game. The mother ant, dragged off and killed, then delivered to a decorated mound, is suddenly bathed in Annachechi's falling tears. Tessiebaby pulls harder on her thumb, raising the skin in withered ridges.

Why is Annachechi crying? But these days it is no good asking Annachechi anything. She will either scream at Tessiebaby till Tessiebaby cries for her to stop, or Annachechi will burst into renewed sobbing. So Tessiebaby sits inside the dusty dark that is her Annachechi's hair and does not ask, and never comes to know that her sister has only just realized that a person who dies of sadness does so by killing herself.

Later, does Tessie understand her sister's tears later, when she is an adult? Perhaps she does. But when she is six-year-old Tessiebaby, trying to piece together a story from information she gathers in trade from neighbour-women, she finds adding tears to the story of beautiful hair results only in an unbeautiful story. And she so badly wants a beautiful story about her beautiful sister. Tessiebaby begins to reason all over again.

First they lived in Cochin. She is sure of this because didn't she once say to Annachechi that she remembers hearing someone crying when they lived in their first home, and what was Annachechi's reply?

'Silly, that was the sound of ships leaving Cochin harbour.'

'Ships? I never saw ships.'

'That's because Saramma told us to never leave the house. She went off but we had to stay shut in all the time.'

'Yes, because Amma likes us to be safe.'

Tessiebaby will see city life next only when she is thirteen herself, and that city will be Madras. She will be sent there on a mission to bring back Annachechi, vanished some eight years in the past. To bring Annachechi back, but not Annachechi's child, the little boy she has somehow made without the help of first getting married to someone. The only bit of the city she will see

·on this failed mission is the inside of a police station. Outside of the illustrated page, she will never again see ships.

Though Tessiebaby is not sure when it is they leave the city and move to the home village in rubber country, she remembers that her sister with the smooth head is unchanged: she does not stop slipping out from their home, into the night.

In rubber country, the smoothness of Annachechi's head gives slow way to pinpoints of black. When Tessie sits on Annachechi's shoulders pretending she is still Tessiebaby and not big girl Tessie Verghese—now going to Lower KG and learning her letters sitting on the ground with a slate and slate pencil—and Annachechi slips on the large rubber tree leaves climbing up the rubber tree hill, and Tessiebaby reaches for hair to grab hold of, there is none. There is just thorny stuff that pokes Tessiebaby's hands. Annachechi sets Tessiebaby down and Tessiebaby does not pretend anymore. They keep climbing the big hill, slipping on leaves, and the only reason Tessiebaby does not cry and insist on returning home is because she is sure there is punishment waiting for Annachechi at home. What part of Annachechi will they cut off next?

Annachechi promises her they are climbing to a big rock. That, Tessiebaby agrees, is a good reason to climb. Along the way, a nice Chettan comes to help. He picks Tessiebaby up and she becomes a baby again, seated upright in the crook of his arm. And he holds his other arm around Annachechi. Things are getting better and better. Tessiebaby lets her pretence fill out a truly elaborate story. The Chettan is the father, and Annachechi is the mother, and Tessiebaby is the baby.

The Chettan could well be the father because it has already been established that fathers appear suddenly. Tessiebaby's father with the broken back appears one day and moves them from Cochin to the village in rubber country that is now their home. Before he moves them from the house in the city, he shouts at them every day. He shouts early in the day, by afternoon he is gone and at night when he returns, he either sleeps quickly or sits quietly. But in the mornings when he wakes, he shouts and pulls away the cover Tessiebaby shares with her sister. The Chettan on the rubber hill appears and carries her in the crook of his arm without shouting.

When her father first appears, it is soon after their mother returns to announce that she will now live permanently with them. Annachechi, who is no longer to be Tessiebaby's 'Little Mother', points to the wizened man who is pressing himself against their mother.

'He is our father.'

Revelations are tumbling so rapidly, one upon another, Tessiebaby standing firmly on four-year-old legs, refuses to believe this. She stands in the kitchen doorway and peers at the two figures who have suddenly materialized in the dark. Annachechi, standing behind Tessiebaby, presses forward, nearly tripping Tessiebaby from the doorway and into the front room. Tessiebaby turns to see her sister's eyes shining in the dark.

Later, Tessie reasoning her way through her sister's beauty, remembers this moment. And she runs to share this memory with yet another neighbour woman.

'That was the first time Annachechi turned beautiful. I was almost going to fall into the room then, but I didn't. She was beautiful, wasn't she?'

And Tessiebaby hears, 'Your Annachechi was a lot of things. But a beauty, she was not.'

Tessiebaby remembers, Annachechi grips her so, and her voice is hoarse.

'Our father is back.'

Tessiebaby whimpers, 'He is killing Amma.'

And yes, their father has his hands wrapped around their mother's neck. Their father shouts at their mother.

'You had to go and have the baby? Just when I lose my job, it is then you decide to burden me with a child I don't need? And you blame me for leaving? And what all have I been hearing from people? Woman, where all have you wandered leaving the children?'

Annachechi holds her hand over Tessiebaby's ears. Tessiebaby wiggles free. She is not convinced the man is really angry. His shouting is so feeble. But she is glad her mother knows to nod and look at the ground. Because otherwise this man might keep shouting about Baby being a burden.

When their father returns to them, to that first home, the one in the city of crying ships, her sister takes her hand and they follow their mother and father down the street, which up to now she has only seen through the window with the bars and the trembling light. They travel till it is dark again and they have left the city in a bus to come to her mother's home village.

In the village, he stops shouting and becomes very quiet. In the village, especially in the village school, Tessiebaby is very important for having come from the city. In the village, she plays in the light outside every moment of the day, and never sees the inside of a dark room unless it is to lie down to sleep in one. In the village, her mother becomes like all other mothers, combs Tessiebaby's hair in the morning, and sends her to school with fried sardines in her tiffin. In the village, their mother remains with them day after day till Tessiebaby stops expecting to see her gone when she returns from school.

So in the afternoon, when after a night of shouting, Tessiebaby runs in from the half-light of the veranda into the one dark room, then back out to the veranda, and from there into the yard and up the rubber tree hill and back, all the while calling—Chechi, Chechi, Annachechi—she feels only disbelief. Her mother scoops her up, presses her hand over Tessiebaby's wailing.

'Don't goooooooo,' Tessiebaby hears in her head, but her mouth makes other sounds in her mother's palm.

Her mother, who has yet to be asked why and where, who has yet to slap her, simply says:

'Enough, Tessie. She is gone. No need for you to chase after her.'

8

The Shape of the Hole in Saramma's Story

Saramma slaps Tessiebaby. And regrets it immediately. To win her daughter back, Saramma offers her a story about Jose Verghese and Saramma John—and Tessie. About hunger. About trying to feed Tessiebaby when there was no food. About tea that boiled in her empty stomach. About stones that cried their hunger in her dreams. She leaves much out of the story. The shape of what she leaves out is the shape of Annakutty. Tessiebaby turns away from Saramma's story. She hasn't the wisdom to take the story and fill in the shape of the hole, to find her sister there.

Jose Verghese wishes to be kind to his new wife, Saramma John, a girl still in her teens, a girl distantly related to his first wife whose loss he is still mourning. So he tries.

It seems impossible to Saramma that she will ever talk to him, much less learn to love his touch and love him in turn. But she senses his effort to be kind. The first evening in her new home, he seats her on the floor and drags a small metal trunk over to her. It is similar to the one that has travelled with her from her village, even in the dust that covers it. He indicates she should open it. Feeling mutinous rather than shy, she shakes her head no. He opens the box and brings out his dead wife's clothes. A small stack of drab cotton. Who folded them so neatly, she wonders idly. Among them is an astonishing treasure—a length of something slippery she is compelled to touch. Vivid purple and blue, it is a sari. She fingers it and pushes it back into the box. The rest of the box is hers as well.

There is a collection of oddments. A snarl of twigs, she realizes, is a nest. Pictures ripped from magazines. Jose lets his hand pass over the collection; turning what appears to be a wooden spool in his hand, he tries to explain its function. She can hear the first wife speaking through him. Saramma does not want to know more. At the bottom of the box, a collection of polished pebbles. He throws one in the air, grabs for one of those on the ground, and by the time his palm turns to receive the one coming down, it is too late. She thinks him absurd for misjudging her so.

This is how he thinks I plan to spend my time? He thinks this is what I was doing till yesterday?

And she, eager to get to the grown-up work of marriage, reluctantly picks a stone, throws it in the air, makes the catch.

And she loves him, loving him even on those late nights his friends carry him home, his pockets empty and his tongue twisting when she asks him where the money is gone. On good weeks, Jose brings home whole notes. These whole notes convert to coins that pay off any number of shopkeepers. And always there are a few coins still left in hand. On the good weeks, Saramma is more than a little pleased. A note is more money than her father has ever put in her mother's hands.

So what if there are times when the careful hoard of coins pulls her from sleep, requires recounting in the dark, reveals by its feel that the coins are daily fewer in strength? So what, so what, she tells herself—a promise rather than a question.

Her Jose works in the city where land is not divided up endlessly. It is used instead to build a harbour into which the sea pushes ships loaded with the goods of the world. And these goods, Jose likes to tell her, would rot if it weren't for his strength. She pictures his body, the grey hairs springing from the chest and the long hard muscles at the waist that dip and disappear into cloth to emerge knotted at the back of his legs. He is an undulating wave she sees, flowing into a ship to empty it. The iron scent rising from him is the scent of the scrap metal he most often unloads, and laced with that is the nectar scent of ships that sail loaded with bananas.

Sometime, late that first year, there is the glamour of a wooden bed which Jose asks her to describe to the carpenter so that it can be made as she wishes. There is an afternoon of shame as the carpenter works in the house, asking her first to sit on their single chair, which he determines too high for her, then asking her to stand while he measures her legs. And when she reluctantly reveals her dream of a headboard, the carpenter laughs and makes the bed plain. Jose endorses this laughter when he returns from work that evening, laughing along with the carpenter, then taking out a packet of notes and, with licked finger, sliding five of them toward the man.

'From where, oh where do these ideas come into your head, Saramol?'

He takes measure of the bed. Laughing he pulls little Annakutty into the bed and tickles her. Saramma is pleased. She loves to make him laugh. Loves it especially when he calls her mol. Here is the preciousness of being nearly young enough to be his daughter. Annakutty's squeals as she twists herself into the sheet to escape her father's hands make Saramma look away. It will be her turn in the night. And, if she can get him to, afterward she means for him to hand her the rest of that packet.

With the advent of the bed, she understands the reason they have waited for their own child. A bed is needed so she can lie with her baby by her side. No need to hang cloth for a hammock to keep the baby off the floor, away from the rats that dart into the houses from the gutter outside. And Jose must come, in the evenings, to gaze at the little one, his imprint borne by her. A healthy baby kicking freely on a bed, not bound up in a hammock. She argues and pleads, and still her husband pulls out in the moment her hands reach between his legs to cup and tip him into her.

'We have a child,' he tells her.

She rages within herself, thinking of him lying with the woman who got to him before she did.

And much later, when he lies curled toward the wall, she hangs her feet from the bed enjoying the sensation for a moment before walking to where his work shirt hangs from a nail, both pockets empty.

So that is the use he puts the bed to for all the many years till they send him home pressed flat to a pallet hoisted on the shoulders of the able-bodied. For the first time, she pays attention to the talk of men, and under the clatter of their anger, she hears him. His voice is frail. What he says is incomprehensible.

'They did this to me, mol.'

'Who?'

She smiles to encourage him.

'The bosses. Bastards,' he says.

But it is in English. What she hears is a word she knows— 'baskets.' She smiles some more because of the foolishness of what he is saying. He looks at her in reproach.

For days he lies in the bed. When he is able to walk again, she cannot understand why he doesn't return to his work at the docks. This time she listens to the talk of women. They say, 'A hero he is.'

She understands they are laughing at Jose. He is no hero. The man who in past evenings finished his dinner in a rush, stepped out to the stoop and was not finished lighting his first cigarette before other men gathered around him, who knew to take a quiet hum and grow it to speechifying, then arguing then shouting, has no more companions, sits no more on the stoop, is no more applauded, smokes his cigarette indoors, alone, laid flat on the floor. He is no longer a leader among the men of his neighbourhood. His speeches about trade unionism are now a mumble, and eventually silence, on his lips. During the day, when he sees her looking at him, he settles pain into his face and slips a hand to his back. In the night, he tells her apologetically, 'It's only the big motions that hurt. The small ones are all right.'

Then a little later, 'Lay still mol, otherwise I cannot.'

So she climbs out from under him and balances herself above.

The first night after the baby is born, Saramma lies in bed listening to the rats scuttling in the thatch roof above. The room reeks of her labour. In the kitchen, she can hear Annakutty breathing in sleep. Suddenly the girl is grown into a giant, her breathing meaty and full of life. Saramma's nausea grows. The child next to her startles, limbs springing out as if it would swim in the bed. Then it falls back into a sleep full of snuffling. She lies listening to its irregular breathing and terror grows in her.

Where is Jose? She feels her loneliness keenly. I can't do it alone, she pleads. Then she is angry: wasn't it him and his doing? And how was she at twenty-six, and still without a child of her own, to allow him to keep pulling out? How can Jose say she pestered him for the baby? He made the baby inside her, and she remembers his eyes shining in admiration when she rose above him.

In the four years she continues in the city, Saramma takes charge. Before the return of her bleeding, before Tessiebaby can complete her first year, Saramma sells the bed. It rises on two pairs of human legs and walks right out the door, laughing at her as it goes.

She hears Jose asking her from long ago in the past, 'From where, oh where do these ideas come into your head, Saramol?'

Annakutty is taken out of school and kept home to watch the baby. Saramma takes up work as a washerwoman in the houses along the waterfront. Jose leaves. Then he returns. Empty handed. He repeats this till Saramma grows weary from the fear that builds with each departure, and weary from the hopes dashed with each return, and weary especially from the long wait in between.

One night, Saramma screams for the neighbours to come. Though they crowd in the doorway, they do not stop Jose. Her legs locked, he rides her through air, afloat on the straw mat, the ends of which she still clutches, but which no longer covers the coins and notes saved to pay the rent. The neighbours watch as

Jose kicks himself free of her. She marvels that anger at her should straighten his back for the first time in months. He leaves with the money. She locks the door against him, pulls her daughter to the thin stuff in her breast and looks away from the other child. The time comes when there is nothing in her breast for her daughter.

She asks the women she works for if they will allow her to take home the food they give her. The women don't see a problem with the request. Saramma's eyes scan the piece of dried fish and bowl of rice gruel or the banana and two idlis to see how she will stretch this meal. There is nothing to do but feed the baby till she clamps her mouth against more. Then Saramma hands what remains to Annakutty. When she feeds the baby, Saramma feels light-headed from the need to bring the baby's mouthful to her own mouth. The act of pushing the nearly empty leaf plate toward Annakutty debilitates her so that she has energy only for looking out the window. Yet her every nerve remains alive to the sound of Annakutty's cautious chewing. It takes five days for her to tell Annakutty to leave the house when she comes to feed the baby. When she is done feeding Tessiebaby, Saramma crams a whole idli into her mouth. There is no room in her mouth for chewing. She breathes with difficulty.

Again, Saramma approaches the women she works for. Can she bring her children to work with her? Her employers raise their eyebrows. They see trouble headed their way. But aren't they women, as this thing in front of them is, and too soft to fight a disaster even as it looms? They allow that the washerwoman's children can play in the yard while she goes about her work. Saramma and Annakutty take turns carrying the baby on the long walk to the waterfront. There, they move from one house to the next. When meal breaks are called, two leaves are spread on the ground; they squat, eating quickly, quietly. Saramma leaves Annakutty to hers, and feeds Tessiebaby from her own leaf. In the space of morning and afternoon, they consume a day's allotment of meals. With nothing to carry home, they fast through evening and night. But this arrangement is infinitely preferable to the days of stretching one plate of food three ways.

Nine days they feed well, though elsewhere in the land, famine has reigned. And food is yet to be had for any price. On the waterfront, Saramma hurries past men hanging in bunches, their hands empty, or employed in scratching their legs, in swatting one another. She refuses to wonder where Jose is getting his feed from.

On the tenth day, Saramma looks up from the clothes she is washing to see anger on the face of her employer. She follows the woman's eyes to Annakutty perched on a flat stone, bent over a clay pot, scaling fish, silver coins flying in the air, catching and flashing in the loosened waves of her hair. Stupid girl. Saramma will tell the girl to keep her hair tied. If a strand of it finds its way into the cooking. Then Saramma sees the woman's head turn from Annakutty to elsewhere and back to Annakutty. And Saramma sees it too. The boy, the woman's son, watching Annakutty. And the secretive movement of his hand on the checked cloth covering his thigh. Saramma looks again at Annakutty and sees the girl hunch harder into herself. The girl knows, Saramma thinks in astonishment.

The boy's mother calls to him. He replies in a smooth voice, 'Tell this girl to bring me some bath water.'

'I'll do that.' Saramma's words are an appeal.

In the kitchen, water is steaming on the woodstove. She picks the blackened pot up by its lip, pours a steady stream with burning fingers, and curses Annakutty. She jog-sways back to the boy, the bucket sloshing and spilling its content in her haste.

That afternoon, the woman of the house tells Saramma, 'You needn't come again.'

Annakutty's straw mat is no longer rolled up in the mornings. She lays prone on it. It is easy to pretend the girl is ill and unable to eat. A week goes by, and late in the evening, Annakutty whispers to Saramma that she needs help going out. Tipped forward, hands on the ground in front of her to support herself, she labours to push out stool so hard she whimpers as it emerges slimy with blood. The girl begins gasping; her wet eyes, when they find Saramma's, are dilated in fear. Saramma pours water. The girl is too weak to do this for herself. They leave the field together. Saramma hurries home the next day and feeds Annakutty before Tessiebaby. Though the girl's lips are cracked and her mouth a welter of sores, she swallows and Saramma speaks to her softly, urging her to chew or she will lose the meal. Annakutty responds by touching Saramma on the cheek, then pushing the plate back toward her. Saramma flinches from the gratitude in that touch. After that, her days are further broken by multiple trips home to look in on the girl. The tea she allows herself to drink at each of her employer's boils in her belly as she walks.

Walking home, she stops where the neighbourhood dumps its refuse. It is not, she tells herself, what she has come to do. And still her eyes scan the refuse for food discarded from other homes. Her hands turn over the desiccated remains of a mango sucked free of everything but hair standing stiffly out from the seed. Banana peels and egg shells and fish bones. She takes a spiny, unchewed length, dodges the image of the rat that didn't find this bone and places it as cautiously as she might the Eucharistic wafer in her mouth. It crumbles to chalk; long decayed, it yields no juice. She spits it out.

She does not go to work the next morning. She waits till after the cooking smells from the houses around her have given way to the sound of dishes being scoured. She pushes her children to the furthest corner of the room, away from the high barred window that faces the lane outside.

'Stay back,' she whispers, her finger shaking in their faces. 'You are not to come to the door or window. You are to stay back and not look out.'

Tessiebaby's incessant whine—'rice Amma rice'—collapses into dry-eyed weeping. The children cower in the corner. Saramma goes to the house across the way and, standing in the doorway, calls to the woman inside.

'Padmachettathi, it is I, Saramma.'

A tap is turned shut, water trickling away for a few seconds afterwards. The sun, streaky-fingered, is just beginning to paint the sky. The lane behind Saramma and the doorway in which she stands is bright even in this early light. But she cannot see inside the dark house. She is not sure if anyone else has come to the door with Padma. She is afraid of Padma's husband. When she tries to imagine him responding to the request she has come to make, she cannot conjure anything definite. How a man might react to any situation, hers or anyone else's, is outside the scope of what she has pondered in the past.

Padma asks again, 'Is it you, Saramma? You've come early, haven't you?'

Saramma is accosted with a new shame: that of past

ungraciousness toward her neighbour whose welcoming overtures more than ten years in the past she had been both too shy and too proud to respond to. Hesitantly she speaks.

'My children are hungry. Will you give me some rice?'

Three months gone since Jose was last seen in the neighbourhood, carrying out the nightly assault on the doorway of his home, calling out to Saramma to—

'Open the door, or this time, my god knows I speak the truth, I will teach this woman a lesson.'

Padma returns with a square of cloth wrapped into a soft ball only a little bigger than her own fist. Now Saramma swallows hard; her hand midway to the tiny bundle halts.

'I need more. Enough for a week at least.'

Padma leaves her with the ball and Saramma hears her moving somewhere in the other room. It is unclear who she is scolding, whether it is a child, the husband, or a goat that strayed into the kitchen. The irritation in her voice sets the whole house rattling.

These houses all resemble one another. Though Saramma has never been further than this front room and most often when they have conversed in the past, it has been across the gutter and the alley that divides their two front doors from each other, she knows the contents of that room. A modest collection of items arrayed and shined as she might have done in the past in her own home. A collection of no substance, easily blown away.

In her own home, in the backroom kitchen, next to the stove, stands her collection of dented canisters that topple over at the least disturbance. They are empty of cooking oil, rice flour, paddy and salt. She has bargained on there being full containers of food stuff in Padmachettathi's backroom. But the lids banged down and canisters scraping the floor as they are dragged all speak a hollow tin sound. Saramma is afraid. What if Padmachettathi returns with nothing?

There is in her backroom a length of rope on which hangs the daily change of indoor and outdoor clothes. The mundu she starched, pressed and hung on the rope three months earlier still hangs there. Greyed in the first months from exposure to the cooking fire, it is turning yellow now that the fire is no longer lit. When will he return? Three months have been enough punishment for her. She will open the door this time, and if he kicks her, she will lie silently at his feet. Anything is better than standing at this door, waiting for the moment Padmachettathi returns to turn her away.

Padma returns with a newspaper folded into a brick this time. She hands this to Saramma along with a bottle of something warm. It is curds thinned with water. The fragrance of mustard seeds and turmeric rises from it. Chunks of green plantain have been added, giving the mix some substance.

'I will send the bottle back with Annakutty. Right away.'

Padma nods though she can't decipher the mumbled words Saramma speaks. There is no need to understand her words, which are a frail attempt at conveying the apology so eloquently conveyed by her lowered eyes, by her grip on the bottle, by the fact of the mumble, an admission that she no longer has a right even to words. Padma knows the bottle will be returned scrubbed clean. She feels pity, of course. And also curiosity: what must it be like to be this woman in this moment? Padma looks across at Saramma's house, the door apologizes as it opens and shuts softly. She shakes the question off and replaces it with approval for how Saramma is conducting herself.

Watching the front door open, the children's eyes dart toward their mother's entry. The door shuts; something their mother is holding winks at them in the dark. Annakutty moves slowly to light the fire. Even Tessiebaby knows to stop her whimpering.

Saramma makes rice gruel. She sloshes a giant share of the moru into their one plate and hand-feeds the children impatiently. Annakutty takes the food shyly. But Saramma is soured on Annakutty, and reads accusation in the child's failure to meet her eyes over the handful of food she proffers. Annakutty's shyness is wrapped in just one thought: with so much food, will she be allowed to eat her fill? Hunger knifes Saramma as the two girls take it in turn to slurp from her hand. The delay in addressing her own hunger to feed the ungrateful Annakutty brings a tide of anger swimming to Saramma's eyes. She gulps the handful intended for Annakutty. Annakutty meets her eyes in a plea and Saramma thinks, such a craven creature. Her own father cannot remember her. Saramma continues to feed herself and Tessiebaby till the plate is empty.

Then she tells Annakutty, 'You can make more if you are hungry. Tonight, and every morning and every night, you make kanji with this much rice.' She indicates the amount with her hand. 'There is only kanji now, but when I come back, I will bring other food. Maybe only three or four days will go by. If you are careful, there is enough rice here for at least ten days. I will be back before then. You eat in the morning and night. This much. Each time, you give half to Tessiebaby and half to yourself.'

Saramma walks as far as the end of the lane without looking back. She turns, knowing she will find Annakutty's eyes fixed on her. They are. She raises her hand in a small wave, not of greeting or parting, but a wave that indicates Annakutty should step back from the window. The girl's fear, and Saramma's own, can only grow if they hold each other thus. At least avert your eyes. And she averts her own to show the girl how it is done. She walks on, turning the corner and many more, still feeling herself caught in those eyes. Here, on the side of the open road leading out of the city, she rests to prepare for the journey ahead.

Her hands seek the ground, stroking the sun-warmed skin of stones. A shiver passes through her in remembering that it was in this position she released herself to childbirth. She dreams in the heat of the noon-day sun that she has given birth to these stones. She dreams, knowing her dream is just that—a dream. Her children are not stones. Yet under her hands, the stones refuse to be soothed and clamour with the mouths of hungry children. And though she is careful to explain her dreaming as the product of a mind weakened by hunger, something of the dream's danger enters her to stay.

'Oh,' she says aloud at the end of brief weeping, 'to have given birth to stones instead.'

For the first and the last time in her life, Saramma thinks of both Annakutty and Tessiebaby as equally her children. And with that realization comes the knowledge that Annakutty will care for her daughter while she is away. A great shame hastens her on her way—shame she is never able to forgive in herself, and which she holds against the girl in the years to come.

9

Tessiebaby Understands
Her Sister's Tears

Tessiebaby turns from her mother's story, but not before piecing it together with what she remembers. Six-year-old Tessiebaby remembers being four. She remembers her mother leaving. She remembers the dark bars in the window and light streaming from between the bars. The window is next to, and a little bigger than the picture of God with his hands open and light streaming from the hole in each of his hands. She is swung in the air and she can see out to the lane, to the back of a woman who, the more she recedes into the distance, the more clearly is revealed to be their mother.

Tessiebaby's hands grip the bars. Tessiebaby is happy in her very centre, which is filled with the warmth of food. But she lets her lips pout and cheeks fill with sadness because Annachechi is not happy.

There is a buzzing sound from a fly trapped in the light between the bars. Annachechi sets her on the ground where Tessiebaby has only the wall to look at. She cries, and once again Annachechi lifts her to the window, and this time the woman turns and waves to them. Tessiebaby knows about waving and she waves; her hand has little room to wave between the bars. The woman stands still too long and Tessiebaby almost cries 'Amma', but she knows not to. One never calls to someone who is leaving. It can bring bad luck on the journey.

In the years to come, standing at windows, the hour of morning when light shakes off its wavering and gathers substance, Tessie will feel this giddy sense of possibility, the beginning of adventure—and fear tightening in her belly, buzzing in her ear.

That morning, fear is Annachechi's hand tightening around Tessiebaby's middle as the woman turns and keeps walking till there is nothing left to see. The fly continues its buzzing. The children press their faces to the bars: homes no higher than the disappeared woman gather tight on either side of an empty lane, on either side of the space that was her, hemming in her disappeared silhouette and, miracle of miracles, there she is—captured. Tessiebaby waves at the silhouette, which is a little tenuous. So she drops her hand—where is Amma? Then, prompted by Annachechi, waves again till—there she is! And then she isn't.

They watch the empty lane till Tessiebaby begins crying that Annachechi's hands are hurting her. Annachechi puts her down.

Tessiebaby sees that her sister is also crying. It frightens her into anger. 'Your Amma may have died and left you, but mine is coming back.'

The two girls go to the backroom and Annachechi pulls out the twist of newspaper tucked deep in the coconut husk piled up behind the hearth. Wrapped when they were received, the girls don't yet know which kind of toffee they will find inside. They are the chewy kind. The children make a sound of disappointment. The best days are when the shopkeeper man hands Chechi the kind of sweets they call pigeon's egg—egg-shaped and egg-sized, they are pretty—pale blue, pale pink or pale yellow, hard and vaguely sweet. Annakutty sits on the floor with Tessiebaby straddling her lap. First they play the game where Tessiebaby holds one of Annachechi's thumbs in each of her curled fists and arching her back till she can arch no more, she lets herself fall flat onto Annachechi's outstretched legs. She meets Annachechi's eyes and blinks. Now Annachechi blows softly on Tessiebaby's belly. 'Blow some more,' Baby begs. Annachechi shakes her head. 'Your turn,' she says. This makes Baby angry.

'No, you do what Baby says or Baby will tell Amma about the toffees.'

'No, you won't.'

'Baby will tell. The day is coming.' Baby tries her best to frighten with adult words.

There is no way Baby has seen anything. Annakutty knows this. She shrugs and pulls Baby up by her clenched fists, and Baby comes up and blows toffee breath gently on Chechi's face. They play the blowing game, their see-saw contained in their bodies; the words travelling back and forth bore them.

'Baby will tell.'

'Then you won't have any more toffees.'

'Baby can buy her own toffees, why not?'

'When that day comes you will be an old woman with no teeth.'

'Baby will tell. Baby will tell.'

'Don't you have anything else you know to say? Get lost.'

'Amma will give Baby toffees for telling.'

'Amma doesn't even have money for food. The rice we ate today? She begged it from Padmachettathi. What do you think Amma went there for? To beg. And now she's left. Now she'll come only when she's made enough money to give Padmachettathi her rice back.'

'Baby knows all that. Ok?'

'Then why are you talking about toffees. As if Amma could ever buy us toffees.'

'Baby will wait till Amma comes back with rice and toffees, then Baby will tell.'

'Fine, in that case. You do just that. Old woman with no teeth by then. You will just have to suck your toffees while Amma beats me.'

Annakutty switches to the banana tree game. She circles Baby's palm with her forefinger, chanting solemnly, 'He planted the seed and all around he built a fence, the banana tree blossomed and grew a whole stalk.'

The excitement builds. Annachechi's voice switches accordingly. 'One night a robber came. He stole the bananas and ran away.'

Baby shrieks and tries to pull her hand from Annachechi's.

Annachechi continues, tugging gently, first at the thumb, 'Do you know where the robber hides?'

Baby replies for her thumb. 'No.'

Now the forefinger is tugged, then the middle finger, then the ring finger.

'No. No. No.'

Now it is the little finger's turn.

'Do you know where the robber hides?'

Baby's throat seizes shut. Her whole body is shaken by a giant hiccup of delight.

Annachechi replies for her. 'I do.'

Annachechi's fingers run up Tessiebaby's arms to the hollow of her armpit. 'The robber is here, here, here, here, HERE.'

Tessiebaby squeals. She shrieks. She cries.

Tessiebaby turns to the door in alarm. Someone is pushing it open from the outside. It is Padmachettathi.

'Don't you girls have any shame?' Padma shouts her question at Annakutty.

'Your poor mother,' Padma drops her voice. 'Is she gone?'

All the while her eyes dart around the room. Why, it's dismal in here. Not a stick of possession anywhere in sight, and the floor hasn't been swept since how long?

'Amma will come back in a week.'

'Girl. You. Old enough to pick up a broom. Don't you know to keep clean?'

Padma is only halfway in the door. Now she turns and pushes it open to let the sunlight in. It hurries into the dark interior to discover amidst any amount of crumpled paper two girls seated on the dirt floor. One of them appears to be simultaneously fat and thin, a child, terrible in appearance, who squints with rheumy eyes at the unfamiliar sensation of light. The light travels the wayward approach to growing the child's body has taken. She is a series of spheres connected by bent lines. Her head, so abnormally large it appears to wobble on her neck, below which an equally large belly acts as a counterweight. The whole contraption of her held together by the shambling clutch of sticks that are her arms and legs. The wrist and ankle are points of weakness. An ungentle touch will snap them. Her cheeks in their feverish glow are a pleasurable red, but the rest of her skin has the pallor and the raised blebs found in batter left overnight to ferment.

Padma thins her already thin lips and beckons to someone outside the door. Tessiebaby turns away from the woman to hide her face in her sister's long skirt. Annakutty cradles Tessiebaby's head, stroking the wisps of her sister's hair, the faint purple of her palms move lovingly over the child. The sun catches Annakutty from all sides, setting off little fires of entanglement. She ignores the light; her body devotes itself to crooning an inarticulate sound. Tessiebaby is sobbing in her lap.

'Sssssssst.' Padma cocks her chin at someone out in the alley. 'No one here but the children. What a sight. Dust even on the children. Nothing's been cleaned since when? You've seen Saramma come and go these many days. I've even seen the elder girl out and about. But the baby. A sight.'

The other party to her conversation is not interested in crossing the threshold. Man or woman, the figure hangs back. The children, wrapped tight in each other, don't look up.

'All this time she didn't say a word. I thought, she wants to be that way, let her be. Turned her face away when I tried to ask her about Jose. Till this morning. How was I to know? Thought she must be making money working in those houses.'

'She's been living on whatever Jose gives her,' comes the reply. It is an old woman's voice. It quavers.

'Such goings on here for the past one year. Josechettan pleading at the door and that hussy locking it against him. Why should he give her anything?'

'People don't do because they should. They just do.'

Padma shakes her head. An emphatic no. In the beginning of the trouble between Jose and Saramma, Padma's sympathy was with Saramma. But a woman cannot endlessly turn a man away. One turns a man away to teach him a lesson. But if he is the type who won't learn, then one has to swallow that sorrow and take him back as he is. Saramma's greatest sin in Padma's eyes: to not have known the importance of consulting Padma, who older-wiser would have advised reconciliation.

'I don't live across the way from her for nothing. I was there when he came, not to give her money, but to take. Took her thali. Later, two bangles. And I don't think he brought any money back from the sale. Never seen thinner bangles in my life.'

When the elder woman doesn't reply to this, an annoyed Padma tosses out, 'Well, what do you think of that?'

'I think you've been scared your husband would go Jose's way. It's what all you women worry about. You thank God everyday that it's Saramma who took the beating and not you.'

The old woman's laughter, whether because this is how she always laughs or because she is attempting to contain it, is a prolonged huffing.

Padma waits the laughter out. She aims to go another round with the old woman and lines up her arguments accordingly:

That Saramma, she acted alone. But wasn't it the neighbourhood women who had to do penance for Saramma's sins? Wasn't it they who had to demonstrate to their doubt-filled men that they were not cast in the same mould as the faithless Saramma? It was they. They, who slid to the side and hung their heads while their men sent a fist or the dinner plate flying in a bid to try Josechettan's injury on for size. *Let's play a game: I'll be Josechettan and you won't be his wife.*

'It's come to this,' Padma retorts. 'When was the last time these children ate?'

The old woman is seemingly silenced.

Years of quiet from that Saramma. And now she comes to beg

for food. Why now, is what Padma can't figure out. The time of shortage has been over for a year. A time, pray god, that will never come again. No grain in the market, no grain anywhere in the land. What times we have all lived through. No, she can't say lived through. It was all so recently, it is hard to be certain that those times are in the past.

'Vishnu, Vishnu,' Padma mutters aloud. She looks inside the little room, at the huddled girls, then over to the shrine containing their God—haggard, no beauty anywhere in the image. The sorrow on his face is understandable given that he, despite being a god, is somehow strung on two pieces of wood. But why does he have to be ugly?

They like to tell a joke, the Christians. The dying Hindu and the dying Christian. The dying Hindu calls to his god. When he does not appear in the instant, he supplicates another, then another and so on. Meanwhile the gods, jostling one another to come to the man's aid, give up in exasperation as the man cycling too quickly through his list gasps his last.

'Vishnu, Vishnu,' Padma mutters again.

The joke ends with the dying Christian calling to his one god whose timely appearance is the result of his free passage, uncrowded by other gods.

Padma makes a face. The famine is over. Though Christians and Hindus alike suffered the dole lines, she believes the Hindus fared better, if only in spirit. She cannot imagine the comfort to be gotten from the one God when he was himself a starved man. Fish and rice is what he ate while he walked the earth, and had, according to the stories told about him, the ability to convert a few fish to baskets full, capable of feeding thousands. Padma is too well mannered to laugh in the face of such stories. But she has always wanted to ask, why fish? Wouldn't the hungry have preferred prawn biryani, and meat-fry? Padma's mouth waters. A year since the hunger; no one is eating meat yet.

'I gave her food. Rice enough for ten-twelve meals. This whole time, I wondered how she was managing. Must have been eating the stuff the government gave. You're mad if you think that hero Jose gave her anything. Me? I was happy to see her finally ask. Only then can I give. If someone never asks, how can one just give?

'Maybe. Maybe. I ate that foreign stuff myself. Didn't agree with me. Decided much better to stay hungry than to eat something that I have to shit a stream of immediately. A person can eat just about anything. But only to a point. What's the use if food doesn't stay in the belly long enough to warm it a bit. A periodic lesson in hunger, that's what all of us need.'

'Then Saramma is learning her lesson now.'

'Part of the lesson is you don't wait for someone to ask. Much more important to learn to give than to learn to ask.'

The words, like her emotions, swell in Padma's chest and come spewing out:

'She never. Not once did I. The child was born and not a mouthful of paysam distributed to us neighbours in celebration. And she had that child after Josechettan's accident. Isn't that something? A whole village full of her relations descended here for the celebration to get fed on whose earnings? Such foolishness. Who fed her children today is what I want to know? Not the relations. Not the useless hero of a husband of hers. Me. I gave more than she asked. Took what I had prepared for my children to eat when they return from school and gave it.'

'Then you did the right thing.'

'People should think, shouldn't they, before they decide they are going to incite others to riot? I told my man, you stay away from Jose. You think it was easy living across the street from that nonsense? Gathered a crowd of no-goods every evening. All lounging out there, talking big about striking. I told my husband, "We have children to raise." You know how old my children were three years ago when they brought our hero back on that stretcher? My youngest wasn't even six then.'

'Yes, you kept your man clear of trouble. Seems everyone except Jose managed to stay clear of trouble.'

'It takes a strong woman.'

'Ah, that's what it takes.'

'If you have something to say?'

'No, nothing. What would I have to say?'

'Jose knew what he was walking into. They said go to the construction zone and he went. Yes, he thought a big crowd of his followers was going with him. Fool of a man. He could have turned back when he saw no one behind him. At no one's insistence. He walked into danger at no one's insistence.'

'Why don't you go inside and see to those children now? All that was a long time ago, no need to carry on. What is done and gone, let it be done and gone.'

'Easy for you to say.'

But Padma is happy to be released. She leaves off standing with one foot in the doorway. She walks all the way into the interior dark.

The thin voice quavers after her. 'Cheap you all are. They did him in and bought you all off for cheap. If you're willing to work for a packet of idlis, they'll work you for a packet of idlis.'

Padma flings herself out the door. 'What did you say?'

'Nothing. Nothing.'

'Old woman, go home and rest your mouth.' Padma shuts the door behind her this time.

From the other side of the door. 'All of you eating well on the raise they bought you off with. No one to stand with the man when he went to face the boss. Plenty gathered to hear him speak, to say they were with him. But when the time came, no one. Nothing. He'll never work again. Not with the bosses making sure of that. And you wait these three years. Famine's been and gone in that time. You wait till Jose's wife comes to tell you her children are starving. Then some rice handed over and you think some great act of holiness has been performed.'

Padma wonders how much of the exchange the elder girl has heard. She is gruff as she asks, 'Where did your mother go then?'

Padmachettathi is pretty in a frightening sort of way. Her hair is straight and shiny, parted so exactly in the centre, her features so exactly balanced, and her mouth full of straight teeth is easily at least one or two teeth too full. Yes, she is pretty. But her smile is frightening.

The children shrink from her. They worry the toffee tucked in the back of their mouths. What if she asks them where this toffee has come from? Tessiebaby sucks harder, louder. When Annakutty speaks, it is past the scratchy dripping of sweet in her throat. She makes a wringing motion with her hands to convey her helplessness. She cannot be answerable for Saramma.

'Amma went. Somewhere. We don't know.'

'Somewhere? You don't know? Then what do you know, eh? Do you know where your father is? No? She's run off then, leaving us to worry about the two of you, eh?'

'No, not like that. She will be back soon. A few days only. She said so. She prayed with us and asked God to bring her back in three days.'

Annakutty doesn't add, before the rice is all gone.

Where could she have gone? Not to the family, or she would have taken the children. What woman would return to her family leaving her children? Padma's eyes have had their fill of studying these rooms. She would like to touch what her eyes have studied. Open the trunks. No secrets there, she knows. Who in these parts has anything to conceal? Living across the way from Saramma, doesn't she already know at what hour, no, what minute of which night in which season Jose took off with the woman's two measly bangles. And the single chain and thali which he snapped from around her neck. Past midnight it was. And just before Onam. Padma relishes the thought. No, it's not to discover anything new in these trunks that she sets out now to open them. It is to touch the familiar, to confirm the known. Padma's eyes cross in her excitement.

Aaah, poor woman. Left with not only a baby, maybe three years old at most, the little meagre thing, but also this black thing from the first wife, fourteen, fifteen years old, ready to be married off and look at her sitting in a blouse so tight it's split open under her arm. Through that opening. One dark breast. Visible for all the world to see. Cheee.

'Girl, put some decent clothes on.'

'Ammai, I will.' Annakutty's voice is mild.

Outside, the old woman's voice rises. 'A hero he was, and foolish only for trying for a better life for the likes of you.'

Annakutty feels herself shrinking. She shrinks to compensate for the fact that she is a reminder to all of her father. And she shrinks from the shame of being ashamed of her father. And she shrinks because she is growing. She keeps herself inside the house, or close to the house to hide the growing. It is by shrinking that she bears the eyes of the shopkeeper who gives her sweets.

'For the little one,' he says.

Shrinking compresses her voice. Padma has to lean forward to hear the girl. Padma screams the louder to punish the girl whose efforts to erase herself have not proven enough.

'Open the trunk. There must be something else in there for you to wear. You can't be sitting here in that torn blouse. See, there is cloth in the seams of your blouse. Take it off and I will let it out for you.'

The old voice outside, now closer to the shut door, comes from lips pressed to the door.

'What all did you buy yourself with that money in the last three years, eh? Everything from hair oil to new tiffin boxes, and that bicycle your husband rides. Next you'll want convent school for the children.'

'Old woman, are you saying something?'

'Nothing you don't already know.'

The door shakes as the body leaning against it shakes. A moment later, the sound of huffing laughter recedes.

Annakutty opens the trunk. Her father's shirts are still there. Turning her back, she removes her blouse and slips into one of her father's shirts.

'I will come again with the blouse fixed.' Padma flashes her ferocious smile. But she means it kindly. 'You don't worry. Your ammai is here to make sure you don't go hungry till your mother returns.'

The two girls look at each other, then at the shut door. Annakutty sticks her tongue out at the door and Tessiebaby squeals in delight but dares not imitate her.

A stir at the back of the stove. The coconut husks arranged there in a pyramid teeter as the room releases its long-held breath; the pile tumbles to the floor. A modest store of goods that have escaped Padma's scrutiny lies exposed, gently signalling its presence to the girls. The shopkeeper man's other gifts: a scrap of new cloth Annakutty doesn't know what to do with, a string of beads that glimmers the colours of the rainbow trapped within, an orange plastic doll moulded of a piece. Its dress is painted red.

Annakutty bolts the door behind Padmachettathi, brings the plastic doll to Tessiebaby, and they play. Annakutty shows Tessiebaby everything about the plastic doll that makes it attractive. Legs are pulled apart and the smooth plastic between them is pointed out and giggled over. Then Annachechi shows Tessiebaby that her own elbow folded plumps the flesh and divides it by a single crease. From here girls piss. Then Annachechi flicks open her thumb and waggles it. Here is where a man pisses from. The thumb dives into the crease. He pisses inside a woman if he feels like it. The buzzing of the fly hurts Tessiebaby's ears. She is filled with disbelief. She pushes the doll away and refuses to play Annachechi's game. The two retire to separate corners of the house.

Eventually Annakutty rises from the window and takes a broom to sweep the floor. She sweeps the floor bent from the waist, sweeping a half circle to the left and a half circle to the right. Three pairs of half circles and the breadth of the room has been swept once. She steps forward and works the breadth again, steps forward and now the length of the room is done. The front room is even smaller, hasn't the complication of stove ash, woodpile and a tumbled avalanche of coconut husk. But here Tessiebaby sits interrupting Annakutty's paired half circles. She approaches Baby with a twig drawn from the broom, slashes the air near Baby's bottom meaningfully. Still Baby does not budge; she does not even flinch. She pretends to whisper a secret in the orange doll's ears. Annakutty can hear that it is gibberish. She takes up the broom with a sigh and draws her half circles on the mud floor, not in swathes that take in the breadth of the room, but by walking a spiral path that radiates from Baby, hunched over the doll. When Annakutty is done, the floor is marked in overlapping petals, Tessiebaby the centre of a flower; and still Tessiebaby pretends disinterest.

Annakutty has backed herself up to the front door. She straightens and throws a shy glance at the girl caught in the broken piece of mirrored glass hung inside the door. Turning away from this girl, she pretends to be troubled by the smile caught on her face. But how beautiful this girl is in her father's shirt that billows white. How wonderfully her face and hair shine. And now this girl will step out the front door and be noticed. *He* will come walking past her door and notice her. She will look down as she sweeps the leaves from the gutter. But this time she will not shrink. She will not hunch her shoulders and draw in her chest. He will not pretend that he does not see her. He will stare at her wearing her father's shirt, and when she turns from the waist and the shirt turns with her, he will think of a net swung out from land to the sea.

10

(with her last breath)

My stepmother tells me to remove my half-sari. I do. Why do I hand it to her so meekly? I am not meek.

Saramma rips the cloth. She throws the pieces to the floor. She steps on them and reaches for me.

I stand in my petticoat skirt. Her face looms in front of me. Heat rips my waist. The chord reels in her hands. My skirt is spun. I am spun. Feet tangle in cloth. I am thrown to the floor. She will trample me.

Cold. I can feel it coming from far away. My skin breaks, shivers escape. My scalp prickles. The hair is growing, but not fast enough to cover me. And here is the cold now. A cloud cover for me.

She points to my blouse. I return her look. She tugs at the hooks. Her fingers are warm. I want her to leave her hands there. I want her to speak tenderly. The back of her hands knuckle my breast. My blouse is ripped from me.

And is this rain that pours down my father's cheek? Rain pours from his eyes. No, the rain is outside. The window is blown open in the rain. Rain snakes on the flat glass panes. There are fat tears

74

on my father's face. I want to mock him, laugh out loud, but I am crying instead. Is this me?

Look at me. I am naked.

She thinks without clothes I have nowhere to go. She thinks I will not step out of the door, will not dare to be seen in this village of hers. She thinks she will keep me home now. But back in the city when she shaved my head, did she manage to keep me home then?

Why do I need clothes? My body is enough for me to walk out of this home. I will feel the cold of this weather she creates for me.

But Saramma screams, 'Catch her. Where is the girl going? Jose, I told you. You didn't believe me. Now you see her. Now you see her go.'

11

The Women Remember

Jansy has a headache. She almost always has a headache. She holds her head and moans, 'Amme. Endamme.'

'Calling your mother, are you?'

The woman who enters Jansy's kitchen is tiny, not more than a child in height. Her white hair is a halo of frizz that stands up around an intricately lined face. Her right cheek bulges and her lips shine wet with red spit. Valli shifts the wad in her mouth to her left cheek and stands self-consciously.

This kitchen is unlike anything in her home. The counter is topped with smooth grey stone. Light pouring in from the window strikes the counter in a sheet and splashes off the surface, dazzling her. But Valli has been many times in this strange kitchen with its white walls and grey stone and wooden shelves loaded with as much foodstuff as she expects the biggest stores in Kottayam must carry on their shelves. She has swept behind the gas cylinder which, set on a steel tray with cunning steel wheels, slides out from under the counter with ease, yielding to her broom as the spaces behind the clay stove in her kitchen do—the amber rustle of desiccated cockroaches, beetles and occasionally the silver flash that is the tip of a rat's tail. Besides, Valli is of more use to this kitchen than the kitchen is to her. Amuma, as Valli is known in the neighbourhood, is self-conscious but not nervous.

She knows she can leave any time she chooses, which is more than Jansy is free to do. *Like a dog kept in her cage*—this is how Valli, who shouts at the dogs kept in their cage at the entrance to Jansy and Devasi's property, sums up Jansy's life. Valli can chew the betel leaf and nut and spit wherever in the forest she pleases. If she is not hungry, she can spend the day in the shade of the bridge, her feet sunk in cool creek water to ease their swelling.

That was where she was when the rain blew in, and that was where she had planned to stay till evening. Her stomach needed nothing this day. Two rupees' worth of betel nut chewed creek-side had killed her hunger. At eleven in the morning, her favourite time of day, the languor of the mouthful was just creeping through her body when her heart constricted. She nearly called out. In the conversation of two men—it was Devasi and Jonikutty, released from the solemn duty of prayer and on the way to the coffeehouse—as they swayed overhead, she heard the news: Annakutty, dead.

A blur of movement materialized in the rain, splashed in the mud and made its darting way between the men on the bridge. The men cursed the child as they retied their mundu, which had come loose in the fierce gust little Kunjukuttan's airplane game had raised. Shamefaced laughter followed. The flash reappeared between them, arms winged and body tilted at the waist, its entire being straining toward the 'rrroooooo' sound of the airplane that issued from pursed lips. Valli waited till the child, whirring like a top set loose, was called home to his mother, and waited some more for the men to run their girlish way across the bridge. Then, plucking a large hyacinth leaf to hold over her head, she made her way to Devasi's home, past the baying of the idiot dogs—'shut up'—mad from their confinement, and into the kitchen where she found the woman, Jansy, cowering by her gleaming stove, eyes blind with pain.

'Amuma, is that you?'

Valli stands at the door, then turns her head to the side, purses her lips and issues a stream of red into the courtyard.

'There are dishes in the back kitchen. Not many. But when you are done here, if you will go to Annachechi's . . .' Jansy hesitates, but is unwilling to acknowledge whatever special bond this old tribal woman may have formed with the eccentric Annachechi. She merely sums up, 'You know, of course.'

'I came when I heard.'

'It was last night. I haven't been yet. Oh, if this headache would only let up. Devasiachan found the child crying on the steps this morning. I was leading the cow out to her calves, and I heard such a mad rush of running and shouting. I almost thought the rain had brought the hillside down. Oh, but this pain hasn't let go since.'

'Why doesn't Jansy Kochamma take one of those white tablets then? Amuma is here. You sit. I will tidy up here and go over to the other house.'

'No, don't go. There will be no cooking in that kitchen. Even the coffee I had to make and send from here. I've asked them to bring four of the chickens from her coop. So that's next. Then who knows?'

'What about the girl? Has anyone seen to the girl? If nothing's been cooked there, she will have to be called here to eat.'

Valli speaks with concern she feels is her right. After all,

Annachechi had consulted Valli on everything from four-year-old Nina's refusal to unscrew her thumb from her mouth, to nearly twelve-year-old Nina's impossible astronaut ambitions. The application of bitter gourd had easily rendered the thumb no longer delectable. And as for the fear that the girl thought too much of herself and wanted what was beyond the earth itself, Valli had to disagree with Annachechi: 'Why shouldn't the girl dream whatever takes her fancy? Let it be the Americans who kill her dreams. She will find out soon enough what we all know—they went up top some mountain and took pictures of old rocks and called it the moon.'

'Oh, this headache will kill me. And ask the boy outside to stop that sound.'

Valli calls out to Kunjukuttan, 'Kunjukuttan, back already? Didn't your amma just call you home? Jansyammai wants you to make your noise elsewhere. Listen, will you go see if Nina has eaten anything since morning? Has she had her coffee yet?'

Ignoring the old tribal woman, Kunjukuttan flies his plane to Jansy.

'Rrroooooo Jansyammai, Jansyammai, I saved Devasi Uncle, who brings our milk and Teacher Sir, too.'

'Go on Kunjukuttan, and call Nina to come here and eat.'

'Jansyammai, it was with one single jump I landed in front of them. To save them. After that, one single kick and I hit the snake on the head. One single hit, like this. With a big-big stick. From the big-big tree. Then the snake, he took one single bite. And rrroooooo I flew down in my plane and gave one single kick more. I killed that snake. Just like that. Then they asked me, how old are you, Kunjukuttan. Then I told Teacher Sir, two and a half. Ha ha ha. Ha ha ha. I fooled them. I am already four years old and I will not go to school.'

'Kunjukuttan, you are such a big boy. You must be four years old at least. Now listen to Jansyammai and go tell Nina to come here. Don't ask her anything. Just tell her to come to Jansyammai's house. And Kunjukuttan, tell the men to only kill four hens. No need to empty the coop yet. You try to be helpful, but who knows what people will say afterwards. They will say anything that comes to their mind. As if we don't have enough to meet our own needs. Plenty of hens here. Probably end up having to kill from here as well. God knows four hens will only feed a handful. There will be plenty who show up if there is a feeding to be had. They'll be the ones. After they show up empty-handed and fill up their stomachs. They'll say we stole someone else's hens.'

'Jansyammai, you stole hens?'

'Get out of here, child. I have enough of a headache without your nonsense to add to it. People from around here can be trusted to open their mouths at any age, to spew whatever they want to empty from their heads.'

'Then I am leaving. I will leave with one-single jump. See. Have you seen? One-single jump. Then I land with one-single hop. See? One-single kick and the snake is dead. Then rrrooooo. I will not tell Ninachechi anything. I will not tell her.'

Valli mutters something muffled by the juice gathered in her mouth. She shakes water from the last gleaming pot, announces the dishes done by setting the pot with a clatter on top of the pile, and steps over to the door, past the woman sunk to the floor with her head in her hand. She spits from the door and turns back to the woman. Valli knows the cure for this woman's headache. Jansy needs to walk from this house, its ash-shined pots, counter, kitchen, children and husband. She needs to walk to where she can spend the day in the shade under the bridge, dangle her feet in a pool of sun and then a pool of rain, stave off hunger by feeding on glimpses of the young men come to bathe there among the reeds. Then at sundown, she should allow not hunger but thirst to drive her to the Shop. Three quick glasses of toddy and three slow ones drunk in the gathering dark. Valli has not experienced a headache in years.

Jansy would never accept an invitation to such an excursion, which is not the reason why Valli fails to issue it. Charity is all well and good, and Valli practices it when she takes home and shares with her man a meal too hearty by far for her to consume by herself. But picking her way carefully among the stones scattered by the creek, bending to turn them over in search of the little crabs that emerge in the rainy season is a happiness Valli cannot imagine halving or packing. Besides, the young men who twist and turn in the sun like freshly caught fish—the young men whose gauze-thin towels cling when wet to their thighs so the brown shines through—who fail to see the old woman nodding on the rock on the other side of their curtain of reeds, they would never fail to see Jansy. Jansy will have to live with her headache.

'Listen to the noise from the Junction. What is going on there this early in the morning? Amuma, I can put up with that child's rrroooooo sound, but what is this Malayalam they are speaking into loudspeakers.' Jansy shakes her head in disbelief. A political rally at this hour? What is the cause? Who is listening to this broken Malayalam?

Valli ignores Jansy. She is staring hard at the shaking in the grass ahead. Here comes a clutch of hens, a tousled bunch hung from curled claws; their necks plucked of heads sway lightly as they come up the path, past the hysterical dogs. But Jansy has disappeared into her bedroom, where Valli knows she will lie with cloth tied around her forehead. She will refuse the tablets Valli brings her. The women, four of them, who have come with the hens, will stand at the door and whisper into the darkened room. The two who have only just now crossed over from girlhood will know enough to hide their buck-toothed excitement behind their hands. With feet splayed from gripping the bumpy terrain of her floor at home, a third woman will caress the foreign nature of a floor laid on the level. Then there will be one who sniffs her disdain of a woman who lies in bed at eleven in the afternoon.

'Tea,' they will argue in whispers. 'No, coffee is what will cure her.' And their whispered concern will not conceal their longing to enter Jansy's model kitchen to touch Jansy's pots and pans.

Jansy's face will remain turned to the wall. The women won't see that it is pierced by a thousand red-hot nails. They are welcome to her pots and pans if they will only leave off whispering at her door. But they're talkers, the people around here. And full of opinions. If one wants silence, if one wants to be left alone, it can never be.

Valli plucks the hens clean and leaves them on the back steps, and begins the work of sweeping the yard. The women's cooking noises, their opinionated camaraderie carries through the kitchen's open window.

'She stayed away from her father when it was his time.'

'Manju, I doubt anyone will come.'

'Anyone? Why talk about anyone, Leela? No one will come. Neither from the mother's or the father's side. She destroyed her parents. No one will come.'

'You speak the truth. None from her family will care to come.

And I doubt even Thambichettan's family will have anything to do with coming here.'

'Remember she turned his funeral into a joke. Singing some song from a film.'

'Remember his brother told her to get up from the floor and leave the house.'

'She didn't leave.'

'Why would she leave? It was her house, Manju.'

'No, it wasn't. It was Thambichettan's house. It's been in his family for generations. It was he who brought her here. From somewhere. Madras? He found her somewhere far from her people. They will have to be told anyway.'

'Her people won't come. As for the house, she was married to him, wasn't she? It doesn't matter who or what before she married Thambichettan. After marriage, all that is his became hers.'

'Leela, you are getting all these new ideas from where? You think because some years back the court said women have a share in their parent's estate, they automatically have one in the husband's.'

The buck-toothed two are working industriously. Their young ears sharpened to this talk, and their hands hoping by their labour to pay for this insight into the adult world. How ashamed they are of their ignorance. Thank God for Annachechi's timely death, which is teaching them so much.

'I don't know anything about what the court says.' Leela sniffs, then pronounces: 'But I do know right from wrong. Annachechi might have had her problems with her parents—her mother, I've heard, was her stepmother—might have made her mistakes in life as we all have, but she stuck by who she was. And she was as faithful and loyal a wife as any one-legged man could hope to find.

Thambichettan got himself a treasure when he married her. And the little girl she raised. That Nina gets good marks in school, looks clean and smart, and if you ask her to make a cup of tea, she knows how to. How many of us have children who can do all that? And how did the child come to be this way? An old woman gave herself at the end of her life to raising this child.'

Leela finishes up without bothering to drop her voice. She barely glances over at the two backs—so slim, elegant and (sniff) too pliant by far. 'She did not leave the search for the child, did she? She and Thambi spent hard-earned money these last days, putting advertisements in the newspapers, even far away in Delhi. I know what people thought of that, but as for me, I consider it a good thing.'

'Listen you; I never had a problem with her searching for the child. Wouldn't we all search for a child if it was lost? But did she lose the child or did she sell the child? Huh? And as for marriage, I'm surprised you don't know: very unlikely those two were married. She never set foot in church. How would they've gotten married then?'

'What do you know of what really happened, Manju? Thambichettan found her in Madras according to you. How do we know what happened in Madras?'

'Things happened right near here, Leela, and not fifty years ago. Her people are from these parts, and it was after some earlier troubles, the kind of troubles which land a girl in a mess, that she ended up far from here, in Madras. Sent there, she was.'

'Oh, now you are going to tell me she ran naked through the streets. I've heard it all before and I don't believe it.'

The buck-toothed two forget the task at hand. The knife, the rubber cover for the thumb and the beans for the sambar fall away. Forgetting how important it is to remain hidden if they are to be allowed to remain in this company, they let their mouths fall open to issue competing rounds of ayyos.

'Ayyo.'

'Ay-yai-yyo.'

Annachechi running naked through the streets. They shudder to think of her breasts flapping. The rest of it they cannot imagine. Neither one can remember a time when they have bathed free of the coarse drawers they slip off at the end of a bath, exchanging stale for fresh after first tying their towels around their waist— the cloth of both the stale and fresh drawers speckled in grey. Mould cannot help growing on cloth the climate of their bodies and the climate of the land never allow to fully dry.

A frenzy of horror at where their excited minds have dragged them. Guppy-faced, their mouths, like their eyes, round to issue fresh Ay-yai-yyos.

'Ayyo.'

'Ay-yai-yyo.'

'Girls!' Splay-footed, Manju searches for a grip on this ground which she realizes with some irritation is as smooth in the kitchen as it is in the rest of the house, as smooth as Leela's smooth words. No grip here, and she comes to her toes ready to launch into something, but what. She settles for scolding.

'Are the beans going to chop themselves? Cook themselves? Come come.' Then in a more pacifistic tone, 'Let's not talk ill of the dead.'

'Who, me? What are you saying, Manju? I, talk ill of Annachechi? Who was saying her family will not come? Not me.'

'What's ill in what I have said? Her family will not come. That's the truth. They turned their backs on her when she . . .'

Again, splay-footed woman stops herself. Then restarts. This time she will not be stopped. She speaks earnestly.

'If it was only the child. It goes back a long ways. To the days when they lived in the city. You don't know all this, because it happened Kuravalangad side. That's near where I grew up. They were city people first and returned to her stepmother's village when things didn't work out for them there. Even then people talked about her. When they came from the city, she was maybe sixteen. A wild thing! She was shaved bald in the city. They said her stepmother did it to bring her in line.'

Shaved her bald? The younger of the two girls gives her head a shake to feel the oiled rope hanging there. 'Manjuchechi, really?'

Splay-foot gives her a disinterested glance. 'Thing is, Leela, she was a handful right from the start. It was the year after the famine, no, maybe two years after the famine that I was born. My parents called me a famine baby. The Americans were sending wheat in shiploads during the famine. Annakutty's family came from the city around the time of the big fight between the Americans and the Soviet Union and that other little country.'

'Cuba.' The rope of hair is swung again.

This time Manju gives her a sharp look. The girl is silenced. She hunches over the flick-flick of the knife against her rubber thumb. Beans, cut on the slant, rapid-mound the wicker tray into which she fires them. She wants to prove herself worthy of this company and this conversation. This girl has only just realized how truly unimportant the Cuban Missile Crisis is outside the question paper she mugged up for in her school days, how truly unimportant in the real lives lived by real women.

'After their return from the city, there was an episode when she was caught with a man. She'd been meeting him after the household went to sleep. Her stepmother locked her clothes up. So you know what she did? Just walked out of the house. Tell me what you would do with a girl like that? Was I already six then? What I remember is there was a meeting in church for the girls. I didn't go. My sister went. Maybe it was only for the older girls. The priest was at the meeting to tell the girls how they should behave. Annachechi, her place was at least two villages away, but we heard about it all the way in our area.

'The church advised her father to send her to the convent in Madras. She was sent to become a nun. Later we found out about the child she had there. Not rumours, mind you. She told us herself she had a child.

'Who knows, people said, if the child was from the man in her home village, the one she was meeting at night, and she went to Madras pregnant, or if she found someone in Madras and got pregnant there. Her father just shut his mouth. Rumour even had it that it was a priest. No one saw the child except the sister—that Tessie—who was sent to Madras. Was it to help with the birth? No, it was later. When the child was sold. To foreigners.'

The two girls have moved from the green beans to the hard skin of the pumpkin. Each one sits on the floor and slashes at a pumpkin she holds in a tight embrace. A priest, thinks one. But how could she go out naked, thinks the other. Outside, Valli is seething. She marches to the window ready to tell these women a thing or two. She looks in, then looks away. She sucks hard at her mouth. There is nothing there to spit.

Valli is from the north—north of everything, certainly north of these Kuravalangad side people, north of the centre, Kottayam, which, if people around here are to be believed, is the centre of the universe. North even of that furthest outpost, Kannur. So far north, it is a place believed to be uninhabited. Her mother slung the baby Valli on her back while she pruned, and later in the season plucked the pods from gnarled and knotted coffee bushes. Then came the tea season. The baby, now too old to be slung, was just old enough to be taught the value of betel nut in warding off hunger. Valli's been chewing ever since. Chewing and spitting as often as she has the little bit of cash necessary to purchase the fixings.

These Kottayam-side people, who think their Malayalam the best, who speak as if every word slips from their mouth coated in gold and honey, they came north during Valli's childhood. They came in the belief that they were entering wilderness. Accordingly, they set to taming it. They prospered by working the people who recognized them as the meanest, stingiest skinflints ever to appear in the guise of human beings. As a child, Valli watched her people deal with their supposed betters. The settlers held their nose around Valli's people, but were forced to step back when the people aimed thin streams of red betel juice inches from their feet. Now that life has brought Valli south to Kottayam—the land of these very serpents—and confined her there in her old age, she finds her skill in spitting, perfected early in childhood, is all the armour necessary to survive here.

No betel juice in her mouth, she clears her throat with vehemence, gathers a hard knot of phlegm and spits. The women inside make a face but don't look up. Valli sinks into the shade under the eaves. It's been decades since this moisture trickled from her eyes. The morning's work, uncompensated for, no meal when the woman of the house lies in bed, leaves her feeling weak. Valli too lies full length, listening to the conversation from within, opens her eye to a blank sky and lets the tears roll to the ground.

Valli remembers Annakutty. When she first saw the shy bride of thirty-three, Valli had laughed in her face, and in turn been surprised when Annakutty joined her. They continued their laughter while turning over rocks in search of crabs. Poor people's meat. Hut-dweller meat. Kottayam-side people disdained it. Annakutty and Valli. A woman new to the taste of happiness and a woman practiced in turning rocks over in the search for it, one with straight back, one hunched under hers, cooked the bite-sized crabs out in the open and ate from each other's hands.

12

The Crowd at the Junction

An old man, sucked thin, a little bent, faces a microphone, composes himself before beginning. He harangues an invisible enemy; his speech tears the air. An equally invisible audience is riveted by the power of his speech. The man's one arm is thrust behind his back, where unseen, it clenches and unclenches. Anger, though a useful tool in the struggle for working class liberation, can make this man appear spastic. With his other, more measured hand, he thrusts at the air, stabs an accusing finger at the invisible enemy.

'Comrades,' he cries, 'we mustn't forget.'

The air crackles and moans; the microphone strains to do justice to this man's fervour. Behind the speechmaker, on the makeshift stage, two men in crisp white sit on two metal folding chairs. An old-fashioned black cotton umbrella is open overhead, its handle tied to the back of a chair. One of the men yawns, rests his elbow on his knee and re-props his chin on his fist. The other man is young and exceptionally handsome. An awareness of his beauty catches him in the middle of the speech he is rehearsing under his breath, and he rights himself, angles his face so the light reflects off his smooth cheeks.

At the barbershop across the way, Unnikrishnan lathers his newest customer. He curses the need of those across the street to rehearse speeches he will be subjected to again in the evening. He curses the two still lingering in the shop though he finished barbering them an hour before. The rain is thin now and they could walk out into it, past the speechmakers haranguing the empty street, and head home. But they sit, riveted by the contents of his modest collection of magazines. The verbiage within focuses on male fitness, the illustrations for which are supplied by the female form, tightly clad and always in an aspect of repose.

'Ridiculous.'

'At least they should have done something about the stubble on her leg.'

'You should see those girls in Bangalore. Such smooth legs. What is wrong with our girls in Kerala?'

'What is wrong is they keep themselves so covered up, they have no idea themselves what they look like. This one probably showed up to have her picture taken with her mother in tow, changed into the mini skirt at the studio, and never realized her legs look like that.'

'Let the girl be. What is wrong is the magazines in Kerala using a girl like that. Black prickles on chunky legs. Look. On every page it is the same girl. Same legs. Oh God, here she has a cat on her lap. What is that supposed to be? Is that supposed to make us think what it's like to sit on her chunky lap? The girls in Bangalore, their legs are white like milk.'

'Shut up about the girls in Bangalore. What's a newly married man doing ogling girls in Bangalore?'

'My interest isn't in the girls. Don't get me wrong. I'm a student of human behaviour, which is the kind of thing your mind is too small to understand.'

'Oh ho, that's it then? You're studying human behaviour?'

'It makes no difference to me what you think. When I visit Bangalore, I sit at the mall. Ideal place to study the crowd. Mainly I'm there to study the men who are ogling the girls. Such pathetic creatures.'

'You've heard it said, the man with two diseased legs shouldn't make fun of the man with one diseased leg . . .'

'Who's got a diseased leg, who's making fun of anyone? Me, you're accusing? I sympathize with them. I may not be in their situation, but I understand their situation. What else are they to do? What are the chances of anyone getting a look at anything here in Kerala? Every last girl here wanders the livelong day in that gown thing—what do they call it—trailing to her toes. Then she shows up in bed at night wearing the same thing. Bloody hell. I tell you, it turns the Malayali man into a pathetic fool who will settle for anything he can get.'

A movement outside as the speechmaker concludes and returns to his seat. He nods at the youngster for whose benefit they've connected the microphones in the rain, running the wires clear from the other end of the junction, off the main located at Party HQ, location also of the area's fish shop. The handsome one rises and returns the nod, not unamiably, but neither amiably. His frightened smile stretches his skin tight so his skull peers from his face, replacing the pretty there. He soldiers on to stage front, nodding to the left and right at what he both wants to imagine is a real crowd and which, once imagined, he wants nothing more than to make vanish. On reaching the microphone he grasps it, nearly bending it. The crowd roars its approval and he croaks back. Promptly the crowd gives up on him, and he is left staring through the inattentive rain at the empty road, and a hop of the eye away, the barbershop and bus stop. His training is in the power to summon or banish a crowd at will. But what of the recalcitrant crowd?

He begins his speech in earnest.

His two superiors settle to the extent they can on their hard chairs. He'll do fine at the actual event later in the evening. He, meanwhile, is repeating the same speech as his predecessor.

'Comrades, we mustn't forget.'

He finds his stride; his hands in a sudden fit of inspiration remember to do what his mentors' had done. He stabs at the air with one, then the other. Ah, that's the way it's done. But no, it is a mistake. He is immediately buffeted by his twin imaginings. He twitches and starts to the continual antics of the appearing and disappearing crowd. His speech stops and starts accordingly. It is hard for the two old ones behind him to preserve their confidence in his future, much less to keep from nodding off to such a staccato tempo as he is effecting. Midway through the speech, his sense of himself as beautiful and deserving of stage and audience flickers on then off. And this too is part of his training: to summon and banish himself at will.

'What a hero he is. What is it that our hero does not want us to forget?'

'Didn't you see the Kallen Chothi memorial was covered in red on your way here? That glorified mess of cement isn't memorial enough for these guys. So they cover it in red. It's that time of the year again. I was running to get out of the rain, not interested in sightseeing. A shave, I thought, would be a good excuse to get away from all those women. Annakutty—remember that Thambi, used to drive his autorickshaw with just the one leg, died last year, his wife she was—met her end last night. All morning it's been nothing but fuss with women running this way and that. Praying, clapping, singing non-stop. It seems she was an important figure to the poor women around here. A bit of a hero.'

'You mean a heroine. Listen to our hero there going on about not forgetting. He and his kind must have done up Kallen's gravestone last night or maybe early this morning. Don't know why they bother. God knows we've all forgotten.'

'What have we forgotten?'

'The Kallen incident. It's been fifty years maybe.'

'I know what you're talking about. More like a hundred years. My uncle is a sympathizer himself, so he keeps all these stories going. This is the one about the rubber tapper. The strike, isn't it?'

'This Kallen wasn't even a big leader.'

'But when the strike was broken, he was one of the few who held out.'

'Low-caste types! Actually all of them are potential hoodlums. Big ones. Little ones. Makes no differences. They're all ready to attack at a moment's notice.'

'A group of them did attack one of the landowners. Who was it they were after?'

'The Olayathil family, my father's cousins actually.'

'My uncle didn't tell me that.'

'It's been fifty, hundred years. We remember in our family because our people were involved.'

'My uncle said the owners got together and went after the remaining strikers.'

'They hid out in the forest.'

'The owners or the strikers?'

'The strikers of course. They were hidden, but the owners knew where. Probably one of their own betrayed them. That's the low-caste type for you. As you said, it was a case of most of the strikers being done with the agitation. They no doubt wanted done with the so-called leaders who got them into the mess in the first place.'

'So then?'

'They flushed them out and went after this Kallen. He was part of, or maybe even led the attack on the Olayathils. They made him pay.'

'My uncle told me this part.'

'They cut him.'

'With a machete. Split his stomach open.'

'Like chopping wood.'

'He tried to get up and run. His guts leaking out.'

'He held onto his guts with his hands, pushed them back into his belly when he got up to run. That's when the eldest Olayathil kicked him back down. Held him down there, his foot ground inside the man. Looked him in the face and ground him down.'

'He died right there on the ground with his guts hanging out. Writhing. Everyone watching. Imagine that.'

'No need. Matters from the past are best left in the past. If our hero had his way, these days would become those days.'

Across the street the handsome one finishes his speech.

'Comrades,' he exhorts the entrenched hordes, 'we must not forget.'

He's done well. He waits the appropriate amount of time for the applause that he alone hears to die out. This is a crucial point in his training: a well delivered speech will be applauded loud and long, and it is a mistake to walk away without turning this appreciation toward agitation. But he is at the end of his speech and can think only to repeat it. He begins again.

'Comrades, we must not forget.'

Chairs scrape behind him. From both sides he is seized. He smiles and nods at the rain, hurrying along the street. He is dragged backward to his seat. He consoles himself: he will have another chance. This is just a rehearsal.

Unnikrishnan turns the face in his hands this way and that. A jab with the towel clears away a last fleck of foam caught in the rather handsome cleft that his razor has just revealed. Then he twists the neck, cracking it once, twice, and shoots two puffs of powder that drift and settle ever so gently on skin, bumpy and pink. He declares the job well done and steps from in front of the mirror.

The face pulls forward and peers into the mirror, watches the throat in the mirror swallow hard. After a long moment, the face smiles at what it sees. The beard is gone. He looks less priest-like already. The face studies the reflection of the two seated behind him on the waiting-bench, notes they are men, full grown, but seated like youngsters, shoulder to shoulder, turning the pages of the magazine spread open across both their laps.

'Kids,' he says mockingly, 'we must not forget.'

They look up and frown at the man who pays Unnikrishnan and leaves.

'I am closing the shop.' Unnikrishnan shoos the young men out into the rain. A motorcycle speeds away; two men sprint for the cover of trees.

Unnikrishnan leans his forehead against the inside of the door he has shut. He is remembering a young woman walking in just such a rain. A rain that swallowed her, but not before every piece of her had been examined. He remembers she walked with her hands hanging down at her sides and her open palms flashed white. Her eyes looked up and they flashed white. And almost and almost he and they in the crowd saw only how naked those eyes were. How naked those hands. And almost and almost, the younger him those many years ago did not lift his eyes to the naked breast and the naked thighs, to burn everything of her that curved and hollowed and twisted in the long ago rain to the crowd's whispered chant: mad girl mad girl.

They have been ashamed, him and the crowd, all these years. His shame has remained with him as silence. Silence on the night he removed the clothes from his wife's body for the first time, eyes shut against the white palms of those hands and the white defiance of those eyes. His shame was with him each time Thambichettan entered his shop, filled it with sound, then more sound, lifted his chin for Unnikrishnan's razor and had to be told to be silent or get cut. And Unnikrishnan's shame was with him when he went to ask at Thambichettan's house, if he a Hindu would be permitted to shave his old friend one last time. Shame filled him as he moved in silence, lifting the chin to expose the silent throat as she stood by, she whom he was never able to see without seeing her walking toward him, then away from him, hands hanging at the side, palms and eyes flashing reply to the whispers of mad girl mad girl. And shame it is that urges his daughters in his voice full of silence, to cover up cover up. What is the meaning of this kind of skirt?

Is there a way to deal with shame other than in silence? He was young then and old now. He remembers her; he does not remember any of those who gathered with him to line the roadside three and four deep as she walked by that day. Her hands hanging, and when they stepped toward her, two or three in the crowd with lengths of cloth held open to cover her, her hands found stones on the ground. He remembers her bending, squatting, the way her knees pointed and her thighs flattened so she became a blade. Did the others see this as well? How did they go on to love their wives and their daughters? In silence or in anger? Is there another way for him, and they, who stood that day and watched her scrabble in the mud for stones to fill her lap? She stood up and the stones rolled off her. She walked to where someone stood with outstretched cloth, tore at it and bent again to her stones. She gathered them into cloth.

Outside, the hordes remain, are held in the rain by the force of imagination of the three who have fled the stage. The speechmaker's words from earlier swim the street. Rain-soaked and bilged, the words tip over and disintegrate before they sink.

'The mutual animosity of caste, religion and sectarianism and the related bad rituals . . . leftist activities lifted up Kerala from such a condition to present-day state . . . reminding us . . . the ebbs and flows of the progress of Kerala . . . to learn and teach it . . . a heavy blow on landlords and retrogressive forces . . . strong public agitation . . . At the international level . . . Inferiority complex banished . . . So we remember and learn from . . . Kallen.'

Somewhere beyond the ripples spreading from the drowned speech, trees brush one another as they bend to the whispering of two men.

'Yes, but how can you even say that?'

'Why not? It's the truth. I can say it.'

'Women do not.'

'Yes, they do. I tell you they do.'

'You have a wife. How can you say that?'

'Yes, that's what my wife said. Till I took her hand in mine and showed her the truth.'

'Your wife? How?'

'On our honeymoon.'

'In Bangalore?'

'We were in line at the museum. She had this crazy idea that we had to visit all the cultural centres, see art, study history. I tell you—our Kerala girls are like that.'

'Yes. Yes. But what happened at the museum?'

'Long line, see. We're both waiting. It's just about forever. No one's pushing or anything. Mind you, it's a museum, not a bus stop. We were definitely experiencing some kind of higher thinking, I tell you.'

'Yes. Yes. But what happened?'

'So it's not so crowded and no pushing, but long wait. So I have trouble grasping it, see, when it happens.'

'What? What happens?'

'This girl. In front of me, eh? So I can't see her. That's my bad luck, because she's really something to see from the back. If her breasts, I was thinking, are anything like her shake-shake bottom. I'm thinking this. Wouldn't dream of doing a thing, when you know, so casually, you wouldn't believe how casually, she just leans back and sticks that shake-shake right onto me.'

'Are you mad?'

'Mad? No, not me. It's what I'm telling you. Girls do enjoy it. There are girls like that. Leans right back against me. Sits it on top of me. Well, I get my pole out in a hurry. The whole weight of her. I sort of had to, you know, brace myself.'

'Then?'

'So then I take my hand, and just with the two fingers, mind you, I nudge her. A little nibble. Like this. I can just about hear her moan at this point. She wiggles that bottom of hers then. Looking for my hand to do it again.'

'On your honeymoon? You bastard.'

'No-no-no. You still don't get it, do you? The thrill for me is in finding out how people think, not in feeling up some woman. You don't believe me?'

'No.'

'Well, listen to this. Just the day before the museum thing, I was arguing with Elsie about just this. She wouldn't believe me that there are these women—no, let me rephrase that—plenty of women who want it like that. So you know what I do? I just lean back in line a bit and whisper into Elsie's ear.'

'What?'

'What do you mean "what"? The proof. That's what I told Elsie. I've got me the proof. Then I took Elsie's hand and guided it over to that beauteous bottom, and Elsie's two fingers did the rest.'

'Nudge?'

'Yes, a little nudge and the bottom's wiggling all over again.'

'You're a bastard.'

'No, my friend, I'm a student of human behaviour. And now you see it.'

'Now I see a bastard.'

And though the trees bend hard to the task, there are no more words to hear, just scuffling, till suddenly, as when a gunshot flushes from cover the dumb beast, the two explode into the open, roll around in the clearing, chase each other past what they must not forget. They are laughing as they run.

'He'll get you. The ghost of Kallen is coming to get you. Look out now.'

The one whose uncle is a sympathizer bends and fills his hand with something from the ground. He rises to throw it. But a similar something is already winging toward him, he turns and it catches him with a squelch on the back of his head. His companion has had the same idea. His own something lobbed as he turned lands short of its mark, and oozes red at the base of a tree trunk. Unexpectedly, he is upset.

'Get lost,' he yells to his companion.

His lips turn down. Red bleeds from paper pennants rained to the ground, lying in sodden clumps on a slab of cement.

13

(with her last breath)

My love, you've missed the greening by just a day. I look for you. I see above me the bare branches of the trees by the gate—so shy; each new leaf has emerged thin as plastic, so thin, light passes through. The trees look filled with stars; strung, like the trees at church, with Christmas lights. But it's not night. Only eleven o'clock. The day is just settling in all our stomachs.

I am on the path that used to bring me to you. Remember this tree by the gate? It was so bare, and the ground nearby was strewn with shit and the rubble someone heaped up there. But now. Now you've missed the change.

On the path I hear whispering. I look from under my eyelids at the faces of those who watch me. I see the man whose cheeks stand up on his face. How absurd, I thought when we first saw him on this path. I meant to point him out to you then, and we were to share the joke. If not for his moustache, you know what I think, I think he would be exposed as a child.

I see the dogs chasing after one another through bushes and almost your arm circles mine to pull me out of danger. But you are not here with me. Those days when we were together, I was pretending. I was not really afraid of dogs. You knew it was pretence. It was our game. So you would bring your arms around me. And now I am afraid.

Here, see, it is husband. Behind him—wife. Can't see her under the bowl of her umbrella. She is armed against the sun. But what does she have to defend her from her husband? Wife has a voice that booms small. She booms small at the husband's back. She sways and drags and booms, and he throws back over his shoulder that she should shut up. Not really. That's just what I would say if I were a husband. She says, Husband, my brother has taken the best part of the land. Let us measure again. He throws the knife with a lazy hand, over the shoulder, blind throw, laces her lips. Not really.

He might be your father. She might be your mother. They might step from the crowd, face me, she, take the knife, and he, unlace her lips. They might face me and speak as one: 'shameless girl, mad girl.' Not really. No one along this path need do anything. All has been done. You are gone.

It's the time of year for the pinwheel flowers to bloom. Not yet. I stop to touch the buds. Today the pointed tips are frilling. It is the time of unfurling. So surprising when, after all that anticipation, they open and the petals are single, there is no scent, the sap is bitter and stains my fingertips. I am crushing the buds. Why should they open and betray every expectation?

At least the touch-me-not plant behaves predictably. I trample them, and they fold like girls in church folding to the priest. Last Sunday, the priest blessed me with the cross, bringing it down on top of my head. His ungentle touch. He pushed down with all his might. I pushed back with my head. Foul man. He was the first to falter. He tried to lift the cross and it tangled in the net on my head. Now there will be another rule for girls in church. Scarves should be made of plain cloth and not net-and-lace.

How will I go to church on Sunday?

They've taken my clothes from me. Dear one, they have hurt me. How will I go anywhere?

I will walk this path and pass people and let them pass me. I will walk this path in a dream. Dreaming, I will not see them.

No, I will not dream. I will walk this path and pass people and let them pass me. If I can do it on Wednesday, I can do it on Thursday, then Friday, then Saturday, Sunday. I will do it by using my feet and hands and tongue and eyes. I will listen to the noise of the whispering and turn it into the smell of their souls putrefying inside their bodies. I will burn them with my eyes; scorch them till their skin ashes white, as white as the powder they paste on their faces, necks, breasts. I will push Joseph and Tessa and Sudha from the mike, and I will take the mike in my hands and sing. How terrible my song will be. You know I can't sing. You know you teased me and forced me and I sang and you laughed at me and it was no good my crying and telling you, 'Didn't I say I couldn't sing? Why did you make me?'

How will I walk this path?

Now it rains lightly. Now it rains ropes. Now ropes of rain braid my hair that isn't.

Now the path is empty. Someone is calling me, asking me to step inside and take shelter. Is this kindness? Will she push me when my foot lifts to step over the threshold? Can I tell her how hungry I am?

This morning we ate puttu with kadala. You know how I love puttu. I would have liked to eat bananas with the puttu. What I craved was something a little sweet. The taste of honey has been in my mouth for days and I must find food to match the taste. What is the good of taste in the mouth? What I need is to swallow. But Saramma, she always knows when I want something. She removed the plate from right in front of me. Just in the same way she took Tessiebaby from me after she returned. Just the same way she took father from me. You from me.

I left the table and thought I would wander this path in search of honey. I long for a comb of honey to squeeze in my fist. Oh, to trickle something sweet down my throat. For something to burn thick in my belly.

I hear the sound of water. But it is not the creek at the end of the path I hear. It is rain outside a window. I am inside. It is rain pouring in from the window. Someone, quick, close the window.

Have I left the path then? Whose bed do I lie in? Have I been shown kindness? Then why this pain that inflames?

I am covered in rain. I am covered in people's stares. Someone is stoking a fire; the iron pipe is at the mouth. This is cruel of them, to blow into the pipe, to blow on the fire, to fan the small flame. It leaps. People, don't you see the fire is leaping in me? Brothers and sisters, dear ones, you burn me.

A man loves me. Don't you know a man loves me?

14

Father Paul Starts Over Again

If the freshly shaven Father Paul, rocketing down the highway to the head office in Palai is to have a chance of making sense of himself, much less of making sense to his Superior, he knows what he needs to do. He must rehearse, practice, crack the books as he never did the textbooks in Rome, by which he means he must crack his thoughts, or at least marshal them, and his arguments, of course. Rehearse, he commands himself. Head down to protect newly exposed and sensitive skin from the grit flying at him from the road, Father Paul does just that: he rehearses.

Paul Vadakel here. Father, may I enter? Good evening, Father Thayiparambil. Thank you, Father. Yes, Father. Well, Father. They are also well, Father. Father, I have come with regard, Father, to speak with regard, to explain to you Father—a certain matter. Father, you know me for the last twenty-two years. From before I came to the church as a small boy of fourteen you know me. I thought this was a way for me to choose my own family instead of having to live with the one I was born into. All of us boys after the lights were turned out, joking together. That

106

Tharackan fellow was so good at doing imitations. Such a hunger we had to be together. I came three years in a row to summer camp. I am sure you thought it was the result of the good work you were doing to help us recognize our calling. Refugees—that's what we were.

No, no, no. This isn't right.

Father, I hail from a family devout in their adherence to the church. You have been present for long years in my formation as a priest. Through the difficult times when I returned . . . when I was returned . . . when I came to this parish.

Never mind that business in the past. No one else even remembers it. Start over again, Paul.

Y ou must take me seriously, Father. Father, you know me throughout my formation. So you will take me seriously, Father, when I announce to you my resignation. Your expression is clouded. You are troubled, Father. You don't know what to make of this news. It is, Father, because I know well what decision you will take with regard to a controversial parishioner. You have objected to—have been objecting to—my continuing interest in her spiritual welfare. Her presence is no more, Father.

You are laughing at me Father. You, who know me for twelve years of my formation. You will take my resigning from this hypocritical institution seriously. This grave decision.

Start over, Paul. Enough of trying to speak in English. Start over in Malayalam.

I n Malayalam then: it is I. Father, I bring news of the passing. The passing. A parishioner. Passing. No, not of our sister

Rajamma's. Her suffering continues. Yes, she is still refusing the medicine. She suffers such pain. Her people are very concerned, but I believe their admiration contributes to the miserable state in which she is choosing to spend her last days. I counselled her family to accept morphine, but immediate tears from her. Like a waterfall.

What is this? Not supposed to be about Rajamma's suffering. One more time.

It is I. Father, I want to inform you that Annakutty has died. Annakutty Edanolil, wife of the one-legged Thambi. The church helped him find employment with the loan for the vehicle, Father. Father it was a quick illness. There was no time for the anointing of the sick. This should be no problem. I have prayed over her body and others from the neighbourhood have joined in praying the rosary. I have taken her sister's phone number. I have phoned her sister to inform with regard to her demise.

What is this? English again? Stick to Malayalam, Paul.

Her sister has taken the news well. Actually, her sister was most concerned about her daughter. The child is about twelve years old. The child was being raised by Annakutty in the absence of the child's mother, who is in the Gulf for some years now. Actually this woman did not take the news well, Father. I am not sure what made me tell you that she had. In fact, she had not. She kept demanding that I put her child on the phone. Of course, seeing as I made the call from the ISO booth at the Junction, there was no possibility of my placing this child in connection with her mother.

I assured the mother the child was being fed and in other regards well taken care of by the many women who have come to oversee the preparation of the body. Numerous times the call was interrupted Father by a loud crashing. Then this sister of Annakutty's would take the phone up again and explain to me that she had just thrown it at this or that person.

Yes, Father, perhaps it runs in the blood.

No, Father, I am not expecting you to be concerned about the arrangements. I am simply informing you, Father, that I am handling my duties as per my duties. I mean that I am handling myself all of the duties. Just to inform you the vigil is throughout this night with a funeral to be tomorrow, myself officiating. We are only awaiting the arrival of the family member whom I just mentioned.

What do you mean you will not allow the funeral, Father? Father, this woman was baptized in the Catholic faith. In the Kochi diocese, I believe. But she's been in our diocese since her marriage to a member of my parish. He was himself a member of our parish since his birth in these parts. He was born in 1929. I remember the details of his death certificate that I was witness to. He himself passed away just a year ago, Father. Myself officiating at that funeral, my first funeral.

No, Father Thayiparambil. I have not seen her baptism certificate. But in my time spent with her, I have come to know the details of her life. Such particulars as her birthplace in Kochi and then her mother's passing, and the difficult life she lived without her mother's guidance.

No, Father Thayiparambil. The church-given marriage certificate does not exist. This is as it is, as you know from the grief it caused you when Thambi chose for the marriage to be held outside the church.

No, Father Thayiparambil. The marriage was not registered afterwards with the church.

Yes, Father Thayiparambil, it is Annakutty I was having difficulty persuading to allow the girl in her care to attend Sunday school.

No, Father Thayiparambil, I was not able at the last instance to persuade her to allow me to pray for her soul.

Nineteen forty-five, she was born, Father. If you can imagine.

Of course, Father. You don't have to imagine. You were yourself born prior to that. But my point Father was how difficult those times must have been. How much more difficult those times, forming people so they have clung to mistaken precepts. Not you. Of course not you, Father. But surely the times were such . . . such . . . what she must have had to live through were such events as would make faith, not impossible, Father, never impossible, but yes, difficult.

The truth about her marriage, Father? She refused marriage in the church.

It was a legal marriage.

I am certain, Father.

There was never a sense of her hiding anything from me, Father, so I never felt the need to probe.

You are right, Father. She refused every sacrament the church offered her. She refused the sacrament of marriage, the sacrament of redemption, finally the sacrament of absolution.

But Father, this is one truth. There is also the truth of her hunger, Father. For justice. To hunger and thirst for justice, as she did, is at the centre of our faith. She embodied this spiritual hunger. Father, I myself have not let food or water pass my lips since the news of her passing. In fact, my last meal was yesterday afternoon as I had withdrawn to my room prior to the dinner bell with the intention of pursuing some private reading.

No, Father, I have not made a practice of withdrawing.

What you have heard from Father Kuriakose is not true. Father Kuriakose has ulterior reasons for speaking poorly of me.

Father, it is simply that this is the only time when I am not either teaching at St Anthony's or working with the upliftment effort at Little Flowers.

Yes, Father, the work with the tribals is going well.

With regard to my choosing to not eat. I am choosing hunger as a way of struggle. The immediate struggle, Father, is sometimes greater than the spiritual struggle. In this instance, the struggle is against social injustice. My faith calls me to this struggle. It calls me to hunger.

Father, I shall undertake a hunger strike, with your permission Father.

Until?

I shall strike, Father, until there is a resolution to the question of truth that you have raised. You ask what truth there is in Annakutty's life. I shall fast till I can ascertain this truth, present to you this truth, expand our understanding in the church of what truth there is in the suffering lives of our brethren. Our sister, Annakutty.

Father, it is you who wish to exaggerate. You wish to exaggerate the precision of history. You wish to exaggerate the order of the life she lived. What came first, second and third. Perhaps Father, for her, third came first and second came last and the first was the middle.

No, Father, it is not my hunger that makes me speak, as you say, in a muddle. Life does not have a pure grammar, Father—a past, present, future, strung one after the other. She whispered to me, Father. Yesterday afternoon, she whispered the greatest truth there is. She said she never stopped loving her lost son. She said this erased all distinctions of time. Hers was a life lived in the constant. A continuous tense. No grammar for her. She said her past was her present, her present was her present and her future was her present. Don't you see, Father? Have we ever been called, Father, to anything else? To anything less than immutable love?

Yes, of course I see the danger in obsessing. By obsession, you mean that she was living in the past.

Not the past? You say—in the past that could have been. Again, you exaggerate. You play with words. You invent grammar. I do not know of any such tense. You say she was trapped by the idea of a life that could have been. But, Father, hers was no obsession with what could have been.

In that event, she would have wanted nothing less than to rewrite her past. This is what we in the church have done. We have rewritten the past. In our version, she should never have had the child, so the child disappears.

He was stolen, Father. And aid was given in this matter by our own church. There was a desire to wash our hands clean at the expense of the spiritual tie of a mother to her son. It is we who wish away the sins of our past. Not she. Even today. I understand that even today a certain person continues as an ordained priest. Despite the role he played. And this role, it is known to all—he fathered the child. I have said it now. There, I have said it. Is this inevitable that he should continue as a priest? Even today, I would say this is not inevitable. It was her faith that called Annakutty to act as she did, to act even against the church.

Yes, I am unclear about the circumstances. It was never from her that I heard these matters. But I know as everyone else does. I do not judge. Rather, I commit the grave error you ascribe to her of wishing away what cannot be wished away. I wish the church never . . . She, on the other hand . . . How can I explain this to you? She accepted the past. But it was never inevitable for her. She accepted the present, even the future, but never as inevitable. Don't you see, Father, we choose what determines us? There is nothing inevitable in any moment we live, nothing that says we cannot love as she loved her son, even in his absence. Isn't this what I have been working to convey at Little Flowers? Yes, yes it is. But I never understood it till last night, never understood it when I was preparing for my ordination, no, not till this moment. And now I cannot make you understand.

What application for us? The application it has for us is that we can choose what we want to do. Even I, I can choose. We do not have to adhere to anyone who tells us that she is an outcaste from the church. And I, I can determine who and what I am in the church.

How can I make you understand, Father, what I saw yesterday afternoon. I saw a woman who lived on hope. Because if there is nothing inevitable about any moment we live, then surely you see, Father, we have every reason to hope.

I will tell you something that perhaps no one else knows. She told me that she placed her hand on his back. Can you imagine that back—a child's back is such a small thing, a small part of what is already small. She must have stooped to place her hand there. With her hand there, she gave her little son a push toward the future. It was at a railway station. She gave him the push that sent him away from her. She set him on the road he was to travel. The road she has travelled. The same road. It binds them. They have never been apart since. She and he have travelled this road since. Can you imagine?

She said the moment his back moved away from her hand, she

knew it was a mistake. And she is convinced that he too feels the error. That he is surely angry at her. Annakutty told me that she knows her son will not accept their separation as inevitable. She said to me that if she set him on that road, then surely it leads back to her. Can you imagine that? I cannot. I spent the night trying to imagine how he would return to her in the short time she had remaining. I was shaken to think that she could imagine it.

You know, for the past year, she has been advertising in newspapers. Yes, she did this years ago as well. I thought last night, her faith will be rewarded. She will surely live till she sets eyes on him again. Until this moment, here and now, I had not understood—her reward is her faith.

Is this not an exemplary life—a life lived in faith?

No, her faith was not in herself. Her faith is demonstrated in a life of peaceful struggle against oppression. It is the same faith we are all taught to uphold, and few of us understand. I too wish to protest as she did, and will begin with a hunger strike.

Until?

I will undertake this hunger strike without your permission if necessary, until the church agrees to granting Annakutty Edanolil a Catholic burial.

No, her faith was never to my knowledge a faith based in the name we have given our saviour, Jesus Christ. She herself told me her god was in the return of her son. I understood this to mean that she saw god in everything: in the presence of her son before he was lost to her, in his absence afterwards, and in the idea of his return. Her god was in the love that was constant through all three of these periods of her life. I see no inconsistency in understanding god as a creation wherein each of us is to bear faith to our inner nature and to the god within.

I do not mean that god is our creation. No, of course *we* are his creation. But our understanding of him is our creation. Nothing precludes her faith in her god from being substantive in the same way that my faith in my god is substantive. The two are the same.

And faith. Faith is a tree you climb. You climb it so you can see farther than you would from the ground. Her faith was a huge tree. She saw farther.

Let me explain it like this. She climbed a mountain and it led to other mountains. We think we have only this mountain to climb. I am trained to think that way. Teach the women at Little Flowers, set up community meetings, climb the mountain of their ignorance. But now I know. When I get to the top, I will not be done. There will be other mountains. From the top, I will see the other mountains. When I finish wrestling with one set of questions, others will spring up, bigger.

Yes, I mean trees. But also mountains. I am not being clear, but you know what I am saying. You are quarrelling with my words. Why don't you quarrel with my ideas instead?

Yes, as a matter of fact I do believe in her god: I believe her son will return. And furthermore, she believed in my god. In Jesus Christ, her saviour.

No, she never used the words Jesus Christ.

But to go back to obsession. We obsess. I will say it: you obsess over the Kingdom that is to come. You teach little children to say, 'thy kingdom come'. But what if the kingdom is already here?

Father, I read all night. I have been preparing even prior to last night for the eventuality that you would deny her a Catholic burial.

No, it's true I was not expecting her to die. But, Father, she believed she was dying.

No, as I said before, she never asked for absolution. No, she did not want a Catholic burial. It is I who ask. It is I who need to know, what purpose my faith.

In my readings, Father, of canonical law, I saw that under certain circumstances, even at the funeral of heretics, a mass may be said. Here in Kerala our church is ready to force absolution on those who are professed atheists. Why? Politics. Politics is what brings us to the bedside of any member of the Communist Party whose frightened wife allows us to be present at his last hour. In the fight to reclaim a Communist, which is to say the fight to claim power, any canonical law can be bent. The church is ready to play the political game. She lived by her faith, Father. All I can bring you from my readings is:

What does it profit, my brethren, if someone says he has faith, but he has not works . . . So faith by itself, if it has no works, is dead.

Yes, Father Thayiparambil. James 2: 14-18.

Father, what purpose my faith if I cannot come to you and persuade you we have wronged Annakutty Edanolil through much of her life. In her death, we must demonstrate the meaning of our faith and correct the grave injustice done to her.

Father, we must not only bury her. We must continue the search for her son. Our church is a powerful institution. A worldwide church. Years of standing at the right bedsides. Accruing enormous amounts of power. Let us put this power to the service of our faith. If we choose to, we can right the wrongs of the past; we can see the kingdom that is here in the life of Annakutty. Father, we can find the child. If we want to, we can find him in no time at all. He can be here tomorrow. He can be here for the funeral. It is only up to us.

Yes, Father, this was her dying request of me. To find him. And I am no priest if I don't.

Father Paul Vadakel is covered in dust. He has ridden thirty kilometres to arrive at the Provincial House's gates. He eases his motorbike inside and looks at the long approach to the building's front door.

Inside, the Provincial is gathering up papers, settling them on his desk. In another moment, the Provincial, one Father Thayiparambil, will gather his robes, and then himself. He is a big man whose skull has been brought to prominence by the years that have vanished his hair. It will take him time to move the heavy bones of his legs from under the desk he is seated at, to swivel toward the door, and aided by one of the younger seminarians, rise and walk from the room, pushing his cane ahead of him. It will take him time to arrive at the evening vespers. The bell calling the seminarians and priests has not ceased its ringing. It is calling Father Paul as well.

At that moment, if someone were to look out from inside the Palai Diocesan Centre, he would have seen a man, barely out of his childhood, step away from a length of bulging metal, pause next to it and adjust the cassock that's twisted along the short column of his body.

In another moment, the bell will cease its calling, and the man in the cassock will begin the long walk up the path to the front door.

But just at present there is no one looking out a window, to note the man hunch his shoulders in an attempt to stop trembling. No one to note that when he straightens, the air around him seems to be vibrating, that he is sobbing at the strangeness of what is filling him: so this is faith?

15

(with her last breath)

I knew you the first time I saw you. In the convent parlour, that room full of embroidery, and girls sitting, knees pressed together, you were the one whose eyes I fell into. You looked like me. All burnt you were on the inside. I thought that's me sitting there with Bihari eyes. Later they burnt you on the outside as well.

When I saw you that first time I couldn't help but think how ugly you were. Your eyes, so small and folded over. Did someone feel when you were a baby that you were looking too hard? Did they take your face in their hands and pull the lids down, so your eyes opened only half as wide? It seemed to me they had failed. Inside your few lashes, as soft as fern, your eyes glittered like water in the far bottom of the well.

You were ugly. Your shoulders were broad. Your legs were short and bowed. Where was your neck? The hair you wore curved over the forehead told me you thought you were beautiful. I knew you were not there wanting to become a nun. Your clothes were thick and striped and full of colour. I wanted your clothes.

I was frightened. Sent away. I did everything to ensure they would send me away and, when they did, I wanted to fall on my knees and beg my father and Saramma to let me stay. Instead, I hid my fear and came into the parlour and saw you sitting there in between all those girls so eager to be married to a man dead ten thousand years on a cross. You, sent to this marriage because there were no parents to stop it, and I, sent to it because my parents willed it.

And I recognized you. Both of us, girls with no dowry to bring to the convent, we would work in the kitchen and the laundry while the others with their sacks of gold, and their land waiting to be bequeathed to the church, they would live a life apart from us.

'How it rains. Outside, the water must be rising.'

Your parents knew how to make the journey in water, did they not? Growing up in your parts, did they expect the river when it came for them? Did the animals tell them? Did the rats run out into the open and did the cows low in the fields and refuse to pull the plough? Did your father's foot sink into mud one morning as he stepped out of your home? Did the baby refuse his feed that day? Did your mother say, God is absconding? How did they know? What were the signs that prepared them?

Here, no matter how high the water gets, we have our hills to climb. We don't go in a flood. We don't. We go lying down in our beds. But where do we go? They say God is watching over us. And if he is, then it will be as they say—Mavelinaadu: a kingdom with a king and happy subjects, mothers feeding their children. But if God is absconding, then there is nothing to prepare for. Go any which way the path takes you.

You told me, Bihari girl, that your parents drowned in the flood. But I didn't think to ask you how. Your parents, your brothers and sisters and aunts and uncles, grandparents and dogs, cats and cows—how?

Your father tied you, his favourite, to his shoulders and trod water till the river rose high enough to transfer you to the top of the highest tree. He tied you there.

'Catch,' he called to you. 'Hold on. Stay alive.'

You watched the dogs, cats, cows, grandparents, aunts, uncles, brothers, sisters, mother and, finally, your father wave goodbye. You must have wondered at the gape-mouthed glubbering of those goodbyes. You watched whole trees, huts, stretches of tar road, bridges of stone come riding the weeping river to knock the dogs, cats, cows, grandparents, aunts, uncles, brothers, sisters, mother, and in the end your father, free of their goodbyes.

Your father dodged what came at him, shouted all kinds of nonsense at you.

'Remember we want this for you.'

'Remember,' he commanded as a chunk of his chest was hacked from him. 'Remember to call to us when you need us. We will come to help you.'

When he was all but pulverized, he still oozed words.

'Remember you are never alone in this world. We go with you everywhere you go.'

'Remember,' he shouted when he was just a head bobbing in the water, 'we have always loved you.'

And when he was five bubbles—you counted—dancing on top of the red river, he sobbed to you: 'Remember to never forget us. Remember to live for all of us.'

You loved to tell this story. And I listened though it kept me awake at night. But I forgot to ask you, how? You saw them cross over. How did they do it?

And I never told you that I very nearly drowned once. But in the end, I pulled back; I didn't know how to cross over.

I told you I had a love when I was a girl, living in Cochin. I would lay waiting for him at my window. Through the bars I hung my hand for him to touch. In that city, in the lane we lived in, others saw my hand and touched it in the night. Others pulled me to come. I knew only his hand. I told you that, didn't I? I waited for him in the dark. Till the day they took me away, there I waited. Bihari girl, when was it that he stopped coming? Was it after they shaved my head? Yes, it was after. Here's a truth I didn't tell you. Though I knew only his hand, there were so many others at whose touch I shook. To be desired. I wanted that.

When they took him from me, I did not want to love again. I knew I could. But I wouldn't admit to such knowledge. I studied myself in the mirror, the pale skin the razor exposed on my head, the dark skin of my face. I walked to where my father took me once to see a palace strung in lights in the middle of the water. I wondered how it was possible that the time of my childhood had come to an end and how it could be that here I was in another time, standing on the water's edge, gathering stones to fill my skirt. The water did not rise. Didn't I tell you?—here the waters don't take you. Not even when you offer yourself.

The palace lights came on one by one. They tossed in the lake—lit, then snuffed by the waves. I prayed for the waves to come toss me. I stared into the dark till I woke to see fishermen slip from many boats and enter water. They held on to the edges of one net. Boats and men pulled apart to spread the net, then danced back tight to close it. Into the boats they hauled fish, splashing, twisting and writhing in the morning light. My stomach grumbled. I had come to die and had lived. Bihari girl, I lived.

After that I knew how. The thing I had done without knowing I was doing it—the thing of living—now I not only knew I was living, I knew how. And this knowing never tripped me up, the way knowing I am breathing stops my breath, restarts it, frays it. Knowing how to live is a path with no obstructions.

On that day, knowing how to live, I remembered, I can love again. And I did. In Saramma's village I loved again. It is why Saramma stripped my clothes from me. It is how I was sent to the nuns. It is how I loved you, Bihari girl, your priest, my lost child. It is through knowing how to live that I lost my child.

Bihari girl, you were taken from the top of the tree and put on a train. The waters, still full of bloated bodies, parted on either side, and you travelled all the way to Madras. Because, they said, God is calling you.

We used to laugh, point to each other and repeat, 'God is calling you.'

You and I, up on top of the stairs that led to the pigeon shit-covered chapel roof. Lying there because it was the one place we could laugh together. We laughed most of all to think of all the people, even animals—a state full of Bihari people and animals— God had to knock from the earth so you could hear his call.

Bihari girl, you taught me to laugh. It took a long time, but I learned to laugh at me.

In return, I hurried past the locked door, past your moans, past the sound of your baby coming too soon into the world, the sound of your leaving, so slow.

It was easy. I pretended to not know you.

Three days and you did not rise in fulfilment of the scriptures. You are not seated at the right hand of the Father. You do not receive my prayers. But you alone are the only one. When the moaning stopped, I was taken from the laundry and given your job in the kitchen.

The girls in the kitchen stared at me.

I only said, 'What are you staring at?'

They looked away.

'The Sisters killed her,' I said.

It was too late to say such things. The girls scurried to the far wall. They stood in a row, their backs to that sooty wall.

I said, 'She was going to have a baby. They found out and killed her. Watch out you don't have babies.'

The girls opened their eyes wide. But their ears were closed. It was easy. They pretended to not know me. And there was the length of that entire kitchen between us.

'Mother Claudia ordered it,' I said. 'The oil that tipped onto her. It was not an accident. It was from this pan they threw the oil on her.'

'This pan,' I shouted at them and shook the pan.

One girl returned to the rice she was pounding. She pounded alone. Though her rhythm was off, the sound filled the kitchen. I thought to tell her about the priest. I wanted to say something that would make her return to the wall. Another girl separated from the wall, and took up position across from the first girl. The wooden pounding stick picked up speed. Their arms flashed as they threw the pounding stick in turn, flash, it flies high, thump, it raises a fine mist of flour.

I couldn't think what their now-smooth rhythm, the piston-like movement of their arms reminded me of.

'The priest,' I choked. They did not turn to look at me.

I thought of the train that brought me to the convent. I thought of how even as I hated Saramma for sending me away, I was also pleased to be on a train.

I took the priest to our laughter on the chapel roof. I tried to teach him to laugh. In memory of you, we tried to laugh. We couldn't. We made my son in sorrow. Is it any wonder I lost him?

I hid my pregnancy, but there was no hiding my labour. When my son came, the nuns were at my bedside. I was pushing him out. I could feel him emerging. Then I felt them pushing. They tried to push him back inside me. They were going to smother him.

Though you were long gone, I heard your voice repeat your father's nonsense: 'Remember to call to us when you need us. We will come to help you. Remember you are never alone in this world. We go with you everywhere you go. Remember we have always loved you. Remember to never forget us. Remember to live for us.'

I felt you then. You and all your people. Crossing. And with you my son was crossing too. I felt your father tie my son to me. I heard him. 'Catch. Hold on. Stay alive.'

How did it feel when they tried to kill my son? It felt like all the times I heard the sound of rice in someone else's hand, rice in someone else's mouth. Spit in my mouth. Hunger in my stomach. Death entering me. It felt like all the times I did not want to cross over. I wanted my son. That is what I felt then.

My arms were tied, my feet tied. I screamed at the nuns.

'I know what you did to her. It was not an accident. You emptied the cooking oil on her. Don't take him from me.'

They would have killed my son.

I screamed, 'I will tell the world what you did to her.'

They left me alone with my son.

Three days in a room and you never rose again. Your name was Bihari girl.

16

An Impression in the Sheet

Tessie is not done with being angry at Father Paul. In the hours that have elapsed since she spoke with him on the phone, she has accomplished much. She has shed hysterical tears to get the Filipino nurse off her back. More tears, and she has arranged for a leave from work and purchased a middle-of-the-night ticket that will get her to her sister's village by morning of the next day. In the midst of this tremendous flurry of activity, she has kept alive a conversation with the priest. It is a simple conversation. He is silent, and she repeats over and over in her mind what she should have shouted at him when she had the chance. 'You want to know who I am? I am my Annachechi's Tessiebaby.'

Back at home, at the end of her work shift, she has her husband Santosh for an audience. 'I shouted at the priest, "Who are you to say such a thing?" Maybe,' she tells Santosh, 'it was wrong to speak to a priest like that. But I spoke from shock. He should have understood. He shouted back at me, "Who are you?" A strange thing for a priest to ask a woman he knows well enough.'

Tessie doesn't tell her husband that she threw the phone. That the priest's voice continued to make noises from the floor.

'Why should I,' she asks her husband, 'tell this priest anything about *who I am*. He knows who I am. He's called me at the hospital twice before.'

Tessie doesn't tell her husband her reason for throwing the phone. The priest's question, she is certain, was an accusation. She is a failed someone, someone who didn't come to her sister's bedside while she lay dying.

Tessie tells herself, he doesn't know that I have done worse than fail to attend at my sister's bedside. He doesn't know that she was my elder sister, but the years we were just the two of us, there were nights I called her my little mother.

He wants to know who I am. First and last, I am my Annachechi's Tessiebaby. She loved me and I hurt her.

The day Annachechi turned away from the empty train tracks, she looked at me like she would kill me.

For months my father had twisted at me to go to her, to tell her to come home. But to first leave the baby somewhere. Then suddenly there was another choice. Somebody who wanted the baby. The Sisters at the convent arranged it and gave father the money. When I was barely older than Nina is now, maybe thirteen, I went alone to meet my sister. It is a day and a night's journey by train. In the morning, I sat with my face pressed to the bars on the train window. There was only a five-minute stop at that station, and I had been told by father I must hurry to get off before the train went on to the main station in Madras. I kept searching the station and wouldn't get off till I finally saw her, a woman, standing far back on the platform. She was looking right at me. I realized, this woman knows me. She made no movement to come to the train. I got off and I carried my box and went to her. I looked by her side for the child, but he wasn't there. I stood for a moment not knowing what to do next. The train signalled its departure.

I had carried bananas wrapped in paper from home—a stalk so big I had left it on the train when I stepped off with the box. I left my box at her feet and hurried back to the train to bring them to her. The second time I staggered over to her, she threw her arms around me and I cried to have my sister back again.

Yes, I was thirteen then. She was twenty-four. I had not seen her in seven years. I had never seen the child. She gave birth to the child when she was at the convent.

Father had written to tell her that people were making life difficult for me. He asked her how she thought I would ever get married. He said she would have to come home without the child, and only then could he arrange for me to marry. I went to see her, full of doubts about father's thinking. But within a day of seeing how she lived, I wanted to go home and resume my life. I wanted to sit in my own house and eat food that we eat at home. I wanted to be done with her misery, done with her love for the boy. Sometimes hugging him till he cried. Then pushing him away. I told her what father taught me to say. I told her about the boys at school who called me names when I walked by them.

Father thought it would be better to never tell her about the money. He planned to send her to school with the money. He must have thought he would make good his lie that she was in Madras for her studies. Later he sent me to school with the money. But no good came of it. In his lifetime he saw neither of us married. She never gave people a chance to accept father's story about her living in Madras to study. She told everyone who would listen about the child. 'My Lost Boy.' She almost never called him by his name. If Thambichettan hadn't taken her into his home, she would still be sitting on the bench outside the District Police office, waiting for the DSP to give her news of her boy.

She never forgave father to the end. As for forgiving me . . . we never talked about it. So I don't know.

Certainly she never forgave herself. Of her part in it, she said: 'I made a mistake.'

Somehow I cannot say the words 'I made a mistake'. I don't know whether that is because I don't quite believe it is a mistake or because I'm unable to admit a mistake when I make one. I think to admit it a mistake I have to first imagine what life would have been like if she'd kept the boy. All I can imagine is her continuing to live in that dark room and all of us, even the boy, hating her.

All I know is I was the one to urge her to meet with the German woman; I was the one who sat on a train, memorizing all the words the nuns and my father gave me to persuade her to give the child away. I was the one who said, the boys at school call me names. And when she looked at me as if none of what I said meant anything to her, I said, 'They call me your sister.'

The foreigners. They disappeared with the child. They never contacted the nuns after they took the child. We were supposed to be told when they arrived in Delhi, and where they would go from there.

Father said Annachechi shouldn't have filed the complaint at the police station.

'They heard in Delhi,' he said, 'when they arrived there—that the woman had gone mad and wanted her child back. Of course they never wrote. They took the child and left the country. They had paid for him. What else were they to do?'

Father was right. They made an agreement with Annachechi to take the child, to make him their son. Then they heard in Delhi, maybe from the nuns at the convent, maybe from the police themselves that she had changed her mind and they hurried away with the child. What else were they to do?

Amma only said, 'Everyone gets the child they deserve.'

I was never sure what she meant by that. Did Annachechi get the child she deserved? Her lost child? Or did the Germans get the child they deserved?

He was a beautiful child. He had hair that fell onto his face. I teased him and called him a movie star. When he smiled, his mouth opened to show both the top and bottom teeth. They were perfectly even teeth, matched in size, not like that of anyone in our family. There were almost dimples in his chin. His eyes were slanted. I only saw him for a few days before she handed him to them. And I was too young to really feel anything for him. And I have to tell the truth, those days I mostly thought of myself. I mostly worried about what was to happen to me. So much had gone wrong with my life already. They were saying Annachechi had corrupted one of the novices in the convent. They were saying this other novice killed herself because Annachechi and she were in love with the same man. The boys in school whispered when I walked past. They whispered things about what Annachechi was doing in Madras. What I did not want was for things to keep going wrong. I wanted to do something to make my life better, or at least to make it not any worse.

Annachechi hated me for what I did. She turned from the train that had disappeared down the tracks, turned from chasing it,

turned toward me who was chasing after her. Her hair was in her
face. There was spit flying from her mouth. She wasn't crying yet.

'Give me back my son.'

Those were her words.

She took my daughter as a favour to me. There was no way I
could have brought Nina with me to Dubai. I earn enough, but
when am I ever home? I work every extra shift they give me.
Santosh says, make the money now. If there is a war, like the one
in Kuwait, then we will have to leave. There is no knowing what
the future holds. This way Nina could be safe with Annachechi.
And somewhere in the back of my mind I thought, this way I will
give her back her child.

We went to the police station in Thambaram. From the start
she did it all wrong. People used to say about Annachechi that she
never learned how to behave. People used to say Annachechi was
always too sure of what was owed to her.

It took her one minute of pacing the corridor to barge into the
Inspector's office. He asked her if she had taken money for the
child. She jumped on him and scratched him. They put her in jail
for the rest of the day and then for the night. We had tickets to
return to father and mother, leaving from Thambaram station
that night. I was supposed to have a different life from that point
on. Instead, I stayed all night outside the police station. In the
morning, they called me inside and told me to take Annachechi.
Her head and arms were covered in bruises. I was afraid that the
police had done something to her.

'Annachechi,' I said, 'you are hurt.'

She looked at me. Her eyes were full of pleading. Then I saw the marks on her arms were bite marks. It was she who had hurt herself.

'Take her,' they said. 'The woman is an animal.'

I was frightened of her.

She refused to come with me. She made the police call the nuns. Right then, she lost any chance of the nuns helping her. Nuns are powerful people. If they want, they can have the priest or even the bishop speak for them. But in this case, they had no need. We heard the police speak to them. The side of the phone conversation we heard was filled with what people in the village call tail wagging.

'Sister, the bishop has been so kind this year. The water tank is working beautifully. It is the bishop's good work that keeps the people in the slums from fighting with each other.'

'No Sister, we don't expect much from the government. That will be the day, Sister.'

'If those boys are seen climbing that wall again . . . Sister, you only have to tell us.'

What did Annachechi think would happen? Who were we to go to the police with a complaint against the nuns? The police were Hindus. Inspector Saar was sometimes addressed as Narayanan Saar.

I said, 'Narayanan Saar.'

I said, 'Inspector Saar.'

I was thirteen then. I knew well enough how to talk to a man with that much power. If Annachechi ever knew, she certainly forgot that day. Everything that came out of her mouth was abuse.

'Dog,' she called him.

'Bitches,' she called loud enough for her voice to carry to the nuns on the other end of the phone line. 'Give me back My Lost Boy.'

Narayanan Saar put the phone down and turned to us. 'I just spoke to the Sister in charge of the orphanage and also to the Mother Superior at the convent. Both of them tell me a couple from somewhere outside India came to them for a child. This couple did not select any of the children shown to them at the orphanage. They asked for an older orphan. The sisters were disappointed. They had no older child for the couple. But the Sisters say they told the couple about a girl from Kerala, who is doing domestic service in the Selaiyur area, who has a child she wants to give for adoption.'

Annachechi shook her head.

'Hold on. Hold on.' Narayanan Saar pointed his stick at one of those standing next to Annachechi. The man moved closer to Annachechi.

'The Sisters tell me they don't know for sure if the couple did anything with the information. But they did give the foreign couple the name and address of this woman from Kerala. That would be you, my dear.'

Annachechi didn't leap up and try to kill him like I thought she would.

'The Sisters tell me after that they never heard from the couple again. They say they do not know where the couple came from. They say they do not know if the couple met with the girl in Selaiyur. They say they do not know where the couple went.'

The Inspector Saar sent a jeep to the home of the woman who had translated between Annachechi and the German woman. By then it was late in the morning. I needed to eat and I needed to relieve myself. I was too frightened to speak of my needs. The police brought the translator and questioned her.

This woman was in our house just two days previously. Now she would not look at us. She said that she was hired by the couple. She said she did not know anything about the nuns. She said she was surprised when the couple came to her house to hire her. She said her father was surprised too because she had never done any such work before. Perhaps the couple came to know of her because she had such good marks in the English exams three years in a row at her college. She said her picture had come in the paper three years in a row. I wanted to ask her if the college she attended was run by the nuns. I managed to keep quiet. But I needn't have bothered. Annachechi had already begun shouting at her.

The police asked her if the couple were from Germany.

Annachechi answered for her, 'Yes, yes. They are Germans. This girl herself said to me two days ago in my house they are from Germany. They will be easy to find. They work in Delhi for the government of their country.'

The girl only raised her eyebrows at Annachechi and said very softly, 'We spoke in English the whole time. They were not very good in English. So of course they are from somewhere else. But I don't know from where. If they spoke German, I don't know anything about that. I don't speak German and don't know it when it is spoken. Anyway if they spoke German, it does not mean they are German. Many people in other countries speak German as well.'

Before she left, the girl looked at us and said directly to Annachechi, 'You agreed the child should go with them on the day I came to your house. Then why have you changed your mind? Even if it was your child, aren't you glad someone who can take care of him has agreed to have him?'

Again Annachechi surprised me by being silent.

I had the same question: why was Annachechi changing her mind like this? But I didn't like the way this girl was speaking.

The only thing of any significance I said that day at the police station was: 'The child is my sister's.' I shook as I said it.

From the police station, we were taken in a jeep to the area where Annachechi rented her room. The three men who were with us laughed every time a bump in the road threw us from side to side.

They said, 'Malayali girls—have to control them. Look, they are such spitfires.'

I was afraid the one man who said this would put his hand on me. He kept it on Annachechi's back. I saw him rubbing circles there.

Before they left us, standing in the muddy lane outside Annachechi's room, they shouted they would be back to check that we were gone from the town.

All along the stairs to Annachechi's room and in front of every home on that lane, people had crowded together to see Annachechi and I return.

They called to us when the police left: 'What happened? Where is your son? Did you give him then?'

These were the same people who crowded outside the door when the German woman and the translator came to talk about the child. They knew. But they made their eyes full of unknowing and asked repeatedly, 'Did you give him then?'

They asked as if the previous day they hadn't said: 'It is the right thing to do. It will be a good life such as none of us can give our children. He is powerfully lucky. The Goddess is with him.'

Inside, the room was as we had left it. Everything bundled and packed. The kitchen pots tied into a basket and the shelves empty save for newspaper lining and cockroach eggs. A day of dust was gathered on the two plates and glasses left for washing in the kitchen bucket. Annachechi's mattress was tied and ready for the journey home. Only Madhu's was lying unrolled on the floor. In that thin mattress, in the one sheet spread on it, there was still an impression of him. In the little twists in the sheet, the places where the mattress sank. Not very deep.

I began crying as I remembered him whom I had not thought of since he left. I fell to my knees and cried knowing he was crying somewhere. I was frightened for him. Only Annachechi sat and stroked the outline of him in the sheet, never crying herself, scolding me.

'Stop it before I slap you.'

17

Bus Stop Love

How was it that Annakutty met Thambi? Or the question could be asked in this way—how was it that Annakutty met with happiness again? Nina didn't know how to ask the question in this, the second way. But she often asked her Peramma—how? And because the one word covered it all, Peramma answered her by telling her how she let happiness come into her life. On a bus. It was on a bus from Thambaram to Pondicherry.

Annakutty is somewhere mid-bounce when she knows it: someone is watching me. She doesn't think it, feels it in the sudden mid-bounce lightening of her self. Warmth spreading over her face. It is there in the feeling of his gaze, so steady, she has been caught unaware in it, till mid-bounce the gaze jumps, skitters, attempts to regain its hold, is intrusive. She comes down hard on her seat. A man, she thinks scornfully.

Contemptuous as she is of anything weak in herself, she pulls her hand back to her lap, stops it from plucking at her sari end, tosses her chin and cuts her eyes sideways at him. Then she fixes

136

her sight on the land peeling loose from the bus window, falling away into evening's void. Despicable—this land.

The man withdraws his attention. He too fixes his eyes out the window at his side. He too stares at the evening gathering force out there in empty stretches of land. Land so filled with possibility he longs to lie there and pull darkness around him. And around her. He dares not hope. And he does.

The bus rushes them through town lights hard at work, past people drawn from the dark to piled-up wares on wet streets. Annakutty strains her eyes to catch every detail—of vegetables, their colours spilling from storefronts, of glass cases filled with every shape of sweets, of coiled ropes and plastic buckets, their untidy arrangement on dusty shelves from which they threaten to spill. She wills her eyes to interest themselves in these details. Are these sweets as good as the ones in The Dolly Star Bakery, and should she pay ten paisa for the roasted peas the boy outside is pressing to her window? The boy is insistent.

'Mother, buy one packet for your journey.'

She is unable to do the necessary fumble, reach past the drawstring at her waist to dig from there the small weight of coins resting in the divide of her belly and her thighs. And she is hungry, so hungry.

No longer allowed past the gates at Thambaram police station, she'd spent the day outside. She'd starved herself, as she does every Tuesday, waiting for the DSP to emerge from inside. He did not come out of the building.

So this Tuesday passed without the weekly confrontation that let her know she was still her son's mother. DSP Saar did not emerge from the building's tall door, walk the front path with head averted from the woman crouched at the gate, his pink mouth contorting, directing the lesser someone who followed close behind carrying his briefcase, and sheaves of paper bundled in red string. *Where in those papers is her son?*

Sst, the sound of a match being struck. She did not jump.

He did not, on reaching the gate, toss the match, never looking at her, yet careful to miss her. He did not, sucking on his cigarette, climb into the jeep. The guard at the gate did not hold himself in readiness to spring on her. The broom criss-crossing the dry earth of the police station's yard did not cease sounding its shoosh-shoosh, so the sweeper could watch the drama of the mad woman's crouch and spring. And Annakutty did not spring from her crouch. The broom sweeping, swept on. It has been years since Annakutty last sprang on the DSP.

She did not scream at DSP Saar, 'My son. My Madhu.' But then she has not screamed at him in years. Years of the DSP whisking himself away while she's sunk into silence. She understands there will come a day when he will pause, smile and greet her, and she won't even whisper the words, 'My son.' She will agree instead that it looks like rain is on the way. Or she will disagree with him, arguing that rain is yet weeks away. She has divined her future while eavesdropping on just such exchanges between DSP Saar and other supplicants, who crouch like her at the gate, but who unlike her have shaken loose the burden of their anger. These supplicants, whose daughters have been murdered by their husbands. Or, the second floor addition to whose homes have slid, the adhesive quality of adulterated cement not up to the task of keeping the weight of genuine bricks from burying alive their elderly parents. Or these other supplicants, whose crops have been razed, or poison poured into whose wells so that their infants have died of slow starvation, or died more quickly, foaming at the mouth and convulsing first. These supplicants have made peace with the fact that they have survived and keep on surviving.

Those who have not made peace—principal among them, ones whose sons have disappeared caterwauling into DSP Saar's care—have learned to wait for the day when they might.

The Constable marched in front of the gate, from left to right with a click and pivot of his heel, then right to left. He did not look her way, and eventually she dozed. She never strayed far in her noonday dreaming from her hunger, and from the heat of the sun beating down on her back. Never so far as to dream of touching her son, of spreading her hand across the span of his back. But then it has been years since she has dreamt even of his face.

This Tuesday, the Constable was quiet, morose even. He did not laugh at her when she finally got up from the ground and walked away, carrying with her the dust settled in her garments.

The boy with the roasted peas is ahead of her bus window. She can hear his voice: 'Mother, buy five paisa's worth for your journey.'

The strength of effort required to maintain an interest in that frayed rope, which dangles that bunch of bananas, black splotches on red peel, from the eaves of this shop, had nearly failed her as she debated paying the boy a coin. And if she had allowed herself to be distracted, then what? She cannot think. She feels herself grow rigid from one moment to the next, till her eyes stare unblinking and the black splotches grow to cover the red and grow still more to entirely cover over her vision. A moment later the bus jolts forward. Much later she relaxes into sleep. Four hours of journey before she is home.

140 | *Mridula Koshy*

A month of Tuesdays follows that bus ride. A month in which the DSP Saar absents himself from the police station. She reasons it makes no difference whether she murmurs 'My son' to the Constable or to the DSP.

The other petitioners, squatting in the dust with her, say DSP Saar has been transferred to some other station. Some say he has been caught. But she has difficulty with the details of what scandal it is that he is caught in. She is terrified at the thought of another man in DSP Saar's place, terrified of having to start over again with the pouncing and screaming and hoping that she might persuade the man to open his files and look there for her son. The Constable stops in his click-march-click to say, Saar is in Delhi. And laughing, nearly adds, looking for your son there. But he will not hurt her needlessly. She smiles back at the Constable.

Dusk, that month of Tuesdays, the man never fails to be present somewhere in the crowd at the Thambaram bus station. Buses pull in and out, their metal sides shuddering as they await her decision—admit defeat and board, or stay to fight some more. But there is no decision left to be made. It has been years since she's stayed back to surprise DSP Saar on a Wednesday. Mad woman materializing in the dust to pounce—'My son.'

When she boards the homebound Pondicherry bus, the man follows soon after. Her sense of him somewhere in the crowd coheres into the shape of his body, the crutch laid first on the floor of the bus, the arms straining and the cheeks puffing as he launches himself up the three steps in a series of one legged hops. He sits across the aisle from her. Sometimes, when this seat is taken, he sits ahead of her. He never sits behind her. She is grateful.

At the bus station: 'Who is he?'

'Who?'

'The one that?'

'Who?'

Shame floods Annakutty. She is silent. Then spits it out: 'He. The one who has only one leg.'

'Who? The cripple?'

'The one. He's always on the bus.' And weakly, 'I am just wondering.'

'He lost his leg in a factory.'

'No, he didn't. He lost it rolling logs.'

'No it was something else.'

'None of you know.'

One girl giggles and has this to say, 'I know, but I can't say.'

The group of girls—the giggler, annoyed that she is being ignored, is the last to join in—turn to look at Annakutty expectantly. The one Annakutty thinks might be the prettiest in a bunch of what must be the prettiest girls she has ever seen, the one who pretended at first to not know who Annakutty was asking about, opens her mouth wide. The sound issued from there takes time to gather meaning.

'Why?'

The pretty girl wants to know, Why?

Annakutty is confused. She doesn't know why she has asked about the man. Her wraithlike self, briefly sharpened to life in the late-evening, dust-glimmering wait at the bus stop, fades for the girls even before she steps back.

Just as the giggler throws out, 'To think the mad woman knows to speak.'

There is another giggle, and the girls swing back to their

interrupted chat. Their necks bend to one another. Their foreheads touch in a tight circle. Bound, yet liquid—their hair is jet, burdened with clumps of pink and orange. Each oiled head with its splash of sunlight at the crown is the light and dark centre of an elaborate flower that sways, face bared to the sky. Its petals—the skirts spilled billowing from the girls' waists. A confection of colours. A flower. A group of girls. The mad woman sidles away, hurling silent abuse at the colours, the flower, the girls.

The bus, theirs, arrives. Annakutty makes ready to board. The flower breaks apart. Petals scatter, and in the scattering, one petal touches Annakutty lightly on her upper arm.

'He is Malayali, like you. He says from the same place you are from.'

A shiver travels from this touch, gently flipping its tail against Annakutty's innards. Is she mocking Annakutty? No. Left to her devices, this petal pities the mad woman.

They board the bus, the girls, then Annakutty, then the man. Does he know? Did he overhear her questioning the flower-girls? The shiver is still there. No longer a pleasure. It is sharpening its teeth on her entrails.

The man is merry. He laughs to himself as he balances on his one foot, seizes the rails on either side of the bus and jumps, skipping the lowest step, landing on the step above. He skips the step above that to land on the floor of the bus. Annakutty draws in her breath, outraged. He is showing off for her. And as suddenly, she begins crying. She turns her face to the window. He seats himself across the aisle from her.

At the signal crossing, the light flashes red and the bus, grinding and screeching, comes to a halt. There is an interminable wait. The dread grows in her that he will never cross the aisle. He does.

The bus starts up again to the signal's clamouring sound. There is confusion. Is the signal urging the bus to stay or leave? The bus stands still, and another and then another train hoots past. When finally the bus pulls over the tracks, the green fields outside the window have given way to dark. The two of them have learned to breathe together, to endure the silence between their breaths.

Outside the window, silhouettes come briefly to life, are shown in the glancing shine of the bus headlight to possess human features, to walk streets that are like any other streets. These strangers make purchases on these streets and Annakutty studies it all; she studies even the pitch dark between towns. Her eyes don't hurt. They are bright and wet.

She is able to look away from the window, to look straight ahead, to ask him, 'Is it true, you are a Malayali?'

'From the next village from your mother's. I know who you are.'

Then they return to the silence that continues with them into the next hour and the next. Then she asks him his name, and how it is that he knows who she is. He tells her that all he meant to say was that he knows her parents. She asks him how he knows her parents and finally, how her parents are, whether her sister, Tessiebaby is married.

'Does she have a baby of her own now?'

'That's me,' Nina exclaimed each time Peramma reached this place in the story.

Peramma spoke sharply, 'You were not born for another ten, twelve years. Girl, you were nothing then.'

Adopting a darkness she didn't feel, Nina muttered, 'Well, we all come from nothing. And eventually, some of us will actually become something.'

'What is it with you, Nina? You say whatever nonsense comes into your head?'

Nina's ears burned in response to the good rubbing administered to them by her Peramma's hands.

'What is it with me? What is it with me?' She danced around the dining table, darting every which way to dodge this pain that clung to her. 'Ask yourself, what it is with you, Peramma? You've hurt me,' she wailed. 'And for no reason.'

'Not for no reason. If ever there was a child given every happiness and who for no reason went searching for unhappiness, it is you. Here then is a taste of unhappiness.'

'You've hurt me. My ears will fall off. You've pinched them so hard. Even the Sisters don't pinch us like that.'

Peramma could not let Nina's wailing be the last word in this matter. She continued her muttering: 'Given everything and ungrateful doesn't begin to describe her. A philosopher. She must go and be a philosopher. Explains that something comes from nothing. To me. And she, she will be something. And this—"Some of us become something." And others? I want the girl to tell me, what do others become? Eleven years old and a philosopher. And cries like a waterfall.'

Nina circled back around the dining table to Peramma. She lay her head on Peramma's lap. 'How?' she asked again. Thambi was dead six months. Nina's *how* and the story told in response was the riddle to their grief.

Peramma was mollified. Still, she added before continuing with the story, 'Nina girl, without first tasting the bitter, you cannot talk about the sweet.'

Nina remained, head on lap.

Peramma was satisfied. She added, 'Philosophy is only for

those who have experienced sorrow. Don't think you can build it from joy.'

Peramma stroked the head on her lap. The head could see no connection between sorrow and anything else, but it loved what was coming next. The head burrowed into the cloth, the thin bones underneath. This was Peramma's cue to continue.

Thambi tells Annakutty his name. He tells her how old he is. He is forty-seven. He tells her he is one-legged. As if, Annakutty thinks, I cannot see this as well as everyone else. He waits in silence for a spell. As if, Annakutty thinks, I will gather up my bag and self and leave. Thambi continues talking. He gives her news of her family. As much as she wants to hear his words, her mind keeps wandering. She hears very little. Why, she keeps thinking, is he talking to me?

'Your father is not well.' She hears this. And also, 'Your mother takes good care of him. Your sister is not married. It worries your mother no end. Your father also.'

Annakutty can't bring herself to care about any of this.

'What do they say about me?'

'Your father boasts to everyone that you work in Pondicherry College.'

'Ha. I work as a peon. I do everything from making the tea to sweeping the floor.'

'Your father likes to say how educated you are.'

'My father had nothing to do with that.'

'That may be. He never says he is the reason you are educated. He is only proud that you have done so well.'

'If I have my pre-degree, it is only through my own determination and labour. The nuns at the convent made sure we attended class.

But very few of us passed with a certificate. And when I was sent to the convent I had not been inside a school for years. It was my father who stood by while I was kept home from school. After I left the convent, my father may have sent me money to pay for the tuition, but it is I who went from door to door asking if anyone would teach a skill to a twenty-three-year-old woman, an unmarried mother, sent as a girl to become a nun. Yes, I took typing classes with my father's money.'

'I know who you are.' He speaks eagerly. He wants to forestall what else she might say of her suffering. He wants to say, There is no need for you to suffer. I will suffer for you.

She fires back, 'You don't know anything.'

What he wishes to forestall in her speech, he finds himself speaking. 'In our area and even in the nearby areas, people know you had a son once. That, and you never came home.'

Thambi gives these words the same even-handed treatment he has given all his earlier words. He banishes eagerness from his voice. When she does not look up from her lap, he speaks again.

'Your mother made a match for your sister three times in the last few months. All three from the area near us. This is a mistake because in no time someone interferes and raises the issue of the child.'

Annakutty braces her arms against the seat in front of her, turns and looks directly at him.

'You are wrong to say I *had* a son. I have a son.'

'Yes. You have a son.'

'I don't know anything about my sister.'

'Yes.'

'My son was stolen from me.'

'Yes.'

Then she turns away and once again they ride the bus in silence. And only after a long while does Thambi say, 'People are wrong to treat you this way.'

'I cannot go home.'

'I wasn't telling you to go home.'

It's on the tip of her tongue to say, what are you telling me to do then? Instead, out comes the anguished, 'Why don't you offer to marry my sister, then?'

Though he doesn't reply to this, he appears to not be displeased. He appears to be considering what she has said.

'I am not responsible for my sister not getting married. In the first place it was her who came to me with . . .'

The crutch Thambi leaned against the seatback in front of them lifts from the floor in minute hops, chattering incessantly. It's too much—the man, his crutch. She is ready to ask him to return to his seat across the aisle, leave her in hers. The seat is now occupied by a couple. Never mind that. The bus is full of other empty seats. He'll just have to find himself one.

Across the aisle, the woman seated where Thambi was seated earlier taps her man's shoulder reproachfully. She, leaning on it, has found no comfort there. He turns his vacant eyes to meet her plea. Intelligence awakened, his eyes shine. He slides away from her, along the seat, till his back comes to rest against the window. She stretches her neck and lays it and her head on the lap he makes for her.

'Then you and Perappan got married. And then after many more years Perappan found my father for my mother and arranged for them to marry. And then came I.'

'No, not you.'

'Well, get to that part. But first say the part with the moon. And you forgot to scold me about saying you and Perappan were married.'

'Hold your tongue girl. It is I who am telling the story.'

In reply, Nina once again burrowed into the shallow lap her head was laid in. Cued, her aunt continued.

All the rest of the night Annakutty looks out the window in fear. Low in the sky, dangling within the bent frame of the window at her side, an orange slice of light holds aloft a dark sphere. The sphere weighing down the light and the crescent of light, easy with the weight, are both determined. To do what? Annakutty doesn't know. Thambi and Annakutty remain seated side by side, the two thinking their separate and same thoughts.

At the next stop, three boys head for the seat ahead of Annakutty and Thambi. Flinging himself into the aisle seat, one of the boys reaches his hand around the back of his head. The other two send their hands to their heads. Hands pat the inch of air above all three unruffled coifs. Thambi, with all the diffidence of the balding man, brings his hand to his head.

'This part is new,' said Nina in her muffled voice. Her face was still in her Peramma's lap.

Annakutty didn't reply.

She sat lost in thought.

'Soon after that, you got off the bus and got married?'

There was no more scolding to be done. Annakutty spoke from habit. 'We never married, your Perappan and I.'

Annakutty sat lost in thought.

'That's why you never had children?'

'Marriage is not the only way to have children.'

Annakutty sat lost in thought

'But you had me.'

'Exactly. We had you.'

Annakutty sat lost in thought.

'Then that's the end of the story.'

Annakutty nearly cried at that. Her grief over Thambi's death was softening the old boundaries of the stories she told, and now the stories were leaking new meanings.

'The three of them,' she said.

'They were show-offs, weren't they? Hero types, patting their hair, like the boys do in school. But the Sisters say if they catch a boy with a comb in his pocket, they will make him wear a ribbon in his hair. Only they've never really done it. Not yet. Anyway, you never told me about this part of the story before.'

Annakutty sat lost in thought. The backs of three heads bobbing in front of her.

'The three boys,' she repeated. 'I didn't know till then. That thing they did with pretending to comb their hair. And Thambi hardly had any hair he could pretend with. He just had to pretend with his shining head.'

Nina nodded sagely, waited expectantly.

'I don't think I knew till then. Eight years had passed since I lost my son. I didn't know till that night that he was no longer four. I just didn't know—that he was ten-eleven-twelve now. I knew. But I didn't know to think about what that meant. That he was tall, I knew. That he was tall like a twelve year old. But that he would care about how he looked. That he would want to comb his hair when it was ruffled. That he would have friends. That he would grow old. That he might lose the hair he cared about.'

Nina stopped listening. She thought instead about the Lost Boy arching his back and pissing into the bath oil and about him walking toward the train, looking for the wooden horse Peramma had promised him he would find on board, about him forgetting to look back at Peramma, about the crumpled sheets on the mattress back in the room from which he was gone.

She thought about the stories of him told over and over by her aunt and by herself. She pictured him, his legs and arms and the shape of his head, and it was the shape of the child worn into her brain and the shape of her filling the shape of the child, and she decided she did not want to hear any more. Peramma kept talking and Nina thought about the Lost Boy coming back, getting off the plane from Germany, of her waving to him from her side of the glass window upstairs at the airport where you paid fifty rupees to see the planes land. And she saw him wave back from the ground. She saw the speck of him break apart into arms and legs and face and saw the hand separate from the arm and dive into his pocket and hold high the perfect German marble she would win from him. Now she saw only the marble. It shone. She felt certain of his return.

'When he returns, I will win that marble.'

And Peramma kept talking.

'It was around then I added the years to his age. I didn't stop noticing four-year-old boys. But I also noticed the twelve-year-old boys. Not the way they looked or how tall they were. I tried to pay attention to what they talked about, what they laughed over, how they thought and what they felt. It was hard because they were not like him. Not like he was when he left.'

18

Bus Stop Love: 2

'Tell me about the marble. About the Lost Boy and the marble.'
'It was like this.'
'And about the boy Shekhar.'
'Yes, Madhu used to talk about the boy, Shekhar.'
'And Perappan wanted you to marry him, but you wouldn't.'
'That's right.'
'So you told him about the boy Shekhar and the marble and the Lost Boy.'
'Yes I told him. On the bus. Two years we rode that bus till he convinced me to ride the bus back here to his home.'
'But you never married him. And why didn't you, Peramma?'
'We had a marriage of sorts. Just a cup of tea and no asking father and Saramma for permission, no dowry, no Jesus. A Party marriage. At that place your Perappan spent so much time at. At the junction, in the Party Headquarters.'
'But first he had to ask you and ask you?'
'Yes, your Perappan asked me and asked me.'
'Like in the movies? With a song he sang to you? With a big bunch of flowers? Did he say, "Will you marry me?"'

'No.'

'Then what?'

'He asked me and asked me. Always on the bus, he asked me, "What do you want, Anna?"'

'What do you want, Anna?'

'What do I want? What makes you think there is anything I want? That too from you?'

'No, from life, from your future? You want to keep sitting outside the police station? Why only once a week then? Why not every day? Oh, you'll tell me you have to earn a living, and once a week is when you have a holiday from work?'

'No, that's not it.'

'Why not sit outside the station every day and beg? You'll get food. Or the mosque nearby will take you in at night. Plenty of women there. Mind you, they are old. But why not—you will be old in time. I hear they feed the women.'

'It's not safe.'

'It's not safe?'

'You don't think I've thought of these possibilities? There is no place a woman is safe if she doesn't earn. I should know. For as long as I was a dependent, I was told I would have to pay. With my body if necessary. I got this message from everyone. My father. He certainly looked the other way. Wept his tears, but looked the other way. And Saramma. She hated me. I don't know why she hated me. I think she didn't even like herself for hating me. So she made me pay. In any case, she wanted me to be hateful. All those years she was telling everyone how loose my morals were, how hard she was working to keep me under control, she wanted nothing more than for me to be a disgrace. And the

Sisters. They wanted the same. How else to keep their faith? Everyone needs a sinner. Someone to hate. The priest though. He was blameless. I was the one who seduced him. Yes, you might as well hear this.'

'Anna, forget about the mosque. I am asking you to come with me. What I am offering is not anything to do with what's happened to you in the past.'

'Oh that quickly he writes it off. Two words—The Past.'

'Anna.'

'Well.'

'I'll help you find him. Don't you see you will never find him sitting outside the Thambaram station. No matter how many years you sit there.'

'From back in your village you'll help me find him?'

'Anna, there are much more effective ways. You can write, even type. We will send letters to Delhi. I will go with you to speak to different people.'

'Which different people? Do you know any people? And where will the money for all this speaking come from? It costs money to speak, you know. Or will I simply pay as I always have—with a piece of myself?'

'Anna.'

'I would if that's all it took, I would. Don't you think I would?'

'Anna, I will find work. Anything a one-legged man can do, I will do. The house is already there. A place for us to lay our heads, a place of our own. I will go to your father. We will do it like it's supposed to be done. I don't want a child. Your child will be mine. I will help you find him.'

'Will . . . we go to Delhi?'

'Will we?'

'We will go wherever we have to.'

'It can't be.'

'You'll just keep doing this then for the rest of your life? This. It has no meaning.'

'Don't say that.'

'Explain to me what you are doing here.'

'I can't leave. Not for anything.'

'Not to go to a place you can rest, to take help from someone who wants to help you?'

'Here is where he will return.'

'All right then—where is this here? Here in Pondicherry, here on the road between Pondicherry and Madras, or here outside Thambaram police station? Oh, wait a minute, he didn't leave from the police station, did he? He left from the train station. So why don't you move to the train station. There are many who live like that.'

'My son had a friend. Actually, he had many friends. But there was this one—Shekhar. Shekhar was perfect. Shekhar was so tall. Shekhar was so fast. Shekhar could wrestle like anything. Shekhar had a pencil box with twenty-four coloured pencils in it. Shekhar even came to school riding a horse every day. A white horse. And with his father riding the horse, Shekhar on his lap.'

'Your son was longing for a father.'

'Yes, yes. I knew that. I too dismissed it as fantasy.'

'There was a real Shekhar?'

'I used to listen just to humour him. I used to listen to the stories about the big lunches that came in a car for Shekhar every day. Masala dosa. Too big to fit in a tiffin; it came on a plate covered with a cloth. The driver brought it to the school veranda and the teacher came out and put a chair and table for Shekhar to sit at and eat his lunch. The sambar was so hot and the children would all stand by with their cold curd rice and watch Shekhar eat. Sometimes the driver would bring lunch for the teacher as well.'

'Anna?'

'Listen to me. This Shekhar with his father, who was an army officer, and his mother who came in the car in the afternoon to take him home, wearing her saris and jewellery. This Shekhar was real. I was called to school one day by the teacher. My son had hit a boy very badly. And his name was Shekhar.

'I went to the school and, yes, he had hit this boy who looked like he might have a family somewhere with some money. I don't know. The children all wore uniforms. His was made from good cloth. It was newish looking even though the year was nearly finished. Maybe they stitched him a new one because he grew recently. Maybe there was even a horse and tiffin and car and jewellery.'

'No.'

'Probably not. After all the school wasn't a rich one. But there was a marble. They had fought over this marble. I had given Madhu the marble. It was part of the collection of things the woman left with me as a gift for him.'

'The woman?'

'Yes, the German woman. She came twice. Once to see him. He was asleep. Again she came. He was awake this time, but I sent him outside. Next time it was at the train station when I sent him away.'

'She gave you gifts for him?'

'The second time she came. It was hurriedly, without anyone

else with her. She gave me clothes for him, biscuits, sweets, other things. I had no intention of giving any of it to him. She wanted me to tell him what was going to happen soon. She wanted me to tell him because she couldn't speak with him. I think she spoke German. Maybe it was another language. I don't know the difference between German and any other language. But this girl who was with her the first time, a Malayali girl who spoke only English, no German, so who knows, she said the woman was German. Afterward the girl tried to say at the police station that the woman was not necessarily from Germany. She was. The Germany woman insisted I should tell Madhu that she was going to be his new mother. She insisted I give him the sweets and the biscuits. His birthday was just a few months before. I had not even been able to buy him a cake. And she left all this for him so that he would be happy to go with her.'

'And a marble?'

'A bag full of marbles. I put everything away. The next day he found one underneath something. Must have rolled its way there. I let him have it. I told him I had bought it for him. I was changing my mind already. I wasn't going to let her have him. I was so confused at that time. I didn't know what I should do.'

'Anna, what happened then?'

'I sent him away.'

'No, what happened with the marble and Shekhar?'

'Oh, the marble. He took it to school. He took it there and probably he showed it to everyone. It wasn't like any marble you can buy anywhere around here. It was clearly foreign. And I think this boy Shekhar tried to say it was his. It couldn't be Madhu's.

'I asked Madhu afterwards what had happened. He said they were playing with it, rolling it between them on the bench at school, and whenever it fell from the bench, Shekhar said Madhu had to get it for him. It seems when they play with Shekhar's ball, that's the rule. Whether Madhu throws the ball and misses or Shekhar, it is Madhu who has to collect it. I know how that game is played. One person in the game is the master and the other the servant. For Madhu this marble meant he was not the servant. He beat up the boy with the nice uniform. Whether he rode to school on a horse or not, I don't know. But his new-looking uniform had blood on the front. I told Kuttiamma Principal not to bother with punishment for Madhu. I told her Madhu is going away. He won't be coming to school anymore.'

'You decided.'

'I thought, maybe the other children know. The thing the adults held against Madhu. Maybe they've heard from somewhere Madhu is a bastard. And if the children know, then soon Madhu will be told.

'No, I never decided. I changed my mind again and again, a thousand times. I lay awake all night. I touched him, all over, every bit of him, the last night. I put my nose to his nose and I breathed him. I thought of how I made him in my body. How could I ever let him part from me? But I did.'

'In the end Nina, your Perappan showed me how stupid I was to live alone. How completely stupid to try to do everything alone. How I was better off with him than without him. Maybe we are all better off with one another than without.

'I said to your Perappan that day, "You seem to be a happy man." He opened his eyes wide, like this, in surprise, and said, "No. But I have been searching."

'Eh, Nina girl? Is that enough philosophy for you?'

'Yes, enough.'

19

(with her last breath)

It was a long time ago I put my hand on your back, gave you a push, sent you into the world. Your feet walking away from me must have made the sound of footsteps. I didn't hear them in the din of the train station. When was it I woke to their sound, circling the earth back to me?

I've kept the faith. In place of you, it is all I've had.

In this rain I don't hear you. Will you not come then?

When you come I will cry.

O my son. My son, my son. O lost to me—my son, my son.

Yes, I ran from you the moment I made you. I ran so hard, I lost you. Why should you come?

Madhu, I gave you up. But I never gave up loving you. Will you not come?

It is how I have loved you, knowing you would return.

O my son. My son, my son Madhu—my son, my son.

I learnt from the father you never had, I learnt from Thambi, to feel something beside myself. I feel you searching. You will come.

I hear the sun shines silver in the north. I cannot imagine such a sun. But I can feel the shine of it on your skin. I know you, your words in that other tongue.

You will never come.

If I could, I would go back to the beginning. But I can't. I can only go to the end. I will search for you there.

You will never come.

It is the end.

Now you must come.

You. You will be my heaven.

You will never come.

When I am no more, I will live in you then.

20

Uneasy Return

Forty-three years in time separate two women as they pack to return to their daughters. It is 1961 when Saramma John Verghese returns to Cochin, to her daughter, Tessiebaby, and her stepdaughter, Annakutty. The grown-up Tessiebaby, now Tessie Scaria, returns from Dubai to her daughter, Nina Scaria in 2004. Both mothers set out on their journeys from their children so they could find the means to care for their children; they left with every intention of returning. Then why this uneasiness?

Tessie Scaria hurries to pack. She remembers to pack tampons. No such thing available at her destination. Yet, such a cheap convenience, how can it not be available? A wad of cotton, easily swallowed by the septic tank the latrine empties into, no need for newspaper-wrapped bundles to be safeguarded from stray dogs and male eyes till they are burnt in the compost pit. Some government scheme. Tribals to dig compost heaps. Why don't they just organize a municipal garbage pickup? It's the Communists. Interested only in the tribals. And compost pits. Of course, the jungle her sister lives in—not even a proper road leading up to the house—would never qualify as a municipality.

Lived in. The jungle her sister lived in. Tessie feels like slapping herself. She continues instead to scold the Communists. What's a woman in need of a tampon to do in Kerala? In 2004? She yelps softly as the zipper on her suitcase catches her finger. Nothing. A woman is to do nothing.

Saramma John Verghese hurries to pack. She has been living in the Young Master's shed for ten months now. Leaving it weekly for the long walk home, arriving in Cochin past midday, a stay overnight with the children, and then the walk back in the early hours of the next morning. Saramma will do this no more. She is packing to leave this shed, to return to her daughter.

She bundles her clothes. Stands still as she works something out to herself. Then she hurries with the bundle to the garbage pit. In the dark, she stumbles at its edge, changes her mind and hurries back to the shed. She will leave the clothes in the shed after all. Perhaps the labourers, when they discover her gone, will make use of her clothes. More likely they will shun the clothes as they have shunned her. Or burn the clothes in the pit. She shrugs. Why, they might have happily burnt her in the pit. Well, it makes no difference to her now. She is leaving.

She knows what they say: prostitute from the city. Even that she is the devil, and Young Master's sold himself to the devil. Only once did she forget to tidy away her basket of clothes and cooking vessels in the shed where the Young Master housed her. She'd left as she did every morning to make way for his labourers. She returned in the afternoon to basket and contents trampled, torn, crushed, spat upon and left in the centre of the shed for her to find. *That's how the powerless behave.* She was free and they were not. Why begrudge them the expression of their frustration?

Chinks of light peep in from between the boards that make up the walls of the shed. Nearly morning. She must hurry.

And it wasn't that they shunned her so much as they feared her. So afraid, they pretended she wasn't there. And this perfectly mirrored her sense of herself.

Altogether, non-existence has pleased her. Days of the most exhilarating loneliness. And nights, the Young Master came to her shed, ensuring more such days were hers to have.

She unwraps the bundle she had meant for the pit and begins arranging the items within. Will they trample these today or will they understand her gesture? Her presence was a humiliation to the fathers and young husbands among the labourers. They should have been grateful instead. The nights he had failed to come had frightened her. She, and they—the husbands and fathers—they were united, those nights, by their helplessness. Weren't they?

Saramma shakes her head in anger. Why is she thinking of the nights Young Master found his way to others? She tries to return to the memory of the afternoons she spent wandering this land, the ecstasy of freedom from want and obligation. It had come to her in those wanderings that no one in any of the stories she had ever heard as a child, certainly not the biblical ones, no one in her childhood home nor in her adult life, certainly not Jose, who gave up his belief in the solidarity of workers to replace it with a drunken confusion of guilt toward his family, no one has lived the life she lives—freed from living for others.

She is free to leave this shed and the man who kept her in it. And the daughters of the men who toil on this land, those young girls who are not free, as their parents are not free, they will have to once again resume their nightly services to him.

And her clothes she will leave because it is inconceivable that Jose should ever smell him on her. Or that she should smell him while with Jose. Yes, that is why she is discarding these clothes. A fresh change of clothes, purchased just for this departure. She knows how to do these things. The change of clothes has been with her for three months now.

And the four sets she is leaving behind—she cannot throw them in the heap that lies smouldering behind the shed. Burn them? No, some girl must wear them. And when the Young Master finds his way to that girl, as he surely will, then he will remember Saramma.

Nina's mother carries a light blue plastic suitcase. It is small. Tessie lifts it with some difficulty. She is ashamed of its dented surface. It is increasingly difficult to pull the lid shut so it meets the body of the suitcase exactly. If the two don't meet exactly, the latch doesn't shut. At the airport she anticipates having to open it numerous times. In her purse she has a length of plastic twine against the possibility of the suitcase refusing to shut.

It is late at night. She is outside her apartment. She sets the suitcase down beside her and waits for her husband to pull the car around to the front. She does a mental check of what is inside. Tampons. They are for Nina. She started menstruating soon after Tessie's last visit home. Annachechi had told her this over the phone. She had spoken disapprovingly.

'You should have thought to talk to her about it.'

'But I did. I did.'

She had shown Nina on the last visit with the aid of a scarf how she was to fold the cloth.

'Like this, a triangle, then in half, and half, and half.'

'But where will I get the cloth from?'

'You must ask your Peramma. She saves scraps from her tailoring for just this.'

'You mean Peramma?'

'I don't know. Actually, no. She used to. Not now. After you become older it stops.'

'How old? Do you also?'

'Never mind that. When you ask her, she will take from what she saved in the past.'

'But what if I am at school?'

'Then you must ask your teacher. The cloth is only when it starts. So you have something immediately. Later your Peramma will buy you something you can just throw away after you use it. Don't have to wash. Wrap it in newspaper and leave it on the bathroom floor. When you have a chance you take it to the compost pit.'

'I know about pads.'

'You know?'

Tessiebaby's mother steps onto the road. Night is just giving way to morning. A little breeze is valiantly trying to fill the void in time between the two. It pick-picks at the palm trees, creating an in-between time music. It is with a sense of disquiet that Saramma pauses under the last palm trees and listens to this music. Four sets of clothing, each item spread open on the floor, three blackened cooking pots spaced apart, some bangles and toiletries arranged neatly on the shelf, where the labourers when they come at dawn will find them. This day will begin for them with the visible signs of her life lived in their room. Instead of complying with their requirement that she erase herself from the room, she has left them with a gift: I was never here. The fact that I can leave—leave my clothes, my slippers, my tin of powder—should tell you I was never here. I am free to come and go as you are not. You are always in the room.

The floor has been swept clean. The bedding tossed into the compost heap. She has remembered to pack—herself. She walks empty-handed. Her dignity is intact. She examines herself to make sure of this. Her mundu is just so. Her chetti is spotless, like her mundu. She has taken the trouble to fan the starched pleats of her upper garment so a little crown rides her bottom. She regrets how thin she has become in the years of struggle, the months of walking the road. But her buttocks ride high as they always have. The little crown lifts and dips behind her.

Of this much she is certain: when she stepped off the road a year ago, stepped onto this land, she lost nothing. She had not wanted to walk any further. It was that simple. She had set out to do the heroic, the impossible, to walk wherever the road took her, wherever there existed the possibility of finding a means of providing for herself, for her daughter and for that other child, wherever it was that she could get away from her neighbours' eyes. If the road brought her to such a place sooner than she had anticipated, then what need was there to brave on? Unnecessary heroism? Pah.

Recent visits home have found a voluble Padmachettathi.

'I cannot do any more. You can pay me all you want, the girl will not listen. Walks away even as I talk to her. What will your little one learn from all this?

'There is a boy who talks to her outside the door. I watch to make sure he doesn't go in. If I don't keep an eye, who knows.

'And you better keep an eye on that Jose. He is doing some sort of job in a hotel. One of those places where all kinds of women are seen. Yes, by the bus stand.

'Oh the police just get their share from those women. You and I can't know the kind of appetite such women have for men, especially married men. They'll just pick your Jose off if you don't collect him from there. You know a man, what can happen to him if you don't see to his needs.

'The little one was sick again last week. If it happens again, I will send my husband to inform Jose.'

'Yes, yes,' Saramma had said as she left to walk the road back to Young Master's.

On the road that led her from Padmachettathi's scandalized admonitions to the freedom of life in the shed as a nobody with nothing for which she was responsible, Saramma thought, Yes, yes, send your husband, inform mine. The road drew her closer each time she walked it to the eventuality of a day when she could not rouse herself to return home. *Send for him.* And she let Jose's daughter's too-tight blouses get tighter while she shopped for a fresh change of clothes in which to return to her husband.

Yes, she tells herself, yes, my conscience is clear. But there is that twinge again. That Annakutty, she thinks. The girl knows more than is good for her. She winces, then spits.

Nina's mother worries that she will be stopped and checked when she walks through the airport's green channel. She turns to her husband, seated in the driver's seat.

'This once when there is nothing to declare, they will stop me. I am sure. That's the way it works, isn't it?'

It's true that this once there isn't the battery powered scissors she smuggled in last time that cut of their own accord and were to spare Annachechi's rheumatism. Nor the handheld video games which emerged from between towels to meet Nina's scorn.

'Made in China. You know we get that here.'

This time the customs agents will stop her. They will find tucked between towels not the mini electronic dictionary or the Chopper Mixer Grinder, or the DVD player. No, they will find tampons. Boxes of them. They will rifle through her suitcase, rip open a box, hold one aloft and guffaw.

'Now, what's this we've got here? Where's the battery on this thing?'

Tessie drags the suitcase out of the trunk of the car and turns with it to the trolley she has lined up kerbside. The brakes on the trolley don't work. The suitcase manages to half land on it before the trolley slips forward leaving the suitcase on the ground. After three tries, her wrist throbbing, she throws the suitcase on and makes a grab for the trolley. Santosh remains at the wheel. Her breath is shallow and tight in her chest. She checks. The suitcase hasn't come open. She scolds herself. I am being so silly. It's not like I don't know how to do this. I've gone home before. I can go home this time as well.

'Tell Nina-mol I'll come next time.'

'I'll do no such thing. She comes back with me. You'll see her here in a week.'

At the same time Tessie thinks, why did I pack boxes of everything? Boxes of biscuits, boxes of jam, boxes of sweets, boxes of tampons. Clothes she's been gathering as she does between visits—always two sizes too big. Because who knows when the next visit.

They look for a moment at each other. Her eyes are dilated. He knows this woman well enough to know she is afraid. He has no time, neither to reason with her, nor to comfort her. It is a long drive home. He needs to arrive before the shuttle service from work comes to pick him up. The car is for her commute to work. And unless she was to quit the job, sell the car, move to shared housing . . . he frowns. The list is long. She won't bring Nina here. He waves—a quick, brisk wave as he pulls away from her standing there, watching him with her air of recrimination. He knows this woman well enough to know that this is her habitual air around everything and everybody.

She probably holds it against her sister for dying when she had only recently declared Annachechi would go strong for another ten years. Even half that number would have been enough to see Nina through schooling and in some college hostel. A boarding school is where Nina will have to go now. A little earlier than he had wanted. But what choice is there? He could send her to his people, but this is where he will compromise—he will allow Tessie to have her way. Tessie will not want to take the chance of exposing Nina to the possibility of his people's criticisms of her sister.

On the rare occasion they return to Kerala together, she does not accompany him for long to his family. Even a short stay begins with a numbing harangue on the drive there.

'When we get there, don't just sit there with a newspaper. Don't think I don't know what you are doing when you hide behind the newspaper. You heard me. I said "hide". You hide behind the newspaper till I leave with Nina. Once we are gone, it is then you are free to lay your head on your mother's lap. It is then you are free to be a baby. Still you ask me, "Why do you always rush off?" You want to have it both ways. You want to blame me for leaving, and you want me to leave. What nonsense is that? What kind of fool do you take me for? Listen, I didn't marry your mother's son. I married a man. A husband, a father you are. And you go on being your mother's son.'

And on and on and on. Santosh laughs. A little uncomfortably.

Watching the speck of him inside the car, pulling from the kerb, now getting swallowed up in traffic, Tessie imagines this is what he is doing—laughing at her.

Through the entire security check process and the inevitable rope-tying when the open suitcase finally refuses to close, and this just as she hands it over to the baggage collector, Tessie continues to fret over the tampons. When she dozes briefly on the flight, she dreams there's a crowd with her in the tiny bathroom. Watching her insert a tampon, they smile and shake their heads. She looks at what her hands are doing and realizes she is inserting not one but fistfuls of tampons. She wakes and forces a laugh from herself. She is getting worked up over nothing.

She will tell Nina, 'It changes you Nina, but not in any bad way. You just have to be careful how you behave.' Should she add, 'Especially around boys.' No need. 'You just have to be careful. Be conscious you are a girl. Now you have grown up.'

She feels almost kindly toward her husband who has so little idea of anything. Not of what is in her suitcase, nor even of what it is to have a daughter.

Dozing again, a memory comes to her in a dream, of a woman seated in a dark room. Tessie is little again. She and Annachechi are peering at the woman from the doorway. This is how they greet this woman's periodic incursions into their lives, by standing far back from her. They watch her as she dozes, sitting in the chair. Then Annachechi brings food and later oil to rub the woman's feet and legs. The woman says she has walked a long way

to come to them. In the memory, Tessie can feel her baby-self
wanting to call all the children in the neighbourhood to come see
her mother. But now someone else enters the dark room of her
dream and Tessiebaby no longer wants to call anyone. The
someone else is a man. Who? The woman is seated across from
the man. Annachechi whispers to Tessie it is their father. How
hard it must be to be their father, so old and thin and frightened-
looking. Suddenly Tessiebaby feels a strong dislike for the beauty
of the woman.

Their father talks earnestly to their mother. Then he stands up
and places his hands on their mother's shoulders and pulls her up.
He wrings their mother's neck. And still Annachechi holds
Tessiebaby back at the door. Tessiebaby is sobbing to go save
their mother. But no, Annachechi has her tight. Their father is
not hurting their mother. Because, look, their mother is smiling
her small smile. Their father is loving their mother like Tessiebaby
has never been loved. His hands are around their mother's neck,
climbing her hair and loosening it. Annachechi is pulling
Tessiebaby away from the door now.

Saramma turns to look backward one last time. She can no
longer see the coconut trees that mark the boundary line of the
land. Just the curve of the road, the dip of it, the tilt of the planet
toward his piece of land. She sighs and walks on, compact, strong
enough to fight the urge to turn back to the shed, and yet unsure
of herself. Unsure especially of how she will handle the future.
Ahead lies much that will require her active intervention. Jose has
called her back. But once she returns, he is as likely to leave again
as he is to stay. She will have to get him to quit the city and move
with her to her brother's land. It will be a humiliation for him to

live in his wife's village. But better to live again on land than in a miserable alleyway, and one that requires payment, monthly. It is impossible to know what use Jose will be on her brother's land. But she must return with him. Or the humiliation will be hers as well. It is a confirmed fact that he is of no use in the city for all that he says he has a job now. How long can a man his age work in a hotel, hustling orders and cleaning up after customers. It is the kind of work that belongs to boys. And idle, the city offers much mischief.

Mischief. Her lips twitch. She plods on. Mischief is everywhere, and now she knows it's inside her as well. This is something she plans to keep hidden from Jose. It will be best if he does not ask too many questions. What she needs to do is convince Jose that it is for the girl they move from the city. Jose's daughter for certain has been up to mischief. She is best off in the countryside. Away from that boy in Padmachettathi's story. Girls have to be protected. They cannot on their own strength decide, as Saramma has, to leave a man, to leave two men if need be, to turn to a man, to return to another one. Saramma stops, struck by the rightness of everything she has done.

She searches for a prayer. The lion and the lamb. No, it is the lion and the snake. She shakes her head, trying to remember old lessons. 'Even the snakes have their holes and the birds the sky.' Tears spring to her eyes. It has been a hard year and she has rarely cried, she who has repeatedly walked this shelterless road. The right prayer comes to her between her tears.

'Surely,' she murmurs to herself, 'goodness and mercy shall follow me all the days of my life . . . Or is it to the ends of the earth?'

Saramma laughs with satisfaction. A year ago, she was

abandoned by all. She did not think to pray then. Now she prays when there are so many paths open to her.

She decides that between them, she and the girl will be enough help to her brother to justify their occupying space on his land. And then her brother must be persuaded to part with a little bit of the land. She won't ask for it outright. Tenancy on favourable terms. It is a small amount he has. But what was she given as her share when they sent her off at seventeen to wed a man more than twice her age, one who took ten years to give her a child and then only after acting the fool, fighting a one-man fight against the whole harbour, returning home with a broken back, giving her the child to make himself a man again in her eyes? They couldn't have thought that was all they owed her? Her brothers? Her mother? She nearly sobs. Her mother. She would like nothing better than to return home to lay herself next to her mother, to fall asleep with her mother's fingers raking her hair.

Where is the bathroom? Now Tessie sees an arrow accompanying the outlined image of a woman—an oval, a triangle, two sticks for legs. The arrow points to the right; the arrow pointing down indicates the escalator onto which her fellow passengers have crammed themselves; they seem unable to pull apart and occupy any space greater than the airless interior of their economy class experience. Even now the goldfish in the reception area of the Hospital, transferred more than a year ago to a larger tank, continue to swim the outline of their original tank. Tessie has spent some time trying to persuade them out of this circuit by tapping on the glass and making fish faces at them. So far they have not been persuaded.

Tessie has been holding herself since immediately after the car pulled her away from the apartment, some ten or more hours in the past. She rushes into the bathroom, past the attendant who holds out a basket of toilet paper squares. The attendant withdraws the extended arm as the woman nearly knocks the basket over in her haste. She glowers at the back of the woman who enters the stall with a slam and urinates noisily and at length. Malayalis, the attendant thinks. There will be plenty of cleaning to do after the woman leaves. Probably sleeps on a mattress stuffed with Gulf money and won't help herself to a piece of toilet paper because she is afraid of being asked for a tip.

Tessie, done hovering in the air over the toilet pinches her lips at the droplets sprayed all over the rim. She is already behaving like an Indian. She thinks to rinse the seat clean. She searches for and finds the plastic mug tucked behind the toilet. With difficulty she extricates it, then recoils in horror. A pad wrapped in toilet paper and stuffed within the mug uncurls slowly, agonizingly, till letting out a final sigh it rests belly up, its bloody innards exposed.

Tessie pays the woman outside for her toilet paper, retreats to the same stall and wipes her mess clean. She pushes the mug back behind the toilet.

Outside the bathroom, the escalator is, if anything, more crowded than ever. Have more flights landed, disgorging more humans trained in the circumspect behaviour of goldfish? Predictably the baggage is not on the carousel yet. Her flight-mates—their rigid shoulders pressed together to keep her out—defeat her attempts to find a place ringside. No late-comers allowed.

Suddenly, seemingly of one accord, the crowd breaks up. There is a great deal of noise and Tessie gets swallowed up by it till she can hear nothing.

'What's happening?' she asks the person next to her.

He stares at her, his face is smooth one moment and the next, the mud of it is churned in the riverine flow from his eyes. He makes no sound as his face collapses, only the eyes remain fixed on her with something like outraged disbelief. What have I done, she wonders. It seems nearly everyone is crying as they walk away from the baggage wending its way past them. And now the baggage, piled one on top of another as the conveyor belt's capacity to hold comes to an end, begins tumbling to the airport floor. And now the crowd is not walking. Its tight weave which had unravelled in the first moments of noise and confusion has reasserted itself, and all of it is running together to the same point on the other side of the hall. Tessie remains behind. She doesn't see the elevator door tucked behind the escalator open to disgorge an impossible number of men and their shared burden. But from far she sees the body, so draped in flowers it is a mass of orange and red, borne high above the crowd. An anxiety to touch this thing, held above her reach, seizes her. Even as her hand clutches air, the rest of the crowd too, moving in unison, raise their hands and clutch at air. The bier is whisked from her sight quicker than she can draw a breath. She holds hard to her sides as she bends over.

Annachechi. But how? What is her body—here? Why—the crowd?

The body re-emerges from behind a pillar, then exits, still afloat on raised arms, through the distant doors that lead out of the airport hall. The crowd shouts: 'Comrade Nayanar Zindabad.' The crowd outside roars its response. Lal Salaam. Lal Salaam.

Tessie continues to stand, her mouth agape. Not her sister, thank God, not her sister. Someone else has died. Comrade Nayanar? Yes, she remembers who that is. He used to be the

Chief Minister. He must have died. That must be his body, smothered in garlands. Oh but her sister. Yes, she too. Far from here.

Returning for their bags, people mop at their faces with handkerchiefs that are absurdly large. They hurry in an ordered fashion to collect their luggage. They are considerate but brisk. Suddenly it seems everyone has a larger purpose than getting to their relatives and homes. Bags and suitcases in hand, they hurry from the airport. No officials to stop them; all are outside those doors. They hurry to mourn. Tessie moves slowly as if the air is something impermeable, something she has to part before her. She does this to reach her suitcase. When she has it in her hand, she sets it down, crumbles to the ground and looks about her for a handkerchief. Tessie is finally free to cry.

She weeps, thinking of her sister at sixteen. So softly her sister breathes over Tessiebaby: 'Be quiet. I have to throw away the bloody cloth. I will be back soon.' Her sister has explained to Tessiebaby, 'It doesn't matter when the red comes. It only comes for a few days every month and we have so much more inside us.' Tessiebaby can hear the blood inside her sister.

And she can hear the Chettan outside, urging her sister to hurry.

Now their mother is lighting the lamp. Now Tessiebaby thinks she should say something in warning. Now their mother shouts to their father.

'Catch her. Where is the girl going? Jose, I told you. You didn't believe me. Now you see her. Now you see her go.'

Now Tessie knows to say, 'Please don't go.'

21

The Vigil

Valli goes looking for Nina. It is the morning after a night of vigil at Annakutty's bedside. Nina's mother will be here soon, and the girl is nowhere to be found.

'Nina girl, where are you? Troubling Amuma like this. Come out now. That is enough drama from you. What is wrong with you, girl? You come out from where you are if you want a feeding.'

Valli was told by the prayerful gathered around Annakutty that Nina hadn't been seen since when she went off early in the morning, presumably to see her friends off at the school bus stop. Valli wanders in the direction of the main road, crosses the little matchstick bridge and follows the creek a distance. She is high on the embankment and has to squint hard, training one eye straight ahead on the lookout for Nina, and the other eye below where the creek bank should be crawling with dinner. But it isn't. The crabs have been picked off. Or they never emerged. There are frogs, but it requires fashioning a trap to catch them

Valli calls again, 'Nina. Girl, show yourself.' In an inspired moment she adds, 'You are not acting as your Peramma would want.'

Then she drops to the ground. The stirring in the bushes below is possibly Nina, but more likely it is those creatures from elsewhere. Ugly things. As only Malayalis can be. Black and coarse for all that they have gone somewhere far from here and pasted themselves with powder and cream. She can smell them. Two young ones. Wonderfully smelly, sweet and sick. They've been spending a fair portion of the past many days creek-side, disturbing Valli's solitude. She peers out at them now. They are seated, sides pressed together, on the rock, their bare feet paddling the water, their seats wet and growing wetter, their tongues writhing in each other's mouths.

'Chee,' Valli spits out at them. 'What will Malayalis think of next?'

She jumps up to throw a stick at them. Like dogs in heat. They will have to be beaten to separate them. Valli relishes the thought. But disappointingly, the two spring apart and glare back at her.

'Hey,' the fellow shouts while the girl hangs behind him, laughing and buttoning her blouse.

'Hey,' Valli shouts back at them. She slides down the muddy slope and comes up to them, a smile on her face.

'Malayalam?' She asks a number of times before they understand her, and the fellow nods but talks nonsense to her.

'Thdsjhouiujwelkkj.'

'A little money,' she tries again, rubbing her palms together. She wishes the girl would come out from behind the fellow. He seems a complete idiot.

'Malayalam, Malayalam,' she shouts.

Then she uses her English. She hates Little Flowers. But there is some use to what her daughter-in-law has learnt there and come home and repeated.

'Please. Thank you. Yes. No. Good Morning.'

'To buy some rice,' she wheedles.

'Kilo Kilo.'

She remembers the word is the same in Malayalam and English. She shakes one finger in his idiot face to show him.

'One.'

His jaw hangs slacker still and she thinks, What do they feed these children to make them so weak? Again she rubs her palms, then holding her hand under his nose she presses her fingertips together and rubs them. The fellow is a fool.

In exasperation she shouts, 'Paisa. Paisa. Rupee. Rupee.'

The girl makes some noises of her own. 'Guywhjihioiko.'

Then the fellow fishes a two-rupee coin out of his pocket and puts it in Valli's outstretched hand. This is too much for Valli, who shoots an arm to snatch from the ground and fling at the fool the frog she has by the hind leg. He jumps and screams an idiot sound. Valli spits.

'Idiot Malayali.'

For good measure, she throws the two-rupee coin into the creek and calls after the couple who, backs turned, are skulking off toward the bridge.

'You think it's possible to buy anything with a two-rupee coin? You think you can buy two grains of rice with a two-rupee coin? How much do you eat every day? Must be 200 rupees of rice every day. Has anyone ever seen fat like yours? Is that how it is in America? You eat two rupees of rice and grow fat like that? Listen, here we only have Malayali rice. Two rupees won't even give you a mouthful, much less that pot belly you were pushing at your girlfriend. How does your little thing make it past that belly to get inside her?'

'Chee,' she gives over from shouting and mutters. 'Chee. No wonder he was sticking his fat tongue inside her.'

Valli whirls.

It is Nina—her laughter rustling from deep within a bush. The next moment, Nina attempts to jump out at Amuma, but her laughter sends her sprawling to the ground at Amuma's feet.

'Girl,' Valli scolds Nina. 'Girl. What are you doing sitting here spying on this Malayali filth. I tell you, they all want to claim they are American and know to stick their tongue inside each other's mouths. But you know it is only a Malayali who will think of such an absurdity.'

Nina is disappointed she hasn't frightened Amuma. But springing on Amuma to frighten her is an old game, and one that Nina regularly loses even though Amuma is most often dozing when Nina jumps out at her. Nina moves swiftly from disappointment to sagacity, a kind of worldliness allowed her in her games with Amuma.

'It is like the astronauts when they landed on the moon to stick the American flag there. What did they see—the Malayalis had already set up a chaya shop there.'

'Chaya?' She pretends to try to sell a cup to Amuma.

'Chaya? Hot chaya? Kapi? Hot kapi?' Then, feeling wicked, she carries on, 'Kisses? You want hot kisses? Only two rupees.'

'Keep quiet, girl.'

But Nina cannot stop herself. It feels almost as if she is crying— this wickedness that is pouring out of her.

'You know Amuma,' she says, the tears just the other side of her lids, 'when the American astronauts landed on the moon, they said, "Yes, we'll have some tea." And the Malayalis, you know what they did?' Now Nina feels completely miserable. 'They stuck their tongues inside the astronauts' mouths. They spat and spat inside their mouths. They hated the astronauts and they hated their mouths. So they spat and spat.'

Valli gives her a knowing look. 'Enough,' she says. 'Have you eaten anything today?'

'No one gave me anything to eat. Everyone forgot me. Yesterday night, I took food from the house, even though you are not supposed to cook or eat at home. But what was I supposed to do?'

She wails it again. 'What was I supposed to do?'

In a rush, she speaks her grief with astronauts and people, who forgetting her go around sticking their tongues in each other's mouths, children who are sent off to school with morning tea in their bellies, children who don't have to go to the moon to get their tea.

'I was awake all night the night Peramma died. I was scared but I stayed with her and was brave. Sister Agnes says you can't be brave unless you are afraid. If you carry the cross even when you are afraid, if you do the difficult thing, failing a test instead of cheating, then you are a brave person. To be good you have to first be tested. But even Sister Agnes cannot have done what I did yesterday night. I was brave.'

Valli sits down on the ground and pulls Nina to her. Nina's wailing subsides to sobbing. Finally she is hiccupping.

'I want Peramma to come back. I just wish she would come back. I have such bad thoughts. I think, if she'll only come back, I promise to never become an astronaut. And, certainly, when I grow up I'll never kiss a boy like that.

'And Amuma?' She checks to see how well Amuma is listening to her. Is she dozing? A warm sun is shining on them. It is warmth made watery by a recent rain that sparkles a thousand little friendly suns on every surface. And there are two little suns in Amuma's eyes. She is listening. Nina almost tells her the worst bit of thinking she's been worrying over. Would she be willing to promise never to want her mother again if it meant she could have Peramma back? But she wouldn't. She wouldn't. As much as she would rather live forever with Peramma, she also knows she cannot allow her Amma out of her life.

She feels miserable in her power to choose her mother over her Peramma. She tells Amuma so. 'I want Amma.'

And Nina begins wailing again. Valli rocks her on her lap, taking the brunt of the ground's wetness into her thin shanks. Her bones will ache tonight.

'There, there girl.' Her crooning is scratchy. 'It doesn't matter. It doesn't matter. Aren't you your mother's child? Your mother's own child? Your mother's only child? Your mother's honey child?'

They sit like this till the warmth of Nina's body is absorbed into Valli's. Nina slips into Amuma's hand the slip of paper Peramma has entrusted her with.

'Peramma said these are the words for her son when he comes back. Only, I don't know if I have to live here without Amma and without Peramma till he comes. If I go away from here, how do I give him these words?'

'Your Peramma wrote a letter to her son?'

'Not a whole letter. Just a few words. I asked her what I have to do to give him these words. But she went back to sleep without answering.'

Valli unpacks the tightly folded piece of paper, studies it thoughtfully. But it is undecipherable. Valli cannot read the words Annakutty has scribed there. The literacy volunteers from Little Flowers have yet to persuade Valli to take up slate and pencil.

'Do you know what it says, Nina?'

'Yes. It's only four words.'

'Never mind the words. I am glad you've given me this, Nina.'

Nina hesitates. She hasn't meant for Amuma to think that she's given her the piece of paper. The next moment she feels the burden of it lift from her.

'You will give this to him, won't you? When he comes, if I am not here, then you will always be here.'

Valli folds the sheet of notepaper back along its creases and folds it into the cloth at her waist, tucking it in deep from where she allows it to slip past her thighs and fall to the earth. Reaching under her body she scratches earth over it.

'Yes, Nina, I will always be here.'

'Amuma, Peramma told me they will bury her far from where they buried Perappan in the church. They won't do that, will they? They'll bury her with him, and they'll write her name below his name, won't they? We can add these words too.'

'Is that what she wanted?'

'Yes, she said the words are for him to read when he comes. But how will he read in Malayalam? He speaks only German, you know. There was more she said, a lot I couldn't understand. She said she was having a hard time remembering the real things.'

'Was she talking about him—the lost one?'

'I don't know. Yes, she was. She was talking about how it is impossible to remember everything, to know how things really are, and impossible to know what else will happen, so we just have to imagine it. She said imagining what is real is the most important thing. She said what is real comes from our mind. She said, if it is real, then you will remember it. Then she said, remembering it will make it real. She said after she lost her son, she still had her memory of him, so she put it into her memory that he would return. She said, if it is real, you can remember not only the things that have happened, but also remember the things that are going to happen.

'She didn't say anything more about her son. She talked all about the chickens and goats, the rain, the church and girls laughing, and so many other things. I fell asleep when she was talking and her words came into my dreams; I saw all the things she was talking about. Her son too. I saw him last night. He was a stranger. And in front of our house, the chickens and goats were running everywhere. But I didn't like it. He knew many things I didn't know and he didn't know many things I know. You know Kunjukuttan was also in my dream, pissing in the ditch in front of our house. But the stranger in my dream, he wasn't a very nice man. He made everything seem strange. You know, in Elsie's house, they have baby goats now. He didn't even know how to feed them banana peels properly. But the thing about my dream, Amuma, is how real it was. So real I am sure it will happen.'

Nina sighs once, dramatically. Then once more. This time it is a little tiredly.

'Last night before Peramma died, I tried to ask her questions. Peramma never answered. She said my name a few times, but she never saw me. She wasn't even talking to me, except when she wanted to complain that I hadn't closed the window against the rain.'

Nina settles deeper in Amuma's lap; she is almost smiling. The little piece of paper she's clutched for a whole day and night is gone. The puzzle of what her Peramma had babbled to her is losing its importance. Banished too is what has had her wandering restlessly from one place to the next: the dread of wondering if her mother will come. She is content sitting in Amuma's uncomfortable lap. She remembers past happiness. Hard on the heels of remembering will come the crash into disbelief—never to touch Peramma again.

But first: 'Thambi Perappan used to say so many things about Peramma that I loved to listen to. He said she had skin that did battle with light. He said her skin fought and defeated the sun. He said tomorrow the sun will not come out. When we need light, we will have to look at Peramma. I used to wish he would say that about me. Perappan could say words that were not true till when he said them. Then they became true. Peramma's skin had light hidden in it. If you looked, there was light to see. Her skin caught the sun, it did.

'When the sun goes down, it is like a drawing of the sun going down. I used to make that drawing when I was little. In my drawing, only a bit of the sun showed between triangle mountains, and the sun always had two eyes and a nose and a smile on its face.'

'Is that right?'

'When I was little, I made the drawing of the sun with the smile on its face by imagining about the sun. If I had looked outside the window at the sun, then I would have never been able to draw the sun the way it really is. That sun is too hard to draw, all wavy lines. And where does it begin or end anyway? I told Peramma about how hard it is to draw the real sun. And when something is too difficult to draw exactly the way it is, then you draw it the way you imagine it. I wanted her to know that I understood about how you remember what is real. She said imagining what is real is the most important thing of all.'

'Is that right?'

'Yes.' And Nina begins trembling. It is coming now: Peramma is gone. And it is coming now: where is she gone?

'Why don't I take you to Jansyammai's house. I'll fry an egg. Bull's eye. And you can eat it on a banana leaf plate. And you can have a cup of hot chaya. Will you like that? Will you like Amuma to feed you?'

'Yes.'

22

Nina Dreams for Annakutty

The stranger steps down one, two, three steps. He is free of the house. He crosses the yard in five more. There is a ditch, a boy is pissing into it. The boy's back arches and he smiles triumphantly at the stranger from over his shoulder. The boy speaks, but the stranger does not understand him. The language, to the stranger's ear, is babble. The boy prompts the stranger with his eyes and with a forward push of his head to observe his swordsmanship. He carves the sunlight with the stream he brandishes. He carves it in a K.

(Is this our Kunjukuttan?)

The stranger hurries away from the babble, hurries past a few small houses, or rather, a series of huts. There is a little creek and a bridge that he crosses. Several hens run ahead of him, some other animals have to be shooed away. Someone rescues him from the persistence of one goat. Someone else says the goats have just given birth. He is offered bananas the size of fingers to eat. He eats till he is full and the crowd that's gathered insists he eat more. He eats more. He is led to a tidy little structure, palm-woven and bound together with rope, open to the sky. He hands his peels one by one to the nanny goats that have been rounded up and are now penned in the shed with the baby goats. A tremendous bleating follows him as he walks away.

He passes a whitewashed building on his right. The land gives steeply here and he is propelled almost at a run. The man who rescued him from the goat says, 'Not here,' indicating the church.

(Then where?)

He is at the end of the rain-rutted path. The mud and gravel washed downhill by the rain has created a berm at its end. He is led around it, and around the other face of the church, to the single paved street running through town. A scraggly market stretches along the street. Little trucks in various stages of being loaded or unloaded (it is hard for him to know which) are parked in front of shops. The shops are dark for all that they appear to be missing the wall that fronts the street. He comments on the missing wall, and is told it is there in old wood panels that are pleated to the side. And yes, he sees the wood, pleated and carved. How old? Someone in the crowd says a hundred, maybe two hundred years old. Next, he asks about the trucks, and it seems they are being loaded for the journey to Kochi, where they will offload these stalks of green bananas for shipping to the world. He says something about never seeing such true greens in his life and people nod. It is impossible, he thinks, for these people to know how remarkable the fields are, how pure the green of paddy. He walks on past the shops filled with shoes, umbrellas, jewellery of the cheapest sort. The air is full of gnats. There are even a few bees to pollinate the flowers that grow everywhere.

He turns to his rescuer from before: 'God is absconding, but all his creation is here.' His rescuer immediately becomes very serious and speaks carefully, as if he is lifting and examining his words in some internal space before speaking them. But this is the effect of his speaking in English, a language he is not comfortable with. After some time, perhaps exhausted by English, his rescuer begins to sound crazed, insisting that all religions are one, that God is one, that he lives his life as a testament to God. But the stranger explains that what he had said was meant as a joke, just a response to the tourism slogan constantly invoked: God's Own Country; a slogan that had him itching to ask, But where is God?

Now someone else, an ancient, speaks. It is shocking to hear him speak English and in an accent of such neutrality. He says, 'You are your mother's son.' The stranger digs deep in his pocket and rubs the marble he keeps there for luck. The stranger shakes his head.

Is it to indicate he doesn't understand the meaning of the old man's words?

And still shaking his head, he steps out on the empty road leading out of town. The land falling away on either side of the road has the air of a woman exhausted by her own unremitting beauty. He feels a headache coming on. A cluster of girls walking by avoids his eyes. He finds it strange that they giggle so provocatively. But when he steps toward them, they scatter like the hens did outside the house. He is angry enough to want to take not one but two or three steps toward the prettiest one in the bunch. To maybe make an obscene gesture.

But the crowd is still with him. They hem him in and angle him off the road toward a fairly dense grove of trees. It is practically a wilderness. Strange, he thinks, since there is little land that goes uncultivated here. Often what appears at a distance to be matted green, on closer look is combed into rows. Not this.

The crowd is huge now. Maybe a hundred or more. Young and

almost entirely male. They push amongst themselves, but are silent. They seem to be looking for a reaction from him. He studies where she is laid to rest for another moment. Someone explains the larger slab is for a man who died in a strike. So he makes a show of studying that for a bit. When he turns to walk back, the crowd hollers. They jump in the air. The stranger reacts with alarm, shrinking into himself. He is afraid they will hoist him on to their shoulders. The song they break into seems to him an inarticulate hee-hawing. No words in this song.

He turns over in his mind the words she left him:

> *Annakutty Verghese*
> *1945–2004*
> *I live in you*

PART TWO

18–19 May, 2004
A small city in the Midwest, United States

Amma, I'm remembering everything:

suitcase. it might have been a box.
name. did i have one?
box. it was a box, not a suitcase
chameleon airport search hole magician train swing name name name
My name is Asa Gardner

1

Suitcase

He is a beast equipped with hands. She is square and chubby. His. Not a beast, a darling.

Asa sudses the shampoo into his daughter's hair. Noel is jerked up by her head so she comes to her six-year-old toes, then let go to rock back onto her heels, which is when her arms fling up from her sides and flail the air. She carefully avoids grabbing onto his body, reaches for him with the squeaky, 'Papa you're going to make me fall.'

Her reluctance to touch him enrages him, as does the angle at which she holds her face—turned away from him. All he is trying for is to get Noel clean. Clean enough so LeAnn, when she gets here, will not have this to complain about.

Not that LeAnn ever actually complains. Not when the weekend passes so quick, it leaves him with little time to bathe Noel or get her to do her homework or feed her a LeAnn-style meal. The goodness that is LeAnn precludes complaint. The women in his life, Asa feels his way cautiously through this thought, they forgive him. Abruptly he leaves off thinking. To do, to do, hums in his head instead. To do: the mess that was breakfast will need to be cleared from the table before LeAnn gets here. But the first order of business is getting the sticky out of Noel's hair.

And the breakfast—not to be avoided—will have to be the next order of business. Carcass of waffle. Pool of syrup. LeAnn doesn't consider waffles from the freezer a proper meal. How does she do it? How does she let him know this without complaining?

Once though, on those mornings when they had woken up, the three of them in the same bed, his waffles were good enough then. He lets that bit of falsehood stand for a second. No, the truth is, on those other mornings, being three together did not so much make frozen meals acceptable as give LeAnn something in return for her willingness to live with the unacceptable. Being together cancelled out everything else: the garbage piling up week after week, his failure to remember to put it out for the weekly pickup just something they laughed about together.

'What's happened to the man of this house?'

'You're the man in this house.'

'I look like a man to you?'

And she stretched in bed, the length of her undulating to show him what she was.

'You make the big bucks.'

No note of sourness in this statement. He made money. Some. Sometimes. Enough. The deal they had struck did not require him to do more. And she made money. 'Enough and more.' It was her language when they talked money.

'That's prehistoric, Asa'.

'Okay, fine. This prehistoric man wants to remind his liberated wife the garbage is put out on Tuesdays. The prehistoric man would also like to point out to the liberated woman she is nagging him in prehistoric style.'

They ate waffles, frozen or otherwise, without needing to weigh the love in their meals. Now she is someone else.

Someone who simply notes with what could almost sound like sympathy: 'Oh waffles. Look in the box marked appliances. My grandma's old waffle iron is in there.'

'Got me there,' he replies. 'The wrong breakfast. Oh, and why have I allowed eight months to pass without opening boxes?'

She watches him from inside that terrible LeAnn silence. When he's brought it up to her, how much he hates the silence—'Why don't you say something instead of sitting there with that judgemental look?'—she tells him that she is just gathering her thoughts, getting ready to say something.

'Anyway, why would you stick your grandma's waffle iron in a box of appliances for me?'

'I have another one, Asa. It's not like I've given it away to someone I don't know. It's not like I'll never see it again.'

Or another time she might have said: 'Oh Noe, I can tell you haven't had a bath in two days. You all must have had some fun.'

'Some? What do you mean by SOME fun?'

Is that how he talks to her and is that how she talks to him? Have they talked like this?

Or this. Did she say this once: 'Never mind. We'll get to the homework at home. Noe, yes?'

There was of course little chance that the three-hour drive home would end with anything other than Noel being carried straight to bed. Standing on this side of the front door, getting her shoes laced or jacket buttoned, Noel was a wreck.

Nearly every visit ends with her wrapped around her mother's legs chanting from the depths of a trance, 'Can't we just stay here? This one time? Can't we, mama, can't we, can't we? Please?'

Please, oh please. Oh please, oh please . . . on and on and on till Asa wants to peel her from her mother's legs, and shake her till she opens her eyes and looks at him.

'It's not your mother.' He wants to put his mouth to her ear, to force the words in. 'It's me.'

Did he actually do that once? To his six-year-old daughter? Did he tell her he was the monster in her life?

Asa is never grateful to Noel for wanting to stay. All it does is draw attention to the misery he has inflicted on her. And on LeAnn. Misery that they are all so gamely living with. There is a complicity between mother and daughter to absolve him of responsibility, to deflect the sort of scrutiny that could find him failed as a father and husband, and worse: find him failed as a human, revealed a monster.

Noel won't even reach for him when she is about to fall in the bathtub. She thinks she has to spare him getting wet. When did she start thinking about him as someone so apart from her, someone to spare contact with her body?

Once, she was a baby and there were three of them together. Asa. LeAnn. The baby. Then, change. Change that never stops changing. We called her Noel, Asa thinks. How did she become Noe? His grandmother was named Noel. She, the baby, was supposed to carry the name. This other name is an interloper. His anger continues its incremental growth. Shrunk into the hardness of a walnut shell and in the belly now, but soon his anger will be as large as the apartment; it will push open the door and send him out into the street where he will not dare find the explosion he longs for.

Noel's hoisted out of the tub, swung over to the rug by the bathroom door. He has thought ahead to this moment and set up the space heater, so in his overheated apartment there is this additional, localized inferno. Noel hates to be cold. Asa does as well.

My daughter, he thinks with satisfaction; his anger is as suddenly dissipated. Then he notes that swinging her out of the tub and over its high sides, he's held her at arm's length, not wanting any of her to drip onto him.

Why was it so different when she was a baby? Was it just that she was a baby then? He had done the bulk of the diaper changes. He'd learned the trick of keeping a fresh wipe ready in the left hand before reaching with the right, to peel back the soiled diaper wedged between baby legs. From one end of the innocent belly, which breached the foam pad she was laid on, she invariably squirted—her little whale spout, a sparkle he caught in the wipe.

'Sweetie,' he asks her, 'how come mommy's changed your name to Noe?'

'Mommy didn't change me,' Noel tells him. 'I wanted to be like my friend Zoë. Zoë and Noe. Get it? It was my idea to become Noe.'

He towels her, and again she is a wobbly doll, tipping heel to toe, arms flung every which way. He forces gentleness into his hands, takes the slowed time of the towel working its way down to toes to think. He smiles at himself for fearing what she admits to so fearlessly: she is changing. He lets himself go slack. She doesn't fear anything, he thinks sadly, least of all me. And I? I fear everything. On her behalf, I fear myself.

It doesn't matter who is changing her, or how. What matters is it is happening away from him. He should want to sink his teeth into his arms, to tear the flesh away, because what really matters is that all the changes are happening because he has allowed them to. He is the architect of change.

'I did this,' he mutters, bending, holding underwear stretched open for legs, so they can, prompted by the appearance of two holes, pick themselves up, one-two, and step in.

'One-two,' he breathes and settles the waistband gently around her belly. She doesn't hear him.

He leaves her sitting on his bed; the heater is redirected to point to her, centred in the turmoil of sheets. The sheets blaze orange. She is a goddess. There must be an Indian goddess who sits in flames. He will have to remember to make the bed before LeAnn gets here.

He heads to the living room, where her little plastic suitcase with its plastic wheels and retractable plastic handle tell the story—again that story. Misery. She and her mother think to tame it with plastic and pink and a smiling expanse of white caught between the plumped lips of a cartoon princess. No, it is not a princess, he sees. It is a mermaid. Ariel. And various sea creatures swimming the painted pink sea. Unzipped, the sea yields Noel's essential possessions that travel with her from her mother to her father and back again. How, he thinks, can a child of six have a suitcase? And how did it come to be his child? How did he let this happen? How, he corrects himself, did he make this happen?

Inside the suitcase, LeAnn has arranged clothes so tops and bottoms, socks or tights are folded into one another. Each of four packages represents a morning or an evening, two of each that his daughter spends with him twice a month. It is no good disrupting the arrangement of these packages. Noel will only wear the clothes in the order to which her mother has submitted them. He knows that if he suggests a different skirt paired with a different T-shirt Noel will frown. And if he suggests that her mother wouldn't disagree with his selection, then Noel will shake her head emphatically.

'It's not mama who chooses. It's me. She packs what I choose.'

The last thing he wants is for his daughter to have to continue defending her mother against her father. He takes a package coordinated in green and blue. Yellow bees are crawling over the frilled socks. 'Summer nearly here,' he notes, lets the suitcase mouth flap shut and heads back to the bedroom.

Noel's seated hunched on the bed, legs drawn up and knees fallen away from her. Just the crown of her head is visible; the rest of her head is tucked in the space between her knees, from where she is peering into herself. She looks up, hearing him enter the room, releases the finger that has pulled the crotch of her underwear aside and brings her knees back together. The rapt inwardness of her expression gives way to a flash of something else. He barely registers its passing, hasn't the time to decipher it when her face settles into a look of cool expectation. Asa keeps his voice free of inflection.

'Everything all right then? Shall we get some clothes on? Or are you due a lotion rub? Your mother didn't say.'

But Noel wants to explain, 'Some soap got in there. It was burning, so I had to see.'

He is immediately irritated out of his studied gentleness. 'What's the matter? Do we have to wash again?'

'I don't know,' she says, and letting her knees fall away, she tugs the underwear aside.

It was a shutter pulled from the outside and a window revealed. A window so small it was a mere peephole. A peephole compelling his eye to look into someone else's home. And as when looking through the wrong end of a peephole, his vision narrowed to the opaque.

No, it was a window on the inside, a window to the world.

Not a window.

No, an eyelid opening to show an eye. Bright, the eye. And open. Opening. An eye opening to see the world.

The world revealing itself from a great distance, spinning.

He thinks about it long after Noel leaves with LeAnn, after he goes out alone into the night and returns to lie on the disordered bed. He thinks as his eyes close into sleep about an aperture opening, a flash of light and his daughter. He thinks, I don't know how to describe her.

Bending next to her on the bed, they had looked at the intricate pleating, at the seam running through a little girl's symmetry.

'It's like a bird's beak.'

There was great gravity in her words. And it was as she said. It was the little beak of the little bird that is his daughter.

High to the right of centre, a fleck of white—soap foam? He licked his finger and extended it, then halted the hand. There was nothing wrong in his reaching to touch her, wipe what was burning her. But all the same he withdrew his hand, shooed her into the bathroom.

Sleep doesn't come to him. He gets up from the bed, strips it and remakes it, tucking everything tight, smoothing the top, climbing in and pulling the cover neatly around him. He doesn't clean the crud from on him. He enjoys a mental swagger when he thinks that by morning a crust will have formed on the snot and blood of his nose, on the cuts across his arm that are already pulling tight, and on the mud splattered across the back of his jeans. He will have to climb into the tub just to soften and melt the carapace he has laboured to acquire.

'Liar,' he accuses himself. 'Chameleon.'

The swagger dissolves because now something, by its stillness, is making its presence felt within him, something that . . . the climbing of which . . . but it is so insurmountable . . . will allow him to understand what aches seeing his daughter with her head bent between her knees. The word transgression comes to him, and he shivers.

Without desiring it, he realizes, it is possible to transgress. Her vulnerability. How can she be so easy with it? How can anyone? How, LeAnn?

Transgress: he loathes himself for coming upon the word. Has LeAnn come upon this word, come upon it as she prepared the suitcase and the child to be left with the father? He despises LeAnn. She would be the type to pretend the word away.

LeAnn had come in the afternoon, come up the stairs too quietly, he had not heard her, had swung up from the sleepy work of a puzzle he and Noel were solving, Noel complaining that he wasn't trying hard enough, he sensing the presence while nodding along with the complaint, then LeAnn, at the door, the light catching in her earrings.

There was the time, the same earrings, at a dinner, he thinks, somewhere out, somewhere meant to resolve something between them, and it wasn't resolved despite her careful dressing up, the earrings that are still ill-suited to her face, its masculine jaw, her height. He had accused her that day of trying to humiliate him when she picked up the bill.

'I invited you. I picked this place. I'll pay.'

'You think I'd agree to come to a place that I couldn't afford?'

And they decided that day to plough ahead, to marry without the sought-for resolution. Probably, he thinks, her pregnancy made him attractive to her. But if so, it was not for the same reasons it made her attractive to him. And he attended the birthing classes, sat circling her belly from behind with his arms, the two of them on a rug with six or eight couples with bellies similarly circled, their competitive instincts fired by the athleticism of what they were riveted to on the classroom's pull-down screen. Hours of sweating and panting compressed into moments, and now they sobered to the rushed conclusion of the story, set in a tub—this detail the only thing completely unrealistic, unacceptable; not for our baby, they thought in unison. But as for the trick with time, it made it possible for them to believe in the heroic ready to be wakened in them.

Asa blinked hard in the darkened room to clear his eyes of moisture, and around him in the dark was the sniffling of women as the camera closed in on the baby's head crowning. There was a momentary pause when the tangled growth on the baby's head and the tangled growth at the opening churned together and the next second the baby emerged, a separate being, after all. A triumph that wrung still more tears from him.

When the moment for heroism came, there was anger that he had not expected, anger that wasn't in the film shown in the classroom. There was anger in the way LeAnn leaned into his chest, bit his shirtfront and tugged and panted, so he knew she was holding back from tearing past the shirt. Anger in the livid red of LeAnn's flesh when finally they laid her on the bed and swung her feet apart. The flesh gave up its tension; tearing, it transferred its anger to the baby, emerging just as red, squalling its refusal to live, the squalling forcing life into its lungs. She was buffeted and pulled and swung and in general maligned, so Asa started again and again in those early moments of her life to plead the cause of his newborn daughter: let her go back, she doesn't want this. Instead, she was set atop LeAnn's belly.

Asa saw the baby was as dark under the red as he. On LeAnn's pale belly, the child was a foreigner. There could be no relationship between the two of them. She could not be LeAnn's. But neither was she his. Her darkness was her own, that of a creature long submerged. Hair whorled on the skin of her cheeks, the imprint of her ascent through other waters. Indefatigable, she inched, still swimming the now spent current of her mother's silver ripples; upland she swam. In her swollen face, her lips pursed in a rose of exertion searched for her mother's nipple. First though, the blind bump of the vessel coming to shore.

Asa was baffled: from where came this child? Whose was it?

When he looked next, the voyager was home. LeAnn and her child reformed as one.

He stood by as the placenta was delivered. The doctor held it up as proudly as she had the baby. Larger than the baby, liverish and purple. Asa was aghast. Was she going to place this mass on LeAnn's belly, as she had earlier the foreigner? He looked to the two nurses. He looked to LeAnn. No one else seemed to care about the question.

'You don't want to claim it for a burial or anything, do you?'

He was offended, but the doctor, busy stitching between his wife's legs, paid him no attention. And when the doctor looked up, Asa turned away quickly.

Now she seemed to know and offered mildly, 'Some communities view the placenta as equally valuable. The soul returns, I have been told, to where the placenta is buried.'

Asa didn't want to know. He didn't want to know about communities, didn't want to know which ones made a soup of it to feed the new mother, and which ones allowed it to be disposed wherever the hospital deposited cartilaginous waste, cancerous growths and amputated limbs left behind from other procedures taking place in other rooms.

LeAnn stood, breathing audibly from her climb up the stairs, her earrings glinting against the dark of her hair and the dark of the corridor behind her. Her extra tall frame in its habitual forward tilt, and in her face her mouth opening in a big O.

'Oh fantastic.'

'What's so fantastic?'

Shush, said the gloomy hallway. Shush, said the gloom. Dim bulbs, strung there in a line stretching away from her, said the same thing: shush.

And her earrings swayed and caught the light and all but said, You liar.

But LeAnn, quick and lithe, leapt in: 'No, I meant how brilliant. The puzzle. How brilliant is that? Noel's just figured out how much she likes puzzles. And you're going to have to be so patient because she's going to insist on completing even the big ones. Aren't you, Noel? Hours and hours.'

'How did you get in without buzzing me?'

'Oh I was going to, but someone came out just as I came up to the door. He held the door open.'

'Not supposed to do that.'

'Yes, I probably shouldn't have encouraged it by going in the door like I did. Young guy. Probably not thinking about safety.'

Asa considered this, then said, 'Those earrings. They're too long for you.'

'You've said that before.'

'The issue with the downstairs door is not safety. At least not my safety. I don't even close this door, which is why you can just walk in.'

'I knocked.'

'I didn't hear a knock. Did you hear a knock, Noel?'

'Well, I knocked.' LeAnn continued smiling.

'Did you hear me say, "Come in?"'

'No. The door's wide open, and I could see you both in here.'

Asa had scattered the puzzle pieces, turned them all right side up, and carefully hanging on to the old solved bits, begun work on the puzzle nearly an hour before, knowing she was due to arrive. He had left the door open. He had wanted her to walk in without knocking, to catch them playing together on the rug. He had wanted her to say 'fantastic' and 'brilliant'. And he had known he would hate her when she did—hate her for participating in his pretence.

'My neighbour downstairs, she had a pizza delivery guy stick a knife to her throat after she buzzed him in.'

LeAnn frowned, pointed her chin at Noel. She spoke, keeping her voice smooth, 'I'm sorry. I didn't know.'

'It was a long time ago. She just told me. It just came up the other day as we were talking.'

They both knew he was lying.

'It might have been in a different building. But she's still quite frightened.'

'I imagine.'

'It's the kind of thing that makes you think twice about safety.'

'Well, what do you say, Noel? Want some help with the puzzle?'

'No, daddy and I are going to finish it by ourselves.'

His bed is shaking; Asa chooses to ignore it. At Noel's age, he too had a suitcase. No, it was a box. There was a language, lost to him now, in which it was a box. The sense of the word though is with him. Box.

Was it cardboard? Plastic? No, he knows. Metal.

Was he the age that she is now when he had a box, and where did he live then?

He would never hurt her. Never willingly, he thinks.

A flare in the window. As if someone outside has struck a match. The light is so meagre. It has to be match light. But his window floats five floors above the ground. There is no one outside, lighting up at his window. But look how the light falters—match light, it has to be—and illuminates, before it is snuffed: a metal box that catches the last flicker of yellow light. He searches the contents spilt from it. The muffled feel of clothes. What is it that he searches for? Something written on a piece of paper, affixed to the box. Something he means to peel off and take with him when he leaves the box. But it's too dark now to see. He's being told to hurry. A crowd of voices is pulling him to leave the box, forget the search, come with them.

No, it's not a box. It is a suitcase. Plastic and pink. She has a suitcase and a burden that travels in the suitcase. Bundled in four—clothes she insists on wearing in a certain order that protects her from him.

Ah, so she does fear him.

Then this is what he searches for. Proof of his child's fear.

No, he insists. This is not about Noel. There is a piece of paper. And a name, written on it. I need to find my name.

2

Name

'She told me his name. She told me his birthday. She said I mustn't change that. As if I would. She told me the names of food, different names of different dishes to feed him at certain times. She talked for a long time about this food. I thought I would tell her the truth, that I did not know anything about such types of food as she is describing. Before I could speak, she understood my thinking.

'She told the translator who said to me: "She just wants you to know about the food. She knows you will not know how to cook it for him."

'Then they both began to argue. I thought I would look for the child. I looked around then. I looked through the open doors that led out from the room we were seated in to other rooms. Maybe there are two such doors.

'I was worried. I thought, what if it proves this child has something wrong with him. In the picture they showed me before I came there, the child is coming out of his chair. His arms are bent at the elbow. When I see the picture I got worried that his one arm looks withered. So I have a little anxiety when I look for the child.

'Through the door directly behind the woman, I see the child sleeping on something that looks like one of those mats made of straw. It is spread on the floor. He was very healthy. I can see that it was only the camera, the angle of it that made his arms funny in that picture.

'His lips are wet and open. His thumb has slipped out of his mouth. In half a moment, I see him pull the thumb back in and suck. I was amused. I think, he is four years old, according to her, his mother, and he is still sucking on his thumb. I didn't mind.

'I didn't want an infant, like a little baby, because I know that I am never meant to be a mother. I never even wanted to pretend with dolls when I am a girl. The girls, they used to play with a real baby they borrowed from one mother in our neighbourhood who was always giving birth to a baby every year. She was happy to give her baby as a toy to the girls. I never wanted to touch that thing. A baby always smelled like cheese and vinegar. I would want to say, not that I ever did, "Why are we playing like this? Come on girls, let's play something else."

'The babies they show me at the orphanage are all the smallest of babies. I was holding one with skin that has wrinkles and I notice he has the chord on his belly. It is oozing. I feel quite sick when I see this, and when I ask if he has an infection, they go on and on about the importance of cleaning the chord for I don't remember how many days and waiting for it to fall. I was completely disgusted. This child, when I saw him, he was charming.

'They said to me before I went to the house, "This woman has a really hard time. They tried to stone her for having this baby."

'I have to tell you I was shocked when I heard this. I don't know if it is true. If such a thing is possible. Even in a place like India. It is 1970, I am thinking. Not in this day and age, right? I am not a person with much faith. Not in the sense of religion. But I think immediately of the Bible. Of Mary Magdalene wiping the feet of the Saviour with her hair. And all these other women directing their poison at her. I think maybe this woman is like a modern-day Mary Magdalene. Those days I was young enough to think of things very simply. I had the feeling that it was the desire to make things complicated, maybe to hide real feelings, the truth of people's feelings, which made everything to become so complicated. When I saw the child it seemed simple to me that I should help her, the woman, and him.

'They argued a lot with each other. The woman and my translator. By now I was living in India for over two years. I have used translators many times. I know that translators only tell you some parts of what is being said. I am prepared for all this so I just look away during the arguing.

'The house is clean, but perhaps it has been cleaned for my visit. There is only a few items in the house, a wooden bench and two chairs, a very large table. Maybe another mat rolled up. Some items like clothes and magazines are arranged in boxes and baskets. The walls have colourful pictures of Jesus and this proves to me that the family is Christian. I did not ask for a particular religion for the child when I talked to the orphanage in-charge. It really doesn't matter to me. But now I think, it is good if the child is the same religion. He will not have to change that.

'There was, of course, no bandage or even some marks on her to show she has been stoned. I could not help it. I looked as soon as we came into that house. All I see when I first come in is this woman is quite something else. She has piles of hair floating all around her face. It makes her look like I am seeing her under the water. Everything about her face—her lips, her eyelids, her cheeks—is all a little swollen. Very attractive. I can see she is the mother of a child.

'But never once while I am there does she cry in front of me. Instead, I notice when she starts to play with her hair that she has pinned many flowers in her hair. I feel a little amazed at her because, in my mind, flowers are for expressing happiness. But I think again about Mary Magdalene and I forgive her because I realize this might be her way of being truthful and straightforward.

'Outside, there must be dozens of people crowding at the door. The people at the door are silent and they are using their bodies to keep out the people behind them. I don't look at their faces because this is as much as I can be involved. I cannot take anybody else's child or help to pay for anybody else's operation or tumour or marriage or education. Our neighbours in Stuttgart said to us when we leave for India that India will be very dirty and there will be cows everywhere because nobody can kill and eat a cow. I laughed then. Before India we were in Peru. I understand how people get strange ideas. They stay right at home, they get bored; they are bound to make up ideas about places they can never see. Our neighbours in Stuttgart should have seen the people pushing at the door. There are not that many cows in India, even if it is true that mostly people don't eat cows. But our old neighbours should see how many people there are who look through this woman's door with the expression on the face. Same expression as our neighbours. Such boredom that drives people to make up excitement.

'After a while a much younger girl stepped out from the kitchen where the child is kept. The child is still sleeping despite all the noise between the translator and the woman. No one says anything about who this young girl is, but she has been crying and I thought for a second that perhaps she is the real mother. But no. I don't think so anymore. After all, she is very young, maybe thirteen. The woman who is the mother never cried. She just argued with the translator. But the young girl who cried said something, and quickly everything about the conversation changed. It became very calm. The young girl went to the main door, and when she closed it, it is a miracle—the people at the door step back and let her close it.

'The woman who is the mother said to me, "You won't cook the food, I know. I just want you to tell him the names of the food he liked. When he grows up he will want to know the names of the food he ate when he was a baby."

'I make a pretence, see, of writing, taking into my hand paper and a pen. I must have had these items in my purse. I must have gone prepared to see the whole thing through. But how do you know to make a spelling for a word from another language? But I was impressed, very much, by this woman making me write the words for the food that she has been feeding him. I know what it is that she wants him to know when he grows up. It is what every mother wants her child to know. That she fed him. She is a very intelligent woman.'

'Mrs Oster, can you tell me her name?'

'No, I can't. Hendrik was very doubtful that we might be in the wrong place at the wrong time. He thought these people are very shady. He was strict that we should not get to know them.

'I listened to him in such matters. He was a good judge of character. I was the innocent in our relationship. He thought when we go to Delhi he will have trouble with the embassy to issue the child with papers. So when I am at the woman's house to see the child for the first time, he is elsewhere making the phone calls. But to make a phone call in this place is impossible and we left two days later with the child, no assurances of anything or how we will leave from Delhi with the child.'

'Can you tell me the child's name?'

'I pretended to write the child's name down with the food she told me about. And I wrote her name. I wrote it down because I did not want to forget her. So you see, despite Hendrik's suspicious nature I have a very open nature. Against all his instructions— return quickly, do not talk about money, don't give information about where we live, no address and such. Despite his instructions, I asked her to spell the name. She was very eager. I was talking of course in English and the translator was telling everything in their language. Suddenly I am surprised because when I ask how she must be spelling her name, the young girl starts to answer. *Before* the translator can speak. The one who is the mother gives her a look and then she spells for me her name and also the child's name. She is very eager. A little bit English they understand. It was not a very long name. She insists to tell me the meaning.'

'Do you have the name?'

'No, I didn't write his name. Only the mother's. What happened was not anything like I wanted. I wanted for the boy to grow up happily in Germany with us. I did not want him to pine for his mother. I did not expect him to forget her. But I would want him to slowly see me as his mother. So I have no intention to tell him who she is and about the food and all she is asking me to write down. I thought one can make a complicated situation like this woman with this child smooth again. For myself. I wrote her name down for myself.

'When I went there I was very curious how I will feel when I see this child for the first time. I went to the door of the room he was sleeping in and I saw it was just a kitchen with dirt for a floor. I saw he was beautiful like all children everywhere are beautiful. Perfectly normal. Even the arm is fine. His eyes were closed and he was asleep on his side. I saw his profile. He had large lids and very much tangled hair. I did not feel anything when I saw him. I noted he was beautiful, that his arms are thin. He was wearing a shirt without sleeves, and his arms are very thin. His shoulder was also thin. He was like a little snail in a shell, but without any covers. I was moved in my heart with pity for him that he must soon leave his mother. But I did not experience the rush of love that a mother is supposed to feel. To be frank, I did not expect to feel anything. So I am not surprised.

'Everything else in India is surprising. But never am I surprised by myself.'

'You said your heart moved with pity for him?'

'You expect I should feel guilty. Why? Because I am going to take him away from that kitchen floor. It must have had a floor of mud, no shelves or cabinets, only some pots, pans, some tins, bags, things in a row on the floor. Everything is neat and tidy, but everything is also black with smoke. The walls are black. There is a window with bars, like you see only in a prison. It is already the twentieth century in Germany. Here they are cooking with wood fire. Those bars are sticky with grease. The dirt caught in the grease has dripped like the ice you see in the winter in the roof of the cave.

'Even before I come to India, I feel that there is a reason for me especially to go. Something that is not related to being Hendrik's wife, the official role you see of somebody married to an official person. I was not there to represent the German government as Hendrik was. I am simply myself on this trip. I feel for the first time, going to India, I too have a reason for living.'

'Mrs Oster, you did write the child's name on that piece of paper?'

'No, of course not. I had no interest in the child's name. It was told to me. A very simple sound. I remember the meaning. It was sweet. It means honey. But it is in a language that I do not know, so now I am old and I have forgotten. Do you know that I can speak five, four languages very well. But certainly not that language.

'I will tell you something I never have told anyone, not of course Hendrik. Even my second husband did not know. I did not tell the second one anything, not the child, not what Hendrik and I tried to do. He never had much respect for Hendrik, in any case. I never have told my children this. It is not the kind of thing one talks about to children. It changes their understanding of their mother. You see, a mother has to be only one thing to her children. Only a mother. She cannot, for example, be something else. Say a woman who has an abortion of her baby.

'That surprises you? That I have a child who I aborted.

'When I was a girl I met Hendrik. His last name was Gottschalk. I used to write Gretchen Gottschalk and play the game of counting the letters. Milk maid, Soldier's maid, Hendrik's maid, Old maid. We were paired together by our classmates because of our heights. Because we both have been to the United States. Hendrik to Ohio, and I to Los Angeles. Which gives me very good English, even compared to him. I have seen Hollywood. We are a pair because, when we live in Germany, we only want to talk about being elsewhere.

'After school I studied to become a kindergarten teacher. He goes to the army. I have to do the abortion. It might be that I should have written to him and informed him. But it is hard to know for certain. And I am quite certain that if it is known, they will never let me become a teacher for the little children who live in Stuttgart. Ha ha. Also I am certain that Hendrik will never marry me. Trust me, he is the type who will never want to simplify any complication he makes.

'Only good thing Hendrik did for me is bring me to America where I meet my second husband. And finally I have my children. You have met them. You must be knowing that they are his children. I cannot, after the abortion, have children. But I have my second husband's children as my own. They have no complication to see me as their mother. They met me when they are very little. Dorothea and Kirstein. Even after their father leaves us, I have continued to be their mother. And their father. They have only me. After their father leaves, I decide no more men. Who will marry an old woman with a rotten womb and two girls who need dance lessons and shoes that are matching their skirts? And of course I have sent them to college, both of them. Ha ha.'

'Mrs Oster, you understand that it is Kirstein and Dorothea who have asked me to speak with you? Your daughters have employed me for this purpose.'

'Of course they know about the little boy. They helped me to find you. You see I placed ads secretly, for years, but it never works. I asked my daughters, you see, to find someone like you. Now you will search for the child. That is your specialization.'

'Yes and no, Mrs Oster. Yes and no.'

'Poor man. You sound so tired. You men, you tire easily. And at your age. It is a shame when an old woman is a match for a young man. If you like I can ask for you a cup of coffee. Yes?'

'Mrs Oster, you were telling me something your daughters don't know. Is that the extent of what you haven't communicated with your daughters?'

'No coffee then? That's okay. I will tell you instead about what I used to dream. This also my daughters don't know. Maybe by now they figured out the abortion. But I used to dream, and I have never told anyone in my whole life. Well, one person. I thought it would help him to stop crying. It didn't of course. And his mother, I told his mother.'

'Mrs Oster?'

'Yes, I am telling you. I told the boy and the mother, and since then only you are hearing it. After the abortion I dream again and again that a baby is holding his arm up to me, is calling me.

'For many days after the abortion, I have bleeding that does not stop. I keep expecting that the doctor, who maybe isn't even a real doctor, has not removed everything. I think of a little arm, if it is still there. I was afraid to look when the blood was flowing, even though such things are not possible, for something to get left behind, to come out. It would be an accusation. Yes, you think so also?

'Suddenly, three days after the abortion, there is so much bleeding I have to stay in the bathroom all day. The blood is very thin and pink and I can't wipe it. It just spreads and I stay on the floor with it. Finally my mother says, "Come out. You cannot use the bathroom only for yourself. There are other people in the family," and so on. So I ask for her help because I cannot manage my situation anymore. It is not possible to hide it anymore. My mother and father do not understand the situation. Rather, they do not accept it. My father slaps me many times. Very hard. My mother sometimes tells him to slap me. Sometimes she screams for him to stop. We are a very educated family. Both my parents are teachers. I have never seen them behave like this.

'They take me to the big hospital. There the doctor has to take everything out from inside me; they must scrape away the last bits of my baby. My body refuses to give the baby. They even scrape away what I have for making another baby. Perhaps my father has asked them to do this. Perhaps he has not. I learned that day how important it is to never tell anyone. No one can accept this. It is too much.

'I dreamed about the baby. Then the dreams stopped. Hendrik, he marries me. Many years afterward, we leave to go to his post in India. Then I dream about the baby again. He is now a little brown baby, my baby. You see, even before we step off the plane I know. I dream even in the plane about a little brown baby.'

'Mrs Oster, it is possible for me to see how you came to adopt this child. You faced hardships that took you to this, this kitchen, this place. I believe it would be a great help not only to your daughters, but also to you if you could tell them what you have shared with me.

'Think about it, Mrs Oster. And if can you tell me what name you gave this child? A little bit by way of specifics. What steps led you to losing this child? It is a fantastic story you tell. That you took in a child; that you lost him in a train station. Now you want to search for him. Altogether, a story that is missing details. Details that would help your daughters to understand, perhaps even assist you.'

'I tell you, I don't know the name. I refused to know the name. And earlier, I made a mistake. You better erase from the notebook my earlier thing I said about writing his name. I never wrote his name. I wrote the names of the food she prepares for him. His mother. I wrote his birth date. But I was honest with her about the name. I told her I will not call the child by that name since it makes more sense to change to a German one.'

'Mrs Oster, my notes indicate you did not write his name. That you had no interest in his name. Let me read to you what I have here: "I had no interest in the child's name. It was told to me. A very simple sound. I remember the meaning. It was sweet. It means honey." This is all you have said about his name. Oh, wait a minute. You also said, "I do not know. I have forgotten." Mrs Oster, if you can try to remember. Some memory of the name. Of course it is a good thing that you have his birth date. It will help tremendously. Any other details of the household. One has to guess whether they would have been able to afford a hospital birth. If the birth was registered, then we are in luck. But a name is important. You said you were immediately outside Madras. I imagine in such a place many births occur in a day. This is after all a very populated country we are talking about.'

'But you have not understood me. I am old and I don't remember. I never took an interest. I went to the child who was asleep that day and he never woke. My heart, it never woke to him. I was not interested in him. I was charmed by him. But I was not interested in him. This probably makes me sound like a bad human being. But I am not that. You see, I wasn't sure when I looked at him. I have never told anyone this. I wasn't sure if this was the child from my dreams. Of course, now I am old and I know there is no such thing as dreams. Dreams, they are not real. That is why we have separate words for what is real and what is dream.

'Of course, now my daughters are worried about me. That I am making phone calls to India. But toll-free numbers. Why are they worried? It costs nothing. Most of the time I speak to boys. The girls, I simply don't waste my time with them. But even the boys are too young. I always ask them how old are they. When they talk, I know they are in India. The Indian accent is unchanged. So many years I am gone from India, but I can recognize the Indian accent. You must know I lived there for years. Now the Indians are explaining to us on the phone about washing machines. We used to have an old lady who did the washing for us. In Delhi. Then there were no machines in India.'

'Mrs Oster, your daughters are not worried about the phone bill. I think you know what they are worried about. Why don't we talk about what is worrying them and what is worrying you.'

'Why, I ask, are they worried? They should not be worried. It is an innocent thing I do. I want to make the correction. I ask the boys their age. I will find the child. Yes, I have to tell the boys everything so they can understand me. Yes, I tell them what I cannot tell my children. I tell them about the dream. That I made such a huge mistake. I believed in this dream of the child calling me. Sometimes a baby covered in blood. Sometimes a baby who is brown.

'The first time I tell this story. Many years ago I tell this story to her. The woman. The child's mother. I walk back to the room after seeing the child. The arguing is over, the door has been shut against the people outside, the other girl is sitting with her crying eyes and the mother is still smiling at me. I have seen the child sleeping and nothing in my heart is moved. But this woman looks so hopefully at me. So I tell her about my dream.

'Maybe the translator, she did a good job. Maybe not. But the woman and I are looking into each other's eyes when I talk. I have a feeling she does not hear the translator whose voice is murmuring behind mine. I have a feeling she understands me. She looks at me with the eyes of the baby in my dream.

'I feel such a powerful interest in her. What you call sympathy. It helps me decide.

'I see she cannot keep the child as I cannot keep mine. I see her child will call to her all her life. I see her child will never return to her, no more than mine will return to me. I see she will be my twin. That, far apart from her, she in that room, I where I go, we will always have each other.'

3

Box

It is no longer still within him. There is no question of climbing up or out of the turbulence that descends in place of the earlier stillness. Asa presses his shaking body into the bed with each breath he draws.

The shaking shakes loose from him, jitters to the floor. He observes it distort the floor, gain a wooden opacity, then fluid again, then turgid, spread its boundaries, seep into the walls, climb to the ceiling, and viscous, settle there. Asa closes and opens his eyes. The ceiling peels. The ends of plaster feelers brush him, closer now, they crush to dust on his skin, so close, the ceiling kisses his heated brow. The room recedes.

He knows this space, a shape-shifting space, the space of his reality, composed of what is true and what he's made up in his mind to replace the lost. It is a space that insists on words.

'Thirty-eight now. Give or take a year.'

Thirty-eight is an estimate; it is the best one he can manage. So then he was born in 19 . . . 1966. But the date? Well, if he knew the date he wouldn't have to estimate anything. If he knew the date he would know so much more. Perhaps.

He remembers this: it was cold when he got to Delhi. So painful, it must have been his first experience of cold. He knows this: cold comes to Delhi somewhere in the end of the year and continues to the beginning. December. January. He lost his family somewhere in that period of year.

The last birthday he celebrated with his family must have occurred at some other time of year. How else to explain that he has no memory of a birthday celebration? Children remember their birthday celebrations, don't they?

And he thinks he might have been four. He remembers answering with his fingers held up to match the fingers held up by an assortment of children surrounding him. Theirs: eight or nine. His: four.

He had to have been four for a fair amount of time when he held up those four fingers. Because wouldn't he remember if he had only just turned four, celebrating the birthday with his mother, brothers, sisters? He must have been nearly five. Nearly five. And this is how he's always thought about it, thinks about it now: worrying at bits and fragments of haze, chewing fog between his teeth.

Some years after that first cold day in Delhi, he is asked his age by a group of adults.

But first he is told to sit down, and does on a chair so light it slides around on the floor. Its seat, woven in plastic cane, is unravelling, opens under him, a hole not big enough for him to fall through, just big enough to grip him. He sits with knees jammed under his chin. The people across the desk and around the room consult each other in whispers. Then turn to him.

His age and name?

He holds up one hand in front of his face. He holds the other up and studies the faces around him through fingers he pops from his fists one by one.

'Chuk-Chuk,' he answers the second question first and works his deliberate way to seven.

'Seven,' he says.

Four fingers is a good place to start the count from. Add to four the three fingers of another hand, and seven is the correct answer. He's been living here nearly as long as he lived there, wherever there is. But not on his own, he reassures himself. He has his brothers at the train station; more brothers than there are fingers on both his hands.

He forces his fingers apart, slips the brothers from between them. He can't allow himself to think about them. Juice Uncle's impressed upon him the need to forget. 'If you want to live the rich life.' And Juice Uncle had wagged his forefinger under Chuk-Chuk's nose.

'You're not my father.' But Chuk-Chuk hadn't the courage to say it aloud. He aimed his muttering at his feet. Yes, Juice Uncle is right. The brothers have nothing to do with the rich life. And what is there to miss about sleeping tangled in legs? Their faces are persistent though.

How is it that Syam comes to him now? Standing behind all these grown-ups who are trying to decide if his papers add up to an American future. Syam the monkey. He hasn't seen Syam since the day he, performing for the gang's late-night amusement, jumping from the rooftop of one coach to the next, slipped and went under the wheels.

If the lady—the one who squeezed his arm, took him by the elbow and jerked him toward this office, then just before pushing him in the door, jerked his entire being up by the ear—if this lady hadn't said 'America', if she had said instead 'school' and 'bed' and 'sisters' and 'family' somewhere right there in Delhi, he would have said, 'no.' And if she had insisted, then he would have waited for his chance to slip out the building and return to his brothers at the train station. And as for Juice Uncle, he would have told him to fuck off.

No, he must leave off thinking about them. He fills his thoughts instead with the details of the Office he is seated in, this place from where he is to fly off into his future.

It is green outside the window and the sun shines through the green. Green streaks toward the sky following a sudden explosion of noise. From within the tree come faint peeps. Chuk-Chuk draws in his breath. Babies! He's wanted a baby parrot to raise for so long. He cranes his neck. Why the explosion of noise? But he is caught in his chair and can't see out.

Besides, he thinks, it's not like he expected he would know his brothers forever. Syam, for instance. He went off and died. All of them had turned away that night, listened in silence to the train gathering speed, then screeching to a halt further down the track as the alarm was sounded. What was it Pankaj said then? 'Let it be. The bastard's been trying to get himself killed since I first met him.' True, the littler ones cried for a bit, but not Chuk-Chuk.

They won't remember me either, he thinks with a pang.

Looping closer and further, as the man circles the neighbourhood, is the lonely sound of his cry to come bring knives for sharpening. Chuk-Chuk sinks incrementally into the grip of his chair, his mind emptying itself as the questions come at him, as the whispers of the men facing him give way to loud argument.

When Asa tries to remember the children he briefly held in the finger-count of his hands, he thinks of the green outside the window, of a voice calling, of his fingers splayed. But their faces elude him. Their names are dead. Whether they ever were is a question. Vertigo seizes him.

'From where?'

Just before they enter the Office of names and birthdates and unravelling chairs, the social worker woman asks him, 'From where?'

He wonders about lying. He shakes his head. He can't say from where. He doesn't know. He lets his eyes follow the length of the dark corridor to the door that leads out of the building, to the bright sunlight beyond. There is a road there that if he takes at a sprint he will surely find his way someplace where he is free of this woman. She jerks him by the ear. She barks at him.

'Look down when you are spoken to.'

Obediently, he looks down. The woman bends to bring her face to his and looks hard into his eyes. His desire to run is only half-formed. Equally formed is the desire for something nameless he wants from her. Something that now makes him thrust his chest at her. She frowns and he shifts his weight from one leg to the other. Anything to cover up how angry he feels. .

'If you don't give the right answer, you will remain here. Someone else, some better child who knows to be smart, will take your place. You know to be smart, don't you?'

Probably the people inside the Office will pay her if they like him. She'll beat him if he refuses to go along with her. But what's a few beatings? The truth is—and he has to give himself a moment at the door to the Office to take in the people seated inside, to take hold of the idea—the truth is, he would half-like to get in a plane, to go where he will ride horses, eat ice cream, wear beautiful shirts striped across the chest in blue and red.

He wants a hat like the one in *Benaam*. The little kidnapped boy with the brave face and the hat. The hat. He wants to dress like the boy, walk like the boy and have a massive hunt launched for him so he can be found, like the boy. He knows there is no chance his father is rich like the father of the *Benaam* boy. No chance his parents are beautiful.

And Pankaj, who runs his route with him at the station, has lectured the lot of them often enough that it's sunk in: 'You never want to go back. Stop wishing and waiting for the worst thing in the world. If you go back, your family, they'll lock you up. I remember what you don't.'

Pankaj clashes his teeth together at the end of the lecture. 'Eat you up, they will.'

Chuk-Chuk hums a song from the movie under his breath, '*Yaara o yaara, mein benaam ho gaya.*' He enters the Office, takes the seat they point him to.

'Train.'

He remembers train. And a few other things that are duly noted at the Office.

'From where?'

He sobs the words: 'I don't know. Don't know from where. I ran away because my mother and father were dead. There was no food to eat, and when I asked the people who lived near us for food, they beat me. I ran a long ways and now I don't know the name of where I ran from. I was four years old then. And I ran to the train station and came to Delhi on a train.'

The Social Worker Lady nods approvingly from the door.

Chuk-Chuk's story, which he knows is untrue in the moment of its first telling, and still untrue when retold in court—never told to David or Marge, for whom the version on paper seemed to suffice—and which story Asa has reminded himself all along is untrue, nevertheless begs to be examined. The woman in the corridor who bent over him and coached him in what to say—did she feed him the whole concoction or did she merely build from material he supplied? Is there an element of truth in any of what was duly noted at the Office, on papers Marge handed him nearly twenty years ago: legal-sized, gummed with grime, the letters on the page typed on some ancient machine, the keys of which must have been pounded, he can read the bumps and indents on the back of each page with his fingertips; and in indigo ink, the Government of India's stamp of approval on one Chuk-Chuk, so known by his orphanage name, Indian Citizen of Unknown Origin, certified Destitute, leaving its shores.

Asa has examined the papers; the bold stamp leaps out at him every time. He has examined the mistakes made by the typist; corrections have been rammed onto the mistakes; the weight of the new letter puncturing the old, the weight of the two puncturing the paper. He has read between the lines the despair of a dying insect, trailing wings and legs till here between Oct and 3 is the dropped wing, elsewhere the legs, embedded into the permeable page.

Some day he will write down for himself only that which he knows is true. Then he will open the file, do more than flip the pages to watch the indigo stamp jump in an up-down blur from one page to the next, nodding its yes-yes-yes; he will rip the pages.

David and Marge were not present at the first interview or even at the court date for which someone put shoes on him, leather that bit his feet. He's told the story of his first shoes to girlfriends along the way; it's never failed to pay off. At court, someone was there to represent David and Marge; and perhaps it was the same someone who then took him on the plane. The queasiness of that ride. The plane landed. He didn't know he was going to do it till too late; he threw up into the hands of the someone who was reaching to unsnap the seatbelt. He was wiped. His mouth sour, his whole being enraged, he clung to the someone.

At the end of the softly beeping hall of lights, they were pointed out to him. He struggled to see: the parents, David and Marge, and the sisters, Margaret and Veronica and Rebecca. Looking like the picture of them. Is it a picture he was shown on the plane or a picture he's seen since? He doesn't know. He saw them, and a tide of them, dozens and dozens more of them, a sea of people wearing red, carrying balloons, red, waving and cheering, louder with each step he took forward.

Did everyone wear red in this country? No, they were here for him, these people must be people related to his new parents, and the picture was righting itself—the space between the sea of red and the parents-sisters widening as they stepped toward him. It came to him then—the part he was to play, and he let go the hand of the someone and took a step alone, and another, and broke into a run and was swept up into the strange arms of the strange woman, the contact with whose body contorted his own, his spine arching and bucking, his feet pushing into her belly, pushing away from her smell and her feel, the hurt of her sight, wrong, wrong, wrong, and so right that his hands laced themselves behind her neck, and he clung for dear life.

Asa hunts under the bed, feeling in the pile of paper there, and retrieving a handful. He begins a list, writing with the stub of a pencil. When he runs—in daylight—into one of his night-time scribbles, he is shamed by the childish handwriting smeared slantwise across the page. In daylight, some of his lists reveal themselves written on top of other, older lists. The soft lead of his pencilled words is blurred, leaving rippled grey stains in place of words on the page. In daylight, he sniggers to distance himself from the memory of finding meaning in these words.

suitcase. it might have been a box.
name. did i have one?

This night, lying flat on his belly, he can picture the box. It is there, not just the word—box—and not the confused overlay of his daughter's pink suitcase over something grey and fuzzy. He is looking down at it. It might even be his hand that hovers somewhere in this picture, holding the metal handle of a small metal box, faded white-gold and dented. It lurches forward and then back. It raps his shin. He feels cold, feels he might begin shaking again.

Marge used to drive him when he was fifteen–sixteen, sometimes for hours, when this cold crept into him. She drove late into the night, heading toward distant towns; streamers of light flailing in the wind, then giving way to sporadic winks. And with the passing hours and the distance covered, these winks of light gave way to nothing. They drove till the corners of Marge's mouth lifted, till she began humming softly under her breath, sometimes 'Michael row your boat ashore', and he uncurled himself from the embarrassment of his foetal position to reply, 'Halleluiah.' Sometimes she attempted the more controversial, 'Servant Song', gauging where he was at by whether or not he joined in.

'*We are pilgrims on a journey. We are family on the road.*'

After the Gardner home bedtime hymns were exhausted, he could allow her to speak to him about the easy things in their lives: Becky's botched attempt at producing a four-course dinner the night before. The secret of good paella, then the secret of good risotto, then the secret joy of cooking alone, a glass of wine in hand.

Marge's out-in-the-open secret this: 'Nothing I long for more than to have you kids out of the kitchen, out of the house.'

This was Marge at her best. Marge, having reached this point in the drive, speaking in an understood code about how much she feared losing him, the son she liked to say she had moved heaven and earth to bring home. Even then he had known the jokes about getting rid of the kids, sending them their every which way, and the actual celebration when Meg, then Ronnie, then Becky departed for college, were all a cover for what could not be said to him: don't leave us. Even then he could never say, not even in the worst of his rages: but what if I am not really here?

What he said: I am leaving. You'll never see me again. I'm turning myself off, you hear. And on cue, they cried: Don't.

Once, at the end of one of these drives, he remembers they stopped by the side of the road, and fell asleep waiting for dawn because Marge had remembered the road travelled through a wetland and was sure that light, when it came, would reveal water fowl. He slept fitfully and woke to find the sun in full blaze. Marge was fiddling with the radio, looking for a signal that wasn't there. Her face was imprinted with the pebbled surface of the car's fake leather seat, and the smile she turned to him was tired. The cruel in him pushed his mouth open, wide, as if to take a bite. He had to struggle to close it.

'I am hungry,' he said.

They were two, three hours from any sort of food. Dutifully, she rummaged in her purse and fished out a cigar someone at the office had handed out. A blue satin ribbon—It's a Boy—slid free, along with the cellophane cover; both were allowed to vanish somewhere on the floor. Her tired smile grew more lopsided; she handed him the cigar.

'Now you can't tell anyone it was your mother who corrupted you, all right?'

He squinted against the sunlight coming through the windshield and asked about the ducks or whatever birds it was she was so keen to show him. She choked on smoke, she was laughing that hard, as she waved at the landscape outside their window. It seemed it was near here that she had swum once on some field trip from school. He added this picture of her to the collection he kept of her childhood.

'We came,' she said, 'to the marshy end of the lake to take a wildlife census. We tiptoed, wanting to not frighten them away.'

He felt shy listening to her girlhood voice. Its earnestness—did she know how much in love he was with her as a girl?

'So, is it the wrong time of year for wildlife?'

'No, Asa. I think they are all dead and gone. Looks like a mill or something over there. And it's probably why all you see is this dried-up gloop.'

And it was true that the ground sloping down from the shoulder of the highway looked like the cracked top of the oatmeal cookies Marge baked. There was nothing wholesome about it though; just a puffiness along the edges of the cracks that looked to him like some kind of sickness.

'Suppuration,' Marge offered, and he shrugged, not knowing the word and not wanting to be told.

'Why are you laughing then?'

'Nothing. Nothing. Just can't believe I waited all night to see this.'

She was pointing to the cracks. There was stillness there that, if you stared at long enough, allowed you access: a quick movement in the shadows, the flicker of life. Chameleons. Dozens of them, in place of the missing birds. He thought lazily about getting himself a tattoo, a chameleon asleep in the crook of his elbow.

Back home, Marge had him work on the cleanup: 'Your mess, you clean up.'

She went to have a lie down, but he could hear her through the bedroom door, murmuring into the phone. The rest of the family were long gone from the house. It was past noon. He hauled the coffee table he had smashed out to the carport. The stereo he had smashed against the coffee table was weirdly in one piece, but inside the wooden shell there was the rattle of things come loose. He left it on the kerb in the hope that someone interested in tinkering with it would take it home. He thought about picking up the phone in the kitchen and listening in to see what Marge was saying about him. He didn't. He wondered whether stereos could be bought singly, in which case it wouldn't, he thought hopefully, cost as much as if he had to replace the whole set.

He knew it was wrong to feel resentful about it, but did anyway. He had only broken one. No doubt he would have to buy a full set. He rinsed the glass of water he was drinking from, then let it drop into the sink where it shattered. He let his hand hang there in the air. A drop elongated from the faucet lip and landed on the hand he watched tremble. He listened for Marge's conversation to end.

He's allowed his mind to drift. He has let the box disintegrate into so much metallic snow; little dots of the image are separating rapidly from one another, opening space in place of coherence.

Again, it is Marge who fills the space, who keeps coming to him these days, crisp in a way she wasn't the years he lived with her. He is not certain why this is—perhaps it is the result of maturity, or distance, or both. In the years living with her, an arid landscape had bound them. At its centre, she was the single bloom, blur-edged in the heat of their proximity. Two decades have passed and there is coolness that finally allows him to see her. And here she is: hopeful. He had always felt in the years with her, and he told her when he left, that she had failed in her responsibility to swallow that hope, to hide it away from him. How dare you hope for me? To which she did not reply.

'Go.'

It was David who said the word. And other things Asa had been humiliated, then frightened by. And he had rushed to leave. What he can see now and acknowledge is relief that she had failed as he had always suspected she would. And this allows him to forgive her as he never could when they were a family.

What was it she used to murmur to him on those drives, when she wasn't making the sort of brittle-bright chatter a girl on a date might, or when she wasn't singing hymns that forced him out of his sulk if only to roll his eyes at her:

'Forever, Asa. We are forever. Nothing can change that, not even you.'

The heat of those statements. The difficulty in seeing where those words came from.

He pushes Marge from his mind and tries to gather back the colours and sounds of his hand swinging the box. Now that the image is gone, he is certain the hand was his. There are no pictures of him till at whatever age he was, maybe seven, maybe eight, when Marge and David met him at the airport and snapped at least a hundred photographs of him. Try as he might, he can't think of what his hand in any of those pictures looked like. He is walking alone in those pictures, a thin shirt, pants pooling at his feet, a little bear purchased by the escort dangling from one hand.

Ah, now he's got the hand. He proceeds with it. He reconstructs the feeling of the sun on his hand, of the metal handle sharp in his palm, then tries for the box, but already self-correction is starting in.

The image is too much like one Marge and David might have shown him some family evening, all four children seated on the floor of the family room, faces turned to a screen on which footage—older than they, jerky and grainy footage of Marge or David's goofy childhood—unspools. Does Marge bring out a big bowl of popcorn? She does. Is it, some of it, burnt? Yes, and what isn't, tastes scorched. Does he complain? Yes, he complains— while black and white and light flickers across their faces, and a pleasant humming and rattling sounds in their ears. On the screen someone pushes someone on a swing. The swing lurches forward toward the camera, carrying aboard and closer-larger by the split-second the chubby cherubic someone. The child is incontrovertibly real—capable of swinging thus and forever because she is ravelled in film.

But more of his box-memory is returning. The hand clutching the box may not be his (he is doubtful again). It may be the replica of the one belonging to the chubby girl clutching the swing's rope. The rhythm of the box swinging may be borrowed from the swing lurching at the camera, but now he knows for sure there was a box because it lies open on the ground, its contents are being examined—by who—for something warm for him to wear. He remembers putting on all the clothes in the box, pulling on two, three, four shorts and as many shirts, one on top of the other in an attempt to get warm. It must have been a small box. It fit in his hands. Four-year-old hands?

He adds '*box*' to his list.

He crosses out '*box*', and writes in its place '*box for school*'. Then crosses out '*box for school*', replacing it with '*school box*'. Little children in India must have carried small metal boxes to school some thirty–forty years ago. They might still carry boxes. He tries to think of images he has seen on the news and a few times in magazines. Nothing comes to mind.

Then: a line of children, teeth flashing in their faces.

Asa changes the channel when India suddenly appears behind the news anchor. Of late, these scraps of India are increasingly on the screen. And most horrifying are the advertisements—for insurance, beverage, home appliances—all featuring full-blown Indian families. Happy families, seated together on sofas, grouped on lawns, smashed together into cars, bizarrely perched on cliff tops. He is riveted.

Occasionally he is unsure if the pictured family might not be Mexican. Usually he knows when it is an Indian family. Mexicans sell beer and are noisy, festive. Indians in these advertisements never sell beer, portray a sober happiness, the father figure almost always in a suit, tie loosened, and the dead give-away—the mother, vibrant in some sort of get-up. Often enough, a dot glares from her forehead.

He studies these families, their skin colour, in particular. Families, not too dark-skinned, definitely not light. Medium

236 | *Mridula Koshy*

brown. He is darker than they are. The skin of his cheek is stretched as tight as the skin of his sisters', has the crispness of theirs, is even more of an apple than theirs in the high polish radiated along the edge of sharp bone. But his skin of a spoilt apple is as black-brown as that of the line of school-children who reappear in their school-children line, doing some sort of conga; each child has arms stiff and straight on the shoulders of the child in front. Look how uniformly ashy all their elbows are despite the gleaming black-brown elsewhere. The conga line is snaking through and around itself, like a needle splitting and turning to thread itself. Children in dark, pleated skirts or pleated shorts, white shirts, smile at him, their tight cheeks exploding the light of joy in their eyes, bouncing it at him, telling him something he wants to understand.

This is not an image from the news. He is in the line-up. But he doesn't know which one he is, and if he concentrates on the question, he will lose the children. He breathes with the ceiling, closing in and receding from himself, shallow breaths, and the children stay with him a few seconds, long enough for him to glimpse little metal boxes swinging in the hands of all that laughter.

'I was there.'

He turns over, presses his face into the sheets, seeking some curled worm of leftover warmth from his daughter's sleep the night before. The sheets are just sheets. They give him nothing. And, even when she is here, she isn't. Refusing his daughter the 'No', the never asking her to put away her plate, to pick up the candy wrappers she strews throughout the apartment—he refuses her substance. Asa shivers.

And if he continues refusing her, then what will she prove to him? In her survival, in her triumphant preservation of her substance, will he find proof of his own substance? But but . . . if she doesn't, and then? He settles the question as he has in the past: she is a tough one, a born survivor. And besides, she has her mother.

In a panic, he returns to the earlier puzzle: where is the box? The hand holding the box?

It was easier when he first took the apartment. Noel was excited to play at housekeeping for her father. And he had responded by purchasing a mop and bucket, cookie dough rolls and sheets she approved for his bed.

'That one will make you feel like you are in a garden, and that will be sooo happy.'

Now, the every-other-weekend visits end with him in the kind of rage that tossed him out the door, chasing after her departure earlier that evening. The kid was a mistake, he thinks. Though he doesn't really mean Noel when he thinks 'kid'. Noel is exempt from that thought. The kid who shouldn't be and Noel who is, exist side by side in his head. He moves between them.

Asa wonders what LeAnn tells herself these days about their separation. What had he promised her when she was expecting?

'Let me be the father. I can love the baby.'

He answers the accusation he imagines in LeAnn's silence: a life without suitcases. Not in my power to give her.

The meaning of me, Asa continues his dog-like circling, tamping the ground of his mind in search of where he will rest. I have no compulsion to inflict pain. Other people separate from their wives and require their daughters to carry suitcases on three-hour drives. He winces, thinking of Noel's carsickness. It doesn't make other people into monsters. To live my life, why should it make me a monster?

'Is this the meaning of me?'

He is overcome by self-pity: to alone be a monster, to alone betray all he loves, to turn the dearest to dust with his touch. He exists so all others who are lacking can still be found human, not monster. As long as there is Asa Gardner, no one else need be a monster.

No, the compulsion is not to inflict pain, not on his daughter. The compulsion is to escape pain. It is the cool wave before sleep, the wave that ushers in sleep, the wave that is sleep.

Sleep hits, he jumps back from the brink. There is a hand pressed to the small of his back. He whispers the one word he remembers. 'Amma.' When the weight remains, light and persistent, he whispers his promise, 'I'm remembering everything.'

He reaches for the pencil and paper and crosses out *'school box'* from his list, and replaces it with *'box'*. Because, would a school box contain clothes to ward off the cold? But what is a suitcase doing in the hands of school children? The list stands as before:

suitcase. it might have been a box.
name. did i have one?
box . it was a box, not a suitcase

Hastily he adds other words to the list; these are words familiar to him, from older lists:

chameleon airport search hole magician train swing name name name

At the top of the page, he writes in large letters: *My name is Asa Gardner.*

The advice of one Mrs Morris, his first teacher in the US, to 'grip the pencil like this and repeat after me while writing, "My name is Asa Gardner"', is a directive to him for all the years since he first sat across from her.

On that day, he had not known his teacher's language. But he knew the name his new parents called him by, and he was pretty sure that although Mrs Morris was kind to him as she showed him how to grip the pencil, there would be punishment either from her or them, or perhaps from both her and them, if he didn't make his pencil write as she had written on the page.

'When we begin,' she explained with weary patience, 'we always begin with our name.' Then she had pointed at herself and said, 'My name is Mrs Morris.' She pointed at him and he repeated after her, the two of them keeping time to the insistent tap of her index finger on his chest, 'My name is Asa Gardner.'

Back then he thought all of this fair enough. The name given to him by his brothers at the train station—Chuk-Chuk—was nonsense. And not what was meant when the men at the Office asked him for his name. Still, he had offered Chuk-Chuk, and the men made faces and shook their heads. The woman in the doorway glared. He sank deeper into the hole in the chair.

'It's not a good name. I know. I'm looking for a different one.'

With grunts and gestures, and with their smiles, the children call to him to come out. He, hair oiled for the journey, now stuck over with dust, and eyes round from strain, is squeezed behind a metal tank, lined along its front with taps. Earlier in the day, the children had tried coaxing the tiny creature with similar grunts and gestures, similar smiles; he had scuttled further back, as far from their reach as he could. But it is getting colder. Night approaches. The crowd of thousands has thinned to one of hundreds. His many shirts and shorts piled one on top of the other cannot ward off the cold. So cold he is that night, he stops crying for his mother, disregards her last admonition to keep the school box with him always, to remember to look for his name printed on the sheet she tore from his school notebook and affixed there. He leaves off trying to peel the paper from the box. He leaves the box in the space behind the water cooler at the end of the railway platform, crawls out, steps toward the boys; the weight of her hand falters on his back. He steps toward the boys, though the lifting of her hand leaves him unmoored. He steps toward them because they wear shirts buttoned askew and pants held to their waists with ropes. No adults among them.

He follows the boys who show him how to climb the girders, to shelter in the space between the dropped ceiling and the real roof of the station platform. He curls there in the friendly pile of bodies. His bare legs, burning from the cold of the metal, seek among the clad legs till someone allows him to push his legs in between theirs. He tucks himself in, the hand on his back, so light now it is a waking dream.

'Amma,' he whispers the one word he will hold on to for the rest of his life. 'I'm remembering everything. I'll tell you all. Only come soon.' And there flashes before him the other woman with the white hair, the toys, the hole in the floor, the man, the town and the long street, the dark room in the building, climbing out of the window. 'Amma,' he whispers again. Then he pushes his mother away to make space for sleep.

In the morning, when the boys ask him again, their language a laughing game he cannot enter, he points to the trains roaring and idling below their rooftop nest; he is helpless to stop the bashful smile that is spreading his face. A joke bubbles in him. A poor one he hopes will win him a place with them.

Chuk Chuk Chuk Chuk Chuk.

The boys laugh. Genuinely friendly boys.

I came on the train, he says.

His baby face, plumped by recent feedings, fear in his eyes paired with the open smile—the recent privileges of a mothered child—win him a place in their midst. They do not grudge him who he has been. Not when he has become as they are. The name they give him is his to keep for the years it takes him to forget nearly every word he has ever known as his. He forgets 'son' and 'food' and the place that is home. And he begins the forgetting with 'Madhu', the name for himself.

4

Search

Afternoons in the suburbs of Los Angeles linger with the absorbed interest of the child, tip of the tongue visible, contemplating the next stroke of paint on paper. This May afternoon lingers, dipping into the sun, splashing light, pooling it on red-tiled rooftops, cream stucco sides, sheeting it across dark, glass-coated buildings. These buildings, not quite high-rises, modest centres of commerce, want nothing to do with the afternoon; the busy hum within relies on a twenty-four hour supply of light so tame it responds to the flick of the switch. Elsewhere though, afternoon penetrates scrub-brush on bare hillsides, and in a building tucked away in one hillside, the crumbling bones of a woman, who sighs in gratitude.

This is a woman whose breasts are covered in skin so soft they are softer than the underside of new leaves, so polleny they film the fingertips of her two daughters as they dress and undress her. Her breasts, flat and empty, withered, hang, but are not pendulous. They are without weight, like paper crumpled and tossed. Like the parachute, which spreads the ground after descent, drab save for a shimmering in pockets of air trapped within; the woman's

242

breasts hang, spread and shimmer. They are silk spilled from seed-pods. Dorothea scoops them in her palms and lifts them to soap underneath. Kirstein keeps a towel ready.

The daughters had picked their way earlier in the morning across the nursing home's tiny pretence of green, carefully avoiding what the wind had scattered about, objects that if stepped on would have rolled them forward and off the narrow diamond-point toes of their shoes. Without speaking of it, the two of them handling their mother's breasts, think of those objects on the lawn, of the split husk, the seed and floss within. The daughters, fetching and carrying and passing back and forth square and round and hard and soft objects over the reclining form of their mother, are as wonderfully content as if they are children once again, watching their mother mix the hot into the cold before slipping them into the womb of a warm bath. The daughters are as happy as they were when as children they begged their mother to let them turn the table: to play that she was the child and they her mother, and she obliged, perching on a miniature chair, her hands obediently at rest on her knees, her knees drawn to her chest, allowing them to feed her spoonfuls of air. No longer children, as old as their mother once was, their mother older than she was, they find their dearest wish granted. The mother has become the child. They arrange her body, feed her and reassure themselves that finally she is not only loving them, but allowing them to love her as well.

'Mom?' they whisper hesitantly. Their mother is asleep. A brisk bit of tidying ensues, and then Dorothea and Kirstein leave the room. They are filled with excitement. In the lobby they sit, knees touching as they whisper, and wait for the appointed hour when they will proceed down the hall, to the right, to meet with Palm Haven's visiting psychiatrist, to find out from him what they already know—their mother, more than a little tired since her most recent stroke, needs only rest and care to cure her of these fantasies about a baby boy who needs her.

Inside her room, Gretchen inches her hips into the patch of sunlight that's crawled away while she napped. 'Dorothea,' she tries calling. The sun-warmed room strains to reply.

She stops the slide of her hips; the patch of sun has found her. Back arched, it rubs against Gretchen's leg, and purrs in response as Gretchen mumbles, 'kitty, here kitty.' Little hairs tingle on Gretchen's calves as the electricity built up in the blanket sets off sparks. Gretchen snaps awake.

'So I never tell her that I almost changed my mind when I saw her child. I agree to take her child. I write her name on the paper. Not the child's. My feeling always was someday I will return to tell her the child grew up well.'

'Mrs Oster, you have her name written down somewhere?'

'The name is of no use to you till you find the child. My daughters are worried that I have made this up. But no. The child is real. I am worried to find the child. How can I return to her without the child?'

'Mrs Oster, let me step out and just speak to your daughters for a bit. We'll talk some more after that. Is that all right, Mrs Oster, if we talk some more?'

'No, stay,' Gretchen tries to call out. But she knows he is not in the room. That he left hours before. That her daughters came and they left too. She is alone. She can feel something climb in her. Is she angry? Why does anger make her want to weep? What is she to do now?

'The man is not a detective.'

Gretchen can see that now.

'I have to tell. If the girls don't want to know, I have to tell someone else. She was quite lovely. Younger than I was. She, in her life, and I, in mine. And now I feel her. I feel her leaving. Is she gone? She was younger than me. But maybe a hard life, it must be, makes her older. Now I feel her. Now. She suffers.

'I have my daughters. It's taken me a whole lifetime to find my daughters, here by my side. Who does she have? I must find him. I must take him by the hand and go to her. There is no other way. I cannot go back empty-handed.

'She will say, "Where is my son?"'

'How can I tell her, "We lost him."'

'But how can I tell Dorothea? How can I tell Kirstein?'

Outside Gretchen's door, the murmuring increases and decreases. The drone of wheels—those of lunch trolleys, wheelchairs and walkers—rumble closer and recede. When will someone come in to talk to her?

Outside, the murmuring continues. Gretchen does not hear Dr Buenning, in his office, advise her daughters that it is not impossible there is some basis to the story their mother tells about the missing child lost at the train station. Perhaps there had been a genuine desire to adopt such a child. Certainly she must have seen homeless children wander the streets of those poor countries she travelled in the years she was married to the diplomat.

'He was a diplomat, wasn't he?'

No. The daughters shake their heads a little embarrassedly.

Oh he wasn't? That was a bit of grandiosity the old woman furnished her story with then.

'He was an accountant, attached to the Embassy.'

'Perhaps he, your mother's first husband, stopped her from taking in one of those poor children that she wanted to. She doesn't have any contact with him. At least this is what I understood from my talk with her. And you don't have any way to reach him?'

'That shouldn't be a concern,' Dr Buenning continues. 'It is more than likely there is some truth in what your mother says. But speculating about the past, what is fact and what is not, or even setting out in some sort of detective fashion to unravel the facts, as your mother seems to want me to do, I just wouldn't advise it. The story is fantastic, even with whatever element of truth there might be. And chasing after it distracts from what really needs to be addressed.'

Kirstein and Dorothea exchange equally triumphant looks. For a moment, Dr Buenning has the sense he is not present in the conversation.

'Your mother,' he explains, addressing both of them, still unsure which of the two is the elder or the leader, they so seamlessly switch from hectoring to hectored, 'has some deep anxieties about her role in your lives, about her role as your mother. What she needs so she can free herself from this delusion of the lost child is consistent encouragement from the two of you. The shift here, to a nursing home, has played a role in undermining her security. Remember, old age does not have to equate with helplessness or anxiety. In her case, once she settles into this place, and it may take some time, she is going to be fine. Meanwhile, you may observe she continues to be a little forgetful, to make up stories to fill in the gaps in her memory. They don't have to be stories of anxiety. Not if you concentrate on reassuring her.'

Back inside the now dark room, the daughters work at reassuring their mother. They transform themselves into murmuring shadows moving through her sleep. Drifting awake for a moment, Gretchen thinks of a distant afternoon in her past and of someone else murmuring. She returns to dreaming. A rift opens in the sky. It is a dark line, unbroken, but jagged. As deep as a canyon. The beating of ten thousand wings fills it with sound. She opens her eyes.

'Is it the time? Birds are migrating.'

'Mom?'

'You are wonderful daughters,' she whispers.

'Mom. Mom,' comes their reply.

'Shhh, shhh now,' they say as she begins to cry.

They stroke her cheeks. They make elaborate efforts to comfort her, raising her upright on her motorized bed, turning the television on, and when she quarrels with that, turning it off, drawing the vertical blinds, then shutting them, settling for turning the rod that sets the slats at a slant, striping them in the last light stopped there at the window. They work hard to look past the restlessness of their mother's legs under the bed covers, the legs that slide there under the covers—surprisingly quick they are for someone so frail.

'You have been such a good mother,' they tell her, their words nearly combative in the jumbled rush of their delivery. They stroke her legs that continue sliding under the sheets. It's not yet time for them to feel exasperated.

'We love you. We love you,' they repeat.

She does not acquiesce.

'We travelled for two days and two nights. He kept his face pressed to the window. If I tried to touch him, to turn him from the window, he goes limp. I let him to be alone. He never cried after the first hour. I was so frightened he would cry. We were in the first class carriage. I tell Hendrik we cannot fly because there can be no privacy on a plane. I thought, on a train you can close the door and stay like it is your own home. But he never cried. I gave him sweets and the toys that I have for him to play. He paid no attention. Just watching all the time from the window, even when it turns so dark. To make him to sleep, I have to pull down the shutter. He sleeps next to me. This gives me hope. Before sleeping, Hendrik takes him to the bathroom. When they come back, he nods to me it is fine. It is like that for two days. Too easy, we are not expecting.

'When we are after Agra, there is only few hours maybe left and Hendrik takes him for one last visit to the bathroom. They do not come back for a long time. I decide to not worry. Hendrik wants to brush the child's teeth. I tell him it doesn't matter about the teeth. But he insists to take the boy. I thought perhaps this is the reason they delay. Perhaps it is hard to teach him to brush if he has not been brushing till that point. I am preparing water and a comb to make the child look nice. Hendrik comes back. But no child. I have a cup full of water and a little comb for dipping in the cup. Hendrik comes back without the baby. I cry and scream and tear his face. He keeps shaking his head like he has no words to say.

'He lost the baby. It is like this. He takes the baby to the station platform. He takes him from the train to use the bigger bathroom on the platform; he loses the baby. How? He has to hold my hand to stop me killing him. He closes the door and does not permit for me to call the police. In the next station, we leave the train. It is Delhi. We are in Delhi.'

'We love you. We love you,' Gretchen's daughters repeat. She acquiesces.

5

Chameleon

The first night, home from the airport, they herd him into his very own room. Early that night he wails, nearly on schedule, hourly. Between wailing he seems to sleep. David says—

'Not to worry. He will soon stop.'

After that he wails every half-hour, then every few minutes till Marge lays a sleeping bag on the floor next to his bed. By morning, he is running a mild fever and she keeps him in bed, where he finally sleeps. Not fitfully, as he has during the night. Mid-day, the fever is still there, low and persistent. She calls the doctor. She takes some aspirin and a glass of juice to the boy. He smiles at her from the bed. He takes the glass and gulps noisily from it. His eyes meet hers over the rim. He puts one hand out, palm to her face, as if he is blind and reading her face with his hand.

The hand is hot and dry. She has a moment to register its feel before he pushes her face away. She reacts without thinking— pushes back at the hand with her face. There is a tussle and she sees him in that split second; his eyes are fearful. He drops his hand abruptly and looks into the glass. She is left with the glossy top of his head. Heat springs in her chest, spreads to her face. He grimaces and she thinks he might bite the glass. She tries to gentle her eyes and smooth her face. She attempts a hand to the top of his head. He is immediately contrite. He takes her hand between his and strokes it. She marvels, and imagines that he marvels, at the contrast between their hands.

She calls David to come up and help her carry the boy to the living room where she can keep an eye on him from the kitchen. All five of them are home that day to help the newcomer to better know them. Becky trails David upstairs, but halts at the doorway. She offers that she can play the piano.

'Because,' she says, 'music will be a way for him to connect. The universal language.'

David tells her she can play as long as the rest of the family can connect to this universal language. Becky sulks in the doorway. She feels herself prickle these days at her father's jokes—their invitation to seal herself shut in his world.

And there is as well her father's hurrying up the stairs, the urgency in her mother's voice as she calls to her father. None of it suits Becky.

Meg and Ronnie had not felt embarrassed as Becky had when the church put together a pancake breakfast to raise money for the adoption. They dressed up to stand behind the steel tables in the church basement and serve the line of well-wishers. Meg wore a suit from her mother's younger days, and Ronnie a pink dress, the skirt of which was made so its accordion pleats would remain knife sharp under any circumstance. Her mother was so distracted by the argument over what shoes the elder girls would wear—not the four inch platforms Ronnie had bought for herself—Becky got away with wearing her painter pants. And she was grateful to be in something other than the ice cream shades the rest of the

family was decked in—did they plan it, all of them, even Dad?—
when at the end of the breakfast, Father Chuck and Mr Carver
pulled them up on stage to receive the blown-up cheque for an
amount much larger than the breakfast had raised. The Sielmans
had stepped in, shiny-headed Mr Sielman and his toothy wife,
with enough so even the plane fare was covered.

More absurd still, her family's failure to be horrified when a
picture of the boy finally arrived—so ugly, so not a baby—along
with yet another sheaf of papers to keep the parents busy for days.

Right at this moment, the elder girls are downstairs putting
pies into the oven, getting ready for the visitors who are expected
to stream in throughout the day. And they are cheerful as they
perform the odious task of being a family for this boy.

Becky decides they must all be pretending. Ronnie, who's never
cared about anyone besides herself, she at least must be pretending.
With Meg, yes, possibly there is something there. And Mom and
Dad? Becky watches them puttering around the boy. Becky is
stoic in the face of the unbelievable.

Marge whispers to David, 'Do you think we should find a way
to let people know to not come? I mean, he is sick. It could be
overwhelming.'

'Impossible.'

He bends to scoop up the boy. Asa lies limp, offering no
resistance, but neither any assistance.

'Up you go.' David speaks gently to the boy. 'I'm not going to
hurt you. There's a TV in the living room for you. Much better
than being in here alone. Don't you think?'

In David's arms, Asa is an ungainly heap. Asa turns his eyes in
appeal to Marge.

'Let me get him, David. He's not so heavy.'

She holds her arms out. Immediately, Asa arches his back and begins flailing. Marge retreats. Then she insists. David proceeds to transfer the boy in his arms to Marge's. Asa lies still. At the door, Becky rolls her eyes, walks over to her father and holds his hand; the two of them follow Marge and her bundle, making slow progress down the stairs to the living room.

The lace cover is removed from the television and it is turned on. Asa visibly cheers up. Straightening from his slump, he pushes the heavy hair off his eyes to follow the action on the screen: a cartoon tiger. It speaks. Even in this itchy-scratchy language, it is easy to recognize the bluff heartiness of a scam.

'I'm Tony the Tiger and for years I've been saying Kellogs Sugar Frosted Flakes are G-r-r-reat.'

A little boy is sitting in the middle of a field of wheat. He is sitting, pulled up to a table, on a fine-looking chair. On the table there are obscure things to eat. The boy though is clearly a boy, exactly as a little boy should be. Chubby. His skin is white. His hair is yellow. It is strange that all of this should be in the middle of a wheat field. Where are the walls and the roof, the house that should surround the boy?

The tiger talks to the boy.

'But I'll bet that you don't even know what they are made of, do you? Well, it's this—the golden goodness of corn.'

The tiger plucks something from the field with his paws. Asa gives his head a baffled shake. Turns to ask, Did you see that? But there is no one there he can ask anything. He leans forward to watch closely. Yes, the tiger is having trouble. The thing will not stay in the tiger's paw. It wants to slide off the flat surface. What is the thing the tiger is holding fumblingly? So he was wrong to think it a field of wheat. It is a field of corn. Asa watches to see if the tiger will drop his awkward treasure. The yellow haired boy never stops smiling, does not lean forward to understand why the ear of corn hasn't ripped the paper of the tiger's paw. Asa sits back in his seat, tries to take his cue from the boy, who is such a boy they have put him in the TV to be a boy. Asa smiles wide. As for the ear of corn, even if it were stuck there with the toughest paste, even then . . . This is certainly a scam and the fool of a boy doesn't know it. Asa tries to hum along with the tiger's singing way of talking. It's easy even if he doesn't know the words. He's always been good at singing.

'Kellogs takes it, flakes it, sweetens it with just the right amount of sugar, then fortifies it with eight vitamins. And the taste, well, you tell'em little buddy.'

And the smiling boy manages words without the least flutter of his lips.

'They're Gr-r-reat.'

A voice next to him, the stupid-girl voice of the stupid girl who keeps staring at Asa, says the same thing as the boy.

'They're Gr-r-reat.'

He is glad to see that the girl cannot manage the trick of smiling while speaking while stretching lips while words issue without any movement of lips. Asa frowns at her. She is supposed to be one of his sisters. She comes and sits next to him on the beautiful velvet sofa they have given him for a seat. He bristles. Smiling at her, he scoots his cross-legged body sideways to nudge her away. He knows why she hates him. She must be what decided them— his new parents—to send for him. What a disappointment to produce girl after girl after girl. Maybe he should be grateful to her for being a stupid girl. Because here he is, isn't he, on the softest of sofas, in the house of the richest people in the world, watching television and drinking juice. His knees press insistently into her side. She frowns. He rocks and his knees jab into her thigh. She gets up hastily.

Something else is starting on the television. My space, he thinks. They gave me this space, put me on the sofa with this blanket over my lap. Why should she come to ruin his TV watching? He continues smiling at her.

'Bitch, my space.'

She pats his shoulder. He shrugs her hand off. The other two sisters come into the room. A glob of something to eat lies inert on a small plate. The tallest of them holds the plate out to Asa.

This one will get married soon. She should. She looks old and tired. That will be one less in the house to figure out.

The thing to eat is in his hand. It is like nothing he has ever seen before. It looks like shit. It smells like soap. He is returned to the plane ride. To the numbers of times this lady or that lady came from this end or that end of the plane, pushing a cart, dispensing trays of inedible things. The tears start in his eyes. He wants to watch TV and he wants them to move so he can do it. He waves his arms at them. Move, he indicates. The two of them stand smiling in the same way the women on the plane did, as if their smile alone is enough. Enough for what? He can't remember where he was headed with that thought. His irritation overwhelms him. It competes with other instincts, and has its way.

'You think your bitch-smiles are better than the TV?'

They keep smiling and the thing in his hand is hot and oozing. His stomach turns.

'He wants you to move. He just shoved me off the sofa.'

'Becky, give him time.'

'Hey, if he's not going to eat that, can I have it?'

The middle girl who has been quiet till now speaks. 'They're really for the guests.'

She has the same horrible way of speaking they all have, as if her mouth is filled with something slippery. She steps forward. Once again the screen is obscured. He wants to kick her. She is big and would probably beat him.

The man who is the father comes into the room. His teeth remain bared for a second after he halts, then they are swallowed, the lips vanish, and his mouth is a slit. His eyebrows fold up together and big pieces of his face turn grey. He is very angry. He speaks loudly. But not too loudly.

'Turn the TV off. This. This. Lies. That crook. A pack of lies. What is happening to us?'

Asa watches the man, then the girls. He holds himself very still. Something bad is going to happen. The man points to the TV and says the same word again and again.

'This. This. This.'

'Daddy,' says the little girl.

She doesn't sound scared. But Asa watches the man; he is careful not to let on he is watching; he moves his eyes, not his head. He gives himself a mental nod of recognition: too smart, you are, aren't you, Chuk-Chuk?

The middle girl hands Asa a glass. The bubbles popping inside tickle his nose. It looks like Limca, but tastes like nothing. A longing in his throat. The sob that lives there is hard to subdue. The station platform. Card games. Who brought the crate? The lovely clinking of a full crate, better than a thousand cycle bells. A bottle apiece. All of them. Some drinking fast. Some drinking slow. He drinks fast. He hates the ones still nursing their bottles. Chuk-Chuk. Someone laughs. Everyone laughs. The stuff is streaming from his nose.

'Chuk-Chuk.'

Did he say it out loud? Better not do that again.

'Asa.'

The angry father crosses the room in two strides. He switches the TV off.

Asa bursts into tears.

'Asa Asa Asa.' He repeats the mantra into his glass. 'It was a mistake. I forgot. I won't say it again. Don't turn the TV off.'

The bubbles keep tickling him. He cries and drinks. The two older girls crowd in and try to take the glass from him. He grips the glass to hold on to it.

'I'm drinking it,' he pleads. 'I like it. I forgot for just a minute. Turn the TV on.'

The little girl says, 'You better turn the TV on. That's what he wants.'

The woman, who is the mother, comes into the room. She sits next to him, carefully puts her arms around him. His skin burns from her touch.

'Aaah,' he cries aloud.

She pats him, each pat branding him. Fire touch—Fire removed—Fire touch.

'Aaah. Aaah. Aaah.'

She snatches her hand away as if it is she who has been burnt. He gives up pretending to drink the salty water and cries in big gulps, swallowing sounds and snot, even his tears, so his eyes strain from the pressure of everything he is swallowing. He flings himself into the woman's body. She touches him all over, stroking his head, rubbing his back in small circles. It doesn't hurt. He stays crumpled into her, holding himself in anticipation of the pain.

The mother murmurs, 'Asa Asa Asa.'

He murmurs the words with her, 'Asa Asa Asa.'

The little girl says, 'Turn on the TV.'

Asa looks up from where he has buried his face in the woman's body. The man is turning something round on the TV and now the TV expands from a pinpoint of light to a full burst of picture. The man turns another knob now. Each turn is a new picture. Like a Dilli Dekho. Each turn is a sharp sound followed by the new picture. Too quick to see.

On the next click they pass a train chugging. Asa yelps.

The little girl again, 'He wants that.'

Asa has only a second to register she's helped him. He makes his face smile at her. She grimaces back, her face reflecting his. He tries to correct his smile.

She mouths something, 'The hippest trip in America.'

'Fine,' says the father. 'As long as we're not watching that crook lying to us every chance he gets.' Though he has put the smile of many teeth back on his face, the father's mouth is muttering to the mother. 'The man's lied to us and we keep giving him the platform from which to do it.'

Asa knows about the kind of anger that belongs to the father; a kind of anger which wants to be known and feared but also wants to pretend that it is not anger. This man wants to frighten everyone, and he wants everyone to love him as well. Asa wonders if the father has changed his mind, if he wants to send him back on the plane. Will the plane take him back to Delhi? Is that man who brought him still waiting where they left him at the airport? What if the man is gone already?

There is no time to puzzle out the father. On the TV a very black man is holding a mike. He is singing. There are many other black men behind this man. They are beating on drums and holding up other instruments, the kind of instruments you see at a wedding. Instruments as big as the men carrying them, plates that clang and bells that blow, to the left to the right. Come and show if you know to dance. Here comes the drum. It jerks a beat from Asa.

Now Asa notices there are women among these black men. They are equally black, which is what made it so hard at first to see them separate from the men. The music makes the people on TV dance. It makes Asa dance, seated on the sofa—a dance that takes his shoulders and head while the rest of him remains in the arms of the woman.

Bright lights on the TV because it is night in there. The father and the sisters stand watching the TV quietly. Asa moves cautiously away from the mother. He pretends it is his dancing that is taking him. She removes her arm. He tries to enjoy himself. His mind is not able to stop worrying.

Stupid. Stupid. He shouts silently at himself. Stop worrying. Start enjoying. He hums with the music. He pushes his hips forward. He will show them what he can do. He points to the TV and says, 'Mohammad Ali.'

They laugh.

He stands up and moves like the black man. He can almost sing like the man.

'Ga Dow.

Ga Dow.

Sayda Hoo Haa.

Sayda Hoo Haa.

Ga Dow Ga Dow Ga Dow Ga Dow.'

The drawing of the train chugs across the screen covering the singers and dancers in a smoke cloud. And everything changes. It's over. He sits back down on the sofa. And the woman pats him.

'Did you see that,' says the little girl. 'He can dance just like them.' Then she dances over to the TV, and once again the TV is blocked. Asa waves his arms at her.

'Oh sorry,' she says.

He thinks, At least she isn't stupid.

She mutters, 'All he ever wants is to watch TV.'

'Becky,' her father says.

'Becky,' Asa repeats after the father, exaggerating the sharpness of the father's voice.

A whole day of visitors come and go in the Gardner home. Asa knows they are there to see him. So he shows them who he is. He is a practised hand at showing people.

When the people from the Office had come into the Exercise Room at the Children's Society, Chuk-Chuk had known it was going to come down to his ability to perform. Though the room was called Exercise Room, the only time he or anyone else ever exercised in it was when visitors came. The boys stood, shortest to tallest; they put on a show.

'Exercise.'

'Is Good For Us.'

And they exercised to demonstrate the good in them: The Stand-a-Tease. The Atten-Shun. And, Sa-Loot.

Asa shows the visitors who he is:

Stand-a-Tease. Hands clasped behind the back and legs spread. Atten-Shun. Arms locked and rigid at the side, palms open and stuck to thighs. Feet together. Knees on fire.

Sa-Loot. The visitors like that.

They smile benevolently. They separate from the wall and cross the rug to tap his cheek. They separate from the wall and shake the new father's hand. They separate from the wall and make a general hubbub.

At the Children's Society, the people from the Office smiled benevolently. They remained behind the invisible line drawn at the door. They handed a box of sweets to Master-ji. 'Give these to the children.'

Now a woman comes across the rug. She lets her hand linger on his cheek. She lets her eyes well up.

At the Children's Society too, sometimes a woman would break away from the huddle at the door and disperse herself in the room. Her sari end trailing her smell everywhere. The glimpses of her belly hurting the eyes locked in Sa-loot. This woman inevitably ended her democratic distribution of herself, her gift of fingertip grazing any and every boy's cheek by singling the one out.

'What is your name son?'

Afterward this would always end in blows as boys crowded close to touch the lone boy's cheek and between smacking sounds coo, 'What is your name son?'

The people from the Office left, taking with them the woman with the wanted smell.

'Son,' the boys murmured in Chuk-Chuk's ear.

He, who in the end, was as cheated as they. No, wrong. He who had been afforded the moment's respite from his longings, while they, they had simply been subject to the public baring of theirs. They, who had shifted, they hoped imperceptibly, waited for their perfection to be noted, swayed to keep from falling as she walked by, shied from the sudden breeze that caught in a corner of the room, blown there when the door clicked shut behind her, twitched as they waited for the signal to kill the fantasy: 'All right boys, disperse.'

The one. He deserved to be torn, gouged, chunked, scraped, chewed, spat upon.

But her smell. Her smell of all good things flitting in the night, not in their dreams, but in the moments of waking between their dreams: her smell of well water she splashed on their bodies, her smell of potatoes she kneaded into bread and of molasses she held in her open palm. Her smell of prettiness that was hers, in the curve of hair caught behind her ear, in the line etched at the corner of her mouth, in her lap and her breasts. And the sobs they saved to weep there.

The crowd of boys took the chosen one into their embrace. They spoke to him, full of the wonder of their own tenderness.

'Son, son. Come home with me son. I will dress you in nice pants and a nice shirt. You can eat sweets. Be smart in school. Your daddy-ji will buy you a car. He will find you a heroine to marry. You can live with us—you and your heroine—eating good food, drinking juice and whisky. Watching TV. If you don't like your heroine, I'm there, aren't I? There are many kisses I know to give. You come to your mummy. I will let you stick your little soo-soo in my cream. Your mummy, I will be.'

Softly softly they spoke their word while pummelling him. They giggled. They pummelled him hard. He gasped and sucked in the gasps.

'Such a darky. Why do the cunts always want a darky to stick inside their cream?'

Master-ji watched the antics of the boys benevolently. They had done well. Eased the visitors' minds about the shabbiness of their clothes, the resin in their ears, the dull grey of their skin, the copper glow of their hair, the grime on the walls. Master-ji hugged the box of sweets—a token of the esteemed visitors' esteem for the work he did to transform these animals into human beings. Though god knows, for all the effort he puts in, some of these boys are future rapists and worse. Yes, yes. He pictured it: the shadowy form springing at him from behind a doorway, the knife gleaming in the dark. He whimpered his delight. Should dispense with the Exercise Room and put them all on a truck to some village to build a road, quarry stones.

In his office, master-ji consumed two sweets. Only one more, he promised himself. Three more and the ache in his belly was no worse. The rest he locked away in his desk till evening when he would take the box home to his wife and children. His beard needed a good wiping. The syrup caught there, itched the sensitive skin around his mouth. But now this itch and the ache of his belly was squeezing moisture from under his lids. He checked the flow. It was no good crying over the inevitability of rape and murder. It was as useless as weeping over the inevitability of moss gathering in rain, of rain dripping in from between tiles blown away in the last storm, or no, it wasn't that they blew away, no, it was that he had needed a few from here to replace those blown away there. There, where? There, where his own roof sheltered his wife, his children. It was useless to weep over other children; his own needed these tears.

Master-ji unfurled his handkerchief, wiped his eyes, offered himself a counter to the inevitability of life: today a would-be rapist was chosen to escape his destiny. A powerful boy. Capable of bending destiny. Wouldn't have known it to look at Chuk-Chuk. No shabbier nor comelier than the rest of the collection, but something compelled Directress Raina herself to pick this wretch to land into the lap of American wealth. No matter if he's taking a few beatings for it now. Soon this boy's life will be filled with boxes of sweets. Master-ji thought with regret of the box locked in his desk. With a determined effort, he pushed himself from the desk and headed back to the Exercise Room to make sure the boys' handiwork remained superficial. The chosen one should ideally continue as he was—neither shabbier nor comelier than he was in the moment of his choosing. The best means of addressing the mysteries of the universe, Directress Raina's movements being chief among them, was to remain unchanging, to remain still, very still.

Asa remembers the importance of performance. He does not yelp when the doorbell continues ringing throughout the day. He does not protest when the TV is turned off, and people, their voices flung at him like rocks, come into the room and touch him, or hold themselves far from him, study him secretly, till their secret looks meet his secret looks and he and they pretend to be interested in the food that looks like shit and thankfully does not taste like shit, tastes only a little like soap, and if this is what he will have to eat all the remaining days of his life, it won't matter because he is safe on the velvet sofa; no one will send him back on a plane, not when this many have agreed in their loud voices that he is beautiful and smart and exactly the answer to all their prayers. Asa knows about performance—about equal measures of diffidence and bravado.

So he drops his eyes and looks at his feet and points to the new blue sleep shirt covering his chest and says, 'Asa Asa Asa.'

People's eyes stretch wide, and people's eyes fill with light. Peoples' lips stretch wide, and peoples' teeth shine.

Or, they whisper in horror; they consult one another when the parents leave the room. 'Can this be the boy?' Asa hears the disquiet in their voices. Asa becomes desperate that this should be the boy. He stands up. 'Atten-Shun and Sa-Loot.' He taps at his chest and counters them with,

'Mohammad Ali.'

'Ga Dow

Ga Dow

Sayda Hoo Haa'

The woman who is the mother comes in from the kitchen, she tries to restrain him. The man who is the father says, 'Let him be, Marge. He is a natural-born performer, if I ever saw one. A kick in the pants.'

The man talks to the gathered:

'We said we wanted a child who was unlikely to find a home. We wanted a child we could really help. Who would have known? It is a wonderful thing to see our Asa is so possessed of gifts. Just goes to show you gifts are everywhere. You just gotta look.'

The man talks in a booming voice, but Asa sees him rubbing his hands nervously. We're in this together. Asa can see that. He feels warmly toward the man, who shares with him the goal of convincing these people that he is the boy. The woman, he thinks scornfully, knows nothing.

Asa meets the man's eyes and jumps to his feet. Waggles his forefinger in the air and exhorts the audience, 'They're Gr-r-reat.'

A chorus of 'Amens.'

Asa wants to tell the audience that he is no idiot. I understand this much English already. I know the tiger thinks that boy is the one. And maybe you think so too. You think maybe these people got cheated. They didn't get a Gr-r-reat boy. But me. I am the one. His wretched mouth doesn't produce words they understand.

The man meanwhile continues, warming to his theme: 'This boy is going to teach us a thing or two. Look at him dance, and you won't think him a Gardner. No one here can dance. Our Becky plays the piano, though.'

And the man winks here at the little girl.

'He is a Gardner. Just one day with us and I can see it.'

The man sounds as if he will cry.

'We worked hard to get him here. All of you . . . without your help. How else but? Our son has come home.'

The parade of visitors continues till late into the evening. Bedtime is postponed and the pile of gifts mounts on the table in the front hall. Then, when the gifts threaten to cascade from there, when the lavishness of the display is too much to be borne, then they are allowed to mount atop the bed in the master bedroom.

Asa's fever disappears somewhere along the way. He performs a number of other dances and songs, hastily improvised from the snatches of TV he is allowed between visitors.

'Let him watch,' David insists. 'It is doing him no harm, it is helping with the time change. The earlier he adjusts, the earlier we ship him off to school. That's where he's going to learn to become an American.'

When Asa woke that morning, before the fever and the juice and TV and visitors, there had been a brief snag. He refused to take his pyjamas off. He made a moaning sound of refusal when Marge tried to indicate that he should pull it off from over his head.

'He doesn't know,' Meg said with amusement, 'that these are pyjamas. Probably hasn't the concept.'

'School,' David repeats, remembering the incident, 'is the best place to learn how things work around here. Look at his affinity for this sort of music. He's just amazed by it all. It'll be good for him. He'll see there's a range of kids. He'll figure it out. Kids who look like him. More than we do. That's for sure. Let him watch. It's helping him stay awake. Can't have him falling asleep in school.'

Marge doesn't reply. The dishes in the kitchen are piled high. Not a saucer or cup if another batch of visitors comes in the door. She moves in the direction of the kitchen. David lingers, watching Asa to make sure he stays seated in the sofa, no point in him dancing and singing and further tiring himself. Have to keep that fever banished for good. He moves toward the kitchen. Meg and Ronnie are there, laughing together. First they whisper, and then they laugh.

'What's so funny?'

'Oh dad, it's Asa. He is so cute. I thought he was going to be shy and quiet. But didn't he just crack you up when he did the Soul Train line-up for Mrs Redding. She was so shocked.'

They laugh some more, their heads together, the dishes they are drying in some danger of slipping from their hands. Marge smiles at them.

'You'll have to help him figure out how to behave with different people.'

'How're we supposed to do that?'

Becky is seated in the breakfast nook. Slid so far forward on the bench that she is nearly under the table. Now she sits up and David walks over and kneels by her side.

She sets her chin at him, her face grows redder as she speaks, 'He doesn't know English. All that stuff he is doing is fake. He's just pretending to understand. So how're we supposed to tell him anything?'

'Well, Becky. Shy and quiet he is not. And that's just the way he is. So we've got to accept that.'

Becky shakes her head in the negative. David gets twinkly and turning to the others he addresses them. 'We already got shy and quiet here in Becky.'

He takes Becky's head and tucks it under his armpit. She shrieks immediately. But his knuckles are already buried in the tangle of her hair.

'I'm trying to say something real,' she wails between shrieks.

'And I'm trying to give my baby a noogie on her noggin.'

'Don't want one.'

'All right then,' and he releases her head. 'Tell me. I'm listening.'

'I want you to turn the TV off. You never let me watch TV all day long. Plus it's going to be my show soon and he won't let me turn the channel. I know he won't.'

'Becky,' her mother speaks gently. 'We talked about how it's going to be difficult. Just for the first bit while he adjusts.'

'Yeah, yeah. I know. He's going to grow in love. And we're going to grow in love. And all of us together are going to grow in love. Because when a family grows in number the love grows too.'

Ronnie and Meg bring their heads together over the stack of dried dishes. Their hair falls over their faces. They trade secret smiles behind this curtain.

But Becky sees, and her despair fills the silence: 'Our hearts grow. And grow.'

After supper David carries Asa to his room. He is made ready for bed.

'Well Asa,' a smiling David says, 'your mouth's got a funny smell there. Yup, we're gonna have to address that with this here toothbrush.'

Asa understands the father is finding things wrong with Asa. Maybe, now that the presents are gathered in the parents' bedroom, they will wait for him to sleep, then the man will drive him in their car to the plane. Asa gags on the brush. The man continues to smile while saying words full of scolding. Asa pushes the man's face away. The man takes Asa's hands between his and squeezes.

'No, Asa, that is not okay.'

David shoos the girls out of the bathroom, and tapping at Asa's chin with the toothbrush, repeats, 'Open, Asa. Open.'

He opens his own mouth to show Asa. And, in a moment of inspiration, he washes the toothbrush, and handing it to Asa and pointing to his open mouth, indicates that Asa should brush David's teeth. Asa looks alternately helpless and obtuse. Finally David seats himself on the toilet and pulls Asa into his lap. They struggle in silence. Digging his elbow into David's belly, Asa springs from the lap. The door opens. It is Marge. Asa flies to her side.

'Fine then,' a winded David speaks grimly. 'I don't know how he is going to do at the dentist.'

Asa is better about the toilet. David lifts the toilet lid and Asa manages his aim better now than in the morning. A faint smell of urine wafts from the underwear Asa pulls up. David can't think of whether he's seen Asa enter the bathroom since morning. He starts to call out to Marge, who is waiting outside the bathroom door. He changes his mind. It doesn't matter, he thinks.

'Let's do prayers in Asa's room,' Marge calls to him from the other side of the door.

Asa speaks then, 'Asa Asa Asa.'

And something else, 'My presents. Give me my presents.'

Tears start in his eyes as they look at him with their false smiles.

'My presents.'

He is angry at himself for crying. The woman is trying to touch him again. If he could tell them in their language, he would.

But what comes out instead: 'Give me my presents, bitch.'

His crying bursts from him. He tries to push it down, but the fear refuses to stay within. He has to breathe. He gasps between the sobs and the fear keens forth, concentrating grief into something much more potent. Now he is free to hit and lash. They think they can keep his presents. They think they don't owe him anything for the work he did impressing those people who came and came and came. Why if he had wanted it, he could have made any one of those visitors want him for their own son. He should have. And he hadn't, and these people, with their grinning that comes from possessing a TV and a velvet sofa, think they can keep grinning as they put him on the plane. While he sleeps. He won't let them.

The helplessness mounts around him. Noises are made. He bats at the noises. He makes his own noises. They cock their heads and look at him with intelligence. His noise and theirs, made thin by the house grown silent, TV turned off, the visitors gone—this thin noise saps the strength from him. He lies on the floor and weeps into the carpet that is not at all soft. He searches for his anger.

'Where are the trains,' he roars. 'Where do you keep the trains?'

He points to himself, to the snot running from his nose, the tears from his eyes, to the spit-smeared chin, to the chest and the belly. He points each piece of himself out to them. He circles the whole, drawing in the air with his finger.

'Chuk-Chuk. Chuk-Chuk.'

Becky cries with him.

Ronnie whispers, 'He wants to be wiped.'

Then Marge puts her arm firmly around him. Though he resists, she pulls him tight, pushes his face into her belly.

'He is tired,' she says. 'He wants to be in his old life. Of course the night is hard.'

She soothes him: 'Asa Asa Asa.'

He rumbles and spits his reply.

David lays him on the bed. He lies flat. Marge pulls the cover to his chin.

A slightly scandalised Ronnie says, 'Isn't he going to sit up for prayers?'

Meg answers, trying to keep the distaste out of her voice. 'It is his first real day here. He must be exhausted.'

Marge gives Meg a small smile. They pray. They troop out. Marge, the last one out, turns at the door.

'Goodnight,' she whispers. For a moment after the light is switched off, he is lost to her in the dark. Then his eyes shine from the dark, lock with her eyes, and shift as quickly. She grows afraid.

She had been afraid when the first one, Meg, was born. She had called, the morning after the night her labour began, to tell the manager she wasn't coming in that day to her teller job. The contractions were fifteen, sometimes ten minutes apart by then, and she wanted to be off the phone before the next one hit. She hated the man who delayed her, asking for details of the work left at her station. She longed to tell him the truth dawning on her only just then: 'I am having a baby just to get away from you, and your stupid station, and your stupid job, which is the most meaningless stupid way anyone can think to spend their life. And you can't have a baby so you are stuck. I am not.'

But she didn't scream this at him. She spoke in her best polite voice. She wanted the two weeks paid leave. Only after that would she announce that she was never returning.

The baby came. She was given a name. But the afternoons had no name. Marge was afraid, alone in the house, with the baby. She would leave the child in the cradle, breathing in quick gasps, the eyelids trembling over the eyes' constant scanning of something the infant was purview to in her inner dark. Marge would tiptoe to the kitchen, pour a bowl of cornflakes, or open a can of peaches. Anything more elaborate was likely to be sabotaged by the infant's demand to 'Come now. Come, or else.' Standing in the kitchen, spooning the food into her mouth, her ears straining because isn't that creaking she hears the floor absorbing a whisper of weight, something out there approaching the kitchen doorway. Afraid to turn. Afraid of her baby. She longed to be at her bank window, rubber bands riding her wrists, snapping them around the packets of cash, the drawer at her waist sliding open and shut at the push of her hips; she longed to be acquiescing to the manager's bullying.

Marge stares back at Asa. It is important that she not blink. She knows this instinctively. And she knows this because isn't she a woman now, not the girl she once was? Her eyes water. The lids waver.

'Asa, I can take care of you.'

He hoists his pelvis off the bed, breaks the surface of the sheet drawn tight over his scant frame. He surfaces, a skeletal whale; he surfaces to slam the top of his head back against the headboard. He meets her eyes and slams his head again. Then begins a rhythmic bumping. David is at her side, then past her. She calls out.

'Don't be . . .'

'Nothing, nothing,' he says in reply.

'David.'

His hand is on Asa's bucking frame, now swallowing it, now urging it to comply, to lie flat. He lifts his hand and Asa slams into the headboard. David slings Asa over his shoulders.

'Well, the others slept with us in their time and god knows he's perhaps never had that comfort. So it is off to bed with your mom and dad, Asa. How do you like that?'

In the bedroom Asa sits up in bed, strokes the boxes piled by his side.

'He seems fine now. I'll bring the camp cot up.'

Marge thinks that might work, and in the end, Asa does settle into the cot, pulled up next to their bed, the pile of presents, to the extent they fit, forming a barricade on Asa's other side; what doesn't fit, what repeatedly tumbles off, Asa is persuaded to stack neatly under the cot.

This second night after coming home with them from the airport, Asa sleeps in their bedroom. Marge wakes in the night to a sound coming from something beside her. She thinks it might be Asa working at the wrapping paper. It had been difficult explaining to him the previous night the presents were his to keep, that they would be opened in the morning. The noise is not, as it turns out, the sound of wrapping paper. It is not secretive rustling, not greedy tearing.

The presents are there, neatly stacked under the cot, or piled on Asa's far side. In fact, he proves to never want them opened. It takes several days of Becky working at him, some impatient noises from David before Asa can be persuaded to allow the colourful paper off the boxed T-shirts and shorts, the notebooks, story books—all the practical necessities of raising a boy very nearly at the mid-point of his childhood, brought here to enjoy what remains of his childhood, brought from the kind of place where no doubt enjoyment is an unlikely notion.

The noise that wakes Marge the second night Asa is home is the noise of Asa, held fast in sleep, and still, save for the legs, which are awake and wild. She pushes her way through sleep and reaches her hand over to pat the little boy. He calls out a jumble of words. His legs fling themselves, lifting from the waist, they find her soft places, and kick her.

6

Cat

The phone wakes Asa.

'Noel, darling.'

'Darling Papa.'

'Noel, tell me.'

'I'm back from school.'

'Good. Good.'

'And Mommy is making me eat yucky breakfast. For lunch. Yuck.'

'You didn't finish it this morning?'

'Yuck.'

'What time is it Noel?'

'I don't know Papa.'

'Is it after one?'

'No, Papa. I come home at twelve.'

'So it's after twelve?'

'After twelve comes thirteen, Papa.'

'That's funny, Noel. So is it oatmeal?'

'Yuck.'

'I'm with mommy on this one. You have to eat healthy, grow taller than Papa.'

'But she won't let me put my own sugar.'

'That's probably because you heap it on.'

'You let me put my own syrup on waffles.'

'Well, darling, I'm probably not right to do that. And you know, Noel, if you point that out to me, it may end with me not letting you pour the syrup in the future.'

'The future, Papa.'

She giggles. It is a secret sound. He can see her covering her mouth with one hand, her hair bunching up as she withdraws her head into her neck. He sighs, annoyed by the inexhaustible femaleness of her.

'Oh Papa.'

'Yes, Noel?'

'I don't like school.'

'Uh huh.'

'I want to come live with you.'

'Maybe when school's out. Mommy and I are talking about it.'

'And you can take me to India.'

He places the receiver on the pillow next to him. He is fully awake now, pushes the covers off his body. The phone squeaks. He picks it up and brings it to his ear.

'Are you there, Papa?'

'Noel, yes?'

'Phew. I thought you were like dead.'

'No, Noel. I'm fine. I'm right here.'

'Mommy said to not talk to you about it.'

'About what? Me dying?'

'Silly papa, you're not dying. About how I look. The kids at school say things about why I look like this.'

'Like what?'

'Oh no, she's coming. Can't talk now.'

Her voice moves from the usual inflated excitement with which she speaks to a breathy whisper. He grimaces, not sure which he prefers, her impersonation of a child or her impersonation of an adult.

'Noel, put your mom on.'

'It's okay. She's gone. What I am saying is what the kids at school are saying—that I look like this because I'm black, African-American black. Black like that.'

'Who says—what?'

'I say I'm Indian, like my Papa. They make whooo whooo sounds. You know like Tarzan. I told them not that kind. They still say I am black. They say I couldn't be Indian the way I look. They say it's lucky to be black.'

Asa makes noises, a grunt of assent, something more non-committal a second later.

'What, Papa?'

He can hear LeAnn in the background. He needs to talk to LeAnn. They need to figure out their response to this stuff about Noel looking black. But the impulse is weak and dies. He hears LeAnn pulling Noel off the phone. The sounds of their conspiracy, he thinks. He thinks this lightly. The previous night, its attendant emotions, have passed as if they never were. He tries the language of those emotions on for size. Conspiracy, he thinks again, but the word does not apply. He is relieved. He replaces the receiver on the cradle.

He lies back against the headboard, kicks at the covers, this time to scatter the pieces of paper lying on top of them. The bedding bunches up further. Paper crumples and gathers in the folds. He is elated. These folds are as beautiful as the folds in gowns worn by women in Marge's illustrated bible. There was Ruth, Esther, who else, Mary of course, seated in swirls of blue, the naked baby Jesus in her arms turned to the viewer. He nearly laughs out loud, pretends to wrestle with the bedding. Then mirth-filled and bubbling over, Asa lurches across the room and yanks at the chord to raise the blinds.

Sound rips and light pours in. It is a splendid day outside. He pushes the jammed window open. He sucks in his breath. No wonder he was shivering the night before. Snow on the ground. In May? He shakes his head. Outside, a cat pounces from one floor to the next, using the fire escape structure to climb. Each time it lands on a new stretch of railing, it shakes loose a miniature snow shower. Asa sticks his head out the window and hisses at the cat. It looks at him and pounces once more. Now it is above him. And fine powder falls on his upturned face.

This cat is an inspiring sight, choosing the moment of his eye directed toward it to leap, the leap forcing light to bend and travel the smooth body in ripples. In the alley that hugs the back wall of the apartment building, a row of metal trash cans lie toppled over. So perfect: the inspiring cat has been playing dominos in the night. Asa chuckles. His breath puffs from him, steam-filled. Everything in this day attests to his presence.

Leaving the window open, he hurries through the bedroom into the bathroom. Pulling himself forward, he slaps one hand to the wall, points his penis back into the pot; he takes pleasure in watching himself piss. Done, he turns his face to the mirror and watches the man standing, braced by the one rigid arm. This man has a vague face; its features rubbed dark. A face too long laboured over and as a result a mess. The yellow light from three inflated bulbs screwed to the top of the mirror nearly cures him of his earlier exultance over the sunlight outside his window. Asa shivers his buttocks Watching the action in the mirror, he carefully eases the zip up, and turns his body to fully face the mirror. A faint additional darkness from his nose to his lips. He shoves the hair off the face and brings the nose to the mirror, then snorts.

He remembers lying in bed, covered in blood, mud. Now this faint trace of brown below his nose? Where is the evidence of the evening and night that's past? Wasn't he digging up graves the night before; where are the mouldered leaves and tufts of hair stuck to him?

Or did he go down to the Hungry Tiger, occupy a corner table and grind his way silently through a meal. Did he protest when the chairs were picked up and piled onto the tables? No, he slid his way, brutish, but not, out past the woman, there to give a ride to the bartender with the weary face, backing him out the door, where the sudden cold assaulted Asa, so that two minutes later when he reached his apartment building, dove into the warmth within, the capillaries of his nose, so briefly contracted on the street, expanded again, bringing on a slight drip, and later a brown trickle.

The yellow light in the bathroom nearly returns him to this pet indulgence—the sullied self. But there is no caked carapace of blood, and in any case, it's impossible now. Not when his feet have painted a masterpiece just by kicking the sheets, not when the cat outside's defeated light. And why? He has no need to see himself a beast.

But he is unquiet now.

He thinks about the cat bending light across its body.

'Able to leap tall buildings. Single leap? How does that end? Is it a single leap?'

He dodges from side to side. 'Dodging bullets. Like a Supercat.'

'Supercat?'

His mouth is open, ready to smile at the silly game he is playing when her name magnifies within him. Something's wrong. He is certain of it.

'Marge,' he repeats to himself, and he is again seized with anxiety.

Something's wrong. He can feel it now. Is something wrong with her? He counts mentally. Is it her birthday? And, he remembers, she was there last night, driving him to the wilderness preserve, the lizards in the cracks of the earth, the girl on the swing.

'Nothing's wrong with Marge.'

He nods reassuringly at Asa in the mirror. Asa in the mirror shrugs. Then speaks, 'You fool. Not her birthday. You forgot the other date.'

Another year come and gone. He should have called Marge, not to talk about what happened. No, not to talk about that day, its annual return. No, he should have called just to make certain Marge was all right. That she got through the day. But he didn't call. He let himself forget. Leaving the bathroom, he is back in the bedroom, where he seizes the suitcase from the top of the wardrobe and begins to pack.

He can hear someone weeping. The sound comes to him through the floor. It is Marge, and she is weeping.

That's in the past. He shakes his head. He is not really hearing this. But the weeping is persistent. He lies down on the floor as he did years before, and listens to what he imagines are the muffled sounds of David and Marge. Years ago, when he put his ear to the floorboards, he heard little or nothing and imagined the words and the weeping.

'I was distracted. Oh, David. I let myself be distracted. How could I have been so distracted?'

David replies. More sounds that Asa converts to words and supplies a tone for. His father surely has his arms around his mother. Surely they both weep.

'I have been so filled with pride.'

This is something Marge accuses herself of often. It would be automatic—it serves for all occasions.

'I was filled with wrong. I wanted to prove something. Something about the goodness of me. Not God's goodness that shows us the way. David, I wanted to be the way. The way for my children. And my pride in that, David. I didn't see I was losing her all along.'

He had lain on the floorboard and listened to the accusations Marge levelled against herself till they were levelled against him, till the weeping he heard grew in his ears and he realized it was he who was weeping.

He had stayed in the room. He hadn't gone to the candlelight vigil the church organized at the freeway overpass. He had been afraid of what people were thinking. Were they thinking he had had something to do with it? He shivered. It was quite possible they were thinking what he had thought all day—that it should have been him.

All along, while he raged and made his parents tremble, who in her corner was plotting to do the deed?

He was to blame. Surely he was to blame. And surely Marge would never forgive him. And surely she would. She would come up the stairs and finding him there as she had found him through the previous nine years, she would put her hand on his shoulder, ignore the rigidity there and speak to him of love and family and belonging and the immutability of who they were to one another. Surely she would come.

She didn't.

He rose from the floorboards, as he had many times in the past risen from spying on the half-heard sounds of his parents, quarrelling, laughing together, making love in short bursts of breathing. He rose, as he has risen in the past, from an effort of imagination that failed him. And as in the past, the longer the silence stretched, the louder grew his sobs of rage filling it.

Back then, his parents were never silent for long—neither in their lives, nor in his imagination. They had talked most often of their children. Their children and their God. And he had been satisfied to find he, Asa, was the child they spoke about most often. He had waited for their footsteps outside his door, waited to jump up from the floor and fling himself on the bed in an attitude of despair. He had waited a whole night and into the next day.

Twenty-two years in the past, sixteen-year-old Asa rose from the floorboard as he is rising now, and began to throw clothes into his suitcase. Twenty-two years on, when he is done, there are clothes spilled everywhere. He takes what is in the suitcase and that too is tossed onto the floor. From there he extracts just four of everything and thinks, the same thing I did before and I do now to Noel. There is a satisfying grimness in this thought.

It was Supercat, Asa thinks. I remembered, thanks to the cat.

'What was it like?' Becky urges him. 'When you first met us, who were we? Or before you met us, who did you think we would be? You must have had some ideas about us.'

With each blink of his eyes, his lids press down, and he must renew his effort to keep them open. The questions themselves, her concern for him rounding her eyes, the purpose with which she sits on his bed passing him the joint, taking it back, the steadiness of her hands, relaxes him. Nothing, he thinks, nothing I do can ruin this moment. He can say anything in reply to her, or he can say nothing at all. Whatever he says, or doesn't, will be good and right because she is good and right. He corrects himself. Nothing, he thinks, nothing can ruin this girl. He would have loved to curl himself there on the bed, to pull a pillow to himself, to sleep. He sits instead with his knees pulled to his chin and picks at his face, and this is a useful thing to do. It steadies his hands. It keeps him awake. She doesn't bat his hands away from his face.

'This is what I remember.'

She speaks as if making an announcement. Again he feels himself drown in her great clarity. She is the blue sky inside the room; the quickest of clouds scud by, full of vigour and mission. Soon he will think of something to say to her.

'When I first saw you,' she begins again.

Maybe this is her third or fourth attempt to begin. Against the blue sky there is a great bell. It stands tilted, having just rung; it refuses to return to equipoise. The Liberty Bell? No, it's the bell somewhere else. Ah, Taco Bell. He grins at her and she flashes him her grin. Then they are solemn again. No giggling. He purses his lips to match hers. She rolls another joint. He yawns.

That same afternoon she was dead. The rest of the day stood still, refuting time. When finally there was movement toward night, it was with a sudden lurch. A day and a night, another day of lying on the floor in his room, listening for footsteps. He stepped out of the room late the evening after. In the kitchen, David was a frightening stranger. He pushed Asa back up the stairs. Asa tried to reach for the light switch on the landing. But David pushed him, hand flat against Asa's chest, backward past the light switch into his room.

'Go,' he said, and other frightening words.

'I want to speak with Mom,' Asa started to say, and David shut the door.

In the months before she threw herself off the freeway overpass, Becky had taken to parading on the street outside their home in tight velvet. Asa, watching her from his attic window, had thought she looked classy and troubling. The cat she walked on the leash, he understood, was to draw attention to how cat-like she was. Cheap trick, he had wanted to believe. But he couldn't deny the power of the pairing.

The cat had been part of her dramatic return from college. When they asked her how she had managed to keep a cat in the dormitory, she shrugged, and Asa had thought her clever for getting away without answering. When she unpacked her suitcase, it was filled with crazy velvet outfits that covered her from neck to ankle in one form-fitting piece. These clothes, half a dozen, eight, or ten of them, midnight-blue and black, all variations of the same idea, needed just a tail for her to complete her transformation into the cat she called Sonia.

Rhinestone collars. The cat had a rhinestone collar and so did Becky. She showed Asa, but not her parents. She was no longer speaking with either of them. 'It's what I wore to work,' she told Asa. He nodded. And what had he felt then as he was nodding? Love for his sister, and envy. It would be like her to go to college on scholarship, to enrol in Religious Studies, to send home letters about the church's need to open itself to the idea of women in the priesthood, to distract David and Marge with these asides while she tarted herself up and worked in some bar. *How is it some people are allowed everything?*

Out from the suitcase came books. Beautiful hardcover books of photography. *India, Her Gods and Temples. The Rains Come to Bombay. Colours of the Subcontinent. The Architecture of Old Delhi.* 'I stole them,' she said. And yes, each book was stamped on the inside, Property of UCLA.

'How?'

'Just threw them out the library's upstairs window. I put a rubberband around each one, so it wouldn't fly open and get ruined on landing. Threw them into the bushes. I collected them later, in the dark. See, nothing damaged.'

Becky was not the troublemaker or even trouble-seeker in the family. He was so surprised, he forgot to growl at her for assuming he would be interested in the books. Instead, he looked at his lap where she had piled the books, then opened one and began turning its pages.

'Asa,' she said, 'you need to stop messing around with the question of who you are. Mom and dad are going to try to get you into some kind of college. Maybe Fresno State or San Jose, one of the Cal States if you are lucky.'

She laughed, a silly weak laugh. He should have known then, he who didn't dare even those minor sins his small town afforded him. Listening to that laugh, he should have known she was up to something, something she brought back from the city and wasn't sharing the way she was the books and the joints.

Her last afternoon, she asked him about the books. Had he read them yet?

'No.'

'Look inside, Asa. It's a beautiful place. Even if you weren't from there, you'd think about going. Heck I want to go.'

'Uh-huh.'

'Why not? You don't know where I've been.'

'No.'

He wanted her to tell him. And he didn't. He got up. He sat down.

'I found the formula for travelling without taking one step. You want to know?'

He didn't want to know.

'You let people into your body. And you let yourself out.'

He looked down at the joint in his hand. He'd let it go out. Shit. He snuck a look up at her eyes. She spoke from far away.

'I couldn't do it Mom's way. I couldn't. As soon as I left here, I realized—not that she was wrong, or that her way is wrong—but that I had to find out. And you can't find out without trying other ways.'

He felt out the expression on his face. He tried changing it. His face though wanted only to form itself in fear.

'You let yourself out. Leave and travel. You know, there's a huge place that is you. Most people only ever live in a small part of it. Stay only in the small part, and it's hard to know if where you live is the real you, or if it's somewhere else. You gotta travel to find out. I found my formula, Asa. You let people in. You let yourself out.'

She giggled.

He giggled.

'The only thing is, in my formula, when I let myself out, all the feelings leave as well. One by one. And when all the feelings are gone, sadness remains. Do you know that when you empty yourself, it's a bit risky? Anyone can come in. The crazy ones. This man, he wanted to take a piss. Not on me. You get those too. And he wanted *me* to do it with him. That's all he wanted. For us both to lie down side-by-side and . . . He was paying good money. You don't know what good money is. Never mind. For good money, he wanted us both to. So I did. We did. We lay in bed together and we wet the bed. Like little children. And you know. It was terrible. Isn't that something? Just terrible. Because I thought maybe now I will feel something. That's what he wanted too. I'm pretty sure that's what he wanted. He was so lonely. So I did what he asked. And I don't know if he felt anything. I thought, maybe now I will feel something. But I didn't.'

Asa said 'no' when she asked if he'd do that.

If he'd *ever* do that?

'No.'

Not even with her?

'No.'

'Never mind, Asa. Everyone's got their trip, and that was his. And it's not yours. As it turned out, it wasn't mine either. So what's my trip, huh?'

Did he say something to this? He doesn't know.

'Never mind me, Asa. I have to figure it out for myself. And I have to remember to leave that trail of crumbs. See, I get lost in all that unexplored territory. I get to a new place and I can't remember how I got there. And if you can't remember, then it doesn't matter how real your journey is, or where you came from or where you've gotten to. If you can't remember, then it isn't there anymore. If on the other hand, you can remember, then there you go, it's real. But Asa, you're my little bro. You're not my trail of crumbs. I can't expect that. I should never have asked you. Around here, everyone has to figure it out for themselves.'

A long silence. He thought she would cry when her face crumpled. But she spoke like a waitress in a fluffy white apron, suggesting an add-on to the order.

'Would you like me to explain about around here . . .'

Her voice trailed from its high chirp and restarted. She sounded furious. 'The person who can't figure it out, that person should be punished. She should be punished in the worst way if she gives up. I mean, is anyone else giving up?'

'No,' Asa said. He was shy from his need to agree with her.

Bright. She made her voice bright. He could hear the effort.

'Maybe you'll find a better formula. That's why I got you those books. Why don't you,' she spoke eagerly, 'take a year before you do what mom wants you to? Why don't you go back to where you came from; find out what you can about it? You are lucky, Asa,' she said, 'and I know it's going to sound crazy to you that I am saying this, but I have thought a lot about it, you are lucky you have somewhere to go to and look for answers. If you were from here, can you imagine,' and she laughed again, 'the answer would be staring you in the face.'

7

Here

Outside his apartment building, a cold wind nearly lifts Asa from the street. He wants to tell the children hurrying by with scraps of cardboard and garbage can lids tucked under their arms they'll eat dirt, there's no sliding on slush. A clump of snow slides from the tree he is standing under and lands on his shoulders. He shakes himself, but moisture is already seeping in through the thin flannel shirt he is wearing. No gloves, hat or scarf. Not on him, and not on the children, who continue to pour into the street from their homes. It is the hour children return from school, step briefly into their homes before taking over the street. Adults are absent, locked away for some hours yet. A yellow sky is laid over the earth. Asa sets his suitcase down and looks around him. Where to next?

The children are headed to the steep drive at the end of the block. If it were a sunny day, they would head there still, their skateboards tucked under their arms. Though hatless, they wear puffy jackets more than adequate to the weather, even when worn unzipped. In the absence of light, their silhouettes are that of hulking midgets. In their hurrying, they are refugees. In their

288

scurrying, mice fleeing a town engulfed in flames. Their movement fills Asa with despair. The cold binds him. He stands rooted to the sidewalk. He doesn't know where to go next.

Elsewhere, the snow falls thick. To be precise, in Hamilton. The forests right outside town stand hushed; trees gather strength to bear the weight accumulating on their branches. Asa's daughter wears her hat and mittens and scarf and the lavender jacket with the removable fake fur collar she loves so much. She stamps her feet in the shallow drift at the front door. She jumps into the heaped-up pile where the yard dips near the front gate. In it up to her thighs, she grins and waves mittened stumps. She is stuck. LeAnn comes to extricate her. Back they march up the porch steps. The boots are removed and the snow dumped out of them. LeAnn goes in to get the duct tape. She tucks Noel's snow pants into the boots and tapes the gap between the two shut. Back they go, down the steps, to participate in the mysteries of the landscape.

He could go to Hamilton. He could surprise them. He and LeAnn might work it out—the conversation they need to have about Noel. What is it Noel said the kids at her school were saying? Possibly there are regularly scheduled flights from the airport to Hamilton. If not, if flights have been cancelled due to the weather, he imagines he could get on a chartered flight. He's never been on a chartered flight to anywhere. He's never flown to Hamilton. He drives to Hamilton once a month or so. A three-hour drive, four or even five in bad weather conditions, he's never gone there except by car. Well, he used to go there by car. That is, till he gave up on it, sold it to the mechanic for what was owed him in repair costs. LeAnn offered to pay for a new transmission. When was that—three months ago? He refused her offer. He said he would figure out the Greyhound schedule. He has yet to do that.

He won't go to Hamilton.

He heads to the light rail station, half a mile away. On the freeway overpass, he stops to look down at the traffic. It is sparse. Some trucks on long haul, the occasional car, are all that go by. The chain-link fence he peers through is at least ten feet high and curved toward him at the top. He grasps the links and hangs there, letting his weight sag against the metal. The metal sags back, hanging him over the sidewalk. It hurts his hands to hold on; the steel has turned to ice. He holds on for a moment longer than is possible to bear; he gives the fence an abrupt shake before releasing it. For some time after he steps back from it, the fence makes shuddering music. He turns away, hurrying because he hears the ringing from the station. He rounds the corner at a run. The signal for departure sounds. He stops across the street from the station, bends to catch his breath. It's the yellow line heading the other way, across the river.

At the station, a plump girl leans against the ticket machine.

'Doesn't work.'

'Oh.'

'Means you don't have to pay.'

'Great.'

'Yeah, great for you. I have a pass. It's already paid for, see?'

'Yes, it's too bad.'

'Listen, you wanna buy it? I'll let you have it for five bucks. Its still got two weeks left on it.'

'No, I hardly use the rail. The bus stops closer to home.'

'Come on. Five bucks.'

'I have a car. It's at the mechanic right now. Even if it was at home, I guess I wouldn't be driving it in this weather. Not that the snow is sticking. But who would have thought in May? And, it's not one of those heavy cars. Kind of an embarrassment actually. Ever heard of Renault?'

'Hey, that's cool. You don't have to explain, guy. It's a student pass. I doubt you'd get away with it.'

'Uh, right. What would an almost forty-year-old man be doing with a student pass?'

'You can be a student at forty.'

'Yes, I suppose.'

'Listen, if I were you, I wouldn't go to that end of the station.'

'Just headed for the bench.'

'Sit here, unless you think I'm diseased.'

'No. I mean, sure. Uh, but the benches are all at that end.'

'Well, don't say I didn't warn you. This place is crawling with perverts.'

'You mean that man? With the umbrella?'

She doesn't reply. Her hands are shaking from the cold as she lights her second cigarette. He shifts from one foot to the other, studying her in quick snatches. What is she like under the black puff she is wearing? She is leaking out of her tight jeans. The fat from her cheeks rides high, burying her eyes. Her mouth is attractive, shaped beautifully as the mouths of fat women often are. Asa comes to with a start. She is only a girl. Fifteen at the most. Hard to say. She could be younger by a lot. She's wearing too much makeup. Black everywhere, even on her lips. Her hair is cut like a child's. Straight across the forehead. Again, a quick-snatched look. She's saying something.

'. . . only five bucks for a blow job.'

'Uh, what?'

'Listen, I said the guy there looks fine and all, but he's asking everyone. Might even ask you. Five bucks for a blow job.'

'That man. With the umbrella?'

'Yeah, can you believe five bucks?'

Asa stands unsure of what to do, whether to go or stay. Is she making fun of him? He should never have stopped by her in the first place. But she stands guard at the ticket machine. Of course there's a ticket machine at the other end of the station. But this is the end he came in through.

'I said, can you believe five bucks.'

'Uh.'

'And he's asking everybody.'

Asa looks the other way. She waits him out.

'You don't get it. He'll pay you to give him a blow job. Can you believe five bucks?'

Another yellow line pulls in and Asa is saved from answering her. A group of kids gets off; they come over and surround her. They are noisy and beautiful. They give off a powerful smell. It is mineral and intoxicating. Mixed with sweat, the smell of clay and snow. One of them, a tiny girl, wears thick fur-topped boots, laced high, the tassels at the end of the laces dangle to her insteps. The boots are light-coloured and muddy. Her bare knees and thighs are streaked in pink, as if someone has raked the skin. The rake marks disappear into her rolled up shorts. Asa tries to ease himself out of the crowd.

'He's cute, isn't he?'

He hurries away. But the plump girl is no longer interested in him. She is telling her story in a voice that carries to the whole station. The only person there besides him is the man with the umbrella. Asa chooses the bench one removed from the man. He looks back across the station's length. In the gloom all he can see of the plump girl is the flash of the small disc in her nose. Her story concludes as before.

'Can you believe, five bucks?'

The crowd at the ticket machine shifts and separates. There is one boy for the five girls. They drift toward the end of the station where Asa sits. He is afraid they are looking for a fight with the man with the umbrella. He rehearses what he will say to stop the fight.

'Not here, okay? Take it elsewhere.'

The boy has his arm around the plump girl. Asa is not surprised. The boy is frighteningly handsome in the way of the young athlete; the gifted body, matched by the gifted face. She has a bold walk. Her beauty, Asa decides, is the beauty of her unequalled mind. He flinches when she inserts her tongue in her boyfriend's mouth and proceeds to illustrate a point. She pushes both hands into his waistband and writhes against him. Their locked lips open wide; they separate and she pulls his tongue into her mouth and sucks noisily. Her fans hoot derisively. Asa realizes there will be no fight. Just this. Nothing more.

Their voices continue to carry back to the station as they walk away.

'You my ho.'

The two are the undisputed king and queen of the band.

'Y'all my hos.'

A fresh burst of laughter. They step into the dark without looking back.

Asa moves against the ache in his groin. A disembodied voice announces, 'Four minutes to the arrival of the red line to the Airport. For your safety, please remain behind the white line.'

A minute later, the man with the umbrella gets up and leaves the station. Asa sits alone. After some time, the red line pulls in. He lets it go by. He makes his way back across the street to the indistinct series of cement blocks looming there. The red neon sign announces, ONE-STOP SHOPPING.

An old fashioned graphic of a hand pointing to the front entrance is also outlined in neon. The aisles inside are deserted. Asa pockets a candy bar and walks past the cash register. In the warmth of the carpeted and glassed-in foyer, he stands between the 25c 3-horse carousel ride and the plexiglas cage full of stuffed animals frozen in thrall to the steel claw hoisted over them. He peels his candy bar and chews slowly through it. It is his first meal of the day. He fumbles for a coin and deposits it in the payphone. A voice tells him, 'This call requires $1.50 more. Please deposit $1.50 now and your call will be connected.'

The voice repeats itself while he fumbles for the coins. As he inserts the amount, the voice apologizes, 'I'm sorry, your call cannot be connected. Please try again.'

Another fumble and Marge comes on the line.

'Asa, is it you?'

'Yes, Marge, it's me.'

'So I have a son?'

'Yes, Marge.'

'My long lost son.'

'I called you last week, Marge.'

'I don't remember that, honey.'

'Well, I did. We had this exact same conversation then.'

'Is that right?'

'Yes, Marge. I just wanted to see if everything's okay. Its snowing here, you know? Snowing in May. Can you believe it?'

'Well, it probably snows year-round in the Midwest for all I know. It doesn't ever snow here in California, Asa, you know that.'

'I know, Marge, I wasn't thinking it was snowing there, just checking in. Are you okay?'

'Just fine. Meg and Ronnie are probably going to call next. You children have a habit of piling on.'

Ten minutes later, Asa is still standing in the foyer, afraid of the cold outside, peeling back the wrapper from another candy bar. He ducks when the plump girl and her group come into the store. He pretends to be absorbed in getting rid of the candy wrapper, turning two circles, miming surprise on discovering the garbage can, then lifting the lid. She winks at him. Her nose is dripping and her skin shiny. She rubs her face into her boyfriend's shoulder.

The group is as loud here as they were in the station. The boyfriend gets himself a cart, picks up the fur-booted pixie and swings her in. He is graceful. She yelps; her limbs fling out. She screams then settles into the cart with a mid-air collecting of her parts that has all the intricacy of a paper fan folding into itself. The plump girl is absorbed in this action. The girl in the cart squeals to the plump girl.

'It's my birthday and you haven't kissed me.'

'You beautiful,' the plump girl calls out. She is looking at Asa. The pixie girl is looking at her.

The boyfriend leans his weight on the cart handle till it stands up on its rear wheels; he lets go and it comes down with a crash. The girl inside yelps. He does it again.

'Don't Travis.'

'I'm talking to you,' the plump girl yells to Asa.

The boyfriend nearly loses the cart on this try. It jumps then skids forward. The girl inside screams and falls back. He rights the cart and she begins crying. He grins indulgently at her.

'I'm talking to you,' the plump girl calls again.

This time she is looking at the girl in the cart. The boyfriend is looking at Asa.

Asa wants to say it kindly, You're beautiful too. He doesn't. He sounds the words out to himself, You're just a little older than my daughter. You're all so young. He can hear his voice as Noel would hear it. He sounds ridiculously mournful. Noel, he thinks, such a smart cookie. His gut clenches very quietly. His hand moves to ward off pain that never comes.

'Yeah, you,' she replies, still not looking at him.

Asa looks at her boyfriend as he replies. His voice is caught somewhere. He has a picture in his mind of the chain-link fence along the freeway overpass. He sees himself standing there looking down at the fog lights of the passing cars.

'She's six, my daughter. This will be her last month of kindergarten. Next year, first grade. I can't believe it. And eventually, your age. Of course she's not my daughter. At least not in the biological sense. Just the same. I mean I raised her. Well, till recently. A year ago. LeAnn, we were never very solid. Matter of fact, one of those times we broke it off, she started seeing someone else, she got pregnant. When that didn't work out, I agreed right away, as soon as I found out. I knew right away I wanted to be a father.'

They look solemnly at Asa before they follow the boyfriend toward the door. The cold rushes in with his exit. He leaves, wheeling the cart smartly in front of him. They look like the children they are, thinks Asa. The last one calls softly through the door.

'I just paid you a compliment. Didn't your mother teach you to say thank you.'

The door slides shut. He thinks about going back inside the store and helping himself to a jacket from menswear. Instead, he follows the children out to the parking lot. They can still be heard somewhere, but he does not see them. He calls out after them.

'I'm going to tell my daughter everything. Real soon. As soon as I can figure it out myself.'

It is snowing harder now. He hurries back to the light rail station.

8

Transit Centre

It's supposed to be a forty-five minute journey, including the wait at the transit centre immediately outside downtown. But they have to clear the tracks ahead, and the wait at the transit centre is an hour long.

He waits at the single point of light in the dark station. It is a coffee shop. He takes a seat at the sleek wooden bar running the length of glass separating the shop from the crowd outside. In the seat next to his, a girl is crying softly into her phone. He is impressed by the hushed quality of her grief. It must, he thinks, have something to do with the biology of women that they can cry so easily. In any case, he's chosen the seat in the hope of overhearing the reason for her grief, and she is managing it without a sound. He tries for a few moments, dropping things and picking them up, sliding his chair six inches closer. He gives up. He tunes in to the hum of the shop, and the sweet grief of the song, piped in.

Must be the clouds in my eyes.

Asa is quite happy. He realizes if he waits here long enough, something will happen. Perhaps he will call Marge again. Perhaps he will call his supervisor at work. He has four hours before he is due to punch in. But maybe now is when he should call in to say there is an emergency. He needs to fly to his mother immediately. 'Yes, she is on the West coast. Can you hear me, Ron? Sorry, such a noisy connection, I'm on my way to the airport. Gonna try to get a ticket. It's hard luck if someone isn't actually dead. No, a fall. She took a fall. They told me on the phone, sold out. I told them it is an emergency. Yeah, I'm going to keep trying. Yeah, I'll call and let you know.'

He allows himself to look up at the glass in front of him. Light spreads and withdraws in mercury streaks from across the gnomish face that looks back at him, at first in surprise. He looks down at his cup and blows softly on the foam. A fluff sails the air and lands on the table. He takes ten minutes to tease it into the shape of where he wants to go: 'My name is Asa Gardner.' It's no good. He cannot make himself cry. Imagining Marge with a broken hip doesn't work. Next he imagines an outpouring of sympathy from people. What people? The gnome has no people. He limits himself to imagining Ron's, 'Sure, just let me know, okay?' He remembers Noel will grieve if something were to happen to Grandma. But that grief will not be for her father. Then his heart clenches at the thought of Noel grieving. Idiot. I'm an idiot. He hastily wishes Marge well. Tries to think where he wants to go.

Becky whispers to him, 'You are lucky you have somewhere to go and look for answers.'

'Becky,' he whispers to the man in the glass. 'Where?' And when there is no answer forthcoming, 'What do you want?'

The man in the glass wears an imbecilic look, both vain and reproachful. Asa turns shamefaced to see if anybody is watching him. The girl next to him has long legs. The length of them suggested by her skirt, which has ridden high up her thighs. The feet tucked under the stool swing out and the legs cross themselves. She's aware of him. A shrunken polo shirt vaguely suggestive of a schoolgirl's uniform stretches across her chest and creases at her arm pits. How old could she be? If Becky had stuck around, just a few months or a year, two years more, would she be this girl? It's hard to imagine Becky any age past twenty. Would she sit slushing a straw into a tall glass filled with a childish-looking drink? Like this girl, who has concocted herself into this odd mixture of child and woman?

He leans over and asks the girl, 'Are you married?'

She tries out a sneer. But she isn't very good at it, and her words are almost cheerful. 'Are you a creep?'

He can't imagine Becky in this girl. Becky knew how to sneer. If Becky had lived, she would be older than this girl whose expensive looking hair trails her in feathery wings. Becky's dark hair was straight, and it would be greying now. She would be older than he is—forty-two, to be exact.

On his twenty-first birthday, Asa had done the math, and for the first time he was older than Becky would ever be. He celebrated alone. He had not seen Marge or David or Meg or Ronnie in five years. He got himself drunk, early in the day, sitting in an empty bar, the dark inside fooling him into the sense the ordeal would soon be over, the day would pass. He hadn't eaten in two days.

There was still money in his pocket, left over from his stay at Mrs Silva's. He'd quit the house two days ago, quit the town at the same time in case she sent anyone after him. He took this precaution as a matter of course. In his twenty days with her, no one had come by. If anyone had, he wouldn't have stayed as long as he did. Whom would she send after him and for what? He hadn't taken anything much. He tried to not take from the people who let him in for a day, ten days, even two months once at the Hartmans'. He tried to take no more than the meals they provided him with. He liked to think he left them with their sense of having done the right thing still intact. When he left as he did, without saying goodbye at Mrs Silva's, it was never because he was asked to leave.

He never let himself forget on entering a home that he would eventually leave. Living with Marge and David had taught him to remain in control of the con. No con could last indefinitely. He left before it fell apart. And by con he meant not only the one he practised, but the one he allowed them to practise when he invited them to mother the orphan.

At Mrs Silva's, within minutes of entering her home for the first time, he was hard at work fixing the sink that had been draining slowly for months. She fidgeted, not quite sure how she'd let herself in for this. But then she was like that. A softy. He'd looked about to faint standing outside the grocery store, clearly unsure of how to ask for help.

'Young man, if it's food you need, I'll feed you a meal. I don't believe in giving money to kids.'

The boy turned from the sink with the eagerness of one who wants to pay for his meal.

'It's all right, Ma'am. I think I got it now. My dad was a plumber see. After my mom . . . I was little see, so he had to take me along on his jobs and he learned me a lot about pipes.'

Feed him the one meal, she reminded herself. And give him some of Justin's clothes. The old Pendleton shirts were of sturdy wool, would last into the winter, protect him from the cold if the boy stayed on the street. She shook away the thought of him on the street in winter. They get into shelters in the winter. Don't they? With the heat on full blast in the car, the boy's teeth had not stopped chattering. But a heavier jacket would swallow him up, weigh his thin body down. She fixed him a sandwich with everything she had in the fridge. He had meanwhile crawled into the cupboard under the sink. He made a grab for and failed to get to the plastic bucket he'd lined up ahead of time on the floor next to him. He emerged with splashes of black gunk on his arms and across his shoulders. He held up a shredded plastic bag and more of the gunk and hair—hers—wadded together.

'How did that get in there?'

He turned on the faucet, and threw the switch for the garbage disposal. It made an empty click. 'No problem, I can look into that next.'

'Eat while I get you something to wear.'

He did the quick look down to his feet she was becoming familiar with.

'Please. I can wait to eat.' He looked with distress at her and at his clothes. 'If I can just clean up a little in the bathroom.'

It scorched her, this attempt of his to hold on to the dignity of clean clothes even while he was starving. God knows where a kid like him slept at night. How had he managed the clean clothes she found him in? She looked at the neatly combed hair. Oh the miseries of this world, she thought.

'You just get in the bath and give yourself a cleaning. Soak if you want to. There's towels in the cupboard above the toilet. I'll just get you some clean clothes that belonged to my husband and leave them outside the door.'

She told him the story of the husband while he tore delicately through the sandwich.

'Decided two years ago to go be with his floozy in Brazil. Twenty-four years of life together thrown away just like that.'

'Ma'am,' he looked at her with stricken eyes. She knew she could tell him the whole story, the minute-by-minute grief of the last two years. He was someone who would understand what it was to be thrown away. What had he said about his father? That he packed up house, and on the way out of town, let him off by the side of the highway. She turned the TV off so it wouldn't intrude on what she had to say. He finished the sandwich and the last two pieces of Danish. She regretted the piece she'd eaten with him. She rummaged some more in the fridge. Nothing else there. She could turn the lettuce into a salad if he didn't mind one with just tomatoes. He didn't mind. She tore away the brown ends of the leaves. She helped herself to a beer. She would have to go back to the grocery shop tomorrow. Milk. And juice and eggs.

She told him what it was like to have believed in a man for more than twenty years, 'almost twenty-five', to find out in the last years—she looked angrily at Asa—'I don't know when exactly, two years before or four he'd got himself somebody else. He went every couple of years. He was from there. I went with him last maybe five or six years before. But not every time, I can't go every time. I got to work. And when we was there, it wasn't like I could understand anything that was going on. They all talk that kind of funny language—it's not even Spanish—that I can't understand. So I trust him. I let him go on his own.'

Asa pushed away the empty plate. She rummaged in the grocery bags she had yet to unload. 'Soup? I got some minestrone. Chicken and rice. Some plain tomato. Do you like cream soups?'

'Yes, Ma'am.'

She promised herself she would buy some fruit the next time.

Milk and fruit and cheese. She got the can opener out. He ducked his head, looked at her shyly and ducked his head again.

'Ma'am did something happen to him there?'

Her face twitched.

'You bet something happened to him there. He met somebody there. Imagine, he comes back and lives with me. Without saying a word he carries on living with me like, I don't know, like he don't owe me nothing. He lives here and makes the trips for, I don't know, maybe two or three years. They even got a kid now.'

She kept her back turned while she finished warming the soup. He knew she wasn't crying. She was the type to keep alive on anger. She put the bowl of soup in front of him.

'Why? Because he wants to have a kid. He wants to live in his own country. That's what he said to me. But he never said all the years before.'

Asa fixed the garbage disposal. He raked the leaves just beginning to fall. She would have to keep up with it on her own. Cherry trees at three different ends of the yard. They still had a long ways to go before they were done shedding. Her dog ran circles tearing up the grass, yapping at his rake. He raked old dried-up turds along with the leaves and burnt the lot, squatting next to it to keep warm. The dog wasn't protection for her. She wasn't afraid when she was home alone. She worked graveyard at Dunkin Donuts, and it was security for when she wasn't home. He believed her that she wasn't afraid. She made him feel safe. But the dog, he hated. It followed him everywhere. In the day while she slept, he watched TV with the volume low, slipped into the room she'd given him to use, locked the door behind him and drank. It was tricky keeping the dog out of the room, so it wouldn't yap in there with him. Often enough, the dog found him out and yapped outside the door.

When he left, he took some money from her purse, some from the kitchen where she kept it in a drawer, under the cutlery tray. The clothes dryer he'd taken apart to fix was still strewn in pieces on the basement floor. Under his bed, he lined up the mini sherry bottles—thirty in all—her entire collection.

He'd worried she would discover him drinking. As far as he could tell, she drank nothing but beer. But what if she got another bottle to add to the collection? Then she'd open the cupboard to see he'd been at them. He'd thought of filling the empties with something dark and replacing the bottles. But then the game wouldn't be as exciting. He drank in hasty sips. In the bathroom he gargled with mouthwash and went back to the now heightened mood of television. He left when he got to the last bottle. He left when the suspense around when she would discover her collection gone became unbearable, when he realized the dryer was never going to get fixed, at least not by him, when he could no longer find the many little screws that seemed to roll away on their own, to hide in corners of the basement.

He left because his birthday was coming. He hated to take the money. But he had to throw himself a party. His twenty-first birthday.

'I don't know,' he told the bartender, 'if I'm twenty-one today, or twenty-two, or twenty-three or twenty-four. If this is even my birthday.' The bartender did not offer him a free drink. 'Aren't you supposed to give me a free drink on my twenty-first?'

'Nah, we don't do that.'

The bartender was busy fixing the stools. He'd taken off the seats off and was greasing the chrome poles on which they sat. When he got done with one, he'd put the seat back on and give it a spin. He had a nice rhythm to his work and Asa watched him, lost in it. When he was done, the bartender came over to Asa and nodded significantly. Asa slid off his stool and on to the one next to him. The bartender went to work on the stool he'd just vacated. The two girls practising in the corner beckoned to Asa to come sit at the stage. He shook his head no. The one with the obviously fake hair, extensions to the small of her back, squatted, then parted her knees. Asa looked into his glass. Twenty-one and he had never touched a girl. Not for anything. The bartender grunted as he rose from the ground; upright, he gave the stool one final spin to check it was greased right.

'Cost you a dollar a song. Good way to celebrate the day.'

The man was heavy and old. Working low to the ground hadn't done his back any good. He held it as he hobbled back behind the bar. 'Your way of celebrating—it's a bit early in the day for that isn't it?'

'Okay.'

'You don't want anything to eat?'

'Nope. I never get hungry.'

Asa paid him for the drinks. $22 left in his wallet.

'Don't you even want to see my id?'

'Nah.'

When he staggered out, the light assaulted him, an immensity of time stretched ahead. He needed to sleep. He set off in search of a park, found he didn't need to go far. Asa wasn't lying when he told the bartender he never got hungry. He hadn't eaten in two days. Eating was something that hardly ever occurred to him to do. And not eating served him well. It kept him sixteen.

His emaciated frame, the orphan eyes and diffidence won him a place, if not always in someone's home, then often enough at someone's table. At the table, the only reason to eat was to demonstrate his earlier claim to hunger. In his mind, it was something to take pride in—the thought that he'd killed hunger years before. And starving himself provided him the element of truth so crucial to building his con; it helped him spin stories ever more elaborate.

Standing at the edge of the picnic blanket, his shadow falling over the family of picnickers, he briefly frightened them. The oddness of his frame, loosely connected and shambling, made him a scarecrow, and silhouetted against the sky, he was a menacing one. They strained to see his face. His skin was so dark, the bright shine of the sun behind him melted his features into one. A moment later they were able to see. It was only a boy, after all. He lowered himself to the ground, folding into so slight a creature, they were ashamed. Why, he was just a child. Heavy hair and a thin pointed chin. His mouth was large, his nose and eyes as well. But he was altogether small, and concentrating on seeing him only made him blur.

'Do you mind if I sit here for a moment?'

To the family, he seemed both bashful and proud at the same time. He looked down at the ground a lot. When he took the food they offered, he stepped away as if in apology for impinging. When he turned his back, they could see his shoulders hunch. Was it to ward off the hurt of not being asked to stay? They scolded themselves for the irritation they had felt for his intruding on their fun. They called him back,

'There's more if you need. If you want some more. Help yourself. Here.'

He swallowed hard. He turned his face to the side. Was he

hiding eyes that beseeched for more? He seemed to fight himself as he dragged out the, 'No.'

'We insist,' the family pressed him. They began unpacking containers. He was clearly starving, so thin, the wrists were delicate. That he would adopt clothes with a baggy look endeared him in their eyes. Poor kid, he's trying to look tough. Bet he gets hassled. Oh the vulnerability that couldn't be acknowledged with a word like hassled. And how immaculate the clothes were. The trousers were creased; now they could see the trick of how he did it—with his hands, palming it, then shaping it as he shook his head.

'No, Ma'am. That was a lot of food ma'am.'

They saw he'd devoured everything on his plate. How? When? He must have bolted it.

'And it sure was good. My mom used to make it like that. She always spread the peanut butter to the edges.'

If a sandwich's fixings hadn't been spread to the edges, Asa would have offered appreciatively that his mother 'always piled it in the middle. She knew I liked it like that.'

They made him take a hard-boiled egg. For later.

'My mother taught me how. After it comes to boil, nine minutes with the lid right tight. Turn it off first though. Then it turns out just like this one did—the yolk soft and not all covered with blue. Thank you Ma'am. That was perfect.'

God, he ate that too.

They let him go after that. The man of the family didn't want him around. There was something not quite right with a kid wandering in and shifting everything so suddenly. The man wanted to get back to the adults versus kids board game Asa had interrupted. He particularly didn't like how solemn his wild bunch had become watching this boy. He wasn't interested in his kids learning about life's hardships. Not just yet. And frankly he didn't want to deal with life's hardships. Not today. He knew his wife would let him hear it later. And she did. At the time, anticipating it only made him angrier. He waved threateningly at the boy, shooing him as he would a dog nosing around where it didn't belong. His wife caught a hold of the hand. But the boy was retreating.

Asa knew not to approach large groups. Too many variables. Too many needs. Some of them contradicting others. Becky's death had taught him that. You can't be all things to all people. The effort was enormous and it almost always ended with one person who saw the chameleon change colours– who understood the chameleon was a con. Asa preferred single women and older couples. No children in sight. Once he was in with someone, it was easy going. People almost always wanted to hold onto their beliefs. They fought to prove themselves right.

They'd believed him for the previous five years of his career trawling grocery stores and parks. He imagined he could keep it up for some time yet.

And true enough, they continued believing him: nine years gone and a long ways from Palmdale, California, somewhere in a Midwestern city he'd hitchhiked his way to, the woman answering the helpline believed him.

'I'm going to call the police. Stay on the line with me, okay, hon? Tell me your name again. How old did you say you were? Tell me your phone number. Keep talking, let me know you're there. I'm connecting with the local precinct. They'll send a patrol car out to you. You're near the hardware store. At the entrance to the 405. Can you see what the sign says? Are you at the entrance

for the South Bound or the North Bound? The Lumber Mart? Is
that the hardware store? Okay I have a patrol car on the way. No,
listen they will bring you here.'

The call was disconnected. Fifteen minutes went by and the
tormented voice was back on the line with her.

'Please, I need some help.'

'Listen, you must stay with me this time. You cannot cut the
line.'

'I don't want the police.'

'We're a team, right?'

'He's coming back for me. The man. He. He tried to.'

'You're using a cell phone. Can I have the number?'

'I can't walk anymore. My legs are shaking.'

'Stay where you are. We're going to do one thing at a time. You
stay there, right honey?'

'I can't. He's coming.'

'First thing I need is your number. Give me your number?'

'I can't. It's not.'

'It's not your phone?'

'I can't walk anymore.'

'Tell me your name, okay?'

'My name. I don't know. I don't know. He beat me. It's Asa.
Asa Strong.'

'Okay Asa Strong. We're going to be strong together. I can tell
you how to walk here. Can you walk another four blocks? The
Lumber Mart is four blocks from here. You can walk four blocks
here to the shelter, can't you?'

'He beat me up. He beat me bad. I don't know.'

'Listen you're cutting out. I don't have your number. If it
disconnects, call back and ask for LeAnn, okay.'

The phone disconnected.

W hen Asa Strong walked in, he was covered in bruises. There were fresh cuts on his arms and face. Slash marks from when he raised his arms to protect his face from the knife. There were two small puncture wounds over his collarbone. Luckily the doctor found they were not significant. The slash marks were themselves shallow. LeAnn was not the one who handled the intake, the arrival of the police, or his placement in the shelter adjoining the helpline. But she was called in to see him late the afternoon of that day and went on her own every day after.

She didn't believe his story. And he knew it. Each time he made the story more elaborate for her. It came to include incest, torture, a backyard coop he was kept locked in for years. The story careened so far off course the version in his file, neither of them pretended it was anything but a story.

'My name's not really Asa Strong. It's Asa McAllister.'

She remained silent. She knew they were starting into another version of the truth. Her hope was if she stayed with him long enough, she would see from the shape of the tangle what was covered beneath.

'You must be wondering why someone who looks like me would have a name like this? Me too. I wonder all the time. How I got this name? I don't even know see if I am Mexican or Native, or what. The missionaries, they found me, and finders get to do the naming, see?'

Within a month of his admission to the shelter, he was visited by the police. This time it wasn't to question him further. It was to let him know what they knew. Clearly, he was not the seventeen-year-old he claimed to be. They booked him for carrying false identification. It wasn't enough grounds to hold him. The records showed that, far away in California, his mother had made numerous efforts when he was still underage to have him returned to her. Every return home had resulted in the kid running away. And the residential treatment facilities were no better at holding him. Now of course he was a thirty-year-old adult, and free to go.

Within a few hours of his release, LeAnn answered a call from him on her personal phone. She hadn't given him the number. She could imagine him finding her purse and going through it for her number. She wasn't sure why this didn't bother her. He told her he wasn't seventeen.

'Thirty.'

'I know. Have known. And now, everyone knows.'

'You mad?'

'Let's just say a lot of people are shocked. Some of the kids in particular feel betrayed. They thought you were their friend.'

'You aren't shocked.'

'I don't know . . .'

He wanted to see her. She couldn't agree to that.

'How did you know?'

She knew he wasn't referring to just the issue of his age. 'I know incest and abuse,' she replied. 'It's not the way you talk about it.'

'My sister,' he said, 'she was real.'

'And growing up in India. The things you said about living with a group of boys, about being homeless. That was real too.'

She said it as if it were a statement. But she really wasn't sure.

'I'm not sorry for the life I lead. But I don't want to lead it anymore. I just need a chance.'

She had to quit her job. She quit her boyfriend, her apartment, and most of her friends.

The time she'd asked him why was already in their past.

'Why? Why do you tell these stories?'

When they were still in the shelter, they tended to speak in code. He did not want to admit to anything. She did not want to push him so hard as to lose him. She had no business asking him. She wasn't his counsellor. She handled the calls, hadn't the qualifications to do more. She was violating rules, if not ethics, speaking with him. Her hunch that he was older than his age already put her in conflict with the need to protect the other kids in the facility. But she was very sure he was incapable of the violence that he described having been done to him.

She didn't report him as she should have. She asked him, 'Why?'

He said, 'I don't know who I am. I try on stories, to see if I can fool people into believing that I am somebody. But maybe also to fool me. I don't know. I don't know what my mother looks like. Where she is. When I am near people like you, white people, you know I am not from your group. But when I go to another group they think the same. Black people, Indian people. They all know. So who am I? I want to see if it's possible to try a new game out, one outside of the way people belong together, to see if my game can last. I want to play.'

That late afternoon, she was called over to the shelter end of the agency: 'There's a boy here asking to see you, says he just spoke to you on the helpline.' LeAnn stepped from behind her desk, crossed her name off the dispatch list, informed her supervisor she had been called to the shelter, set her calls on forward and headed out into the sunny courtyard separating the two buildings; she had the feeling, a knowledge in her bones, an impossible thought— rain. It didn't rain that day. At the shelter, she confirmed the call was from the boy, stayed to see him through the first few minutes and returned to her desk. But the thought of rain stayed with her. Afterward, as she came to know him and live with him, this memory of seeing him the first day as if through a sheet of rain, came to mean for her the possibility of holding more than one reality at one time.

She tried to explain this to him. 'Even if you don't know who you are, something in you knows you.'

'You talk like my sister.'

'Look in the mirror. You will see the mother who gave birth to you. See the face in the mirror. It knows your mother. Like she knows it.'

This wasn't enough for Asa. 'My sister said I was lucky to not know. Because I could still find out. She said if I was from here I would already know.'

'Your sister is wrong. You know who you are. You think you don't. And in a very important sense, you don't know. But you can articulate more than one reality Asa. You can know and not know. But your sister is right about another thing. If you want, you can go find out, fill in the picture.'

He played LeAnn the song he and Becky were listening to the last afternoon they spent together. After listening politely to the repeated 'Nothing's Gonna Change My World', she turned him over on his side, and holding him tight, she said: 'Your world is different now. You don't have your sister any more.'

The old Asa who threw furniture tickled awake in him, but he didn't react. He allowed her to keep holding him.

9

Airport

When the red line pulls into the airport, it is nearly seven and pitch black beyond the brightly lit airport station. Passengers rush to get off; there is panic written on many faces. He is in no danger of missing his flight. He gets off the bus slowly, thanking the driver as he steps down to the ground. Asa takes his suitcase to security check. It's small enough to be a carry-on, but he is anticipating the satisfaction of seeing it plastic-wrapped.

The man at the mouth of the screening machine turns to him as a suitcase emerges, 'Yes, what can I help you with?'

'I don't know. I mean, I don't have a ticket yet. Can you help me with that?'

The man doesn't reply right away. He is already wrapping tape on the next suitcase in line, handing it to the owner. Asa tries to think of an explanation for why he doesn't have a ticket yet. Do people always come to airports, ticket in hand? The man looks up at him, remembers he is still there.

'They'll put the tags on at the check-in. We don't do it here anyway.'

'You don't need my ticket?'

'No, it's cool. I just x-ray the luggage. The airline personnel tag it.'

'Oh.'

'So just head over to whichever airline you're going to purchase a ticket from. See?'

'I see.'

A minute later, Asa is still watching the man work. Now he gives Asa a hard look. Asa can't help it. He looks back. There's something exciting about provoking the man.

'You best get going if you want to get your ticket before all the flights fill up.'

'I don't know where I'm going.'

'Well, that is a problem, isn't it?'

He pulls more luggage from the machine, wraps a hard plastic belt around each piece and hands it to its owner. He does his work, studiously ignoring Asa. Minutes go by, and a little reluctantly, Asa turns from the man.

'Have a pleasant journey.'

'Yes, I will, thanks.'

He walks the length of the terminal. It's a small enough one. At the far end, a row of rocking chairs are lined up as if on a porch. He's not sure why this is, till sitting on one, he realizes it might have to do with promoting tourism, or expressing cultural pride, something to do with the Amish or the Mennonite.

He rocks vigorously. It doesn't work to warm him. He is still shivering when he gets up and wanders over to the single food kiosk. He stands in a line of four people, all single travellers with complicated transactions to perform. When it is his turn, he tells the girl he'd like a breakfast bagel. He decides he will be complicated. Can she hold the cheese? He is not very good with dairy. She doesn't reply. He has to slide down the counter and collect the cellophane coated paper bag from a different girl. It is already absorbing an expanding circle of grease. There is cheese in there and it's been microwaved into the egg. There is no doubt about it. He doesn't need to open the bag to confirm this. He wants to throw the bag down on the ground, to dance on top of it. His stomach rumbles loudly as he helps himself to the mustard. He sucks the noise in and holds his breath. The lady next to him spoons sugar into her coffee, gets rid of the plastic straw, slides an extra hand protector into place, works the lid onto the cup, does all this while pretending to not hear his stomach, which keeps leaking its noises. He returns to the rocker to chew the thick rubbery slab of dough. Midway through he decides he's better off saving it for the flight. These days, even the longer flights don't serve meals. At least this is what he's heard.

He approaches three different airline counters and has the same conversation at all of them.

'Yes sir, it's possible to purchase a ticket to New Delhi at this counter.'

'Let me look that up, sir.'

'You're right sir, there is no visa requirement for those who are travelling to India with a P.I.O. card.'

'Yes, you're right sir, it serves as the visa if you are a person of Indian origin.'

'No sir, there are no direct flights to New Delhi.'

'No sir, there are no direct flights to anywhere in India.'

'You'd fly to a hub, sir.'

'The nearest one we connect to is Chicago. But that would put you on a Pacific route. If you prefer the Atlantic route, it is a little shorter in terms of actual flight time, we can fly you to Newark.

There are flights connecting from JFK, as well. But it's a little cheaper out of Newark.'

'Sir, we can book you on a partner airline out of Chicago. But from Newark you fly with us all the way through.'

'Sir, you're best off looking at our website if you are still in the planning stage of your journey.'

'It's a pleasure to serve you, sir.'

Asa sits at the end of a row of fake leather and chrome chairs, all of them clipped to one length of metal, which is in turn bolted to the floor. He is in a deserted part of the airport—a mezzanine level. It is the old viewing gallery. He's picked his seat to allow him to watch the flights taking off and landing. But once seated, he can't draw the chair right up to the window. He remains in his seat, leaning from the waist to lean his forehead against the glass. A child strays over, and leaves, and returns to do what Asa is doing—watching. The next time Asa looks away from the view outside, he is the only one in the area.

His ten minutes on the phone with Marge were easily the best ten minutes of talk they've had in years. His elation from the morning returns in full force as he remembers the conversation. He's done well to come to the airport. He should fly to California to see Marge is what he should do. But it doesn't make sense to fly now and fly in another month again. He's to take Noel to see her grandmother when school's out. He's told Marge on the phone that he will probably have Noel all summer and will need a hand. That she might even think about coming out to help, rather than him leaving work to head to her.

'Bring her and come,' Marge nearly squealed. 'It's been more than a year. And, honey, ever since they, I mean since you—

LeAnn and you, I don't feel like I can call, not the way I used to, just any time I felt like it. And they . . . LeAnn, she never calls.' Marge sounds weepy saying the last.

Asa knows this is not true.

'LeAnn calls every week, like I do, Marge. You forget.' And in a concession to the truth he adds, 'She probably calls more often than I do.'

'I don't forget. I didn't forget the sixteenth. You probably did. I didn't forget.'

'Marge, I remembered.'

'Remembered what? There's nothing to remember.'

Asa could shout at her: your daughter Becky. Your youngest till I came along. It was twenty years ago day before yesterday. Threw herself from the freeway overpass two blocks from our house. You kicked me out. Or David did. You said I killed Becky. Or David did.

'Never mind, Marge. I didn't call to talk about Becky.'

'Who?'

'Marge, don't do this. You can't have it both ways. Either you don't bring her up at all. Put her memory aside as you claim you want to, not that I would argue for that. It's not healthy. Or if you're going to bring her up, then at least you should expect people are going to respond.'

'You don't have to raise your voice. I still have my hearing. I know the memory is a little spotty. But you don't exactly put aside the memory of a life you . . . You can't. She was my daughter. I remember. You just leave me to deal with it the way I deal with it.'

'I didn't bring it up, Marge. You did. We were talking about you forgetting things and you brought it up to prove you remember. And now you've confused yourself about what we were talking about.'

He can hear the soft sound of her crying.

'I'm not confused about anything. I chose you, Asa. That's what I did. Don't forget you are chosen. It's a responsibility. Like when they say if you save a drowning man, you're forever responsible for his life. Don't they say that? It's a responsibility. I won't fail it. I have to put her memory aside. Maybe I am a bad mother to her in death. Same as in life. But how else to continue?'

'How else?'

'I have to continue as your mother. Yours and Ronnie's and Meg's.'

Asa can see this conversation is headed into a whole new tract of wilderness in Marge's mind. On the other hand, the dementia creeping up on her is a blessing. It takes very little manoeuvring for him to move her past the years of recriminations and guilt piled up between them.

'You haven't said, Asa. Son, are you still there?'

'Sorry, Marge. What were you saying?'

'I asked you, if you've called your father.'

'Marge, NO.'

'Don't shout. And why not? I've left him. Or he's left me. Who knows which? Doesn't mean he's left you kids. You call him.'

'No, Marge.'

'You called me to talk about Becky. There now, you've made me say her name. You don't know what it costs me. Call him, son, and see how he's making out. If . . . if he needs anything.'

'Marge, I called to talk about Noel. Today—something she said. Something about India. She's interested. And I don't know . . .' He trails off.

'If you were going to call about Becky, you could have called on the sixteenth. Or even the next day. Why call two days after?'

'Marge, listen to me. I'm calling about Noel. We agreed years ago, didn't we, that it serves no purpose to hash over the past.'

'Well, call your dad. He'll talk to you about Becky. That's all he ever wants to talk about. You can imagine . . .'

'Marge, you know David and I haven't talked in twenty years.'

'It's me he hates. Why doesn't he want to talk to you?'

'Marge, let's talk about something else.'

'That's right. He hates you. Now I remember. He's jealous of you. He thinks I'm in love with you. That I'd give up anything for you. Even him. Well, he proved himself right, didn't he, Asa?'

She laughs uproariously. Asa makes a mental note to call Ronnie and let her know Marge needs to go back in to see her doctor. Her memory loss was sudden, and as quickly it levelled off. It's fine the way it is. He calls her once a month. They usually spend the time on the phone describing a circle around the question of when he called last, with him arguing that it was just a week before and her allowing herself to be persuaded of this. But lately it feels almost as if her personality is shifting—laughter, like in the present instance, seems to bubble from her at the most inappropriate instances. Her tendency to weepiness is increasing as well. But this is more a sign of her willpower weakening. Her grief is always appropriate. She is seventy now. Her weepiness is evidence of how tender she must have been all those years ago when he pushed her to weep and she didn't.

'Marge,' he asks her cautiously, 'can you tell me anything at all that you remember from when I first came to you?'

He doesn't know if he is imagining the instant alertness in her voice.

'What do you mean, anything at all? How you looked?'

'No, Marge. I've seen the pictures. Wasn't there anything I said?'

'Honey, you talked a mile a minute. We were told to expect you might be quiet for a while. To absorb the language. But you weren't shy about using yours.'

'What did I say, Marge?'

'Very little in English, and all of it from what you saw on TV.'

He feels weak with relief. He will stick with the plan to head to the airport, catch a plane to Hamilton and tell Noel the truth. That she is his daughter. But he didn't help make her in her mommy's tummy. But that he's loved her just the same. Always. From the first moment. There were no moments before the first moment. No need, he will tell her, to go to India. Nothing there. And he will call her Noe, if that's what she wants.

'Marge, I want to bring Noel with me this summer to LA.'

'Sweetheart, you already said that.'

'Okay.'

'Sweetheart, there was something else. You used to kick in your sleep. A whole lot of kicking. And when I tried to calm you, you cried like I wasn't there. There was the time the first night. No, the second night. The first night you didn't really sleep. So this had to be the second night. And you were asleep. You said it in English. "Juice Uncle." You said the words as if you were calling for someone. It broke my heart.'

10

Juice Uncle

Mohansingh coaxes the child over; the apple he hands her is hesitantly accepted. Two Children's Welfare Society workers glare at him across her matted head. So what? He returns to the juice machine and to his customers, who've been watching the exchange between him and the child with curiosity, even with some benevolence. They are here now in the early hours of the morning. Done snarling at their children to hurry, they are here with so much time to spare, the track empty yet of their train, why not give the children a treat. Juice—just the thing to wake sleep-staggered children, to restore humanity in parental breasts.

And came the child, with the look of a wild bird. The gummed-feather, maimed look of the chick tumbled from the nest. The parents, the children, were all of them breathing expectantly as Mohansingh took his first then his second then third step toward her. Would she bolt, or would she step forward? They were all of them ready to pounce if she balked, turned, fled. The chase! The excitement of it. But she gripped the ground with her feet, swayed from the exertion, begged with her eyes and held out her hand. A little shift in vision and they saw her: the copper burst—not flecks of flame buried in plumage, but hair leached of colour by hunger; white splotches on her face—not the fledgling's bald spots, but fungus infesting her skin; and the many deltas of brown—not striations in nature but deposits of dirt left on her cheeks by tears that have flowed crossways over her face. They were every one of them ready to peel the extra note from their wallets, to tell the old man to give her a glass of juice as well.

Out of the corner of his eyes, Mohansingh watches the two CWS workers—young men—bend over the little girl. Pants stitched from shiny cloth grip their thighs and buttocks, attesting to aspirations of movie stardom. Smart-looking boys, Mohansingh notes. Made it this far. A few years ago, they were likely wandering this platform, swallowing their fear, trying to feel on their faces a look just this smart as they took it all in: so this is Delhi. Did these children think, coming from a day's or more journey away, that the train station was the whole of Delhi? What happened when, after a day spent wandering the 16 platforms, after watching the hundreds of trains pull in and out, after being spun in the wind that ten-thousand people rushing toward one train, then another create, the newcomer to the city finally made it through the maze and out the station to discover the city was so much more? Once, one of Mohansingh's boys had confided to him that his first day was spent looking at knees.

'I didn't wonder about where I was. I wondered how I would ever see anything when there were so many people and they were all so tall. I came to see,' the boy explained, 'everything that they show you in the movies. All I saw were knees.'

The little girl is bawling at the top of her lungs. Two men, unknown to her, are taking her by the elbow, trying to lead her away.

This girl is intelligent. Maybe this isn't her first day. No, Mohansingh corrects himself. A girl is unlikely to last beyond a day on the platform. The pimps make fast work of them. Even one at six or seven, which is the age this girl looks to be, is fair game. Mohansingh's face pinches. He's watched the trade for half a century now. He hasn't allowed himself to get hardened to this aspect of it.

Her hands, held behind her back, had been worrying at the apple, worrying the skin off it. Her guard down, she hadn't seen them approach. At the first touch of their hands, she had let release the tension stored in her fingers. A little hiccup as prelude, and the mouth opened wide. The apple went rolling away. The Platform Police looked over when she began screaming. Now they look away as Mohansingh scuttles out from behind the juice stand counter to pick up the apple. A quick wipe and the apple is as good as new. He places it in the pyramid display of fruit that fronts his stall.

'You better not put that in my juice.'

He looks up from the arrangement of fruit, at the woman who has spoken. She is an eyeful, he thinks, admiring the heavy arms loaded with bangles. Turn wood and polish it till it gleams and you get arms this smooth, this voluptuous.

'Madam, I wouldn't dream of serving you anything but the best.'

She eyes him suspiciously and yanks hard at the hand of her child who is whining.

'Mummy, not juice. Mummy, I want Frooti.'

Mohansingh has those as well. Also neatly arranged in a pyramid. He promptly plucks a little box and hands it directly to the child. Now Madam is really agitated.

'What are you doing putting that apple back with all the other fruit? And son,' she yanks again at the little boy who is working at the plastic straw glued to the outside of the box, 'give that Frooti back to the Juice Uncle.' She turns from the boy, who if anything works harder at chewing his way through the plastic, turns to Mohansingh, 'I don't like giving him all this boxed stuff. Who knows what all is in there. But then I find out what is natural is being handled like this by you. I don't know what to think.'

'Madam, do you think I will use an apple that's fallen to the ground in juice I make for you? It is only for display.' Behind the counter again, he picks from among his best apples to push into the juicer. 'You will take a little of my special masala?' he asks her and without waiting for a reply pushes the plastic glass toward her.

'No charge,' he smiles at her. But this bit of customer relations is entirely wasted.

She simply glowers from over the rim of the glass.

His boys, all seven of them, have arrived and are waiting behind him, as quietly as if he were a schoolmaster and they his young charges at some proper school. Such well-mannered little creatures. Smart, every one of them. And who made them that way if not Mohansingh? Didn't he, on seeing them wandering the platform, each circuit bringing them closer and closer to his juice stand, take an apple or an orange and extend his hand toward them? Didn't he teach them a way to earn a living picking through the trains for the discards of arriving passengers? Others have trained boys to pick pockets. Not him. And he swells with pride. Here they stand, a testament to the good he has tried to do in this world. They stand snickering and snorting as the woman with the bangles jangles her way through the juice, walks away without paying him, not only for the juice he offered her for free, but also for the packaged drink her son is still sharpening his teeth on.

'I told you boys,' he scolds them with affection, 'not to come when there are customers around.'

'Yeah but.'

'Listen old man, you don't want us taking the loot anywhere else.'

'Yeah, anywhere else, huh?'

'Put you out of business if we don't get you the stuff.'

'Yeah, if we give it to anyone else, then?'

'Oh leave the old man alone.'

'Why? Standing here quietly all this time. Respectfully. Then he cusses us out.'

'Yeah, then he cusses us out.'

'Bugger off.'

'Fuck you then.'

'Yeah, you want me to fuck you?'

'Dog.'

'Yeah.'

The boys unload the bags they placed so quietly on the ground when they arrived. The knobby goods within are the apples, oranges, bananas, chikoos and guavas they have spent the last hour scavenging.

'You are good boys,' Mohansingh pats a boy leaning against his legs.

'Money?' The boy rubs his fingers under Mohansingh's long beard. Mohansingh smiles at the boy pityingly.

'Money?' This time the bravado is gone from the boy's voice, and his hand is a cup held empty.

'I always pay at the end of the day.'

'I haven't eaten since yesterday.'

'You mean you haven't drunk or snorted or huffed since yesterday.'

'No, not that.'

'I told you not to run liquor. I told you to stick to me. You run for them, I won't take fruit from you. Let them feed you. Let them shelter you.'

'You owe me. I brought fruit and you took it. Pay now.'

The other boys have withdrawn, are watching with indifferent expressions.

'Go to the CWS shelter. Go. They'll help you dry out. They'll give you food.'

The boy squats, puts his head down and covers it with his arms. There is no sound in his crying, but he is shaking from it.

Mohansingh has customers at the counter again. The fruit just come in is fed into the juicer as he fills orders. He had spoken the truth to the woman who questioned the hygiene involved in his juice preparations. Rarely is the waxy gloss of fruit in his display pyramid disturbed till they are two or three days past their prime. And then it is usually time to toss them. The good thing about apples and oranges is how long their ruddy shine hides the rot inside.

As quickly as Mohansingh sets to work, the boys melt away. In the last five minutes, a dozen, two dozen trains have arrived in the station, ten thousand or more have stepped off not to journey's end, but journey's beginning. This is what Mohansingh loves to tell the newcomers:

'You're in Delhi now. May your journey be good.'

And what do they say in reply? They don't. They shake their heads in bemusement. They hurry away.

A half-hour later, another lull upon him, Mohansingh steps out to the front of his stall and scans the length of the station in both directions. The station is essentially an oversized tunnel through which tracks and trains enter and exit; at either end, sunlight stands at bay and silhouettes everything within. The roof soars five stories above Mohansingh in a tangle of steel girders that stretches metal breadthwise across 16 platforms. Multiple tracks, laid between the platforms abutting them, carry on beyond the shelter of this roof to where sunlight punctures Mohansingh's vision—carry on for thousands of kilometres, to where Mohansingh cannot see, to the rest of the country.

No, it is impossible to see where those two might be; he is searching for the Child Welfare Society workers. They must still be roaming the platform for their allotted two-hour spell. During this time period, any child found wandering the platform is coaxed or bullied into accompanying them to the Intake Centre they maintain immediately outside the station. From there, the children, if they agree to be led away, are taken to a shelter, fed and cared for till they can be reunited with their family. To Mohansingh's knowledge, few children who accept shelter agree to being reunited with their family. Many more are fleeing their families. In the instances where a child wishes to return, it is inevitable the child will prove to not have in his possession so much as an inkling of where home is, or who his parents are.

'By the big tamarind tree.'

'Where Babu-mian sells cycle tyres.'

'We live near my Aunty and Uncle.'

'I was attending school. When I came home everyone was gone.'

'I was at my sister's wedding. They sent me to the market.'

'They went on a train, but I was playing with my cousin and we forgot to come out from the hiding place, and when I did, the game must have already finished because no one was looking for us, they were gone, and when I went back to the hiding place, even my cousin was gone.'

'Around the corner from my house is the schoolhouse and the master is very good to me. He says I am smart.'

'Near the temple.'

'Near the mosque.'

'Near the wall.'

'Near the jamun tree.'

'Everyone knows the jamun tree. It is lucky we live near it.'

'My mother milks a cow every morning.'

'My father beats me.'

'Kooo Chuk Chuk Chuk.'

'Kooo Chuk Chuk.'

How many years gone by, how many times has Mohansingh asked a boy, where? And had him reply by pointing to the trains, the tracks, and repeat rapidly the nonsense of another language, then shyly offer the universal, the play-sound of the train the child has just stepped off of:

'*Chuk Chuk*'

Mohansingh needs to find someone from CWS before the next rush of customers arrives. It was turning away from the most recent rush that he realized the stumble in his three steps from machine to customer and back was the boy, bent over earlier, now prone on the floor. A quick check: asleep. Nothing worse. Not yet. But this is the ideal moment to get the boy help. And he scans the platform again.

Mohansingh's helped other children before. Always boys. He

hadn't wanted to do more for the girl than give her the apple. There's a way to ordering life, one of which is to steer clear of helping those who can't be helped. Girls cannot be helped. He doesn't fear that taking one into his care will result in his being misunderstood a pimp. After all, who in the hundred thousand passing his stall daily stays around to misunderstand or even to understand. Those who stay—the children, the welfare workers, the vendors, the police, the gangs and pimps—form a world known to itself. But if he were to shelter a girl, he would invite pressure from the pimps to hand her over. What kind of help would he be offering her then? No, he thinks, better for her to fall into that hole on her own. As for the boy laid on his floor, if he were to take him home as he sometimes takes children home for a day or two, for as long as his wife doesn't protest, and she is getting better about that now that their own children are grown and gone, then those for whom the boy runs liquor will be upon him.

It is now four years into the new millennium. In another six years, Delhi will be transformed into a world city. At least, this is the claim of the billboard outside the railway station. 2010 it proclaims. A nightscape provides illustration—bejewelled buildings rising against a moist dark. The same announcement is stuck to the wall of his juice stand. He has a deep antipathy to the poster, but he's allowed it because some government fellow was willing to pay two boys for a day of work plastering the posters everywhere. The boys were so thorough, they'd plastered even the urinals. So considerate, they'd placed the posters just above reach of his stream.

Mohansingh doesn't think he will live to see Delhi become a world city in 2010. He needs a poster to announce 2004. The other years, sixty of them since he first began working at the New Delhi railway station as a ten year old, have fled. The past is grief buried deep in the earth. Layer upon layer of every kind of sorrow man can visit upon man is stacked there. He has the strength to walk on this earth, to make reply to it as the mute beggar crawling about on the platform does—by pointing to his mouth, opening it wide to show the gaping hole in place of a tongue. He has the strength to hear the words of the man, who stands in front of his stand daily, and replies to the question of where he comes from and where he will go, 'Brother, I lost my parents fifty years ago, ever since I wander this earth an orphan.' Mohansingh has endured the past. What he does not have the strength for is the future.

The next time he visits the urinal, he will heft himself if need be so he can send his spray into the future. Before he does that, he needs to shut his shop and walk the child presently laid out on its floor to the CWS shelter.

11

Airport—2

'Juice Uncle?

'Well you might remember what that is, if you just think about it. It's no hardship to think. I do a lot of thinking these days just to remember what's happening to me right here and now. Mind you, I remember the past. I remember my childhood like it is still right there, still happening, so close to me, I can nearly touch it. But what happened last week . . .'

'Marge, can you think of anything else or anyone else from those first days?'

'That was a real person to you, Asa. You should think about it. I often wondered then, but we didn't know to talk about it back then. And I always felt you didn't want to. I should have tried more. But something like you crying that first night—no, the second night—I haven't thought of that since then. One thing came after the other. You don't mind me saying this, Asa, after you came, things just seemed to get busy. And they stayed busy. I couldn't stop long enough to think. I certainly missed a lot of what was important in the middle of that busyness.'

Asa remembers Juice Uncle. He remembers him as a possible figment of his imagination. The man had a beard. He boasted he could be beaten on his belly with a hockey stick. Asa regards the hockey stick with suspicion. Isn't it cricket they play in India? 'Hit me,' he remembers Juice Uncle pointing to his belly. A beard and a hockey stick and 'hit me'. And once, a pack of cards flying in the air. He can see the cards silhouetted against a night sky. Almost, there are stars in the sky. But there is nothing in his memory to confirm that the cards and Juice Uncle are connected in any way. He knows the reason for the name. Juice Uncle sold juice. Not liquor. He was the one who told Asa to go with the lady who sent him to the Office from where they sent him to America.

'Write to me,' Juice Uncle had said. Why hadn't Asa? He should have written to the agency that placed him with the Gardners and asked them to track down the man who brought him to the shelter. There might be a record of the man's name in the files somewhere. Impossible. Ridiculous to think of asking for the whereabouts of someone he knew at age seven as Juice Uncle. And in a place like New Delhi at that.

'I don't remember him.' Asa said this to Marge on the phone, and now says it to himself. He is in the same seat he has been in for two hours. He doesn't want to sit here, playing at sorting the strands of memory in his possession. He is in the airport to be decisive. He needs to get up from the seat, proceed to the counter and purchase a ticket.

What is there to feel so elated about? What did Marge offer him today that she hadn't in the past? Nothing. No, that's not true. Juice Uncle.

He whispers the words 'Juice Uncle', and not knowing he is

going to smile, he does. He feels the smile on his face. He is rising from the chair. He sits back down. It is not too late. He can go back to the agency in Delhi, ask them for the name of the person who brought him there. Although he knows for certain that he and Juice Uncle are not related, he thinks he might lie and tell the agency he is looking for his uncle. Would they have to help him then? Probably not. It might even prejudice them against sharing information with him. What if Juice Uncle was someone they paid to bring them children?

'Juice Uncle,' Asa whispers to himself. He doesn't smile. He turns this piece of puzzle in his head one more time. Again he sees the flash of cards flying.

'Do you want me to tell you, the way I used to when you were little, the story of how you came to us?

'No, Marge.'

'I used to love telling you. And it always calmed you down.'

'I am not angry, Marge.'

'Well, what are you, Asa? You call me up, the strangest thing, two days after. You say you want to talk about what I remember, but you really don't.'

'Marge, the problem with the story you tell is it starts here, where you are. If you are from here, it is a great story. If you are not, then . . . I am your son. But before I was that, what if there was something then too?'

'Don't you think if I'd known, I would have told you? About before. But they gave you to us—no history to go with you. That's how we wanted it. Don't think badly of us, Asa. We wanted to help a child. We had room in our hearts for one more child. I was nearly forty when you came along. Of course now you can have a baby at forty. But then you didn't. And I'd been planning you since I was a little girl. All I ever wanted was to be your mother.'

'You can actually ask—for a child without history?'

'I said to not be angry. Didn't I say, "Don't be angry?" Why are you angry?'

'I'm not angry, Marge.'

'It's not so wrong—what we asked for. We asked for a child without a home or any chance to find one. We wanted to help someone whom no one else might help. Describing you like that—"without history"—is something the people at the agency did.'

'I was living at the railway station when they sent me to you?'

'Asa, you know you were at a shelter for children. The agency we hired found you there. You'd been at the shelter for four months. But before that yes, you lived at the railway station or on the streets nearby. That's somewhere in your records. You do keep those papers carefully, Asa?'

'Yes, I have the papers.'

'It's written there you were likely abandoned at the railway station. I was told by the agency that children older than you are sometimes runaways. But you were six at the shelter, and seven when you came to us.'

'How do you know I was seven? There was no birth certificate.'

'We don't know. Not really. But the Court put it down. They must have had a way of knowing. Based on your height. They may have had other ways. Maybe they questioned you. If you knew about certain events. Then that would place you at a certain age. We don't know for certain. But you have to have a place to start from.'

'That works for trees, Marge, not children.'

'I'd raised three children before you came along. I think you were seven, Asa. I really do. And, Asa, it's hard to hear it. I know it's hard to think you were left there. No one is saying that's what happened for certain. But it's a possibility.'

'I accept I wasn't a runaway at age six. All right, I accept I was six when they put me in the shelter, seven when I was adopted. But why stick with abandoned. What makes you so certain? Maybe I was lost. Or stolen.'

'You and Becky. Both of you. Soon after you came here, she started worrying me with these questions. "What if he is stolen from somebody? Maybe they are searching." She was tender, she was. But mostly I got a chuckle out of her saying this. Reminded me of when I brought Becky home from the hospital. I was gone two weeks. Ronnie looks daggers at me when I get back. So angry. But really so hurt. It's impossible to explain to a three year old why you have to go like that. She wasn't allowed in the hospital. I'm home not two days with Becky when Ronnie starts in on, "Isn't it time to return the baby? Don't they want the baby back at the hospital?" She thought it was like a cup of sugar you borrow.'

'You were saying something else, Marge.'

'Oh yes, Becky. She wanted to know if maybe we shouldn't search. If someone was looking for you, shouldn't we find them and return you. I got a chuckle out of that.'

'Yeah, that Becky, pretty selfish of her.'

'Asa Gardner, that's no way to talk about your sister.'

'I'm joking, Marge.'

'What makes you think I'm not?'

And Marge laughed that new uproarious laugh.

Did he end the call then? No, he didn't. Asa shakes his head. Maybe he should have. But maybe he was right not to. He needs to shed the old Asa, the one who'd rage at Marge if she couldn't drive him somewhere, but never dared tell her about wondering if someone were searching for him. Years of living fraudulently.

'So you asked for a child without history?'

'We asked for a child who was unlikely to be adopted.'

'Unlikely to be saved?'

'Yes, if you put it that way. That makes sense too.'

'So you saved me?'

'You didn't know how to read and write when you came to us.'

'And if I'd known how, in whatever other language, then you would have known to recognize that?'

'Asa, we looked into that. It was absolutely confirmed to us that you didn't know any sort of alphabet. The agency. They checked into it before you even came here. And by the school here. They tested for it. The teacher knows if the child has any sort of prior skills. The lady who administered all the tests, she said at the end that you had no exposure to literacy up to that point.'

'Fine. I was illiterate. But what if I had been literate. In another language. What would you have done about it?'

'Why, Asa, I would have tried to support it. I am your mother. Do you think I wanted for you to not know how to read? I would have found classes. I would have.'

'In Palmdale, California? Classes in some Indian language? I suppose you would have enrolled alongside me.'

'I might have.'

'Right now we could both be having this conversation in another language.'

'Asa.'

'I can see why a kid with a history can be a challenge.'

'So this business of saving me, how has it worked out? Am I saved?'

'Asa, I'm proud of you. You're a responsible and good human being. You care about people. You're a good brother. A good husband. It's not over with LeAnn. I was reading in the paper, there's a section on relationships every Tuesday. Modern Love. Something like that. Different people write it each time. A lovely piece. What was I saying? Oh LeAnn. And you are the most wonderful father. A good enough son. I'm not complaining.'

'David thinks in your rush to save me, he lost his daughter.'

'Asa, David does not believe anything like that. Neither do I. His anger is with me. He doesn't think you had anything to do with Becky. He thinks it was me. Or us. You were a handful, but so was Becky. She was just the quiet kind of handful.'

'Marge, did you ever wonder if there was some third option?'

'Third option?'

'Me illiterate, me saved—that's only two options. Me living in the railway station. Me living in Palmdale.'

Did he end the call then? Nearly he did. He had just one more thing to say.

'Marge, sometimes I think there might be someone out there still searching for me.'

'That's all right, Asa. You can think that. You might think you're being hurtful saying that to me. You're not. I sometimes think we are, I am, just a lab where you test out how hurtful you can be. Maybe this is your way, by pushing out at me, by hurting me, of confirming that you are a bad person, a bad child, who deserves bad things to happen to you. You test me to see if I will give you away like she, her, your mother in India, did. You need me to give you away. You wouldn't want me to prove you are worth keeping. What would that say about her?

'And I very nearly did, Asa. I very nearly gave up on you. But not because you are bad, Asa. You are not. When Becky died, I had to turn my back on you. Do you understand that I had to turn my back on everyone and everything? I went all the way to the end of the world, Asa. I saw over the edge. I very nearly let go then. I can just fall in, I said to myself. But I turned back from the edge. You were there to turn back to. And Ronnie and Meg and even David. I had to come back to all of you. And come back to myself. The years you lived on your own. Believe me, I thought of you. I hoped you would survive like I hoped I would. But I couldn't come find you at that time. Do you understand? Till I made peace with Becky's death, how could I come for you?

'Do you understand what I am saying? I know if your first . . . the other . . . your mother who gave birth to you, if she is somewhere still . . . what I'm trying to say is, she didn't leave you because you are bad. And she didn't leave you because she is bad.

'Asa, if you want to talk about a third way, this is the one I want to tell you about.

'Yes, maybe she's looking for you right now. It doesn't make her a better or worse mother if she is or isn't looking for you. She doesn't have to be perfect to not be bad. And neither do you and neither do I.

'And if I succeed in not letting you push me away, it's not because I succeed where she failed.

'Do you understand what I am saying, Asa? There is a third way to look at this.'

Asa ended the call. He put the phone down.

He heads back upstairs to two of the three counters he had approached earlier.

'What if I don't have a PIO card? What if I used to be an Indian citizen, can I still go back without a visa? How do I get one of those PIO things? It's like our green card, isn't it? Like almost a citizen? But I used to be a citizen. Doesn't that make a difference? I have a copy of my old passport. It was like a gift, see? They gave it to me when they took the original away. I guess my country didn't want me any more. They gave me other papers too. If they really wanted to be generous, you'd think they'd have given me a PIO card. Maybe they don't want me back.'

At both counters he is asked politely to leave. He does so, politely. He goes back to Arrivals, to the waiting area and sits himself in the last row, in an orange chair. It is hard plastic and moulded to be uncomfortable. He begins muttering and can't stop himself.

'Thank you. You have been really helpful. Not your fault I'm here without a visa. It's just now I hear my mother is in India, she's somewhere in India, don't ask me where, she's fallen and broken her hips. I gotta get back there right away. You wouldn't believe how broken up my daughter is about the whole thing. It's her grandma and all. Not strictly her biological grandma, see? I mean, she's my daughter, but not like flesh-and-blood daughter. But that's okay. How does something like that matter? And my mother in India thinks of Noel as her own, which is how I see it.'

The man next to him turns to Asa with a friendly smile.

'Makes you crazy waiting, doesn't it? Wish they'd let us in up to the gates like they used to. Makes me crazy to sit here in front of a TV for an hour.'

'You gotta time it better,' Asa offers. The man takes offence and goes back to watching the screen in front of them.

Asa wishes he were back in the coffee shop listening to music, instead of in front of a TV. The weather announcer comes on, waves his little stick and clouds churn over the blue of the map behind him.

'What's he announcing now?'

The man next to him perks up; he tries Asa again.

'Aw they don't know shit about what's coming our way next. Which flight are you waiting for?'

Asa turns his face away, but not before the man scratches his head in exaggerated puzzlement. White drifts, shaken loose from the man, rock gently in the air before disappearing. Asa can feel the disgust forming on his face. Very deliberately, Asa shifts one seat away.

What was it LeAnn liked to lecture him about? She used to say he knew even when he didn't. 'Even if you don't know who you are, something in you knows you.' And this choice bit, 'Look in the mirror. You will see the mother who gave birth to you.'

Asa tips forward and puts his head down on the back of the hard seat in front of him. He closes his eyes and tries to bring his face to mind. Little flashes come and go; the dandruffy old man's face drifts into his consciousness. He starts to shake his head. For a brief instant he thinks self-pityingly, this is all I have to offer Noel, this face I can't even imagine. No, wait, he thinks, it is my story I don't know, my story so crazy I can't even imagine it. Is this what I'm supposed to hand to Noel—my crazy story, the magician, the man with the stick? Half of it made up. But which half? A gentle weight presses into Asa's back, an old memory of someone's hand rests there. 'Amma,' he replies, 'I'm remembering everything.' In another instant Asa is asleep, dreaming the story of a past he doesn't know, the dream he struggles to find a bearing for in his waking life.

12

Asa Dreams the Story of Everything

The boy is seated in a vehicle of some kind. It bounces a lot, it is large; it seems empty. Is it the back of a truck? There are many curves in the road and mountains in the distance and below the road a steep drop. The boy sees all this from a window, or it is a crack that his face is pushed against. He watches this scene for maybe more than a day. It gets dark outside. But he doesn't remember sleeping, doesn't remember anyone with him.

Later, a man comes. He is very large and the boy can hear his breathing when he comes close. The man's face is large and his clothes are rough. Something is wrong with the man's face. Is it a scar? It's hard to see the man's face clearly. He pushes something like a stick into the boy's mouth and the boy resists him. The boy is gagging. The stick stabs the back of the boy's throat. The room they are in is small, and there is no one else in the room with them. There is a hole on the floor. Maybe the man has chosen this room and maybe dug the hole to push the boy into it. Now the boy is afraid he will be killed. He starts to scream and the man puts his hand over the boy's mouth. The boy throws himself against the door. It flies open. There are many men standing outside the door. They look surprised, then they start to laugh. The man comes from behind and grabs the boy by the middle. The waiting men keep laughing as he hoists the boy and throws him up and catches him and throws him up. He repeats this many times. Everything becomes dark.

The boy wakes up. The place has changed. It is possible many days have passed since the man tried to kill him. Now the boy is in an open field. Except that it is much bigger than a field. It is open in all directions for many miles. There is smoke in the sky. It is very hot, and it is afternoon. A different man is sitting near the boy, and he has a fire lit that he is staring into. When the boy sits up, he is given a glass full of milk. This man feeds the boy from his plate. Then he makes the glass appear and disappear. He does the same trick with the large steel plate from which they are eating. He also makes a strange fruit appear and disappear. The boy asks the man to help him find his mother. The man makes a reply to the boy's pleading. But the man speaks in a language the boy doesn't understand. The man points to the boy's box. The boy opens it and shows the man that it has his clothes in it. The man indicates to the boy that he should shut the box. He shakes his head at the boy and then he gets up and packs his things to leave. He walks away. The boy is afraid to be alone. He follows the man. The land is empty for a long way. Is what they are walking on a road? The man shoos the boy away. The boy doesn't know where else to go so he follows a little ways behind. Sometimes the man stops and picks up small stones from the ground and throws them at the boy.

They walk till night. They enter a large room and the man puts the boy in the corner of the room, covering him with a sheet. The room has no roof. It has a ground and pillars. When he lies down, the boy can see the dark sky. Meanwhile the man starts talking to a group of other men. They are talking about the boy. Although the boy cannot understand their language, he knows this. He tries but fails to keep awake. When he wakes, the man and the other men are gone. The boy cries for a while. Many people come and stare at him. Some of them are very upset and they scold him. One person puts his hands on the boy's head and strokes him gently. Mostly the people watch from a distance, and leave. Finally a woman comes. The boy has not seen a woman in a long time. She gets very angry and grabs the boy by the arm and starts to drag him away. The people watching argue with her. But the boy has a feeling she is right and they are wrong. The boy asks her to take him to his mother. He follows her through many streets in what must be a market. But it's not a very big market. Possibly it's in a small town. She takes him to a light blue building. It has a flat roof. There is a dog tied outside that starts jumping when they approach the entrance. No one comes out to talk to them though the woman calls from the door. Inside there is only one room. She makes the boy enter the room and sit in a chair. Then she leaves, and though the boy waits for her, she never comes back. The boy waits in that room four days or more. No one talks to him but two men come and go and he is fed and they show him a place to lie down in the same room. The men sleep in that room as well. The boy keeps his box by his side all the time.

Eventually he is taken to a larger building which is nearby. There is a room inside and many cots with windows at the head of each one. But the cots are all empty. This time, the men lock the door behind the boy after giving him something like a round bread to eat. There are pieces of something sweet in the bread. There is nowhere to go to the bathroom since the door is locked.

346 | Mridula Koshy

The boy sleeps that night on the floor under one of the cots. When no one comes in the morning, the boy climbs out of one of the windows. Again he is on the same street the woman and he walked many days before. He cannot find anyone he knows.

The boy walks a long time, and when the street ends, he crosses a small bridge over a river. He has to walk carefully by the water because people have been using this place to relieve themselves. There are large rocks strewn about. After a very short while, he sees a jungle and realizes he should turn around. But a man who might be the magician is standing not far ahead, near a hut. The magician walks toward him. The boy sees that, next to the magician's hut, there are two wooden poles stuck far apart in the ground and a third one connecting them at the top. Something is hanging from the third pole, and it is shiny; its skin has been removed. Something drips from it. There are many more structures made of three poles scattered about. There is nothing hanging from them, but all have dark patches in the earth directly below. The boy is filled with dread. He is certain now this is the magician from earlier because he throws a stone at the boy. The boy runs back through the boulders and along the river.

He crosses the bridge and returns to town.

It may be that, by simply walking long enough, he is at the train station. It may be that some people help him find a train station. Eventually he sits on the floor of a train. He is very tired. He has no idea how many days or months have passed since he ran by the riverside. He watches people in the train to see if the magician is among them. He is on the train two days and one night. When the train stops after two days and one night, he is not home.

13

Home

Asa has been awake for some time. He sits holding his head. He knows what he is doing at the airport. He is waiting for a flight. One that originated in New Delhi. That laid over in Frankfurt. One that took off from Frankfurt a few hours in the past. One that won't land at this airport. It will pass overhead on its way west to Los Angeles. It will be delayed when it reroutes itself around the unexpected snowstorm above the Midwest. It will be a long wait for the church folk dressed in red, clutching their red balloons and massing about LAX. (Was it called LAX then?) It will land at LAX in about eight hours. If he finds himself the airline and flight number, he can figure out which gate it will pull into. No, but the old man just reminded him he won't be allowed to wait right at the gate. But he can go as far as Security. No, but he can't go anywhere. He is not at LAX. He is nowhere near LAX. Where he is, there is no flight arriving from Frankfurt.

But the boy walking out of the plane, walking the long way to his new family, he will see Asa waiting for him at the gate. The boy will know Asa when he sees him. He's left the boy a sign in the past. What sign is that? Asa doesn't remember. But that doesn't matter. What did LeAnn tell him?

'Even if you don't know who you are, something in you knows you.'

In the hallway of softly beeping lights, it will come to him, the part he is to play, and he will let go the hand of the man who is his escort. He will take the first step forward, the second, then break free to run into the arms of the woman, pull away from her, and cling to her for dear life. He will do this while looking past it all, to where Asa stands waiting. He will know Asa and Asa will know the boy.

He will meet the boy's eyes over the shoulder of the his new mother and he will tell the boy, 'It will be difficult, you won't be sure what is real, but keep remembering everything and in the end this will become your life.'

The CNN weather forecaster is quite frantic, 'An ice storm.' He indicates with a tapping of his stick that the storm he earlier predicted would travel further north is here to stay. 'Gale force winds.' This time he seems overjoyed. His arm sweeps over the screen. His gestures don't match the map behind him.

Like the sound and the mouth in a Jackie Chan film, Asa thinks sleepily.

From one seat away, the friendly man shakes his head and talks to the screen. 'Man, you nothing. Nothing. You got it all wrong. Rain. You see, it's rain you need on that screen.'

Elsewhere it may be hailing. But the airport is its own weather. A localized drop in temperature. Asa looks past the man, to rain beading silver across the dark glass at the end of their row of seats.

Yet more excitable barking issues from the television. Asa returns his attention to the screen when he hears 'New Delhi.'

'As an unprecedented swell of emotion sweeps.'

Asa looks at the woman on the screen. Definitely Indian, reporting from New Delhi, tricked out like any reporter anywhere. Then why does she look like a refugee standing with that extra large microphone in front of her. Don't they have regular-sized microphones in the third world?

'Former chief minister and Communist Party of India-Marxist leader E.K. Nayanar died yesterday, May 19, 2004.'

He tunes her out when she starts reciting the man's life history.

'He was the longest serving . . . 4,009 days spread across three tenures . . . born into wealth and privilege in British-ruled Malabar . . . considered by the authorities as a recruiting ground for subversives . . . communist ideas sprouting in the country.'

Asa is interested again when the camera leaves the girl with the microphone. It travels to somewhere else in the country.

'Crowds are thronging the airport at Thiruvananthapuram, unmindful of the driving monsoon rain outside.' The camera shoots from high and captures an ocean tide of people rushing in one and then another direction. 'The people are gathered here to give Comrade Nayanar a last red salute, a last Lal Salam.'

Asa looks around him to see if anyone else is paying attention to this. When he looks again at the screen, the action is being shot from inside the crowd. There is a thicket of legs, and the camera points up from knees to catch a flower-decked god-awful display. This must be the dead man in a coffin or a pallet of some sort, swirling above the crowd.

He wishes the woman would get back to New Delhi. And she does.

'One day after his death at the All India Institute of Medical Sciences in New Delhi . . . now in Kerala, hero's funeral for the 85-year-old leader . . .'

And as abruptly, she leaves the graceful-looking building, the tree-lined avenue. 'Later today, the nearly 600-kilometre route that his funeral procession will take from the state capital to his native Kannur district in the north . . .'

The man next to Asa is asleep in his chair. His one hand is trapped between his thighs. Something stirs in Asa. Stirs and loosens. A memory of something tucked between thighs. Not his hand. And not his thighs. No, it was his legs, tucked between the thighs of another boy. And it was cold. He burned from the cold. And a heap of boys. Tossed together. He, tossed in among them. There are no words for remembering this feeling. The man stirs next to him, flings his free arm up in sleep.

Asa gets up from his chair and heads to the door leading outside.

The thing is, he thinks, Noel doesn't have to be lost to be found. She can stay found without ever getting lost.

Asa shakes his head at the door leading outside. It opens to let someone through. And closes. Where, Asa asks himself, is he headed to? He shakes his head again, and tries for the earlier thought. What was it? Yes, that's right. Noel doesn't have to make it without me. Not so that I can find out that I've made it. But Noel must know his story. What he remembers of it, and what he has made up to replace the lost. He must tell her the story of everything he knows to have happened and everything that might have happened before he became her father. It is her story as well, the story of how she came to be his daughter.

His suitcase raps him on the shin when he sweeps through the revolving glass doors. Outside, he shifts the suitcase to his other hand. At the last second, he is unsure of himself. The door completing another revolution exhales a gust that pushes against the small of his back. His legs take over. He steps instinctively into the rain.

Acknowledgements

I am grateful to the following:

The workers at the Barista in Defence Colony, at the Costa Coffee in M and N block of GK and in Green Park, at Café Turtle in Full Circle, at Grand Central Bakery on Fremont, at World Cup inside Powell's City of Books and at Coffeehouse Northwest on Burnside. Here I sat for hours and spent very little and was treated with kindness.

The writing residency at Sangam House and the one funded by ARKO at Toji in South Korea.

S. Anand at Navayana who gave me a desk and sometimes lunch the other ten-plus months of the year.

Tabish Khair, Nisha Susan, Annie Zaidi, Urvashi Butalia, Nilanjana Roy and the members of Riyaz, all of whom read and gave me feedback on earlier versions of the manuscript.

Jessica Woollard, Karthika V.K., Mita Kapur, Ajitha G.S. for fine editing and direction in realizing the potential of the manuscript.

Anita Roy, Roselyne Sibille, Annie Zaidi and Rick Simonson for extraordinary affinity and for sharing their thinking about writing.

Rukhsana Salim, Lata Manchanda and Shazia 'Mona' Jaseem, without whose affectionate care of my children this book would simply not be.

Bhawna Sharma for a home in Delhi.

Devasi achachan, Josie chechi, Lisbeth, James and Maria who laughingly reserved me a permanent sleeping mat on their floor, and whose open-handed generosity provided me not only a base from which to research this novel, but also an enduring sense of home.

~

The website, 'Kerala's First Government' for the speech on page 98, 'The Mutual Animosity . . .', which is excerpted from a longer speech titled 'When the Dream Reddens Again'.

The story of the years the adult Asa spends impersonating children is inspired by the real-life story of the notorious impersonator Frederic Bourdin, nicknamed the Chameleon by the press. 'The Chameleon', David Grann's article in *The New Yorker*, inspired much further reading in this area.